"'Polite'? They are unconscion... yes, I was once a lot like them. ...ng a Wynchester over returning to that world."

Follow @ReadForeverPub on Twitter and join
the conversation using #ReadForever

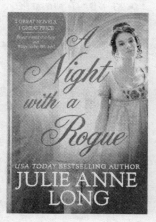

"Well, I hope you've had a lovely meeting. I'll see you all next week. This way to the door, if you please."

"Mother—what—" Philippa hurried to block her. "It hasn't been an hour yet. Damaris barely arrived fifteen minutes ago!"

Mother lifted her chin. "An hour has passed since the *first* carriage arrived. You and Miss Urqhart should learn to heed the clock."

"Mrs. York, this is important." Sybil held up the broadsheet. "We're discussing a wartime cipher—"

"If you bluestockings want to fathom out difficult puzzles, then find Philippa a husband who won't embarrass the family," Mother interrupted. "I don't want to hear a single word about anything else until next Thursday afternoon, at which time you will have precisely one hour to bore each other silly."

The ladies exchanged glances.

"Next week," Florentia murmured in Greek. "We plot our revenge."

Philippa's thwarted friends trudged from the parlor to the front door, this week's undiscussed archery books still clutched in their hands.

Great-Aunt Wynchester paused at the threshold. Her brown eyes glowed intensely from her pale, wrinkled face.

"Don't you worry," she quavered beneath her breath. "If there's a way to stop that bollocks-for-brains, I'll find it."

"You are very sweet," Philippa said. Great-Aunt Wynchester was one of her favorite people. Philippa hoped to be half as bold and confident when she reached her age.

"Come along, Aunt." Chloe looped her arm through her aunt's and helped the older woman to hobble from the room.

Philippa's mother patted her cheek. "You'd be a bluestocking spinster for the rest of your life if I weren't here looking out for you. It's for your own good, darling."

4

Tommy detached her white wig from her head as she and her sister strode through the front door of the grand Wynchester home in semi-fashionable Islington. The disused wing to the left hadn't been touched since Bean had died. On the right was the bright, bustling half of the house, with siblings and servants and smiles everywhere.

Chloe shouted up the marble stairs, "Planning Parlor!"

"I'll ring for tea," Graham's muffled voice called back.

Tommy and Chloe reached the first floor in time to glimpse Elizabeth walking carefully down the corridor, one hand gripping her cane and the other holding her hip.

Some days, she used her sword stick to defend the defenseless. Other days, it was heavily employed to keep Elizabeth upright.

This appeared to be one of the bad days.

Usually, the siblings sat in an order that mirrored their family portrait. Today, Elizabeth arranged herself on a sofa, along with a plethora of pillows.

Tommy and Graham took their customary seats between two tall windows. Chloe preferred to pace the slate floor between the fireplace and the large walnut-and-burl table, taking care to step over chalk-drawn schedules and maps from prior planning sessions.

"Thank God for intrigue," said Elizabeth. "I was growing bored. We haven't had a case to solve in ages."

Graham stared at her. "We finished a mission yesterday."

"As I said." She waved a hand. "Ages."

Graham turned to Chloe. "Well? What is it? Rescue services? Blackmail? Kidnapping?"

"A man is taking credit for a woman's idea," Tommy said flatly.

Her brother blinked.

"I take it back," Elizabeth said dryly. "This isn't a *new* case at all."

"I have to agree," Graham said. "That must happen ten times a day."

"Ten times a second," Chloe corrected.

"Huzzah," said Elizabeth. "'Contravene patriarchal coverture' is exactly the sort of evening activity I was looking forward to. I'm going to need a bigger sword stick."

"Let's begin with something small and grow from there," Tommy suggested. "We have a specific client who needs our help. You all remember meeting Damaris Urqhart last summer?"

"Of course." Graham turned to select a fresh journal from the bookshelf next to his chair. "What does she need us to put a stop to?"

"The Prince Regent's season-opening celebration," Chloe replied.

"'Something small,'" Elizabeth repeated. "I like it."

Graham pulled another volume from his shelf. "This journal contains the notes I've made about each of Prinny's previous galas and celebrations." He paused with his finger on the spine. "Would this have anything to do with a certain Captain Northrup's recent cryptographical achievements?"

"That's right," Tommy said. "Thanks to Damaris, Philippa

collects illuminated manuscripts. Apparently, at some point prior to Chloe and I attending the Thursday afternoon reading circle—"

"*Philippa*," Graham and Elizabeth cooed in tandem.

Tommy glared at them both.

Elizabeth batted her lashes innocently. "How did our dear Philippa look today, Tommy?"

"Like the most beautiful woman in London?" Graham asked with faux earnestness.

"In England," Tommy muttered.

"I could introduce you as...*you*," Chloe reminded her. "Then you wouldn't have to keep pretending to be blustery old Great-Aunt Wynchester."

"I *can't* talk to her as me," Tommy said. "When I get close enough to touch, all of my thoughts jumble and fall out of my head."

"I guess everyone has a weakness," Elizabeth said with a sigh. "Mine is uncontrollable bloodlust."

"Jacob's weakness is baby hedgehogs," Chloe added helpfully. "And romantic poetry."

"Shall we concentrate on the case?" Graham sharpened his pencil. "I should like to read all the coded communications. What do you think Damaris's cipher helped the army to do, precisely?"

"What it helped *Northrup* do," Tommy answered, "is accept honors for plagiarizing Damaris's work."

Graham crossed the room to the wall of biographies and flipped through a journal. "He's to receive a viscountcy, and enjoy a public ceremony on Saturday, the seventeenth of January."

"How is that in your album already?" Chloe asked. "Wasn't the news just announced this morning?"

"I get my news in advance." Graham skimmed his notes.

"Stopping the celebration might be tricky. The sheer number of guards alone—"

"I could hold some off with my rapier," Elizabeth suggested. "And Jacob could release whatever trained creatures are proliferating in the barn this week."

"Bats?" Chloe guessed. "Bloodthirsty bunnies? Pugilistic pigs?"

"We don't need to stop the gala," Tommy said. "We need to prevent Northrup from taking Damaris's credit. The honor should go where it belongs."

"Or nowhere at all," Elizabeth amended. "Don't be surprised if Prinny declines to name rooms in the Royal Military Academy after a bluestocking."

"As long as the fame and fortune don't go to her smug, undeserving uncle," Chloe said. "Ironically, the book used in the fraud contains tales of chivalry."

"Everything about chivalry is ironic," Elizabeth said.

"Prinny already made the announcement," Graham said. "Even if we could prove Captain Northrup unworthy, might Prinny shrug off that detail and continue on with the ceremony?"

"No." Tommy leaned back. "He won't, because of *his* biggest problem."

Graham raised his brows. "Which is what?"

"Us." She smiled. "Prinny might have bested Boney, but no one has ever won a battle against a Wynchester."

5

～～～

*A*bsolutely not," Tommy said to Jacob and Marjorie the following afternoon at tea. She handed a baby hedgehog back to her brother. "Stop meddling."

"Is it difficult when you ask the pieman for a pie?" Jacob pointed out reasonably. "Or when you give your direction to a hackney driver? We call those 'words.' Extremely adept practitioners can advance all the way to 'conversation.' You and Philippa should try it."

Marjorie refreshed the tea. "Tommy's never been in love with a hackney driver or a pieman."

"I've never been in love with any kind of man, no matter how delicious his pies," Tommy said. "I would no sooner fall in love with a man than I would the moon. And the moon is much prettier."

"But not as pretty as Philippa," her cursed siblings sang out.

If she had a pie, she'd toss it at them.

"I'm not enamored," she grumbled.

She was far past enamored. Tommy's romantic thoughts had been filled with no one but Philippa almost from the first moment she saw her.

It might have stayed a passing infatuation if she and Chloe hadn't had to join the reading circle in the course of a prior mission to recover a stolen work of art. In the process, Chloe had fallen in love with conversing with fellow literature enthusiasts — as well as with Philippa's intended suitor.

And Tommy . . . had fallen for Philippa.

"When will Graham and Elizabeth return home?" Tommy asked in an unsubtle attempt to change the subject.

"Who knows?" Jacob turned over the baby hedgehog, which barely filled his palm. He rubbed its belly with a fingertip. The hedgehog responded by closing tight about his finger. "Graham is out gathering intelligence, and Elizabeth . . . is off shopping for rapiers."

Tommy should have joined her. Sword shopping had to be better than suffering through sibling matchmaking while attempting to enjoy an afternoon repast.

How she missed Chloe! After Bean succumbed to smallpox last year, Tommy and Chloe had only grown closer. They'd spent months in a clandestine operation to liberate a stolen item from the Duke of Faircliffe.

And then Chloe married him.

Now she was the *Duchess of Faircliffe*. She wasn't here anymore to eat tea cakes and tickle baby hedgehogs. Her old bedchamber was still down the corridor from Tommy's, but nothing was left inside except unwanted furniture.

That was enough change for one year. Tommy's days were plenty full with missions and pies. She certainly didn't need to add "words" and "conversations" to her busy calendar.

Jacob produced an ornate snuffbox. "I cannot believe that our happy-go-lucky fearless adventuress is scared to talk to a *girl*."

"Woman," Marjorie corrected.

"You have the perfect excuse to approach Philippa." Jacob opened the snuffbox. It did not contain snuff. "We're helping her reading circle."

"I have no reason to talk to her," Tommy said. "The next meeting isn't for a week and we have no news yet anyway."

Jacob arched a brow. "So you'll just pine from afar in the meantime?"

"She's good at it," said Marjorie. "She's been practicing all year."

"Thank you, Marjorie," Tommy murmured.

The truth was, there was no use starting down a path that went nowhere. All good things ended. Especially when it came to people Tommy cared about. She had been orphaned at the age of four. Bean died. Chloe left. It was better to acknowledge relationships were temporary from the start than to get one's hopes and dreams and *feelings* tangled up in the matter.

Tommy was happy to infiltrate asylums and impersonate night watchmen. Resolving situations for clients was something she was good at.

The impossible situations in her own life, however, tended to stay impossible.

"What's the problem? There are no laws against women sleeping with each other," Jacob pointed out.

"Maybe that is the problem," Marjorie said. "Tommy adores breaking laws."

"'Not illegal' isn't the same as 'accepted,' and you know it," Tommy said. "Graham is always deciphering messages in the advertisements. Why do you think the hostess chose to hide the true nature of that Sapphic country house party last month?"

"So men wouldn't attend," Marjorie said without hesitation.

"Probably," Jacob agreed.

Tommy ignored them. It had been an excellent party.

She was no stranger to desire and pleasure. Her lovers weren't looking for anything more than an evening's romp. Fun while it lasted. There was no expectation of gadding about town together in their *real* lives. Most didn't even share their true names.

It was perfectly fine. Tommy didn't need anything else. Or anyone else.

"Besides," she said, "there's no reason to believe Philippa would be interested in me even if I *were* to shower her with words and conversation. She's hunting for a husband. She almost married a duke. To people like the Yorks, rubbing shoulders with an untitled Wynchester—even platonically— is too scandalous to consider."

"She rubs shoulders with *Great-Aunt* Wynchester," Marjorie pointed out.

Tommy sent her a flat look. "Polite Society is not and will never be for me."

"Maybe Philippa doesn't want it either," Jacob suggested.

Tommy picked at her tea cake. "Maybe she does. We don't know. I'd rather never confess my feelings than to see her recoil in horror."

"What if she didn't recoil in horror?" Marjorie said softly.

"I still couldn't keep her," Tommy said. "Losing Philippa would be worse than never having her. If I lost the chance for friendship, I would be left with nothing."

"A simple conversation," Jacob insisted. "Not a sonnet about your admiration of her big brain and bigger bosom, but a regular, ordinary, words-and-ideas conversation about something other than the case. If you do that, I promise to stop hounding you."

Tommy glared at him.

"I promise, too," said Marjorie. "I'll even make the others promise as well. If you talk to Philippa for...fifteen minutes."

"Twenty," Jacob said quickly.

"Talk to Philippa for *twenty minutes*?" Tommy burst out. "About what?"

"Take her a kitten," Jacob suggested. "She likes Tiglet."

"Tiglet is a homing kitten," Tommy reminded him. "If she sets him down, he'll run back to Islington."

"Then you can give him back." Jacob tapped her on the nose. "See? He's a perennial conversation starter."

"I'm not giving her Tiglet," Tommy said firmly.

"You should hurry," said Marjorie. "Graham said she'll be in Hyde Park with her mother within the hour."

"Graham's not even here to be part of the conversation. He..." Tommy narrowed her eyes. "Did he plan this? Did *you* plan this? Am I under attack?"

"You're being manipulated into doing the thing you actually want to do," Jacob said cheerfully. "You cannot go to your grave without having tried at least once."

"I can't walk up to her as Tommy Wynchester. She doesn't *know* Tommy Wynchester, and besides, the daily promenade in Hyde Park is for the haut ton. Her mother wouldn't allow me twenty seconds, even if I were Lady Thomasina. Mrs. York has been very clear that Philippa is only to fraternize with future suitors."

Jacob shrugged. "Then be one."

"Not a boatman," Marjorie said quickly. "Be someone Mrs. York would allow near her daughter."

A crafty smile spread on Jacob's face. "Be Baron Vanderbean."

"The new heir only exists on paper," Tommy reminded him.

Her brother raised his brows. "If no one's seen him, then no one can say you *aren't* him, can they?"

She supposed not.

The Baron Vanderbean who had rescued them all had held a minor peerage in his native Balcovia, a small principality in the Low Countries.

Although Bean had left generous trusts to each of his

adopted children, a society connection was one thing money could not purchase. Before he died, Bean had created a fictitious heir and heiress: Horace and Honoria Wynchester. By maintaining the sponsorship of the new Baron Vanderbean and the chaperonage of his highborn sister, the Wynchester orphans could still enjoy access to places and people that would have snubbed them if they had no titled connection.

Ironic that an imaginary lord held more power than a real woman.

"You want me to be Baron Vanderbean," Tommy repeated.

Just saying the words sent gooseflesh over her skin. Baron Vanderbean was *Bean*.

Bean was dead.

Tommy would do anything to have her father back. She wanted nothing to do with a made-up relative. And she couldn't imagine taking over Bean's name. If she pretended to be his "son," Horace Wynchester, everyone would call her Baron Vanderbean. She wasn't certain she could handle it.

But she also didn't want her family to see her hesitant and meek. Tommy was the one who *did* things. She could be anyone. She just wasn't sure she could do...this.

"It's a bad idea," she said. There. *She* wasn't weak. The *plan* was defective.

"Why?" Jacob asked.

"For one," she replied slowly, "if I play Baron Vanderbean, no one else can do it."

Jacob smirked. "Who else was going to do it?"

Well, fair enough.

Marjorie and Elizabeth were horrid at playing men, and Jacob's dark brown skin made it unlikely for him to be Bean's son by blood. Graham's golden bronze coloring might let him get away with it, but his temperament never would.

Tall, thin, white, curve-less Tommy was the most believable as Bean's male heir.

That wasn't all. She could have more honest interactions with Philippa as a gentleman, rather than dressed as an old lady at her reading circle. Tommy rubbed the back of her neck nervously. *Could* she do it?

"Besides," Jacob said. "The new heir has served his usefulness."

Marjorie picked up a tea cake. "Baron Vanderbean *was* our entrée into society, but now Chloe provides that function. The approval of the Duke and Duchess of Faircliffe carries far more weight than ties to a reclusive foreign lord."

Jacob stopped playing with his hedgehog. "Think about it, Tommy. The baron identity was for any Wynchester who needed it, however we needed it. And the person who needs it is you."

"And maybe Philippa," Marjorie added.

Tommy set down her tea. "Twenty minutes of conversation as Baron Vanderbean, and you'll never mention my tendre for Philippa again?"

Jacob and Marjorie touched their hands to their hearts and lifted their fingers to the sky. The Wynchester salute was how the siblings swore their vows. Both their faces were innocent.

Tommy narrowed her eyes at them.

"Twenty complete minutes," Jacob said. "Of actual words. Not twenty minutes of pining in close proximity."

"It's a promenade," Tommy reminded him. "I'll be lucky to speak to her for *ten* minutes."

Jacob smiled. "Then you'll have to do it twice."

6

Tommy entered Hyde Park with trepidation.

Not because of her disguise. She made a striking and dapper Baron Vanderbean. She'd added deeper laugh lines to her eyes and a hint of shadow along her jaw. Her coat and buckskins were lightly padded, which, even if detected, was very much the current fashion. The cut of her hair would impress any dandy, as would the quality of her attire and the extravagant folds of her neckcloth.

She was tall for a woman and perhaps of average height for a man. In any case, she was astride a stunning steed. The horse's height and breadth helped to muddy Tommy's. She looked the part of a wealthy, fashionable gentleman, but no one would be able to relay accurate details as to her proportions.

Being a man was *easy*.

Twenty minutes with Philippa was the difficult part.

Thus far, she had only managed to progress from "pining from afar" to "pining in proximity." Her current position thirty yards behind the Yorks' barouche gave her a wonderful vantage point for gazing at the back of Philippa's head.

Her lovely head was currently hidden beneath a wide-brimmed bonnet, but Tommy had studied her enough to say with certainty that Philippa's lustrous blond hair was the most spectacular in all of England, and the brain inside of that head perhaps the most singular in the world.

Ah—their carriage was turning. Philippa's profile was now in view.

Could there *be* a finer flush to a delightfully round cheek? Tommy was too far away to see the blue in Philippa's eyes or the curve of her light brown eyelashes, but the *rest* of her curves...Philippa was more than pleasingly plump. Every inch of her looked soft and voluptuous, and oh God, Tommy was never going to be able to coax her horse close enough to attempt conversation.

What would she say? "I like your brain and I'd like to taste your body?"

Perhaps she *should* have brought Tiglet. "Miaow" was likely a better conversational opening than anything Tommy could come up with.

Philippa was so *clever*. She could look at a thing and fathom it out. Tommy liked to read for pleasure, but it was a good day if she could remember the title or plot a year later, much less competently debate literary structure or scientific theory the way Philippa did in her reading circle.

What if Tommy did manage to talk to her, only to discover they had nothing to talk *about*? What if she bored Philippa? What if they didn't have enough in common even to be platonic friends, much less—

She was doing it again. The thing she'd promised herself she wouldn't do: imagining all the ways it could go wrong instead of envisioning how it might go right.

Begin anew.

Tommy had plenty of experience with flirtation. Not as a man, so that was a slight wrinkle. At least, she'd never flirted as a man without the other party *knowing* she was technically a woman, and dear heaven, this was *such* a muddle, absolutely impossible, Jacob and Marjorie were the worst possible siblings for setting the unattainable objective of—

Philippa's eyes met Tommy's!

Briefly. Just as her carriage was turning from one gravel path to another. Soon Tommy's horse was turning, too, and she was no longer within Philippa's line of sight.

But for one glorious second...

"All right," she scolded herself under her breath. "Tommy is a coward around Philippa, but *you* are Baron Vanderbean. Baron Vanderbean doesn't give a fig what the Yorks think of him. He's Baron Vanderbean. He outranks them! Just ride over. Everyone *else* is mingling. It's the reason they came. Baron Vanderbean would not be afraid of a simple 'How do you do.'"

Before she lost her nerve, Tommy gripped the reins and spurred her horse alongside the Yorks' barouche.

And *then* she lost her nerve.

Philippa looked at her again, really looked at her, and it was that night in Chloe's ballroom all over, when Tommy had tried to talk to Philippa at the Faircliffe end-of-season gala, and only succeeded in blushing hot enough to melt the cosmetics from her face and then running away.

It had not been her finest moment.

And she'd just repeated it.

Tommy had ceased all forward progress altogether. In a matter of minutes, her horse was no longer beside the Yorks' barouche, but fifty yards behind.

She couldn't do it. She *shouldn't* do it. They hadn't been formally presented to each other, and greeting Philippa without an introduction was an appalling breach of etiquette.

What's more, Tommy wasn't a lord any more than she was Miss Thomasina. Flirting as "Horace" would be easier from society's perspective, but she still wouldn't be courting Philippa as *Tommy*. So what was the use?

Perhaps she should just go home.

She—

Would never hear the end of it from her siblings if she gave up now. Graham's infinite associates were doubtlessly watching every angle of the promenade.

Tommy let out a shaky breath. She was being foolish.

Philippa was not afraid to be Philippa. She wore more lace on her person than most people owned in their entire wardrobe. Philippa was the bluestockingest ringleader of the bluestockingest reading circle in existence. Philippa was proud to be Philippa.

Tommy could give fake Baron Vanderbean a *little* bit of mettle.

One conversation. She straightened her spine and set her hat at a rakish angle. Twenty minutes.

7

~~~

Philippa gripped her lace overdress in her fists and tried not to go slowly mad at the glacial pace of her mother's carriage.

"What is the point of driving around and around the park, purposefully never going anywhere?" she burst out.

"To see and be seen," came her mother's clipped voice. "I've told you a thousand times."

"I could stand in the middle of the grass," Philippa said. "Give everyone a nice long gander and then go home and do something reasonable with my time."

"See and be seen and *converse*," her mother amended.

"There's the Kimball carriage up ahead." Philippa leaned forward. "Gracie must be inside. I could talk to her."

"See and be seen and converse with *men*," Mother said in vexation. "Marriageable, *titled* men. You almost landed a duke, darling, so I shan't accept anything less than a lord. You know you can manage it. You're just being lazy."

Philippa *did* know she could do it. Rather, her dowry would accomplish it for her. It didn't really matter what sort of woman was going round in circles in Hyde Park.

She wasn't delaying her fate out of laziness. She avoided it because she didn't *want* it. Why must she choose a husband based on rank? Could not intelligence and character be relevant qualities as well? Should she not bear *some* modicum of affection for the man who would beget heirs upon her for the next untold number of years?

"Don't make that expression," chided her mother.

"I'm not making any expression," Philippa answered. Indeed, she was often accused of displaying no emotion at all, regardless of the circumstance.

"I know what your lack of expression *means*," said her mother. "It means you are displeased with your parents' guidance."

Did it mean that? It might mean that.

Mother gasped. "Never say you've fallen in love with a commoner."

Philippa sighed and shook her head.

No, she would never make that claim. She had *tried* to fall in love. *Yearned* to fall in love. But no matter how attractive the man or how pretty his words, there were no butterflies in her stomach or flutters in her chest. She was never light-headed or giddy or speechless or trembling with passion when waltzing with the lords her mother selected for her.

Philippa's heart didn't pitter-patter or leap for joy or skip a beat or any of the other things it was supposed to do. It just carried on, day after day, year after year, performing the same steady, predictable routine without excitement or drama, or making any deviation from what it had always done.

Much like Philippa. Even if it made her want to scream.

"Pinch your cheeks," said her mother. "Lord Whiddleburr is riding by."

Philippa did not pinch her cheeks.

She didn't care about the old marquess, and he didn't care about her. Whether they wound up at the altar had nothing to do with the color of her cheeks.

He nodded at Philippa and her mother.

Philippa pretended she didn't see him.

Mother waved vigorously enough to nearly tumble from the carriage.

Lord Whiddleburr wisely continued on.

"Blast," whispered her mother. "He rode right past."

Another bullet, dodged.

It was difficult to believe that people *wanted* to do this. Hyde Park was relatively sparse at the moment, but during the height of the London season, riders and pedestrians and carriages would fill the park, going round and round in circles for three solid hours every afternoon.

If there was any advantage to being married off against her will at the end of the season, it was the relief that she need no longer parade herself about like a show horse.

"What if I didn't marry?" she asked tentatively.

Her mother recoiled as though her daughter had just sprouted antlers *and* unfashionable freckles.

"Not *marry*?" she spluttered. "Of *course* you'll marry. *Every* woman wants to *marry*. The trick is selecting the right *husband*. He must be perfect in every way. *Titled*, Philippa. You'll belong to him for the rest of your life. That's a long time to spend shackled to the wrong man."

True enough.

Philippa never saw her mother and father in the same room at the same time. Perhaps they were the same person. Perhaps Philippa could wed herself.

"I want you to wed a man you admire," Mother continued. "Someone with wide shoulders and a strong jaw."

As much as she appreciated that her mother wanted her to secure a husband she *liked*, Philippa had never once judged a man by the width of his shoulders or the strength of his jaw. She found swooning over such details as nonsensical as a gentleman choosing a bride based on whether she pinched her cheeks for color.

"Oh!" Mother rapped her knuckles against Philippa's leg. "Straighten your spine. Here comes Lord Dalrymple."

Philippa straightened her spine. She would be forced to endure countless mind-deadening afternoons like this one until some hapless lord was dazzled enough by her fortune to offer for her hand. It might as well be Dalrymple.

It might as well be anyone.

"Good afternoon, Mrs. York, Miss York," said Lord Dalrymple. "How do you do today?"

Mother fluttered her hands and gurgled something incoherent, then unsubtly elbowed Philippa's side so that she would flutter her eyelashes and gurgle, too.

Why? Were men biologically predisposed to favor women who looked as though they were blinking dust from their eyes?

"We're fine," said Philippa. "The squab makes sitting still for three hours somewhat bearable."

Mother's elbow ground harder into her ribs.

"That's . . . wonderful," said Lord Dalrymple. "I always say, a fine lady should be placed in a fine perch."

"Like a chicken?" asked Philippa.

Her mother's elbow was definitely going to bruise her.

"You look lovely today," Mother cooed at Dalrymple. "Is that a new hat?"

Who cared if it was new or not? Eighty-three percent of the men present wore exactly the same hat. They were all copying each other, now that Brummell had fled to France.

Philippa was half convinced these promenades were just an excuse to while away the time for people who had nothing better to do at home. She calculated the probability of connecting with another human in any meaningful way while trotting about in circles to be abysmally close to none.

"It *is* a new hat," said Lord Dalrymple with obvious pride.

"You look impossibly handsome," Mother gushed, giving Philippa an extra jab with her elbow. "Doesn't he, darling? What wide shoulders and a strong jaw."

Philippa tilted her head to consider him.

She supposed he looked good. All gentlemen looked...tolerable. *They* were not the problem. Philippa was. She and her mother could agree on that much at least.

"You look like a print from a fashion repository," Philippa said.

Perhaps it was not the fluttery, gooey singsong Mother had hoped for, but Lord Dalrymple seemed pleased.

"That is what *I* said to my valet just this morning. I could be in a Cruikshank." He puffed up his chest.

Was Philippa supposed to be attracted to a puffed-up chest? Was he crowing like a cockerel because he thought Philippa was his future hen? Was that the real reason for feathers in one's bonnet? To signal which species of bird one was playing at?

"*Bok-bok-bok*," said Philippa.

Lord Dalrymple blinked. "I beg your pardon?"

"She said your valet is fortunate to gaze upon your visage every day, and she hopes to see you next Saturday at the Rosbotham soirée," Mother said quickly.

This was a gross mistranslation of Philippa's chicken noises.

"I...may attend," said Dalrymple, backing away. "I see someone up ahead. Good day, ladies."

"What is wrong with you?" Mother hissed. "He is *unmarried* and an *earl*."

Dalrymple was also not yet far enough away for this comment to go unheard. He glanced over his shoulder.

Philippa flapped one of her bonnet feathers at him.

The earl fled without a backward glance.

"You must waltz with him at the soirée," said Mother. "And flirt properly this time."

"I don't *want* to dance with a man who aspires to look like a caricature," said Philippa.

Her mother sighed. "I thought you were clever, darling. Is the world truly so difficult to understand?"

No. That was the problem. Philippa understood perfectly well what her role was destined to be, and the steps to take to achieve it.

Be an obedient daughter. Follow society's rules and expectations. Be a proper young lady. Attract a suitor. Become his betrothed. Get married. Be his wife. Have his children. Send her own daughters down the same path regardless of their wishes, no deviations allowed.

Become despondent.

Philippa was a busy, bookish spinster of means, who hosted wonderful bluestocking gatherings every week, in the beautiful Grosvenor Square town house she'd lived in all of her life. Why would she give that up for a man? As much as she longed for adventure, there were some stories she'd rather not unfold. Such as losing the best parts of being Philippa.

"Good afternoon," came a rich tenor. "I don't suppose you could point me in the direction of the loveliest bluestocking in Hyde Park?"

In tandem, Philippa and her mother jerked their gazes toward the unfamiliar voice.

A slender, well-dressed gentleman sat astride a handsome steed, easily keeping pace with the Yorks' carriage. He had dark hair and laughing brown eyes and lips that seemed in constant danger of turning up in a smile.

In short: He was attractive. Objectively handsome. It was an inarguable fact.

Philippa waited for a flutter in her heart or in her stomach or in any other region that could flutter.

Nothing.

As usual, her body was broken. No matter how often she placed herself in the paths of eligible bachelors and tried her best to obey the rules, she had never felt the flutterings of desire she read so much about. Other friends developed new *tendres* every fortnight. Philippa yearned for a romance of her own.

The gentleman saw her looking at him, and at this, his lips did curve into a smile.

It was a fine smile. An excellent smile.

It just...did nothing.

There was no hope.

Philippa had glimpsed the handsome stranger once or twice this afternoon during their endless laps about the park. He looked vaguely familiar, as if they might have crossed paths at Gunter's or Almack's, but she did not know his name.

Speaking without an introduction was—according to Mother—an appalling breach of etiquette. Blatantly alluding to his potential interest in Philippa, however, was a magic balm that healed all rifts in decorum. And if she were being honest, referring to her *mind* rather than her rosy cheeks had caught her attention as well.

"Ohh." Mother fluttered her hands and her eyelids and the entire carriage. "I daresay your search is over. Of course you must mean my Philippa. But you have us at a disadvantage, young man. I don't believe we've met."

"You may have met my father," the gentleman replied. "Baron Vanderbean."

Mother's gasp could be interpreted as either delight or dismay. She had a horror of the entire Wynchester family...but "Baron" was indeed a title.

"Of *course* I knew your father," Mother gushed.

She had never met the man.

"I have long desired to meet the new Baron Vanderbean," Mother continued. "I am overjoyed to have my wish granted at long last."

This was a bald-faced lie, but at least it let Philippa know how her mother expected the conversation to proceed.

"You have a nice horse," Philippa offered. "It's very… equine."

Mother closed her eyes.

Baron Vanderbean widened his, and lowered his voice to a whisper. "Did you notice that, too? I wonder if he enjoys his lot in life. What do you think my horse really wants?"

Philippa blinked.

Baron Vanderbean smiled back at her expectantly.

"Maybe he hates being a horse," she said. "Maybe he thinks walking about in circles is a dreadful use of his time. Maybe he'd rather be home reading."

Mother opened her eyes. "Horses cannot *read*, Philippa."

"How do we know?" asked Baron Vanderbean good-naturedly. "I, for one, have never invited a horse into my library in order to find out. The moment I return home, I shall rectify this error at once."

"I hope your library is on the ground floor," said Philippa. "It would add insult to injury to expect your horse to clop up stairs to have a look about, only to discover your taste in books is not in alignment with his."

"Or that the books are in the wrong language," Baron Vanderbean added. "It would be the height of presumption for me to presume an Arabian horse prefers his novels in English."

"It would be the height of presumption to presume he prefers novels at all," Philippa answered.

Baron Vanderbean grinned at her.

Philippa's breath caught. Was this *banter*? Was she *bantering*?

"What makes you think your horse doesn't enjoy history tomes or natural philosophy?" she asked archly. "Is it his long hair? The way he shakes his tail? His curling eyelashes?"

Baron Vanderbean tapped the side of his jaw. "I have not performed a comprehensive study to correlate eyelash shape with literature preferences. You have sent me in an entirely new direction of inquiry, and I am afraid I must depart at once in order to address this very pressing oversight. I shall report back with my findings, the first of which is that *your* eyelashes are very pleasing indeed."

Report...back?

After one conversation with Philippa, Baron Vanderbean wanted to have...another?

"Tell him you'll be here tomorrow," Mother whispered.

"I'll be here tomorrow," Philippa parroted.

There. She was a bird, after all.

Perhaps there *was* hope.

Baron Vanderbean touched the brim of his hat. "Until tomorrow, then."

She stared after the handsome lord as he rode away. Not to flirt with a young lady in the next carriage, but to gallop out of the park altogether, as though his inane conversation with Philippa was the entire reason he had come.

"You did it," her mother breathed. "You chased him off in a way that makes him actually want to come back."

"He was probably being polite," Philippa said.

"He didn't seem polite," Mother replied. "Approaching us without an introduction was impertinent in the first degree. He let *you* be impertinent and bluestocking-ish, too. Do you think the baron means to court you?"

Of course he didn't.

Did he?

8

Tommy couldn't hear the galloping of her horse's hooves over the pounding of her own heart as she raced back home to the safety of Islington and away from the curious eyes of the ton.

She'd done it. She'd spoken to Philippa!

Yes, yes, Philippa thought she was Horace Wynchester, the new Baron Vanderbean, but the only detail that mattered was that Tommy had pranced right up to her and said how-do-you-do and a hundred other things without garbling her words or tumbling from her horse.

And now—she had to do it again! She'd told Philippa she'd be *back*. And Philippa had said, "I'll be here tomorrow." Ha! It wasn't exactly a lover's assignation, but Tommy would take it. She never actually thought she'd manage to speak to Philippa at all, much less have a second such encounter planned for the very next day.

The moment she arrived at home, she tossed the reins to a footman and dashed up the path to the front door.

"Mr. Hastings, I did it!" she called out in glee. It was all she could do not to take the poor butler by the hands and dance him about at his post.

"What did you do?" Graham's disembodied voice

shouted down from the first floor. "Come upstairs and tell me!"

Tommy took the stairs by twos and skidded into the Planning Parlor with a smile so wide, her cheeks were already starting to ache. "I talked to Philippa!"

Graham stopped organizing his albums. "*You* talked to her? Or... who are you exactly, at the moment?"

"Pah." Tommy waved this aside. "I had to pretend I'm the new Baron Vanderbean to overcome my nerves. Bean was never nervous. His heir would not embarrass him."

"'Horace' acquitted himself nicely?"

"Horace *flirted*. A shameful rake, that new heir. Choosy, too. Eyes only for Miss York. Who, I might add, ended our Hyde Park tête-à-tête with, 'I'll be here tomorrow.'"

"Ooh," Graham said appreciatively. "She *enjoyed* your flirting, Horace, you old rascal."

Tommy beamed at him.

"Just think," her brother said. "You could have done this last July instead of spending an entire year in a cowardly puddle of nerves."

"Don't ruin this for me," Tommy warned. "I am quite pleased with myself at the moment."

"As you should be." Jacob strode into the room with a mouse peeking from his jacket pocket. "Marjorie and I didn't think you had it in you."

"I knew she did," Marjorie protested loudly as she entered the room. "I had a side bet with Elizabeth."

Tommy's jaw dropped. "You *wagered* on whether I'd speak to Philippa?"

"I stopped wagering with them months ago," Graham muttered. "You cost me *so* many quid."

Marjorie and Jacob took their usual seats, though it didn't look right. The family always sat in the same order as their cherished family portrait—an oil painting of Puck and six fellow imps cavorting about a fire in a magical wood—just as they had done for nineteen years.

The canvas had been their first purchase as a family. For many of the siblings, their first purchase at all. It was more than art. It symbolized the team they had become, and the long future of togetherness that awaited them.

Their happy tradition of arranging themselves like the painting had ceased last summer, when Bean had died. It had become even less familiar once Chloe left home to live with Faircliffe. There were blank spaces now. In the parlor, in their home, and in Tommy's heart.

"Wait." She turned to Graham. "I cost you money?"

"Forty-six quid," he said morosely.

Elizabeth stepped into the parlor and jangled a heavy coin purse. "Ah, the sweet, sweet sound of victory."

Tommy stood next to Graham and whirled on the others. "You bet *against* me, you knaves!"

"And won." Elizabeth jangled her coin purse. "Time and again."

"Not today," Marjorie informed her. "She did it. Er, Baron Vanderbean, that is."

Elizabeth dropped her mouth open and widened her eyes. "Horace Wynchester, you sly dog. Never have I been happier to lose a wager in my life. I mean it."

"Congratulations, Tommy." Marjorie reached for the bell pull. "I'll ring for cakes and champagne."

"New bet," said Jacob. "How long until she tells Philippa she's not actually a baron?"

"No bets," Tommy said firmly. "I'll never tell her."

Elizabeth shook her sword stick. "Didn't you *just* prove that the world wouldn't end if you tried for what you want?"

"It won't end for the Horace Wynchesters of the world,"

Tommy corrected. "I have proven repeatedly that I will expire on the spot before I am able to approach Philippa as myself."

"But don't you want her to know who you are?" Jacob's pocket wiggled. The little mouse...was a *bat*. "Wouldn't it be even nicer if the person she hoped to see tomorrow was Tommy Wynchester?"

Tommy *did* want that. Bean had loved her for herself, and so did her siblings. But no one else would.

Bean was gone. Chloe had also gone. It hurt too much to lose someone she cared about. It would sting to be rejected by someone who didn't know her well at all. And it would hurt even more to be rejected by someone who *did* know the real Tommy. It wasn't worth it.

She might not feel like a woman, but she was one, physically. Which meant she didn't have the same freedom to flirt and fail like would-be rakehells did at society balls. Not with someone like Philippa. Tommy wouldn't want to be Horace Wynchester permanently any more than she wished to live her life as a lady, but indulging her masculine side afforded her the freedom to court Philippa openly.

A ride or two in Hyde Park as a baron wouldn't risk much. Then Philippa could return to her vaunted world, and Tommy could return to the more shadowy corners, where she needn't hide who she was behind a waistcoat and a title.

"I am perfectly happy just as things are," Tommy told her siblings. "We have each other. What else could we need?"

"We love you, too," said Marjorie.

Graham grinned at Tommy. "Wynchesters forever."

All five siblings touched their hands to their hearts and raised their fingers to the sky.

9

At noon, Philippa found herself once again alone in the dining room. Usually, such meals were unbearable. Today, she was consumed with thoughts of Baron Vanderbean. What was he doing at this moment? Would he take meals with his scandalous wards?

Philippa paused with her forkful of sliced fruits halfway to her mouth. *Did* the Wynchesters ever take meals together? Were they ever home long enough for such a formal event to occur? Or were they always off on one adventure or another, like the chivalric knights in her illuminated manuscripts?

She could imagine Baron Vanderbean in gleaming armor. He had looked magnificent upon his horse, and of all the pretty maidens in the park, he had chosen Philippa to rescue from boredom. Why had he done it? Would he do it again?

Whatever his motives, she was certain he did not return his gelding to the mews and immediately question his equines about their literary preferences. The image brought a smile to her face. A smile! By herself in the dining room! The baron's effect on her was magical indeed. He made her feel less lonely, even when she was all alone.

Philippa finished her dessert. She sipped her wine, but never more than that. She liked to remain in full control of her body. It was the one thing she *did* control.

As she left the drawing room, she peeked through the ground-floor rooms in search of her parents. They took their meals separately, Mother in her private chamber and Father in his study. Nonetheless, one or the other occasionally ventured downstairs. Mother, to entertain guests. Father, to read his paper by the superior light of the cerulean sitting room.

"Upstairs, I'm afraid," Underwood murmured from his post at the door when Philippa neared the sitting room.

She sighed. "Thank you."

There was no sense pretending she was poking her head into doorways because it amused her. Underwood had watched her toddle in search of her parents from the moment she could walk.

As an adult, Philippa was far more likely to escape into a book. In fact, now was as good a time as any to take a closer look at her Northrup manuscript.

Glimpsing the reused paper in the binding of Philippa's book had given Damaris the idea for the cipher. Perhaps Philippa paging back through it would spark an idea of how to help.

And it could help to keep her mind off whether handsome Baron Vanderbean really would return to Hyde Park today.

She cleared the combs and brushes from her dressing table and placed the manuscript in the center. Her dressing room was a poor substitute for a library, but it made a serviceable private study.

This second volume of Sir Reginald's collected tales of English chivalry was in wretched condition. Philippa pulled on gloves and wished she'd purchased pristine copies of all four volumes before her parents had forbidden new acquisitions.

She eased open the cover as gently as she could. The meticulously crafted binding had begun to crack and peel on the interior side of the cover, revealing tantalizing glimpses of other text beneath.

Manuscript binders often reused older material. There was even a word for scraping the text off old parchment and covering it with new text: *palimpsest*. Parchment reused in that manner tended to become part of the primary pages. These were never meant to be seen beneath the binding.

It was fascinating to think she might glimpse a page from an ancient manuscript. Wouldn't that be exciting?

With the tip of a clean quill, she nudged a torn edge of the interior binding aside to reveal a bit more.

What she could see of the exposed section appeared to be penned in a style similar to the finished manuscript. No forgotten medieval treasures today, then. It didn't appear to be scraps, but an unbroken piece of parchment. She wondered if something had happened to an original draft of something or other. Perhaps a cat had spilled ink on part of the page, or a leaky roof had ruined part of a book.

She eased the loose fragments aside a little more with her quill.

Was the text penned by Sir Reginald? Did he always reuse his own discarded papers, or might Philippa's manuscript be special?

She longed to liberate the hidden page, but could not do so without destroying the binding.

"Drat." Philippa pulled off her gloves and leaned back.

If she owned a duplicate copy in better condition, *then*

perhaps she could justify destroying an ancient manuscript in the name of satisfying her curiosity. Better yet, she ought to acquire the entire collection.

Her parents might have prohibited making bluestocking *acquisitions*, but that didn't prevent one from sending a few inquiries, did it? She could find out which collectors owned the highest-quality items, and plan for—

The door to her dressing room burst open.

"What are you doing?" demanded her mother. "We must depart for our promenade within the hour!"

Philippa leapt to her feet to block the manuscript from view. "It's not a promenade if we're in a carriage."

"We won't be in a carriage," Mother answered. "I want everyone to have an unobstructed view of Baron Vanderbean singling you out for conversation."

Philippa had been trying *so hard* not to think about him, in itself a new occurrence. When had she ever obsessed about a man? Yet here she was. What if Vanderbean didn't come? What if he did, and this time their conversation was as disastrous as all of her previous interactions with other men? What if he regretted having singled her out, and the entire ton had an unobstructed view of dapper Baron Vanderbean fleeing from Philippa at speed?

"Where is your maid?" fretted her mother. "We simply do not have time for—"

"I'm already ready," Philippa replied. She'd been ready for hours. "I offered Octavia a well-deserved respite."

"A *respite*?" Mother flapped her hands in agitation. "When you're...you're..." Her voice trailed off and her arms dropped back to her sides.

Philippa was indeed presentable.

Not because of any eagerness to travel in slow, mind-deadening circles for three excruciating hours, but because

she *liked* to be presentable. And…just in case Baron Vanderbean *did* make good on his promise to speak with her
again.

"Well…good," said Mother. "You are indeed lovely, darling. Any man should be lucky to make you his bride. Come.
We should be on our way."

"We wouldn't wish to seem desperate and overeager,"
Philippa said.

"How about this," said Mother. "I will select the five most
eligible titled lords, and you can choose the one with the
best library."

It was comments such as these that made it difficult to stay
vexed with her parents. They wanted the best for Philippa,
if limited to their narrow definition of "best." They believed
proximity to a sufficiently grand library would make up for
misery in every other aspect of her life.

Philippa hoped they were right.

"What I would like, even more than a well-appointed
library," she said softly, "is a husband I can tolerate."

"Humph," said her mother. "One needn't tolerate one's
husband. With luck, you'll rarely see him. It's one's *marriage*
one must tolerate. A lofty title and a large library will serve
just fine."

Mother might be mercenary, but she wasn't *wrong*. To
Philippa's future husband, a young bride and a large dowry in
exchange for a few books would be an excellent transaction.
They saw such matches made every week at Almack's, when
the season was in swing.

"I have an idea," Mother announced.

"Heaven save me," Philippa muttered under her breath.

"It involves that Baron Vanderbean," Mother continued.

Philippa's eyebrows rose. She was surprised a Wynchester
would figure into her mother's plans.

"It's not ideal," Mother said. "He's *foreign*, and in possession of the lowest possible title."

Philippa nodded. "True. If one discounts knights and baronets and military officers and—"

"He's young," Mother interrupted, "and a bit raffish. But...after failing to marry the Duke of Faircliffe last season as expected, *your* image is also tarnished."

"Have the offers from fortune hunters dried up?" Philippa asked in surprise.

"Those will never dry up," Mother said. "They also don't count. Fortune hunters are not real people."

"The Duke of Faircliffe was a fortune hunter," Philippa reminded her.

"The Duke of Faircliffe is a *duke*," Mother retorted, as though a dukedom cured everything.

Philippa supposed, in Polite Society, it did.

Even if the Balcovian baron hadn't been "foreign" and a Wynchester, his delighted willingness to entertain Philippa's awkward, extended equine metaphor had lost him favor with her mother. The baron also seemed to *like* Philippa's oddness, which made him a little odd as well.

That trait was perhaps Philippa's favorite thing about him.

"Therefore," Mother announced, "you should welcome Baron Vanderbean's flirtations."

Philippa stared at her. "You want me to marry Baron Vanderbean?"

How curious. The notion did not fill her with the revulsion her mother's schemes usually provoked. Although Philippa didn't know Baron Vanderbean well enough to categorically state that she *wanted* him, their brief interaction was by far the highlight of Philippa's five years on the marriage mart. If further acquaintance with the baron proved just as—

"Of course you cannot marry Baron Vanderbean," Mother said. "You're to use him as a stepping-stone and marry someone else."

"Use him," Philippa repeated. "To marry someone else."

"Someone *better*," Mother clarified, as though Philippa might not be following along with the plan. "A baron's attention should catch the eye of a viscount. A viscount's attention could catch the eye of an earl. An earl's attention could catch the eye of a marquess. And a marquess's attention could catch the eye of a duke!"

"*Are* there any unmarried dukes now that Faircliffe's been taken?" Philippa asked.

"Marry someone other than Vanderbean," Mother snapped. "I will accept a viscount at this point, as long as he is respectable and English."

"And has a nice library," Philippa added. "They really should add that to *Debrett's*."

"Listen carefully," Mother said. "The advantage of Baron Vanderbean is his title and his wealth. He doesn't *need* your dowry. Gossips will jump to the conclusion he's actually interested in *you*."

"So illogical," Philippa murmured. "What must he be thinking?"

"The *disadvantage* of Baron Vanderbean...is that he is a Wynchester," Mother concluded. "You're to lead him on without reeling him in. Keep him interested but not quite ready to pounce, until you have a better offer on the line."

"And if he offers, tell him, 'No, I shall betroth myself instead to someone less foreign and higher ranking'?"

"Exactly," Mother said with satisfaction. "His interest will help to increase your popularity, which can open up countless better opportunities."

"I think we could count them." Philippa tried to edge her

mother out of her dressing room. "There are eight unmarried lords above the rank of baron, only half of which are currently in town. This is a very ambitious plan."

"I will accept heirs apparent," Mother said begrudgingly. "Many of those are here in London. According to the scandal columns, several gentlemen's clubs remain open year-round. You could still be a duchess."

"No more dukes."

"Then a countess or marchioness." Mother cast her gaze over Philippa and smiled. "Once you've an acceptable gentleman or two in the wings, perhaps we can allow *two* hours per week with your little reading circle."

Philippa jerked her eyes toward her mother's. "If I'm being courted, I can have some of my freedoms back?"

"Courted by the *right* gentleman," Mother reminded her firmly.

An important distinction. Philippa dropped her gaze. It was impossible.

"However," her mother said craftily, "if you *do* manage to secure and sustain Baron Vanderbean's interest, I shall relay this to your father as a sincere effort of good faith."

"Why does it feel like blackmail?" Philippa muttered. She wished her father would speak to her himself. There was a thing or two she'd like to tell him.

"Everyone extorts everyone else all the time, darling."

"Do they?" Philippa said doubtfully.

Her mother pursed her lips. "That's what a society *is*. A group of people with agreed-upon methods of social extortion. 'Do this, or suffer the consequences.' We call it 'proper comportment' so that it sounds nice. You cannot fight it. It's just the way things are."

The way things are. Philippa was so *tired* of the way things were.

A footman appeared in the doorway to Philippa's dressing room.

"Pardon the intrusion," he said. "There's a caller for Miss York."

A caller for Philippa? On a Saturday?

She held out her hand for the card. Her mother snatched it from the footman's fingers.

"Baron Vanderbean is here." Mother breathed in wonder.

10

*M*other flapped the baron's calling card toward Philippa's face. "Darling, this is splendid. *You* are splendid. Come, come. He isn't standing at the front door, is he? I was clear that anyone with a title is to be shown into my cerulean sitting room."

The footman inclined his head. "The baron awaits in your cerulean sitting room."

"Well, don't just stand there. Is someone making tea?"

"He may not have time or interest in tea," Philippa said. "You told me a proper call from a gentleman should not last more than twenty minutes."

"Surely it cannot take our kitchen twenty minutes to make a pot of tea," Mother said. "And everyone is interested in sandwiches and cakes. And perhaps fruit and a bit of cheese. See to it at once. I shan't have him saying our hospitality was lacking."

The footman disappeared to do her bidding.

Mother reached over to pinch Philippa's cheeks.

"Ouch." Philippa ducked away. "I thought I wasn't trying to ensnare him."

"*He* doesn't know that." Mother grabbed Philippa by the

elbow and steered her toward the corridor. "Make haste, make haste. There's a baron in our sitting room."

When Philippa and her mother arrived in the sitting room, he was looking out the windows with his hat in his hands. As before, his lean form was outfitted in a finely tailored coat and tight pantaloons. He stood a good four or five inches taller than Philippa.

Objectively handsome, she reminded herself, and waited to feel the promised flutter.

Her cold dead heart remained cold and dead.

Upon hearing them arrive, Baron Vanderbean turned from the window and made a fabulous leg. "Mrs. York. Miss York."

"You still have your *hat*?" Mother gasped. "What can our butler be thinking? I will summon him at once and—"

"No need," the baron said. "I shan't be staying."

Philippa thought her mother might expire on the spot.

"In fact," he continued, "I am on my way to Hyde Park. My phaeton is spacious and comfortable. It would be my honor and privilege if Miss York would like to join me."

Mother's excitement was palpable. "Of course we'll come! A phaeton—that's just the thing. Everyone will see us. I'll ring for our bonnets at once."

Any hope of enjoying the baron's company evaporated. Mother would be far too eager to put the gears of her machinations in motion. Never mind that a phaeton was a carriage meant for two.

Baron Vanderbean's eyes met Philippa's.

Everyone said her face was blank and unreadable. How she wished she could transmit her thoughts silently.

He winked.

"I would love for you to join us, madam." His expression was the perfect combination of chagrined and earnest.

"Though I admit, I was also hoping for an opportunity to get to know your daughter. As you observed, a phaeton is quite high and open, making the entire park our chaperone. I would hate to take you from your busy schedule."

Philippa was surprised and impressed that Baron Vanderbean had managed to interpret her expression after all.

"I'm not busy," Mother assured Baron Vanderbean. "I was just saying to Philippa, what I wished for most was a long, leisurely—"

Two maids and a footman rushed into the room carrying heavy trays.

"Your tea, madam," panted one of the maids.

"Were we quick enough?" the other whispered.

"Of *course* you must have your long, leisurely tea," said Baron Vanderbean, taking in the mountains of cakes and sandwiches. "I would not dream of interrupting your plans. Shall I return your daughter in thirty minutes?"

Mother pressed her lips together, visibly weighing her desire to insert herself into the situation against her even more fervent desire to keep Baron Vanderbean dangling on the proverbial hook for as long as possible.

"You may keep her for one hour," Mother said at last. "And not a moment longer."

Philippa stared at her in disbelief. Mother was allowing Baron Vanderbean to spirit Philippa away for an entire hour? What were they supposed to *talk* about for an hour?

Unimportant, she realized. For Mother, the outing had nothing to do with the baron's intentions, and everything to do with the number of eyes glimpsing the two together—and increasing the probability that gossip of Philippa's apparent desirability would be all over London by morning.

Baron Vanderbean's forwardness was playing right into Mother's hands.

"Take the pink bonnet with the ostrich feathers," Mother said. It was the most colorful bonnet in Philippa's collection. The dramatic feathers alone were enough to command attention.

It could give them something to talk about when Philippa failed to banter properly.

She curtseyed. "Enjoy your tea, Mother."

A private outing without constant interruptions and remonstrations had not even crossed her mind as a possibility, but now that it was within reach, she would do nothing to jeopardize it.

After buttoning her favorite green velvet pelisse and tying on her least favorite ostrich feather bonnet, Philippa followed the baron to his phaeton.

His brown eyes held hers as he handed her up into the carriage.

The strange excitement humming beneath Philippa's skin was surely due to the novelty of the situation. Wasn't it?

As Baron Vanderbean lifted the reins, his eyes twinkled with mischief. "We have an hour before we're missed. Hyde Park? Or should we attempt to catch the balloon launch at Vauxhall? The pilot is a friend of mine and would let us on board if I beg."

A burst of longing shot through her. Being *in* a balloon had never occurred to her. That sort of reckless antic must occur to Wynchesters all the time. Their lives were an unending series of adventures. The sorts of things Philippa read about, but never actually happened to her.

Saying yes would almost be worth her parents' ire and the inevitable punishment.

"Hyde Park, I'm afraid," she said with regret. "I'd wager my mother is peeking between the curtains to make certain we trot off in the right direction. Or is sending notes to all of our neighbors."

"Next time, then," Baron Vanderbean answered cheerfully, as though rides in hot-air balloons were as common as drives in the park.

He thought there *would* be a next time, Philippa realized with a start. She hadn't yet stared at him blankly and said all the wrong things for an hour. He simply assumed they'd get on well and that he'd be happy to repeat the encounter.

Perhaps Baron Vanderbean's relatives had said kind things about her. Chloe, or even Great-Aunt Wynchester, with whom Philippa never felt self-conscious.

Perhaps Philippa was thinking far too much about a man she wasn't going to marry.

"Have you ascertained your horse's reading preferences?" she asked.

There. That would keep the topic on nothing at all.

"I *did* inquire," said Baron Vanderbean. "He declined to tell me."

"He declined to tell you? Or you don't speak horse?"

"I'll have you know 'horse' is a species, not a language. He would be miffed to hear you conflate the two. Tulip happens to speak my Balcovian dialect."

"Your horse is a Balcovian Arabian?" Philippa said skeptically.

"I said he *speaks* it. Tulip is a clever horse. And yes, he's a Balcovian Arabian. Haven't you ever been two things at once?"

"I suppose we're all many things at once," she admitted.

"Just so." The baron's deep brown eyes were strangely intense. He blinked and smiled, and his expression became sunny and teasing once again. "Did you visit your mews to ensure it's stocked with your animals' preferred reading material?"

"I'm not allowed to go," she replied. "Or I *would* have taken them a few books, if only to make the space cheerier."

"I'll slip in when no one's looking and leave a volume or two about," Baron Vanderbean promised. He guided his carriage toward the park. "If you had to guess, would your beasts lean more toward novels, biographies, or poetry?"

Her horses had shown no sparks of interest when Philippa entered the carriage with her usual purchases. It would have to be something unusual.

"Poetry," she decided.

Tulip nickered, as though in approval.

The baron gave a sharp nod. "Consider it done. My brother Jacob is an expert in the subject. He will have fine recommendations. What about you? Is there anything you long to add to your collection?"

"The Northrup manuscripts," she replied without hesitation.

He frowned. "I thought you already had one."

Was *that* the reason he'd wanted to be alone with her today? To discuss what to do about Damaris's dreadful uncle? Of course it was. Philippa's cheeks heated. While she had been thinking about the baron, he had been thinking about the case. She must do the same.

"I have a copy of the second volume," she said, "but it is in poor condition. Just this morning, I discovered—"

But they'd reached the park. From the moment they drove through the open gates, all of Mother's wildest matchmaking dreams started to come true.

Heads that never turned Philippa's way, turned Philippa's way. Persons who never slowed their fine carriages for more than a brief *how do you do*, no matter how Mother tried to engage them, paused to gawp at Philippa and her handsome companion.

She found herself performing introduction after introduction, as if Miss York the inveterate wallflower gadding about town with a charming, raffish baron was perfectly commonplace.

For his part, Baron Vanderbean seemed cross with the attention, as though he really had hoped for an uninterrupted hour of conversation with Philippa.

"My apologies," he said after greeting one of the patronesses of Almack's. "I did not realize my presence would cause such a fuss."

Mother had realized it. She hoped he would keep causing fusses until Philippa landed an English lord.

"It's no bother," Philippa assured him. Then she remembered that Baron Vanderbean's father had had a reputation for being reclusive. Given this was the first week most of society had ever glimpsed the new baron, it was reasonable to assume he was just as private. So far, he hadn't sought anyone's attention but Philippa's. "At least, it's no bother to me."

"As long as *you're* happy," he said softly. "The offer to float away still stands."

"That would be unlikely to cause *less* of a stir," she said.

"The bigger the stir, the more amusing I find it," he said with a grin so mischievous she could almost believe he meant it. That his discomfort was not with all the unusual attention, but annoyance at being pulled away from Philippa for even a moment.

It was flattering...and improbable. Yet she wanted so much for it to be true.

"How haven't we met before?" she blurted out. "Have you been in Balcovia all of this time, and only just arrived?"

She recognized the impertinence of her question after it was already out of her mouth. She had essentially just accused him of failing to attend his own father's funeral last year. Of course, the notice might not have reached him in time, but still—she had not meant to remind him of tragedy.

The baron lifted the reins and coaxed the carriage faster. "I've been...around."

She'd said the wrong thing again. Even after his mourning period had ended, society invitations were their own paradox. One needed to know someone in order to be introduced to someone else, which could keep even a dashing lord like Baron Vanderbean stuck on the outside.

"I'm sorry," she said. "You asked me here today to discuss Damaris's case for the cipher, not your personal affairs. I have no right to pry."

"I forgot about the case," he replied, his expression serious. "I asked you to accompany me because I wanted to spend time with you."

She gave him a self-deprecating smile. "You couldn't find a better option than a bluestocking?"

"That's *why* I like you." The baron's dark eyes didn't leave hers. "I admire people who are unafraid to think for themselves, and I admire you in particular."

Her breath caught. That was the single nicest thing a man had ever said to her.

"If you have any flaw that I can see," he continued, "it is that you are not quite enough of a bluestocking. A proper bookish spinster would have spoken to my horse directly in his native Balcovian Arabic dialect, rather than impose upon a hapless human baron as middleman."

She giggled and immediately clapped a hand over her mouth.

A *giggle?* Coming from *her?* What was happening? Was she *flirting?*

This was friendship, she told herself. She had never been

friends with a man before. None had ever tried, and to be fair, neither had Philippa. She had always preferred the company of women, though try as she might, she'd never shared the compulsion to become giggly and giddy in the presence of a man.

Except she *had* just giggled in the presence of a man for the first time. What on earth was next?

"Don't cover your mouth," said Baron Vanderbean, his brown eyes warm and intent. "It's one of my favorite parts of your very pretty face."

Oh.

He *did* intend to court her.

Philippa's dead heart hadn't fluttered, but a giggle was a wonderful, terrible sign. She *liked* Baron Vanderbean. She might have welcomed his attentions...if he were the sort of man her parents would permit her to marry.

She could not possibly string this sweet, romantic, happy-go-lucky man along for the next three months, only to cold-bloodedly dash his hopes when she turned her back on him to marry someone "better."

She took a deep breath. "I have a confession."

"So do I," he said, "though I'm likely never to make mine. You first."

"I cannot marry you," she blurted. "My parents have preemptively rejected any future offer. It was kind of you to invite me to the park today, but ultimately a waste of your time. I'm afraid you never had a chance."

He looked at her for a long moment.

Was it too blunt? Of course it was too blunt. Mother constantly harped that Philippa's straightforward, logical thoughts were completely inappropriate. But wasn't fraudulently leading on a perfectly nice man just as inappropriate?

"I knew my admiration of you would go nowhere," he said

at last. A wistful smile flitted at his lips. "Though I might have hoped *Baron Vanderbean* had a chance."

Philippa frowned. "Did you just refer to yourself in the third person?"

"No," Baron Vanderbean replied. "I'm Tommy Wynchester."

11

❦

"Tommy?" Philippa repeated.

Doubt seeped into Tommy's bones. And raw panic.

She hadn't meant to tell the truth. But Philippa had been kind and brave enough to do so. *She* hadn't rejected Baron Vanderbean. Her parents had preemptively done so. Which implied Philippa might not have done, if the decision were up to her.

And since Tommy *wasn't* Baron Vanderbean, and hadn't intended to be him for more than a few stolen moments, it was only fair to show Philippa the same courtesy.

Plus, her siblings were right. Tommy could not go to her grave without presenting herself *as* herself to Philippa at least once. Yet nothing terrified her more than being rejected by the woman she'd loved from afar for so long. Especially not now, in this moment, when they were alone together for the first time, side by side in a carriage, public but private.

Somehow, she managed to nod. "Yes, I'm Tommy."

Philippa was close enough to touch. The softness of her cheek, the silkiness of her hair, a velvet pelisse that hid voluptuous curves Tommy imagined seeing bare. Philippa's hand was *right there*. Inches from Tommy's. Philippa's mouth just a little farther away. Philippa's wide blue eyes... very, very confused.

"Well... Tommy," she said slowly. "If we're to be friends, I suppose you may call me Philippa. Is it a Balcovian custom or a Wynchester custom to be intimate so quickly?"

"Both," Tommy croaked. "I mean neither. That is... I'm not Baron Vanderbean. I'm Tommy Wynchester."

Philippa stared at her, then cackled with glee. "Not Baron Vanderbean! A different Wynchester brother! I hadn't known I could be more delighted with you, and here you are, delighting me beyond all measure. Mother thinks she's pulling the wool over your eyes, and you're not even the man she thinks you are!"

"Er," said Tommy.

Philippa was delighted with her? *Should* Tommy correct her? Did it matter?

"You aren't upset I'm not a baron?" Tommy asked.

"Since we are never to have a courtship, you could be a chimneysweep for all I mind," Philippa pointed out reasonably.

Tommy didn't feel reasonable. There might only be a hand's width of space between her hip and Philippa's, but that was as close as they would ever be.

If Baron Vanderbean wasn't a good enough catch, common Tommy Wynchester was an even more laughable match. To Philippa, it was all a grand jest.

"I feel as though most people *would* mind," Tommy said. "If a baron turned out to be a chimneysweep."

"Then I am honored not to be most people," Philippa answered. "You are certainly unique. Might I inquire *why* you're pretending to be a baron?"

"It's complicated," Tommy hedged.

Philippa nodded. "I figured as much. My life has never been complicated. This is the most exciting turn it has ever taken."

Well, if *that* was all she wanted, then Tommy was an endless store of surprising twists. She could confess her true sex. She could take Philippa's hands in hers and lift them to her lips to kiss them. She could take Philippa into her lap and kiss *her*. She could...

Not do any of those things. Not here in Hyde Park.

Not ever.

A carriage pulled alongside the Wynchester phaeton, revealing the Earl and Countess of Southwell. They made twin expectant expressions at Philippa.

"How do you do, Lady Southwell, Lord Southwell?" she greeted them obediently.

"How do you do, Miss York?" said the countess. "Who is your gentleman?"

"Er," said Tommy.

"Oh, he's not *my* gentleman," Philippa said. "This is Baron Vanderbean."

Tommy coughed into her gloved hand.

"I've already begun," Philippa whispered. "Why stop now?"

"Baron Vanderbean!" The countess sent a look of shock to her husband and drew herself up taller. "I suppose you've informed him of our little soirée tomorrow night?"

"Oh no, Lady Southwell," said Philippa. "I would never be so presumptuous."

"I suppose you wouldn't," said the countess. "I can scarcely credit my eyes at the sight of you with— But none of that is important. Baron Vanderbean, it would be our honor if you were to avail yourself of our hospitality. I'll have a proper invitation sent round this evening."

Before Tommy could reply, the wheels of the Southwell

carriage sped up and whisked them forward to the next encounter.

Tommy snorted. "Why would it be her honor? Not one person has sent Baron Vanderbean an invitation or dropped off a calling card?"

Philippa's eyes sparkled. "It would be her honor because you're here with *me*. By accepting your escort this afternoon, I've inadvertently bested the most celebrated society hostesses. Reclusive Baron Vanderbean! Out in public with a wallflower! They will fight like cockerels to be the first to host you at a private gathering."

"But I'm not Baron Vanderbean," Tommy pointed out.

Philippa arched her brows. "You weren't too concerned about that before you told *me* the truth."

"I'm never concerned about temporary costumes," Tommy admitted. "I'll pretend to be Queen of Balcovia for the afternoon if it amuses me. I just hadn't meant to make you complicit in my schemes."

"Make me complicit in your schemes," Philippa begged. "I want to be an active part in your escapades. You Wynchesters are the most interesting family I have ever met, and I haven't even met all of you. None of you has any idea what it's like to be me."

"I thought you liked being a bluestocking."

"I *love* being a bluestocking," Philippa answered. "But why should 'clever' and 'curious' be synonymous with 'overlooked' and 'left behind'? Why can't I translate ancient Latin texts for my own entertainment and *also* be the queen of the ball?"

"Do you *want* to be the queen of the ball?"

"No." Philippa sighed. "It would involve one of my most abhorred activities: conversing with and dancing attendance upon an endless stream of strange men."

"Coincidentally," said Tommy, "also one of *my* least favorite activities."

"I wish to be the heroine of my own story. I want to have adventures like you. My parents despair of me when I talk this way. They think the only things that interest me are reading books and spending all of my time with ladies."

Tommy's stomach fluttered at the latter. "Is that true?"

"Usually," Philippa admitted. "But my favorite fruit is the pomegranate, and I wouldn't wish to exclusively eat it at every meal. What if there's something out there that's even *better* than pomegranate? How will I know if I don't try new things?"

This was by far the best of all the perspectives on life Tommy had dreamed Philippa might hold. Tommy would be delighted to offer many new experiences, if Philippa was open to the possibility.

That was—Tommy *assumed* an affair with a woman would be a novel experience for Philippa. What if it wasn't? Philippa had famously received dozens of marriage proposals over the years, and had spurned them all. According to Graham's network, Philippa's father had rejected the suitors, but Philippa had never appeared dissatisfied with her unmarried status.

What if Tommy's disguise as a gentleman was the only thing standing in the way of the kiss she longed to take? What if being *Tommy* would make the best possible future?

"I have an idea," Philippa said.

Tommy swallowed. "As do I."

"My mother wants me to use you as a stepping-stone to ensnare a higher-ranked lord." Philippa bit her lip. "What if you did the same thing?"

Tommy blinked. "Ensnare a highly ranked lord?"

Philippa laughed. "No, *I* shall wed the lord. But if your brief acquaintance with me has already given you invitations to places you weren't welcome before, I hereby give you permission to use our friendship to gain entrée wherever you like. We could be partners of a sort."

Partners...of a sort. Yes, that was exactly what Tommy wanted, in exactly the opposite way.

Philippa wanted to marry a lord.

Tommy turned her gaze to the horses.

As a new bride, Chloe had told Tommy that she'd know when she found the right person because neither of them would rather be with anyone else. It was something Bean had told her, before Chloe found Faircliffe and fell in love. A lovely sentiment that in this instance gave Tommy no hope.

Philippa had an entire *peerage* of men she'd rather be with.

She was offering Tommy an unprecedented opportunity to stand by her side...as Philippa met someone else, danced with someone else, flirted with someone else, chose someone else, and married someone else.

The thought of witnessing any part of that made Tommy want to crawl out of her skin.

Especially because Philippa did everything in grand style. Bookish? Meet the leader of a cadre of brilliant bluestockings. Feminine? Philippa could not be swathed in more ringlets and lace without wrapping an entire factory about her person. Beautiful? She could be the muse for a thousand artists.

On a mission to catch a lord? Philippa had caught the Duke of Faircliffe and let him go, like a fisherman tossing an unwanted runt back into the river.

If she wanted to marry a man, it was absolutely going to happen.

Did Tommy want a ringside seat?

Philippa smiled at her. "What do you say?"

Tommy's heart gave a painful pang. The real question was whether she could bear to walk away. This was the woman she longed to be with. If Philippa needed her help, then of course Tommy would give it.

When Philippa inevitably married, at least *she* ought to be happy. Tommy might not be Philippa's fairy-tale hero, but perhaps she could help her find someone who was.

"All right," Tommy said. "I'll help you catch the man you want."

And she would keep her attraction—and her heart—under lock and key for the duration.

"Shall I help you find the woman of your dreams?" Philippa asked.

"No," Tommy said softly. "That won't be necessary."

"Oh, of course not." Philippa chuckled. "What was I thinking? You're not *actually* Baron Vanderbean. One cannot marry using a lord's identity. Good heavens, the courts would make an example out of you for that. Does the baron know you've been impersonating him?"

"I keep no secrets from Baron Vanderbean," Tommy replied. "I can promise he has no objection to the deception."

"Well, that's good," said Philippa. "I would hate to discover someone I trusted was keeping awkward secrets from me."

"Er." Tommy fixed her gaze on the carriage ahead of theirs and gripped the reins tight.

Should she tell Philippa? Tommy was running out of excuses to keep her in the dark. Philippa had proven herself capable of keeping a secret and was clearly game to be a co-conspirator. If it didn't matter whether "Baron Vanderbean" was a Wynchester or a chimneysweep, why would it matter if *he* was a *she?*

Tommy's heart thudded so loudly, it drowned out the hooves and wheels of the surrounding horses and carriages.

Why was it so simple to be someone else, and so difficult to be herself?

Philippa frowned. "What is it?"

"It's me," Tommy blurted out. " 'Tommy' is a nickname."

"I presumed so," said Philippa. "Thomas, I imagine?"

"Thomasina," Tommy whispered, then stiffened her spine and said it louder. "Thomasina Wynchester, at your service."

12

꘏

homasina?" Philippa repeated, not quite certain she'd understood.

The gentleman sitting next to her nodded, his expression wary.

Philippa leaned back and carefully considered his attire, his short hair, and the hint of a beard shadowing his jaw.

" 'Thomasina' as in, you were christened Thomas, but feel as though you are a woman?"

"No," he said. "Thomasina as in, I was born Thomasina. Sometimes I'm more like a man, and sometimes I'm more like a woman, but mostly I feel like...both. And neither. What you're seeing are cosmetics." He gave a crooked smile. "I couldn't grow a beard if my life depended upon it. I've always been more comfortable in men's attire, but beneath these pantaloons, I've the same parts you do."

"Thomasina," Philippa said again in wonder, believing it this time.

A woman. Who felt a little like a man. Did that mean Thomasina was lesbian? No, she hadn't said that. She said she wore disguises. And really, was a costume such a surprise? The Wynchesters were constantly on missions to save this person or right that wrong. Philippa supposed assuming temporary identities should be very much a part of the job. She just hadn't expected the baron to be a woman.

Thomasina gave her a rakish look. "Have you never dreamed of swaggering into a room with a cigar hanging out of your mouth and a glass of port dangling from your hand?"

"N-no..." Philippa answered faintly. "I fear I have not." She could not repress a smile. "I find I am even more pleased to meet you, Miss Thomasina."

"Oh, I'm not Miss Thomasina. Friends and family call me Tommy." She slanted Philippa a sideways look. "You still can, if you like."

"I think I *would* like." Philippa felt a strange little laugh burbling inside of her. "I rather adore that beneath his clothes, 'Baron Vanderbean' is a woman just like me."

"Perhaps not *just* like you," Tommy said.

"Well, you're more daring, that's obvious. I'm glad to have got to know the real you. Knowing you're not a man makes the situation all the more fun."

Tommy's warm brown eyes met hers. "Does it?"

"Of course," Philippa said. "If you *had* been a Thomas, part of me would have always wondered if you really had given up hope of a courtship, or if you were actually biding your time in the hopes of seducing me."

Tommy's cheeks flushed, and she turned to the horses. "Yes. That is definitely a wise and relevant concern to have. Which gentleman do you think *is* trying to seduce you?"

Philippa gazed across the park at all of the riders, pedestrians, and carriages in their relentless circular parade. "None, at the moment. My parents have given me until the end of the season to select a husband, or they'll marry me off to the man of their choice. Frankly, I don't think my mother will last that long. Especially now that her plan to use you to increase my popularity appears to be working."

"How long do you think you have?"

"Mother will decide as soon as everyone 'important' has arrived for the season. I imagine the betrothal contract will come shortly after the Regent's season-opening celebration. It has already been deemed An Event Not To Be Missed."

"Three months," Tommy said.

"Ninety-one days." Philippa rubbed her aching temples. "If Mother holds out that long."

It was just as well that there was no Baron Vanderbean. Philippa didn't need one. She had spent a lifetime being proper and making do with "good enough." Baron Vanderbean would have been *im*proper and unpredictable. Philippa knew what to expect from a marriage of convenience. She'd been training for it her entire life.

She picked at the lace of her bodice. Her cold, dead heart was an advantage. Grand passions were messy and illogical. Philippa liked to understand things. Her choice in husband would affect every aspect of her life. Starting with whether she'd be free to be her bluestocking self...or forced to play the role of society hostess for the rest of her life. Based on her observations, the latter was the most likely.

It wouldn't be a Grand Passion, but these next three months might be her last chance to be herself. To be *better* than herself. To have fun outside of her home. It might be the closest to adventure Philippa could ever get.

She cleared her throat. "I have a proposition. I'm not asking you to play Baron Vanderbean indefinitely—"

"I'll do it," Tommy said. "If I can help you, I will."

A sudden doubt crossed Philippa's mind. "You said no one has ever sent your family an invitation?"

"I said no one from Polite Society has ever sent an invitation to Baron Vanderbean." Tommy paused, then added, "Or to any of us but Chloe."

"Do you know how to mingle with Polite Society?" Philippa asked. Tommy's clothes and accent were impeccable, but if she wasn't used to the beau monde…

"I didn't say I never *attend* society events." Tommy cocked an eyebrow, her brown eyes glinting roguishly. "I said we weren't *invited*."

"Until now." Philippa's chest lightened. The plan was going to work. "Baron Vanderbean will receive a personal invitation from Lord and Lady Southwell this very day."

In fact, it didn't matter how lordly Baron Vanderbean appeared. He was a Balcovian nobleman, not an English one, which would explain away almost any idiosyncrasy. He was also infamously reclusive, and could not be expected to have kept up with the latest changes in fashion or decorum. Any slip would be greeted with delight, as it would provide fodder for the gossips and put the hostess's party on everyone's tongues. It was all good news for Philippa, but…

"Would you prefer to attend a society event as Miss Thomasina?" she asked.

"Blech." Tommy gave a theatrical shudder. "I can think of no worse torture than suffering through society disguised as a proper young lady."

"You're an extraordinary fake baron. Anyone should be charmed," Philippa said. Tommy was fascinating and daring. The quintessential heroine of *her* story, no doubt. "I suppose we'll all find out tomorrow."

Tommy's eyes shone. "You want me to meet you at the party?"

"Meet me?" Philippa smiled. "I'd like to enter on your arm."

13

Tommy held perfectly still as her sister Elizabeth curled Tommy's naturally straight short brown hair into an artfully arranged mess known as the Cherubin. Graham leaned against the doorframe of Tommy's dressing chamber, shaking his head with sham sympathy.

"Not everyone can have natural black curls," Elizabeth said without turning around. "It is rude to brag about handsomeness you were born with."

"I didn't say a word," Graham protested, but the sparkle in his brown eyes betrayed him. "How dreadful it must be to have to burn yourself in pursuit of beauty."

"Be kind," Elizabeth scolded. "We're doing our best."

It was usually Chloe who curled the hard-to-reach bits of Tommy's hair. But when her sister married the Duke of Faircliffe, Tommy had been left on her own. Again. At first, she'd tried to curl her hair herself. The front and sides turned out all right, but in the back, she either burned the hair to a crisp or skipped whole patches altogether.

Elizabeth's hair was naturally curly, so she did not have much experience with curling tongs. On the other hand, she was more patient than almost any other sibling and had assured Tommy she wasn't too busy slashing villains with her rapier to learn a new skill.

She wasn't quite up to Chloe's level—perhaps no one else ever could be—but Elizabeth was a good sister doing her best.

"This is a special occasion," Tommy informed Graham. "I must represent Horace Wynchester, a stylish Balcovian lord."

"Mm-hm," said her brother. "When you chose this romantic hair arrangement, you were definitely thinking of the expectations of the entire beau monde, and not about one specific young lady."

"Where are Jacob and Marjorie?" Tommy demanded. "They promised there would be no more meddling in my romantical entanglements or lack thereof."

"Your first mistake was believing them," Graham said. "I, for one, shall never cease offering my wise counsel."

"If by that you mean 'unsolicited opinions,'" said Elizabeth, "mayhap you're not as wise as you think you are."

Graham smirked. "I predicted Mrs. York would ask Tommy to bring our carriage with the Wynchester crest as a prop for her schemes, didn't I?"

"That's not a prediction," Elizabeth said. "We already knew that the Yorks intend to use Tommy as a stepping-stone."

"Not all of the Yorks," Tommy said. "Philippa doesn't want to use me."

Graham waggled his eyebrows. "Then try harder."

Marjorie skidded into view. "Did I miss it?"

"No," said Tommy. "I won't apply the cosmetics until Elizabeth finishes curling my hair, so as not to accidentally smudge something."

"What you need are side whiskers," Graham said. "Jacob can probably loan you some polecat fur to match your hair."

"First," said Tommy, "never give fashion advice again.

Second, artificial hair is unnecessary. I was clean shaven yesterday. It would raise more eyebrows to sprout polecats on my cheeks today."

Marjorie pulled an armchair closer to where Tommy sat before her dressing table. "I love to watch you turn into a man. It's no wonder Prinny used to spend his mornings watching Brummell do it."

"Beau Brummell was already a man," Graham reminded her.

"And *still* worse at it than Tommy," Marjorie said with pride. "Brummell's toilette took up to five hours, whereas Tommy can become a perfect gentleman in less than forty-five minutes."

Tommy smiled and stretched her legs in their knee breeches out before her.

Elizabeth smacked her on the padded shoulder. "Stop moving. I'm almost done curling your hair."

A footman appeared in the doorway. "Your biscuits, madam," he said to Marjorie.

Graham moved out of the way. "You ordered biscuits to Tommy's boudoir again?"

"It's like watching a performance at the theater," Marjorie explained. She turned to Tommy. "Are you scared?"

"No," Tommy lied.

"Why should she be scared?" Graham scoffed. "Tommy has impersonated everything there is to impersonate, and I've never once seen her hesitate."

"Never once?" Elizabeth asked archly.

"Very well, there were a few false starts before she spoke to Philippa," Graham allowed.

"An entire year of false starts," Marjorie corrected him.

"I did it . . . eventually." A thrill rushed through Tommy. She hadn't just *spoken* to Philippa. Philippa knew the *truth*.

Well, most of the truth.

Part of the truth.

"She now knows the important bit," said Tommy. "That I'm me, and not Baron Vanderbean. And it didn't change a thing."

"That's because she doesn't actually know the important bit," said Marjorie.

"*That* isn't an important bit, because it's irrelevant," Tommy informed her. "She wants to marry a man. I am not a man. Ergo, my feelings are immaterial."

"Feelings are never immaterial," said Elizabeth. "The more you try to hide them, the more volatile they become."

"I don't mind," Tommy insisted. "I never expected to spend time with her at all, and now I'm to pretend to court her for three entire months. Who cares if the only way I can be around her is if I'm dressed as the new Baron Vanderbean?"

"You care," said Graham.

"What if," Marjorie said around a bite of biscuit, "you didn't *pretend* to court her?"

"She doesn't want me to court her," Tommy reminded them. "She wants to use me to attract the attention of a higher-ranking lord."

"Bah," said Marjorie. "That's a boring plan. All spinsters and debutantes want to catch the eye of a lord. Where's her imagination?"

"Hopefully obsessing over Tommy. And if she's not yet, she will be soon." Elizabeth stepped back and replaced the curling tongs in their iron stand.

While waiting for her freshly curled hair to cool, Tommy scooted her stool closer to the looking glass and began to apply deep laugh lines at the corners of her eyes and a light shadow along her jaw.

Elizabeth pulled a chair next to Marjorie. "My turn for biscuits."

Tommy ignored them and concentrated on her cosmetics.

"It *would* be all right, to be a little scared," Graham said.

Tommy ignored him, too. The plan required her to be careless and confident Baron Vanderbean, not hopelessly-in-love-and-trying-not-to-show-it Tommy.

"There's nothing to be nervous about," she assured her brother. "Marjorie's right. The beau monde is predictable and boring. The only time I ever have a little fun is as Great-Aunt Wynchester, and even then, the only interesting moments are the mischief I make myself."

"Make mischief tonight," Marjorie suggested as she bit into a biscuit. "Make it with Philippa."

Tommy set down her cosmetics and reached for her Pomade de Nerole. "Philippa must remain proper if she's to catch a peer."

That was also why Tommy was leaving her flask of gin at home. It was funny when she was with Chloe, but Tommy did not want alcohol tonight.

She wanted to remember every moment with Philippa.

"Oh, drat," drawled Marjorie. "Being improper would spoil her luck? How horrible it would be if Philippa failed to marry a man and instead consoled herself in the arms of her good friend Not Baron Vanderbean."

Tommy glared at her sister in the looking glass as she brushed her new short brown curls toward her forehead and temples.

Marjorie smiled and popped another biscuit into her mouth.

"What Philippa would like," Tommy said, "is for us to prevent Captain Northrup from being lauded for Damaris's accomplishments."

Marjorie nodded. "That's a good courtship gift. I might start with flowers, though."

Tommy was glad Philippa knew who she really was. Glad

and terrified. Tommy wasn't used to being herself outside of the family and hoped she wasn't making a huge mistake. She was supposed to be concentrating on the case, not her feelings for Philippa.

"I see what's happening," said Graham. "You're the white knight twice over. You plan to rescue both maidens."

"We are all saving the day," Tommy said firmly. "The Wynchesters are a family of knights of various colors and genders who save the day together as a team."

"See?" said Elizabeth. "They should have let women write the tales of chivalry. The stories would have been so much better."

Tommy's heart warmed. She could not have asked for a better family than her motley siblings. Even when they argued, it was out of love. And when they joined forces against a common enemy...they were unstoppable.

She wished Chloe were here. It didn't feel like "joining forces" without her. She was the one with the plans. Left alone, Tommy got into scrapes like...being Baron Vander-bean for three months.

That was someone else she missed deeply. The real Bean. Wearing his monogrammed handkerchiefs made her feel closer to him, but at the same time made his loss sharper than ever. The only reason Tommy could play this role for Philippa was because her adoptive father would have wanted Tommy to do whatever she needed to be happy. But no one could replace Bean. Not even "Horace" Wynchester. The loss would hurt less when she could take the costume off.

"We only have three months before Prinny's party," she reminded her siblings.

The seventeenth of January would be here before they knew it. In fact, Northrup could be granted his viscountcy beforehand. Graham's network was gathering intelligence.

"I spoke to Damaris." Elizabeth buffed the serpentine handle of her sword stick with a handkerchief. "She said she doesn't need a room in a military academy named after her."

Graham pulled a journal from his pocket. "What does she want?"

"Acknowledgment. A confession from Captain Northrup to his superiors that he stole her idea, followed by his complete and utter relinquishment of all undeserved glory, titles, or other accolades. And an apology would not go awry, either."

"Oof," said Tommy. "Her likeness on a plaque at a military academy would probably be easier. Any man shameless enough to steal his niece's ideas for fame and fortune is not the sort of man who admits or apologizes for his actions."

"Marjorie can create the plaque," Graham suggested.

"No forgeries," Elizabeth said. "If Damaris wants genuine acknowledgment, then she deserves to have it. The celebration should be in her honor, not Northrup's."

"We'll have to force his hand," Tommy said. The question was how. "If we can find the original plans Damaris drew up, can we prove it's her handwriting and not his?"

"How do we prove which came first?" Elizabeth asked.

"Good point. They're no longer using the cipher," Tommy said. "The war is over. Old messages may no longer be guarded. If we can demonstrate Damaris easily deciphering one, that would prove her familiarity with the cipher."

"Can't *you* affirm she invented it?" Marjorie asked. "You're in the reading circle."

"It was long before Chloe and I attended," Tommy explained. "Apparently Damaris showed Philippa first, and then the others. They *could* come forward and call Captain Northrup a liar—"

"But they're women, and he's Captain Northrup," Elizabeth finished dryly.

"They could swear in a court of law," Marjorie insisted. "Eyewitness testimony."

"It will never come to that," said Tommy. "As a viscount, can't Northrup just claim 'right of privilege' and have the whole thing tossed out?"

Philippa had said she wanted to be part of the escapades. The difficulty was thinking up an escapade that would work. If Northrup could dismiss all charges with a wave of his hand, where did that leave them?

Elizabeth pulled a face. "Damaris said she instructed the reading circle to burn the instructions once they'd committed them to memory, which means she has no evidence of a prior cipher. More importantly, Northrup is her mother's brother, and her mother would not forgive Damaris for bringing formal charges against him, no matter the outcome."

"Captain Northrup won't back down now that there's fame and a title in his future," Graham said. "Worse, he's acting like he already has it. You should see all the purchases he's made on credit in the past few weeks alone. He seems certain that where there's a title, there's a bride with a large dowry."

"He's probably right." Marjorie set down her empty plate. "But we're going to stop him *before* we'd be dragging an innocent down with him."

"Meanwhile…" Elizabeth pointed her sword stick at Tommy. "Baron Vanderbean has a romantic engagement he's definitely not afraid of."

14

⟨F⟩lower in hand, Tommy stepped out of her carriage and
strode up the perfectly swept path of the York residence. The air was crisp and cool. Leaves were beginning to
show signs of gold and orange. She had arrived to escort Philippa to a ball.

Tommy. Philippa. A ball.

It sounded like a fairy tale, and if there was one thing all
fairy tales had in common, it was that nothing went according
to plan.

For one, despite her bravado to Philippa, Tommy *hadn't*
ever been invited to a society ball. She had attended them in
various guises, such as Great-Aunt Wynchester or a liveried
footman, but never as someone fashionable. She knew how to
comport herself in any number of settings, but that was not
the same thing as fitting in.

It was why Great-Aunt Wynchester kept her comments
to the occasional ribald jest at the reading circle. Tommy
wasn't a bluestocking. She hadn't read a hundred books. She
couldn't speak Ancient Greek or write in cipher. She could
drink wine and eat oat cakes and watch the others in silence
like a spectator at a play.

Tonight would be different. She would be onstage. Instead

of watching the show from the audience, the audience would be watching *her*. Judging her. Critiquing Baron Vanderbean. His first public outing with Miss York.

And the person she most wished to impress was...Philippa. Who wanted a real man. Unfortunately, Tommy could not become one fully enough to be an acceptable suitor. Looking the part and even feeling like a man was not sufficient. Especially if Philippa was looking for someone who could father children. But tonight was just a ball. A dance or two. Light flirtation.

Tommy straightened her hat again and fussed with her neckcloth for the tenth time before approaching the front door. Did all men feel this self-conscious when they called upon a lady? Were butlers all around Grosvenor Square peering through slits in the curtains at well-dressed but comically nervous gentlemen who had not yet banged the knocker because they could not decide the proper angle of the sharp black beaver hat upon their head?

The door swung open before Tommy had finished gathering her wits.

"My lord," said the butler. "This way, if you please."

He did not *appear* to be laughing internally at Tommy's anxiousness. Then again, Mr. Underwood had realized Tommy would never knock on her own and had saved her the hassle.

The butler was a good man. Mr. Underwood enjoyed Mozart and waxwork exhibitions, and avoided billiards, pecans, and small children. Tommy had read Graham's compendium on the York family so many times that the spine had broken, and Graham had been obliged to create a second copy. He kept it on a special shelf Tommy was forbidden from touching.

She didn't mind. She kept the tattered original volume upstairs in her bedchamber.

Tommy followed Mr. Underwood toward the same blue sitting room she'd visited the day before. Nothing written in Graham's books could compare to the rush of being invited in person.

"Pinch your cheeks," came a loud hiss from the corridor. Mrs. York to her daughter.

Tommy tried not to smile. She had perhaps spent more time than anyone observing Philippa's pretty face, with great care and attention to detail. Tommy could state with authority that a cold wind and a glass of wine were the only things she had ever witnessed bring a flush to Philippa's cheeks.

Mother and daughter swept into the room.

Rather, Mrs. York bounced across the threshold, while Philippa floated into the sitting room in a sugary cloud of gauze and lace. The white lace trimming the base of the skirt billowed and fluttered, allowing brief glimpses of the toes of Philippa's pink slippers.

She looked good enough to eat. Tommy's heart thudded violently behind its protective layers of cambric and waistcoat and lapels.

"Mrs. York. Miss York." She made her most extravagant bow.

Mrs. York gave a false, high-pitched titter.

Philippa did not change her expression, but her blue eyes shone as they met Tommy's.

"I brought you something," Tommy said.

The corners of Philippa's mouth quirked. "Is it a painting of trolls?"

"Imps," Tommy corrected. "And I would never part with that."

"*Oh.*" Mrs. York waved her hands. "*Must* we recall the horrid 'art' the Duke of Faircliffe gave to Philippa? Baron

Vanderbean, what have you brought? Oh, a lily! Philippa appreciates your gesture, which I think we can all agree is more romantic than anything the Duke of Faircliffe has ever done. A pretty flower is all that is proper. Here, give it to me. I'll ring for a vase at once."

Giving the delicate lily to Mrs. York was significantly less romantic than handing it to her daughter, but Tommy did as instructed.

Philippa appeared neither impressed with the gift nor disappointed that she was apparently not to touch it. Her eyes were not on the tender lily, but on Tommy, taking in every carefully dressed inch, from her freshly shined shoes all the way up to her painstakingly curled locks.

It was not a sexual perusal, Tommy reminded herself firmly. No matter how it felt.

Now that Philippa knew the truth, she was simply curious how the trick was done. Thinking was Philippa's favorite activity. Her clever brain must be whirring madly beneath the deceptively staid golden ringlets, as she calculated and analyzed and developed her theories.

Nonetheless, Tommy's body registered the slow sweep of Philippa's gaze as though it were the caress of a lover's hand.

Ankles and calves hidden inside carefully shined boots. The fit of her breeches and the muscles of her thighs. Her midsection further accented by the smart cut of her tailcoat and waistcoat. The frantic pulse at the base of her throat, hidden beneath the starched fall of a carefully folded cravat.

Tommy would be more than happy to spoil the magic and take off every stitch of clothing if Philippa agreed to do the same. It was not a wish that could come true, but Tommy's brain did not work in the same logical manner as Philippa's.

A Wynchester never let a thing like "impossibility" get in the way of a good dream.

"*There* you are." Mrs. York thrust the lily at a startled maid. "Put that in a vase. We must hurry to the Southwell soirée." She turned toward Tommy. "You brought the coach with the family crest?"

Tommy inclined her head. "As you requested, madam."

Mrs. York clapped her hands. "We shan't waste another moment. Come, come, darling. We must hie at once, whilst the queue is at its longest!"

The Southwell residence was a mere four streets from the York town house. Taking a coach for such a short journey was laughably impractical if one's aim was to join the party quickly.

That was not Mrs. York's aim. The fastest way to spread gossip that her daughter was being courted by a lord was to show the evidence before as many eyes as possible. The queue of fellow guests was a captive audience. It was a remarkably efficient battle plan.

After the ladies arranged themselves in the forward-facing seat, Tommy took the rear-facing seat and knocked behind her head to signal the driver.

"You look lovely tonight," Tommy said to Philippa.

"She looks lovely every night," Mrs. York responded pointedly. "My Philippa is always proper."

Ah. This was less a compliment to her daughter than a subtle rebuke to Baron Vanderbean, whose Wynchester connections were anything but proper.

She inclined her head again to let Mrs. York know the message had been received.

Tommy and Mrs. York were fighting on the same side. Both of them wanted Philippa to make the best possible match, though their criteria differed wildly.

How Tommy wished women could be in the pool of suitors! Not as a decoy, but as a viable option. Someone to be seen, to be considered. Someone who had a chance. Instead, she was the fool in the seat opposite Philippa, trundling along backward, the narrow distance between their knees an uncrossable gulf.

Tonight was not for Tommy, but for Philippa.

After first passing the queue and then crawling along within it for what seemed like an eternity, it was at last their turn to alight onto the pavement.

Philippa met her eyes. "Ready, Baron?"

Tommy smiled back. "I've been ready for longer than you know."

Ready to be at Philippa's side, wherever that might be. Even in a crowded ballroom, with everyone's eyes on them at once. Giddy excitement bubbled within her. This wasn't one of Tommy's daydreams. She was *here*, with Philippa on her arm. In front of hundreds of witnesses. Even Philippa's mother was beaming on Tommy's other side.

Yes, yes, this courtship wasn't *real*, and all three of them were playing their own game of deception, but even a masquerade was more than Tommy had ever imagined she might one day have.

The Southwell butler announced their names together, forever publicly linking them. Mrs. York, Miss York, Baron Vanderbean. Very well, it wasn't *Tommy's* name. She had never minded such details before. She tried not to let it bother her now. At least she was here with Philippa, regardless of alias.

The large chamber was draped with yellow silk and hung with gorgeous chandeliers. The colors made the crowded room seem awash with gold.

At first, Tommy had wanted Chloe to be here tonight. Upon second thought, she had begged all of her siblings *not* to come. She felt awkward enough around Philippa without two brothers and three sisters peering at her from every corner of the ballroom. And she wasn't certain how Horace Wynchester would be received. She didn't want her siblings to witness disrespect to any Baron Vanderbean.

As they passed down the receiving line, Mrs. York ebulliently pointed out Tommy's existence, and her proximity to Philippa. "Good evening, good evening. Why yes, my daughter and I *did* arrive with the baron!"

It was a strange sensation to try to be respectable. Like wearing a waistcoat that didn't quite fit.

Not everyone was thrilled to meet the new baron. Most were courteous, but a few did not bother to hide their disdain of the foreign Wynchester heir. Was *this* one of the reasons Bean had been so reclusive? Were fancy soirées not worth the sideways glances and the pinched noses?

Tommy held herself straighter. She would make Bean proud tonight. She *wasn't* his heir, not in the way she was pretending to be, but she would do her best to represent her temporary title well. To be the sort of man Horace Wynchester ought to be, if he weren't imaginary.

Worthy of Bean, and worthy of Philippa.

Thus far, Tommy's appearance had mostly been met with curiosity. Whispers followed them as they made their way across the crowded ballroom. Likely as much due to Mrs. York's theatrics as anything Tommy had said or done. When they reached the opposite side, Mrs. York pressed a handkerchief to her forehead as though they'd just run the gauntlet.

"I'm going to find the ratafia, darling," she whispered to Philippa. "You two...be conspicuous. There are many eyes to catch tonight."

Mrs. York melted into the crowd, cooing at familiar faces as she went.

Tommy raised a brow. "She's fortunate Baron Vanderbean

isn't the marrying sort. He might have caught on to the dastardly scheme by now."

Philippa shook her head. "Baron Vanderbean would be used to the world of the ton, in which one's worth directly correlates with the worth of one's associates. Why do you think names are called as people arrive? So we can gawp at each other, and see who is with whom, and determine whom we ought to be seen with next. Each name is a feather in the hostess's cap."

"Poor Baron Vanderbean," said Tommy. "Used so heartlessly."

"It is his honor," Philippa reminded her. "A real baron would not waste time talking to a wallflower. He'd fawn over guests even higher ranking than he."

"Then I am glad not to be a real baron." Tommy glanced over Philippa's shoulder in the direction of the refreshment table. "Shall I fetch you some gin or a meat pie?"

Philippa narrowed her eyes. "Neither is on any hostess's menu, so I suspect you are bamming me."

"I happen to like both gin and meat pies," Tommy protested. "Perhaps it is your tastes that are not refined. Meat pies were present at the Duchess of Faircliffe's end-of-season gala."

"Did you attend the gala?" Philippa tilted her head and frowned. "I don't recall seeing you there."

"Er..." This was not the moment to confess Tommy's ill-fated attempt to speak to Philippa while dressed as a woman. "It was a rollicking crush, just like this one. Shall we take a turn about the room?"

"Mother would love that," Philippa agreed.

Tommy made a show of offering her arm.

Philippa made no show at all of curling her fingers around Tommy's elbow. She just...did it, as though strolling with Tommy were a perfectly unremarkable activity that could occur at any moment of any day.

Tommy felt that light touch through her coat and linen sleeves, as though her flesh had just been branded with Philippa's fingerprints forevermore.

"Keep a lookout for stray unwed lords." Philippa's gaze darted about the ballroom. "I didn't want to wed the Duke of Faircliffe, but I hate being a disappointment to my parents. Especially my father. He deals with so much. Marrying well is my sole chance to acquit myself."

Tommy wanted to say, *I am sure you are not a disappointment to your parents*, but parents were complicated beasts. No two were the same. Tommy had ended up alone because she had been orphaned, while Chloe had been abandoned by parents who didn't want her.

Baron Vanderbean—the real Baron Vanderbean—had become their father. Tommy would have done anything to avoid disappointing him. She could not fault Philippa for feeling the same way about her own parents.

As they strolled the perimeter of the ballroom, Philippa said, "I don't suppose there is any news about Damaris's uncle?"

"No, but Graham's informants are searching for evidence. We'll find a way to stop him. Wynchesters never give up on a client."

"Thank you," Philippa said softly. "Our reading circle is a sisterhood. I will do everything in my power to help."

Tommy understood loyalty, and how people who were not of one's blood could become just as important as family. Tommy could not bear to imagine how much Philippa would suffer if her new husband felt such strong ties were "bluestocking nonsense" and beneath them.

"I promise to aid your friends in any way that I can." Tommy took a deep breath. "And I promise to do my best to help you catch the eye of whoever *you*, rather than your parents, wish."

"You are a true gentleman." Philippa gave a small smile.

"I try," Tommy murmured.

"I doubt you have to try at all." Philippa smiled up at Tommy as they strolled the ballroom. "Chivalry seems to come naturally to you."

"Or perhaps the right maiden brings out the best in—"

"Vanderbean!" came low whispers behind them as they passed.

"Don't look." Philippa tightened her hold on Tommy's arm. "They're not talking *to* you. They're talking *about* you. About *us*, rather. Mother's plan is working. Men are noticing me."

Jealousy ripped through Tommy, hot and sour and visceral.

This was what it would mean to keep her promise. To stand aside while actual gentleman after actual gentleman pulled Philippa into his arms. Never knowing which lucky lord would be the one to keep her there forever.

She turned to guide Philippa toward her real destiny. They arrived just as the musicians ended the first song.

"You brought her back before your set was over?" Mrs. York hissed. "The least you could do was dance with her, not just parade her about."

Tommy's limbs turned leaden.

Dance with her?

"You wanted Baron Vanderbean to parade me about," Philippa reminded her mother.

"It doesn't matter," her mother said. "Lord Charsdale asked for a dance. I dislike the gossip I've heard about him, but one cannot cut the heir to an earldom. I shall flag him down. He ought to be happy with half a set. Where did that scoundrel go…"

Philippa looked at Tommy. Her face was blank. Did she want Tommy to ask her to dance?

Tommy wanted to intervene. To say, *Halt! This is my minuet and I mean to have it!* but her throat had gone dry and her lips were stuck together.

It was like Chloe's end-of-season gala, only worse. This was Tommy's "end-of-Philippa" gala, and she *still* couldn't force herself to take the plunge.

"There he is!" Mrs. York gave the least subtle wave Tommy had ever witnessed. "Come, come, lad, look this way, I've—Yes! Here! I've decided to grant you a turn with Philippa, my lord. No, no, she's unoccupied."

Lord Charsdale smirked in Tommy's direction before whisking Philippa onto the dance floor.

Tommy curled her fingers into fists. That smug Lord Charsdale thought Tommy had just been snubbed by Mrs. York and her daughter, when in fact Tommy had managed to cut herself from a set already in progress without any outside assistance, thank you very much.

She stalked from the dance floor, away from the sight of Philippa and Charsdale. If Philippa *didn't* wish to spend much time with Charsdale, then giving him half a set was the lesser evil. Tommy had rescued her by failing to act.

Yes. Exactly. That was what happened.

Tommy should have brought her flask of gin.

She was a good flirt. An excellent flirt. A well-practiced rake. With women who welcomed the sensual attentions of other women.

With Philippa, everything was upside down. Tommy was to *pretend* to be attracted, without letting on that she actually *was* attracted. How could she hide her ardent admiration when they were inches away from each other on a dance floor?

She paused a few yards away from an open doorway. This salon was filled with gentlemen playing whist around square tables or drinking port in comfortable chairs next to the fireplace. She started to enter, then heard her name and stopped before reaching the doorway to step just out of sight.

She'd heard Baron Vanderbean's name, rather.

"...the only acceptable Wynchester."

"If one is willing to accept *any* of them. One cannot comprehend the Duke of Faircliffe's choice in bride."

"He's so indulgent and...and *sweet* to her. They look at each other as though no one else exists. Bad ton, I say."

"*I've* nothing against the duchess—or the baron. Vanderbean inherited his living situation from his father, and we all know what that can be like. Nor have I any complaint against his sister Miss Honoria. My question is why they bother sharing their home with social-climbing orphans."

"Wasn't there some sort of legal trust requiring it?"

"Who do you think is in charge of that trust now? Vanderbean could shoo them out of his house if he wished to."

"Have you jackanapes never heard of honor? A good son follows his sire's wishes."

"Bah. There's a time and a place for honor, and it never requires opening one's home to parasites. If Vanderbean wants a shot at one of the better debutantes, he'd do best to sever those ties."

"It looks like he's after Miss York. Ha! Can you imagine?"

"York ought to exert some control over his wife before she makes them a laughingstock encouraging the likes of Vanderbean."

"*And* his leeches. Every member of that family is unsavory. He shouldn't even be at this ball. No one wants him here."

Tommy stiffened.

They thought she was trash. They thought her entire family was rubbish. They considered Baron Vanderbean sullied by association. *Bean.* And his new heir. The poor imaginary bastard didn't have a chance in hell of impressing anyone.

Yes, he bloody well did!

Tommy would prove it.

15

The minuet had not yet ended, so Tommy took her time traversing the ballroom. Not sulking with her fists clenched and her lower lip jutting out. Nor cowed, with her spine hunched and her head bowed.

Instead, Tommy sauntered as though she *owned* this ball. What did *she* care about the opinions of stuffy, spoiled gentlemen and lordlings? She wasn't even Baron Vanderbean! She was Tommy Wynchester, and she had already accomplished more than these useless nobs' wildest imaginings.

She pretended not to watch Philippa. Instead, Tommy observed the company she was in, and reveled at being a low-born orphan in the middle of a high-class ball. Tommy loved parties. She knew how to make the most of them. This one was full of potential.

Challenge accepted.

This was the Tommy that she was in those late-night Sapphic gatherings with the coy little descriptions so as not to attract the wrong attention. Except here, now, Tommy was free to attract all the attention she could command.

Her pace was slow, deliberate, showy—giving her plenty of time to incline her head at each lady she passed, regardless of age or status. She made certain to return every single gaze with obvious appreciation and reserved her smiles for those who least expected them. Startled whispers and more than a few giggles bubbled coquettishly as she passed.

Baron Vanderbean was no bumbling weakling, afraid to remove his father's pets from his home. Baron Vanderbean was a lucky, rakish, confident gentleman who lived and danced with whomever he damn well pleased. He was *proud* of his family. There was nothing better than being a Wynchester!

Tommy reached Mrs. York at the same moment Lord Charsdale was returning Philippa to her mother.

"Thank you, my lord," gushed Mrs. York. "And now we— Baron, what are you doing here?"

"I've come for my dance, madam," Tommy answered easily, as though it were a foregone conclusion.

"Oh, I'm afraid that isn't possible. Philippa has had *so many* inquiries in her absence. First, we have Lord—"

"I accept." Philippa curved her arm through Tommy's.

"What? Darling, no! There are only fifteen sets, and we've already got six names—"

"Ah," said Philippa. "In that case, I have plenty of sets left."

That's right. Tommy grinned at her. *One shouldn't waste one's chance.*

"But it's a waltz," Mrs. York sputtered. "You should save it for the right man."

"I did," said Philippa. Her eyes met Tommy's.

Her throat went dry. Tommy Wynchester was no "undesirable element." Miss Philippa York was looking at her as though truly seeing her for the first time.

Tommy led her to the dance floor, feeling powerful and invincible. This was the pounding heart of breaching the walls of a castle, of sneaking past armed guards, of breaking into a strongbox full of someone else's secrets.

This was the pounding heart Tommy lived for. The drum-beat of adventure.

This time with Philippa.

"Baron Vanderbean would have caught on to your mother by now."

Philippa winced. "She's marginally more circumspect about every topic except courtship. I hope Baron Vanderbean is not offended."

"Baron Vanderbean loves to dash mothers' dreams," Tommy assured her, wishing it could be more than an act. "Your mother is lucky Baron Vanderbean's aim is to court you, not seduce you."

Philippa's eyes widened.

Tommy lifted Philippa's gloved hand and wished she could touch the soft skin beneath. Philippa placed her other hand on Tommy's shoulder. A waltz. Mayhap the night's only waltz. *Their* waltz. It was already a memory to cherish.

Her palm was on the lace skirt covering Philippa's hip. Those ample curves were soft and inviting beneath Tommy's fingertips. She longed to explore the rest of her body.

Tommy pulled her into the waltz, keeping time with the music. They moved together effortlessly. Tommy was tempted to pull her even closer until their bosoms were near enough to touch. *Improper*, she scolded herself. But improper was exactly what she wanted to be.

"I saw you cut quite a swath amongst the ladies," Philippa said presently.

"Were you watching me?" Tommy arched her eyebrow. "Whatever must Lord Charsdale think of your inattention?"

"What must all of the gentlemen think?" Philippa countered. "You winked at as many married ladies as unmarried ones."

"I winked at no one," Tommy protested. "I simply gave

them an *I-would-wink-at-you-if-we'd-been-properly-introduced* smile with my eyes."

Philippa narrowed hers. "What does a smile like that look like?"

Tommy kept her lips relaxed and made her eyes heavy-lidded, allowing the corners to crinkle meaningfully as she gave an ever-so-slight upward flash to her eyebrows.

Philippa's lips parted.

Tommy's grin widened.

"That's definitely a wink," Philippa said. "It's an eyebrow wink, which I hadn't known could be even more flirtatious than an eye*lid* wink until I saw you do it just now. Is that how you caused so many faint hearts to swoon in your wake?"

"Did they swoon?" Tommy asked innocently. "My attention wasn't on *them*."

"You littered the ballroom with debutantes, spinsters, and *wives*—and you know it," Philippa said. "I think you did it on purpose, just to show me you could."

"Almost right," said Tommy. "It wasn't for your benefit, but for the haughty prigs in the men's card room who believe Baron Vanderbean to be no romantical threat."

"Well. Your seductive prowess offers a marked benefit to me." Philippa darted a glance over each of Tommy's shoulders. "All the young ladies who were fanning their fichus earlier are staring daggers at me now. As soon as our dance is finished, you will be inundated with admirers, but *I* will be the woman you chose first."

"As soon as our *set* is finished," Tommy corrected. "I won't return you to your mother until the last possible second this time."

Philippa's voice softened. "Good."

Tommy tried to remind herself that this wasn't courting. There would be no kisses. It was just a dance or two, as

Philippa had granted countless other men. It was innocent. Mostly.

And because Tommy could not act on her feelings, Philippa need not know that Tommy possessed any.

Such as: Tommy wanted to explore every curve of Philippa's body with her mouth and her hands to see if she felt and tasted as delicious as she looked. Or: The ease with which they danced together was the tiniest of hints at how well their naked flesh might fit together, too.

A lesser rake might lose his step in the waltz. But Tommy was a competent, confident baron, and her rhythm with Philippa never faltered...as long as she reminded herself that it was just a temporary role like any other.

"You know," said Philippa, "tomorrow morning, your poor butler will have to add a second salver on the mantel to collect all the cards and invitations. We've raised each other's currency in tandem."

Unfortunately, no currency in the world could purchase what Tommy wanted most.

She tightened her hold on Philippa's hand. Tommy wanted Philippa to know the fake flirtation was real. She wanted Philippa to *want* a true courtship. She wanted to pull Philippa close, to taste her lips, her tongue, her flesh...She wanted everything she could never have.

But she would have to be content with playing a role. Like the theater, this opera would soon end. The only time they would ever have was now.

Tommy waggled her brows. "You're saying Baron Vanderbean *could* attract a highborn bride?"

"I am watching mothers formulate plans as we speak."

"Then I suppose I shall have to dance with all their daughters, so as not to play favorites," Tommy said airily.

Philippa narrowed her eyes again. "You're *my* pretend suitor."

"And we'll have used up our two sets before the end of the hour," Tommy reminded her. "I cannot imagine your mother wishing to return home until the orchestra plays the last note. As a paragon of chivalry, Baron Vanderbean must do his civic duty and—"

"You *want* to dance with them," Philippa accused.

"I like to dance," Tommy agreed. "I'd rather dance with *you* all night, but it wouldn't have the effect your mother is hoping for." She lowered her voice. "People might think there is Something Sordid between us."

"You make 'sordid' sound like 'wonderful.' "

"It *is* wonderful, when done with the right person." Tommy's voice was husky.

Philippa hesitated. "Are you speaking to me as Tommy or as Baron Vanderbean?"

"For the next few hours, I'm both."

Philippa seemed to consider that. She wore the blank expression that indicated her mind was busy computing facts. She did not appear nearly as appalled or confused by their banter as Tommy might have predicted.

Perhaps there was more to Philippa than Tommy had suspected. If only she could just ask!

Are you sexually attracted to me? was not the sort of question one could gracefully recover from if the answer was no. In fact, Tommy's three months with Philippa could end this very night.

Philippa lowered her eyes. "I'm not used to people flirting with me, even in jest."

Tommy hadn't been joking. She kept her voice serious. "I'm surprised everyone doesn't flirt with you constantly."

"Why would they?" Philippa's eyes lifted to Tommy's again. "I'm a wallflower."

"Oh, you are not."

Philippa's mouth fell open. "I think *I* would know."

"You may not have caught the exact highborn lords your mother wants in the family, but you're beautiful, you're rich, you're the leader of a bluestocking society, you have dozens of friends..." Tommy arched her brows. "Wallflower isn't who you are, it's the role you've chosen to play."

Tommy knew quite a bit about that technique.

Philippa stared at her wordlessly.

"You're a self-appointed wallflower." Tommy turned her in time to the music. "Be careful. Disguises are useful when used strategically, but if you wear them for too long...you can lose who you really are."

"I've always wanted to lose who I really am," Philippa admitted. "That's how I fell in love with books as a child. They gave me the siblings I never had, the friends I never had, the parental adoration I never had, the life I never had. They helped me to survive. I suppose you find that foolish."

"For me it was my sister Chloe," Tommy said. "It started with a shared pie. We all grab on to whatever we can."

"If we're fortunate enough to have something to grab on to," Philippa said. "That's why I'm arranging small community libraries. I want other women and children to have the same opportunity that I had. Everyone deserves an escape. Or to expand their mind, as they prefer. I want others to have *choices*."

"When Chloe and I were at the orphanage, she would have killed for a library," Tommy admitted. "Books were one of the first things she donated after Bean adopted us."

Philippa's eyes softened. "What did *you* donate?"

"Meat pies," Tommy answered without hesitation.

Philippa laughed. "You did not."

"Indirectly," Tommy hedged. "We'd spent years sneaking them in with our pickpocketing spoils. I donated money and equipment to the kitchens, so that stealing suppers would no longer be necessary. The orphanage is a very different place today."

"How I yearn to make a difference, too," Philippa said wistfully.

"You already do." Tommy looked at her in surprise. "Your name is just as synonymous with charity work as it is with your bluestocking circle."

"I donate funds and sew blankets and the like," Philippa said, "which is all very well and useful. But I want to make a bigger difference. A *fundamental* difference. Once everyone has access to local reading libraries, regardless of their wealth or class, I will feel as though I made London better." Her cheeks flushed. "Is that prideful and obnoxious?"

"It's lovely," Tommy admitted. "It's very Wynchestery of you. We are very prideful of our attempts to make London better."

"Attempts?" Philippa scoffed. "If monks still penned illustrated manuscripts, the stories would all be about your family's endless escapades helping the helpless and righting wrongs. It must be marvelous to be a Wynchester."

Tommy's chest filled with love for her siblings. "I sometimes think I am the luckiest person in all of England."

The waltz came to a close. The next song was to be a country dance involving several sets of partners.

"Shall we join them?" Philippa asked.

They could. But Tommy wasn't ready to share Philippa with others just yet. The question was whether Philippa felt the same way.

Tommy gave her most wolfish leer. "How about a turn through the garden instead?"

"Classic," Philippa breathed. "Everyone will think you're angling to steal a kiss."

Stealing a kiss was a splendid idea. The idea that Philippa

was still thinking about how best to attract someone else... less so.

"The garden doors are open," Tommy said. "Come with me. If you get cold, I'll warm you up."

Philippa's forehead furrowed. "You mean you'll loan me your coat?"

"Yes," Tommy agreed. "That is the contingency plan."

A thick border of tall, leafy trees enclosed the small, well-trimmed garden. The sun had long since set, so it was impossible to detect any bursts of autumnal yellow and orange among the green. Clouds diffused the moonlight, bathing the garden in a hazy, magical glow.

The trees blocked the wind, but the cold was already seeping through her clothes. They wouldn't be able to stay outside for more than a few moments.

Tommy touched Philippa's side.

Philippa gasped and froze.

Tommy's hand was exactly where it had been while they were waltzing. Its position was neither salacious nor improper—during a waltz. It was not at all the same out here in the garden, where the loudest melody was the arrhythmic beating of one's heart. Tommy brought her free hand to Philippa's, cradling it for just a second.

She wanted to create a mental map of every facet of Philippa to remember her by. Every dip and curve, every hidden freckle, every blond curl, every expression. Tommy wanted all of it, to hold on to the knowledge in her mind, even after all that was left in her life was a memory. She knew Philippa's face as well as her own, had admired her silhouette from every angle. And now she knew how it felt to dance with her, what her hand felt like in Tommy's. Even if it was all she would ever have. Tentatively, she gave Philippa's fingers another light caress.

Philippa neither jerked back nor leaned closer. She did not slap Tommy's hand away, nor respond in kind. It was impossible to say what Philippa wanted or whether she understood the question Tommy was asking.

Philippa just stared back expressionlessly.

Tommy felt her rakish confidence evaporate. She *wasn't* a baron. Playing the part for a few weeks was well and good, but she had no wish to do so the rest of her life. Bean was Baron Vanderbean. She liked being Tommy. She wanted *Philippa* to like Tommy. But this was neither the time nor place. They could not risk someone stumbling upon them.

What they needed was privacy. A place no one could interrupt them.

And then Tommy could see about stealing a kiss.

Reluctantly, she led Philippa back inside the ballroom. Warmth washed over them—as well as a wave of whispers.

"Men," Philippa said in surprise. "*Gentlemen.* Do you think they're talking about me?"

"Mayhap." Tommy wasn't certain which possibility to wish for. Her jaw hardened. "Those prigs are dreadful gossips. They said Baron Vanderbean is the only acceptable Wynchester. They said the rest of my siblings are worthless ragamuffins who ought to be tossed in the street. They said—"

Did her voice just wobble? Oh God, her throat had gone scratchy. Tommy clicked her teeth closed and stopped speaking, lest any more unwanted divulgences leak out.

"They're imbeciles," Philippa said flatly. She held on tighter to Tommy's arm. "I've committed their names and faces to memory. They will not be receiving smiles or dances or anything else from me."

"You can't say that," said Tommy. "What if one of them is your future husband?"

"He ceased being a contender the moment he insulted your family."

If that was true, Tommy had bad news for Philippa about the entire rest of the beau monde.

"I am eaten alive with envy," Philippa confessed.

"You're *what?*"

"Of your family, to be precise." Philippa gave a lopsided smile. "You were an orphan, and now you're surrounded by a found family of siblings who love you. I live with the same parents I was born to, and it could not be more different. My father rarely speaks to me, and my mother only talks about her eagerness to marry me off. If those—*prigs*, did you say?—aren't clever enough to see how splendid you are, more fool them."

"Thank you," Tommy said softly. "I—"

"Philippa, darling, *there* you are!" Mrs. York burst from the crowd and latched on to her daughter's free arm, tugging her away from Tommy. "What can you be thinking to go out-of-doors in weather like this? No more sets with the baron tonight. Come, come. You must dance to warm those cold fingers. I've been taking names in your absence, and now we have Lord..."

Tommy watched in dismay as Philippa disappeared into the crowd.

The whispers behind her grew louder. She didn't want to hear them. She lifted her chin and strode past. If Philippa were to spend the rest of the night dancing, then so, too, would Tommy.

Even if she could not have the person she longed for most.

16

As Philippa took luncheon by herself in the York dining room, she could not stop thinking about Tommy.

How easy it had been to talk to her. How lovely it had been to dance with her. That moment in the garden, when it had almost felt like—

But no, of course it wasn't that. Philippa had spent the rest of the evening gazing over the shoulders of endless dance partners to watch Tommy conquer debutante after widow after wallflower. How they flirted and smiled and gave full-throated laughs instead of the false little titters Mother insisted were the proper way for young ladies to giggle.

Of course, none of those women had realized Tommy *wasn't* Baron Vanderbean, but Philippa supposed they wouldn't have been any less charmed to know the truth. It certainly hadn't impeded *her*. Philippa's admiration for Tommy grew with every moment in her company.

It was so easy to believe that Tommy was exactly who she pretended to be! Philippa frequently found herself forgetting Tommy wasn't actually a man, even though she knew better. She occasionally even managed to forget Tommy wasn't a real suitor, even though she knew the truth about that, as well.

Mother was in raptures over the ball. The surprise appearance and subsequent popularity of Baron Vanderbean had catapulted Philippa into new heights. She'd had to clamp her lips together not to point out that they'd been social climbing up a dreaded foreign lord. Hangers-on to a Wynchester.

Philippa yearned to be like Tommy's family, part of them, one of them. It had to be better than sitting alone at an empty dining table for the five hundred and sixty-third time this year.

The number would have been even higher if Philippa didn't break her fast in her bedroom.

When she'd finished the final course, she made her usual route through the ground floor in search of her parents.

Underwood handed her a stack of letters and tipped his head meaningfully toward the cerulean sitting room.

Mother? Or Father?

Philippa tried not to feel hurt that neither of them ever came to the dining room in search of *her*. She smoothed her lace overdress and presented herself at the threshold.

Father. Presumably. An open broadsheet hid everything from his lap up. Only his fingers were visible on either side of the newspaper.

Philippa hesitated, then cleared her throat.

Her father did not lower his paper.

Was it too soft? Had he thought her sound the noise of a horse from a passing carriage?

She cleared her throat again, with gusto this time. A very clear, obvious, female throat-clearing. The most theatrically exaggerated throat-clearing ever heard off a London stage.

Father shook his paper pointedly and did not lower it.

Her shoulders sank. He *had* known it was her. Or at least, he'd known it was *someone*, and did not care enough to find out who, even if it was his own daughter.

She wanted to tear the paper from his hands. Would he

notice her then? Or would she be irrelevant and worthless until she landed a lord? The match was as much for Father's sake. Unlike peers, Father actually had to campaign to keep his seat in the House of Commons. A familial connection in the House of Lords could cement his career.

A connection like...the Duke of Faircliffe, whom Philippa had failed to marry when she'd had the chance. Guilt ate at her. Father would have put down the paper if she'd been a more dutiful daughter.

Instead, she'd caused him more stress, just like Mother always did. Philippa sighed and turned away. She would not bother him now. Once she had a husband, Father would be proud of her. She would have proved her worth. Wasn't that what she'd told Tommy she wanted? To be helpful?

She made her way upstairs to her bedchamber and glanced down at the correspondence Underwood had given her. Part of her wondered whether one of the letters would be from Tommy. Why would it be? She wasn't a real baron *or* a real suitor. Nor would she have any idea how constantly she had remained in the forefront of Philippa's mind.

She stepped into her room and closed the door. Philippa *liked* Tommy. There was no one she'd rather find herself in a fake courtship with for the next three months.

Tommy personified fearlessness and freedom. When Tommy saw a wall, she jumped over it or broke right through it. She would have made a marvelous knight in tales of chivalry and adventure.

Unfortunate that she wasn't actually a man. Or a legitimate English lord.

When it came to passion, Philippa's cold dead heart remained resolutely cold and dead, but at least a future with a man like Tommy sounded like a happy one.

The false Baron Vanderbean was charming and clever.

Dashing and bold. Sweet and romantic, even if that part was just pretending. Dancing had been *fun* for the first time in five seasons, all because of the company. Tommy was a delight, no matter what they were doing. Or almost doing. That moment, out in the garden...

But Philippa hadn't meant to spend all night and all morning reliving every moment she'd ever shared with Tommy—who had *not* written a letter. The Wynchesters were hard at work helping Damaris. Philippa ought to attend to her responsibilities, too.

A properly executed husband hunt would appease more than her parents. Marrying a lord would make her project for local libraries more appealing to the rest of Polite Society. Half of her letters were from ladies who had no time for charity—the season would begin in only three months, you see, and there were so many new gowns and accoutrements to arrange. They were certain Philippa understood.

The other half of her correspondence came from antiquities enthusiasts.

Earlier in the week, she had sent letters to her entire list of book collectors inquiring about other copies of the Northrup chivalric tales. Responses were trickling in. Thus far, every seller had the same news:

OUR DEEPEST APOLOGIES.
WE NO LONGER POSSESS THE VOLUME IN QUESTION.

She pushed the letters away and made a frustrated sound in the back of her throat. All the Northrup manuscripts had disappeared over the past half decade?

All of them?

Vaguely, she recalled a persistent attempt to purchase her copy years ago, by some strange collector. He eventually offered prices so high, Philippa had stopped taking him seriously. She was fortunate that his correspondence had been with her, rather than her father, or the illuminated manuscript might have vanished at the first offer.

She would write to him at once. She would also write back to everyone who'd answered and ask where they had sold their manuscript. Someone, somewhere, had to have a copy.

Philippa moved to her dressing table and pushed her creams and hairpins out of the way. She now had twenty inquiries to write.

After she had finished her letters, she took out her battered volume two for further study. Philippa did not want to wreak irreparable damage upon the fragile manuscript— she had a horror of destroying books—but if she wished to extract the mysterious document from the binding, there was no other way.

The gilt-embossed cover was stunning. When closed, even the edges of the pages had been inked and painted with violets and pomegranates and abstract lines and swirls. A fanciful touch, given that the ornamental edges would be out of sight when the book was tucked into a shelf. Opening the volume spread the ivy and swirls into nothing at all.

She picked up a small blade and a clean quill.

This was an act that could not be undone. She hesitated. Harming a rare, priceless book made her hands shake and her stomach feel queasy.

The thin wooden boards inside of the covers were weak. Philippa supposed she was lucky that these were Elizabethan manuscripts, rather than medieval, or they might not have survived. The boards' interior walls were stiff and peeling, even without her interference.

Carefully, she sliced the leather to reveal a folded document beneath. As gingerly as she could, she liberated it from the fore edge. The parchment peeled away as though it had never been glued in place. As though it wasn't part of the binding at all, but a separate hidden page. It had been protected from sunlight and weather and oil from fingers. The painted colors were slightly brighter than those in the manuscript. The paper itself was slightly less yellowed and decorated with elaborate swirling designs.

Nonetheless, the paper was still brittle. Philippa pulled on a pair of gloves before attempting to unfold it. Carefully, she opened the paper as far as she dared without risking it falling apart along the fragile folds.

It was a letter!

" 'To my dearest Agnes,' " she read aloud.

Who was Agnes? Sir Reginald's wife? His daughter?

" 'How I have adored these years together, you and I working side by side at our little table. Each stroke of my pen reminds me of your hand, its art indistinguishable from my own. Each completed volume, identical to the last. I often cannot tell where I end and you begin.' "

Sir Reginald had not created these manuscripts by himself? He and Agnes bound and illustrated them together, side by side at their . . . little table?

" 'To others, copying our words year after year must seem like drudgery. But with you, I have never known a moment's boredom. Our hands are one, as are our hearts and our lives.' "

Well . . . *that* was romantic enough that Philippa discounted the idea the illustrator had penned this letter to his daughter. It must be to his wife. "Our words" and "our hands are one" could certainly be interpreted as two artists illustrating the same text interchangeably. It often occurred with Renaissance painters and their apprentices.

A pang of loneliness filled her. How lovely it must be to

have a shared passion with one's spouse outside of the bedroom. To work side by side on something wonderful. It was a shame Sir Reginald's wife's involvement had been lost to history. Their partnership was just as romantic as any of the tales they'd written inside.

She turned back to the letter.

"'I leave a part of myself in this volume, as I do every time, and I know that you silently do the same. Our names may never be known to anyone but ourselves, but the only esteem I have ever craved is yours. Being known fully to you has always been enough. Yours, Katherine.'"

Philippa blinked.

Katherine?

She quickly revised all of her theories. Sir Reginald hadn't been the artist creating these volumes after all. Agnes and Katherine had. But who were they? Female apprentices? *Were* there female apprentices?

To Philippa's knowledge, illuminated manuscripts had been penned first by monks for centuries, and later by secular artists, but were almost always the exclusive domain of men.

Who were these women? Might they be...no, of course they weren't lovers. If such things were scandalous in modern times, they would be unheard of two centuries before. Any such practitioner certainly wouldn't create physical evidence.

Perhaps Agnes and Katherine were the artist's daughters. Children often assisted the family business, did they not? Although...no mention was made of Sir Reginald himself. In fact, based on the contents of this letter, one could think the sole artists were Agnes and Katherine, and that Sir Reginald had little to do with the illustrations at all.

Mayhap he'd drawn the *first* set, and the ladies made copies. Incredible copies. Copies so skillful and intricate, they appeared penned by the master himself.

Except...Katherine had said, "writing *our* words again year after year."

Our words.

Not "Sir Reginald's words."

It could be a lie or braggadocio, but what would be the point? If she and Agnes worked half as closely together as the letter intimated, Agnes would already know the truth of the matter. These were *their* words, *their* illustrations, *their* books. Philippa's heart beat faster.

The ladies' genius hadn't been "lost" over time. It had been *hidden*.

This was a scandal!

Philippa wiggled atop her dressing stool. Captain Northrup would definitely wish to obtain this document before its contents fell into the wrong hands and sullied his oh-so-important knightly ancestor's spotless legacy.

Perhaps this was the leverage they needed! It was bad breeding to hold a document hostage until one's demands were met...but if Northrup gave Damaris the credit she deserved, that was well worth a little extortion.

As Mother had said: blackmail was a part of life.

The letter had been cleverly hidden. If the previous collectors had taken proper care of this volume, the world still would have no idea that something lay just below the surface. She could not help but wonder if other volumes might also contain secrets.

Philippa closed the book as carefully as she could and patted the pages together until they lined up perfectly. She stared at the flowery motif and the abstract lines and swirls. Or perhaps not so abstract. The design was very similar to the illustrations decorating the hidden letter.

When Katherine said she and Agnes had left "part of themselves" in every book, what if they meant letters similar to the one Philippa had found? If she could acquire the rest of the set, she might uncover even more damning evidence against Sir Reginald. Proof that he was a fraud, just like Captain Northrup. And there were two more women whose credit had been stolen.

She had to talk to Tommy.

If there was anyone who could uncover the true identities of Agnes and Katherine, Philippa put her faith in Graham Wynchester. Unfortunately, now that Baron Vanderbean was in high demand, Mother no longer allowed him to escort Philippa to the park unless Mother herself was present to preen at his side.

Sending her discovery and concerns in a letter was also out of the question. Mother inspected all of Philippa's correspondence before allowing it out of the house—and only if it was in what Mother called "plain English."

Perhaps in the future, Philippa and Tommy could devise a cipher that didn't *look* like an encrypted message, but for now an in-person conversation would have to do.

Was there a supper party or assembly tonight at which they might meet? Mother would have the upcoming weeks' invitations. Philippa wrapped her damaged manuscript in cloth and tied it with string before replacing it on the bottom panel inside her wardrobe.

Then she raced downstairs in search of her mother.

"Philippa, darling," Mother sang out with delight as Philippa skidded into the sitting room. "Don't scurry, it isn't ladylike. Do you know what I have here?" Mother pointed to the piles of correspondence surrounding her on the sofa. "Invitations to *everything*, darling. I know you don't enjoy them, but we simply must say yes to the majority of—"

"Say yes to everything," Philippa interrupted. "I'll go.

It's fine. But the next ball isn't for a week, and I was thinking—"

"A new wardrobe, of course." Mother cast a critical eye over her. "You've worn the same style for longer than is fashionable. Indeed, I regret to inform you that your overabundance of lace has *never* been fashionable. I've just received the latest *Ackermann's* and *La Belle Assemblée*—"

"I like my clothes," said Philippa. "They're pretty. I feel comfortable in them."

"Clothes aren't meant to be *comfortable*, darling. They're meant to look exactly like everyone else's, only better. Here, see this opera gown on page eighteen."

"How about a different activity?" Philippa suggested. "What about—"

"A book," Mother crowed. "I *told* your father you'd choose books over gowns. He merely grunted instead of responding, but I know he feels the same way I do. Very well, Philippa. You've won. I shall allow one more literary acquisition."

Splendid. The very thing she'd begged to do for months, only to discover no private collector in England possessed any of the objects Philippa wished to acquire.

"In exchange," Mother continued, "you must review the expanded list of potential husbands I've made for you, so you can be sure to give them special attention. Have you been practicing fluttering your eyelashes in your mirror like I showed you? Or the flirtatious giggle?"

"No," Philippa said.

"Darling, you really must come at this game with a bit more strategy. It's not chess. It's dominos."

Philippa blinked. "Dominos has more strategy than chess?"

"It has the *right* strategy," Mother explained. "You line up the competition and knock them all out of your way until you're the last one standing."

"That's...not how you play dominos," Philippa said.

"Be the last domino," Mother said gently. "That's all I ask of you. A nice, ivory domino with an entire brood of pips and a husband with a title that makes hearts beat faster."

Philippa wished she could find a man who could wake her frozen heart. In the meantime, all she thought about was Tommy. Whom she was desperate to see...in order to talk about the case. Nothing more.

"Mother," she tried again. "I didn't come to pester you for a new book."

Her mother shook her head in confusion, as though she must have misheard. "You didn't?"

Philippa took a deep breath. "I'd like Baron Vanderbean to escort me to Hyde Park again. I know only the two of us fit comfortably in his phaeton, but it would be a fine opportunity for people to see—"

Mother gasped. "Of *course* people need to see you with him. But not *without* me! No one *else* will have Baron Vanderbean until the Knightsborough gathering next week. We will be the most envied hostesses in the ton!"

"Hostesses?" Philippa repeated blankly. "To what?"

Mother's eyes glittered. "A tea! Not with any of your blue-stockings, darling. We must invite *important* people. I know just the ladies most likely to spread the best gossip."

17

✿

*E*very time Underwood opened the door, Philippa fought the urge to dash from the sitting room to see if the new arrival was Tommy. Her anxiousness—eagerness, whatever this was—had nothing to do with the night before at the ball. Tommy wasn't a *real* suitor.

This strange restlessness under her skin was because she was keen to share her discovery with someone who could actually do something about it. Right?

Philippa was committed to helping Damaris in any way possible. Her friend wasn't the first woman to have her ideas stolen by a man, nor would she be the last. Getting justice for her—a public confession—would feel like winning, just once, for all women everywhere.

And now there were two more names to put on the list! Agnes and Katherine deserved credit for their work, too.

"Miss York," said Lady Newcomb, "how surprising to see you on the dance floor last night."

"And in such an interesting gown," said Mrs. Jarvis. "Every time I see you, you're wrapped in even more lace than the time before."

Philippa stared at them blankly because she knew it would vex them.

This was yet another reason she tried to avoid her mother's teas. Her mother's friends weren't friendly at all. Currently, they were milling about the sitting room, peering at the portraits and Philippa, as if it were all fodder for tomorrow's gossip.

"Is this your morning's correspondence, Mrs. York?" Lady Waddington inquired. "Pity. I would have thought her performance last night would have caused some attention."

Philippa clenched her teeth. The only reason her mother tolerated these people was because they were bon ton.

A wave of awareness rippled through the parlor, and everyone jerked their gazes to the corridor at once.

Baron Vanderbean paused at the threshold as though the doorway were a life-size frame and he, the stunning portrait.

In formal knee breeches with a gold waistcoat peeking from beneath a coat of sharp black superfine, Tommy looked every inch as though she had an appointment with the Queen. Ballroom perfect, except for the wicker basket dangling from her arm.

"Baron Vanderbean!" Mother squealed, nudging her nearest friends.

Tommy swept into the room with just a hint of swagger, striding not toward Philippa but to her mother. After executing an absolutely breathtaking bow, Tommy presented her with a single yellow rose.

"Is this for our darling Philippa?" Mother asked, giddy.

"No." *There* was the rakish smile. "I brought it for you."

Philippa waited for Tommy to add, *To thank you for bringing Philippa into the world* or some such, but it never came. She tried not to feel hurt. Tommy wasn't a suitor. Philippa had to stop thinking of her like one.

Mother blushed and tittered and showed her yellow rose to

all her friends as though Tommy had carried in the moon on her shoulders.

"Introductions," hissed one of the ladies.

"I suppose." Mother sighed disinterestedly, as though she had not spent the past hour bouncing on her toes in anticipation of exactly this moment.

One by one, she introduced Tommy to each of her guests.

And one by one, Tommy charmed them senseless with her particular mix of flattery and flirtation. However many invitations awaited Baron Vanderbean at the Wynchester home, she'd just managed to double the number.

Philippa waited impatiently as Tommy made her slow, deliberate way about the parlor, murmuring compliments and kissing hands and ignoring Philippa.

She didn't *mind*. This was all a lark. She and Tommy were actors on a stage, even if the audience didn't realize they were seeing a performance. Tommy was doing exactly the right thing to please Mother in every way. Philippa could not have scripted it better if she'd tried.

There was no reason to feel slighted at being ignored by a woman pretending to be a man pretending to be her suitor.

Once all Mother's friends were starry-eyed and hanging off Tommy's every word, Tommy turned to Philippa.

"And now," she said, her eyes never leaving Philippa's. "At last my gaze can fall upon the reason I breathe."

Gasps and sighs ricocheted through the sitting room at that completely melodramatic nonsense. No one said such a thing and meant it.

Tommy closed the distance between them in three dramatic strides. She took Philippa's hand. "I have never known another to match your beauty and never will."

Were Philippa's fingers *trembling?* Why were they trembling?

Tommy smiled, as though she knew about the tickling sensation spreading throughout Philippa's entire body. Never dropping her gaze from Philippa's, slowly...ever so slowly...Tommy lifted Philippa's fingers to her parted lips. Tommy kept them there against her warm mouth for several heartbeats longer than was necessary or proper.

Philippa could not have removed her hand if she'd wanted to. She was frozen in place.

"My word," choked Mrs. Jarvis. "I have three unwed daughters I could introduce him to."

Tommy lowered Philippa's hand but did not immediately release it. Instead, Tommy brushed the pad of her thumb lightly across the tender skin, as though memorizing its warmth or sealing in the kiss. Only then did she let go.

No one who had witnessed the interaction would ever believe Baron Vanderbean wasn't actually courting Philippa.

Even *she* had to fight to remember it was all pageantry.

Philippa buried her tenderly kissed hand in the voluminous lace of her skirts. Although Tommy was no longer touching her, the places where Tommy's thumb had brushed Philippa's skin felt slightly warmer than they ought, as though a ray of sunlight had fallen upon her skin.

No one had ever said or done anything so romantic to her before. Philippa supposed hearing such words from another woman should feel peculiar. Strangely, it did not.

The words felt...real.

"I'm glad you came." Her voice did not sound like hers at all. Breathier. Strained. "I begged Mother for this tea, just so we could invite you."

"*Philippa*," Mother whispered with recrimination. "*Much* too forward."

"I'm glad you did." Tommy's smile was slow and seemed

to have been invented just for Philippa. "Since last I saw you, I've spent every moment counting the heartbeats until we could meet again."

Lady Newcomb fluttered an ivory fan near her chest.

"Tea," Mother shrilled in her false-gaiety voice. "It's time for tea. Come along, come along. Baron Vanderbean, you will sit by Philippa, of course. Philippa, you will remember your place and cease embarrassing me."

"It's not embarrassing *me*," Lady Newcomb murmured to Lady Waddington. "If she doesn't want him, *I'll* take him."

Tommy's dark gaze didn't leave Philippa's, but the corners of her mouth twitched. Her eyes sparkled as she deliberately gave Philippa the heavy-lidded rakish eyebrow wink she'd shown her at the ball.

Philippa tried hard not to grin and found herself smiling with her eyes instead. The thought that she could make a similar expression to Tommy's raffish one sent a frisson of naughtiness down her spine. They were sharing a secret joke, a secret gesture. Communicating with no need for words at all.

"Over here," Mother sang and sailed out of the parlor toward the dining room.

Tommy fell back to escort one of the women, much to the lady's tittering delight. Did *they* practice coquettish giggles in front of a looking glass? How did other women manage to make it look so fetching? Philippa turned her gaze away. It didn't matter. She wasn't jealous.

In the dining room, Tommy pulled Philippa's chair out for her, then placed the wicker basket she'd brought just behind the seat.

"What's in the basket?" Philippa whispered.

"A surprise," Tommy whispered back. "Did you really yearn to see me?"

"Desperately," Philippa admitted, and immediately wished she hadn't. She didn't want to give the wrong idea. "I mean, about Damaris. The case. I have news. Maybe."

"No whispering," Mother scolded. "Will you pour the tea, darling?"

"We'll never get a moment alone," Philippa muttered, then rose to pour the tea.

Tommy waited until everyone was served before addressing the entire table in her easy, welcoming manner.

"I suppose you've heard there's another balloon launch tomorrow afternoon at Vauxhall Gardens," she said. "I'll be attending with the Duke and Duchess of Faircliffe. I'd like to invite all of you to pack your blankets and join us for a picnic."

"*Oh*!" Renewed whispers sailed around the table, followed by a chorus of "I'd love to" and "I wouldn't miss it."

Philippa raised her eyebrows at her mother and waited.

Rank was everything to the ton. Mother could not ignore the opportunity to be the public guest of a duke and duchess. Particularly when the friends she competed with had snapped up the invitation in a blink.

"Of course," Mother said. "Will you be sharing a blanket with Philippa and me, or must you sit with the newlyweds?"

Well done. Philippa inclined her head at her mother. If Tommy had been a reluctant suitor, he would find himself hard pressed to intrude upon a groom and his bride rather than accompany the Yorks.

"I wouldn't dream of being anywhere but at Philippa's side," Tommy replied.

Philippa half expected her mother to whisper, "*Much* too forward." The rest of the ladies gazed at Tommy with soppy expressions, as though imagining themselves the recipients of her romantic balderdash.

At least Philippa had the advantage of knowing it was all an act.

She must keep reminding herself of this fact. With Tommy, it was tricky to know what was make-believe and what was not.

Sometimes, it almost felt as though Tommy told the truth at all times and allowed other people to believe what they wished.

When she had confessed that she was not actually Baron Vanderbean—or a man—Philippa had later realized Tommy had never claimed to be Baron Vanderbean in the first place. She'd said the previous baron was her father. Philippa and her mother had taken one look at smart, dashing Tommy and accepted without question that this dapper gentleman must of course be the heir.

"Your mind looks beautiful today," Tommy said.

Philippa slanted a look at her. "Poppycock."

"It's my favorite part of you," Tommy said. "Of course it is beautiful."

Mother made a little chuckle. "Baron Vanderbean has a curious weakness for bluestockings."

"No." Tommy's eyes held Philippa's. "Just one in particular."

The back of Philippa's neck heated, and she dropped her gaze to her tea.

This romantic drivel might not count as a *lie*, per se, because Philippa was in on the joke. Tommy genuinely seemed to want to help in any way that she could. If she was very, very *good* at pretending to be a suitor, well, she was only doing as she'd been asked. Giving Philippa what she wanted.

And the truth was, it was diverting to be the toast of the ton instead of the spinster on the shelf. The boring society nonsense Philippa had long hated was amusing and exciting when she did it with Tommy.

"What is your reading circle's book of the month?" Tommy asked.

"Oh, for heaven's sake." Mother flapped her hand. "No one is interested in that."

"Miss York is," Tommy said. "Therefore I am, too."

"Ohh." Lady Newcomb sighed.

"I'm interested in anything that interests Baron Vanderbean," Mrs. Jarvis gushed. "Even Philippa's dusty old books."

"My daughter *is* clever," Mother grumbled. "I suppose someone was bound to appreciate the trait someday."

Philippa gazed at Tommy. Three months together was not nearly enough time. Now that she'd had a taste of what life could be like with a special…*friend*, or whatever Tommy was becoming, Philippa wanted to keep it always.

But it would have to end. Whomever her parents betrothed her to, it would not be Tommy. All Philippa could do was savor the moments between now and then. With luck, one day she would become one of those shocking old grandmothers, whose best stories began, *When I was your age…*

"Shall I ring for another tray of cucumber sandwiches?" Mother asked.

Lady Newcomb replied, "I couldn't possibly eat another bite."

"You've outdone yourself as always, dear," agreed Mrs. Jarvis.

"I have something for Philippa," Tommy said.

All eyes swung in their direction.

Philippa swallowed. More flowers? Sweets?

Tommy lifted the wicker basket from behind Philippa's chair and placed it on her lap. "Be careful."

Gingerly, Philippa lifted the edge of the lid.

White whiskers popped out, followed by a pink nose and calico fur.

"It's Tiglet!" she squealed, then realized she sounded just like her mother. Perhaps her fluttery affectations weren't fake after all. It was impossible to contain the laugh of delight in Philippa's throat when the kitten rasped his rough tongue against the pad of her finger. She pulled him from the basket and hugged him to her chest. He had grown quite a bit since last she saw him. "Isn't this Chloe's kitten?"

Tommy shook her head. "Jacob's. And now yours, if you'd like him."

Of course she would. Not only was the kitten adorable, but male calico cats were also as rare and unusual as the Wynchesters themselves. Philippa would cherish her temporary companion.

The ladies cooed at the sweet surprise.

Well, all the ladies except Philippa's mother, who looked significantly less pleased with Tiglet than she had with her yellow rose.

"It's a homing kitten," Tommy said under her breath.

"A what?" Philippa whispered back.

"Let him out of a window if you need me," Tommy explained. "It'll be faster than sending a footman."

A *homing* kitten.

Philippa stroked Tiglet's soft fur in wonder. She had devised this encounter because she couldn't send a simple letter. The gift was more than thoughtful—it was practical and useful. Releasing a kitten into the wild was something she could do from the privacy of her bedchamber.

But it also meant Tiglet was one more fun and adorable thing that Philippa wouldn't be able to keep. Between now and the Prince Regent's grand celebration, Damaris would have justice—or not—and Philippa would be betrothed. She would become mistress of someone else's home, and Tiglet...would return to where he was loved.

"If you don't want him..." Tommy said softly.

Philippa cradled Tiglet to her chest. "Too late. He's mine for now."

Tommy met her gaze for a long moment and then tilted her face toward Philippa's mother. "This is such an elegant dining room, Mrs. York. I have never seen such lovely ceiling lunettes. And the trim...Is the ormolu door furniture original?"

Mother puffed out her chest. "Indeed it is." She launched into a lengthy and completely fictive explanation of how she had chosen the house just for those specific features. "Philippa, show Baron Vanderbean the ormolu and the lunettes. But stay inside this room so we can see you."

"Yes, Mother," Philippa said obediently.

Tommy flashed her eyebrows. "Shall we stroll about the room conspicuously?"

"I thought you'd never ask," Philippa whispered.

She rose to her feet, the kitten nestled against her bosom, and made a big show of leading Tommy beneath this ordinary ceiling lunette, then that identical ceiling lunette.

When they reached the farthest point in the room from the chatter of the dining table, Tommy's eyes glittered wickedly and she pitched her voice low. "Alone at last with my fair maiden. Put down the cat so that I can ravish you."

"We're not alone," Philippa said, but her pulse skipped anyway. "There won't be any ravishing."

"Not tonight," Tommy agreed. "Probably. Though I fear it is my sworn duty to change your mind."

"Your sworn duty, or something you *wish* to do?"

Tommy's grin only widened. "Ah. You have seen through me. I wish to ravish you for no other reason than the personal pleasure it would bring both of us."

Philippa's cheeks felt strangely flushed. "You needn't play the rake now, when no one can hear you."

"You can hear me," Tommy said softly.

It was an act. Of course it was an act. But Philippa was reminded of that moment last night in the garden. There had been no music. Just moonlight, and the sound of the wind in the leaves. Tommy had touched Philippa's hip, just as she had when they were waltzing, and for one dizzy moment Philippa had almost thought...

She cleared her throat. "You're incorrigible."

"I've been accused of worse," Tommy replied, and tucked her hands behind her back.

Was it ridiculous to wish that Tommy had not hidden her hands away? That she might touch Philippa again, on the same sensitive spot on her side, just to see whether it would feel like last night all over again, or whether the magic had been a passing fancy?

"I found a letter in my manuscript," Philippa blurted out. Books were a much safer topic.

Tommy gave her all of her attention at once. Or rather, Tommy had already been giving Philippa her full attention, but it sharpened somehow. As though Tommy were a wolf who had just caught the scent of her prey.

"Tell me," she commanded.

Philippa explained her discovery in as condensed a manner as she could manage. How the letter had been hidden, that it had been written by one of the *real* artists of the illuminated manuscript, how all the other copies of the manuscript had been bought up.

"I made a copy of the letter." Philippa turned her back

toward the table and pulled the kitten from her chest in order to retrieve a folded square of foolscap.

Tommy's eyes tracked every movement as Philippa's fingers slid beneath her bodice.

"I'm not an artist like Marjorie." Philippa pulled out the copy. "I'm afraid it's just the text in my ordinary handwriting, with none of the flourishes."

"It's perfect." Tommy reached for the folded square and tucked it inside her coat next to her heart. "Graham shall investigate those names at once. Expect an odious amount of detail in an impressively short period of time."

"What if there's no information to find?" Philippa asked. "Whoever they are, Agnes and Katherine need justice, too. Those poor...women..."

Tommy's hand was rising toward Philippa's bodice. Slowly. Affording Philippa time to knock her hand aside or back away. Which she was definitely going to do. Any moment now. Probably.

Before Philippa could make her decision, Tommy's hand passed Philippa's bosom and stopped at her shoulder, where Tommy lifted an errant kitten hair and tossed it aside.

Of course. Of course it was that.

Why would it be anything else? What was Philippa thinking? Was she *not* thinking? All she ever did was think. Why did her best skill fail her so utterly whenever it came to Tommy?

And...what was wrong with Philippa's breathing? Was her bosom heaving? *Was this a heaving bosom?* Even her heart was behaving erratically. What was happening?

Tommy arched a brow as if she sensed Philippa's turmoil and found it amusing. The heavy-lidded expression was similar to the night before, but somehow even more rakish. The slight quirk of Tommy's lips distracted her in a way she had never been distracted before. She should stop staring at Tommy's mouth at once.

Why couldn't she stop staring at Tommy's mouth?

It felt like Tommy was closer than before. Even closer than they had been in the garden, which was ridiculous because she had been *touching* Philippa in the garden, and here they were standing a foot apart. That was why she'd had all the time in the world to notice Tommy's hand rising toward her bosom.

Shoulder. Tommy had plucked cat hair from Philippa's *shoulder*.

There was nothing less sensual than that.

And yet it had felt as though the light touch were a mere precursor, a hint of something bigger, better. An appetizer before the main course.

Mayhap that was why Philippa was still staring at Tommy's parted lips. Even though the moment had stretched on far beyond what was acceptable or explainable.

She wanted Tommy to do it again; to touch her hip, to pluck cat hair from her bosom. She wanted to know if this electricity crackling between them was all in Philippa's head, or if it was as real as a lightning storm, filling the night with white-hot bursts of power and danger.

Tommy's fingers moved. On the side hidden from Mother's guests.

The slender hand was coming not toward her bodice, or even her side, but just enough forward for Tommy to brush her fingertips up the back of Philippa's hand, from her knuckles to her wrist.

She felt the caress all the way to her toes. In places that weren't even her toes. Every inch of her body seemed alive to the possibility of Tommy's touch...and her cold dead heart gave its first unmistakable flutter. Several flutters. Possible apoplexy.

"Philippa!" Mother called.

"Coming," Philippa replied breathlessly.

She did not move. If Tommy had touched her like this last night in the garden, Philippa might have thought she meant to kiss her.

And if that charged moment had felt anything like this one...

Philippa would have wanted it to happen.

18

❦

$\mathcal{A}$ colorful hot-air balloon lifted a man in a large basket higher into the sky, to the delight of a thousand-person crowd. Despite the rollicking spectacle, Tommy's attention was on the woman next to her. Philippa always looked stunning, but she was even more beautiful with wonder lighting her eyes.

"Just think how much better this event would have been," Tommy murmured in Philippa's ear, "if you would have let me stuff Captain Northrup in there and send him out to sea."

Philippa elbowed her.

They had not had a moment alone since arriving at Vauxhall Gardens. The York blanket was squeezed between Marjorie and Elizabeth, who were communicating in silent hand gestures, and Chloe and Faircliffe, who were the very picture of romantic contentment. Their gazes were so intent on each other, they barely noticed the colorful flying balloon, much less Tommy choking down Mrs. York's cucumber sandwiches on the blanket behind them.

Tommy wished she and Philippa could snuggle shoulder-to-shoulder, lying on a blanket amidst a crowd of thousands, but with eyes only for each other.

Stroking Philippa's hand yesterday had been a calculated

risk...though Tommy still wasn't certain what she had learned. Philippa hadn't simpered or batted her eyelashes, but nor had she reacted unfavorably.

It gave Tommy a glimmer of hope.

At the moment, Philippa looked calmly oblivious to both the very-much-in-love couple on the blanket next to them, as well as to her mother prattling on about her daughter's future opportunities as though Tommy didn't exist. Perhaps after three and twenty years of similar scenes, she had learned not to let it bother her.

At the moment, one of Philippa's hands was *right there* at Tommy's side. How she wished she could entwine their fingers! It was torture being so close and yet unable to touch.

"Ooh," the spectators breathed as the balloon rose higher.

The knuckles of Philippa's hand brushed against Tommy's.

She froze, her heartbeat accelerating. Had Philippa touched her on purpose? Or was it an accident? Was the brush of fingers part of the masquerade? It wouldn't be much of a sham courtship if Philippa didn't pretend to be courted. Tommy let out a slow breath. Was that all yesterday had been? Tolerating the touch of Tommy's hand because it helped to better convey the fiction of their romance to their audience?

But Tommy had taken great care *not* to be seen yesterday. And who was watching them now? Every face was tilted toward the sky.

Maybe the soft brush of fingers meant nothing. Or maybe...*Maybe*...

The spectators cheered as the pilot of the balloon waved goodbye

"Goodbye, Captain Knave-thrup," Tommy called under her breath. "Never return."

"If only it were so simple," Philippa murmured back.

When the trees blocked the view of the balloon, the

audience packed up their picnics and began to disperse. Some no doubt returned home, whereas others took advantage of Vauxhall's twelve acres of pleasure gardens.

And some waited to be presented to Baron Vanderbean.

"Philippa, introduce your gentleman to me."

"Not so reclusive anymore, eh, Vanderbean?"

"So *this* handsome fellow is the heir we've been eager to meet."

"You won't let Miss York take *all* your attention, will you?"

For the next quarter hour, Tommy bowed at and flattered men and women of the ton. It was amusing that they were so eager to meet her. A few hopeful debutantes openly glared at Philippa while waiting their turn to be introduced.

These were the same people who turned up their noses at the idea of being friendly to someone beneath their station. The sort who acted as though they didn't notice children like Tommy in the street. As far as Tommy was concerned, the real Baron Vanderbean outranked all of these self-important nobs.

Mrs. York was cock-a-hoop over the attention.

In fact, everyone's plans were working. The ton got to meet the new baron. Mrs. York had more eyes on her daughter than ever before. Philippa could pretend to be following instructions in order to milk a few more weeks of freedom.

And Tommy...Tommy had Philippa, if only for a short while.

Tommy was used to temporary. Forever was for other people. People like her could only snatch the little moments when they were lucky enough to get them, and do their best to hold them close.

"*Well*," said Mrs. York as many of the spectators drifted away. "At least *that's* over."

She did not appear the least bit vexed. Tommy half expected

Mrs. York to sprout tail feathers to rival a peacock at the attention and jealous looks she and Philippa had been given. Tommy exchanged a look with her siblings.

Philippa turned to Tommy. "Now we have you all to ourselves again."

She suddenly screwed up her face and twitched as though she were sneezing into a sandstorm.

"What are you doing?" Tommy whispered.

"She thinks she's batting her eyes," said Mrs. York. "I *told* her to practice in the looking glass."

Tommy was thrilled. Being flirted with terribly was leagues better than not being flirted with at all.

"It's charming," she assured Philippa. "Probably only to me. Therefore, I cannot recommend deploying that particular expression again. But rest assured that with Baron Vanderbean, it indeed had its desired impact."

Philippa's face was skeptical. She dropped her voice to a whisper. "What might you know about my desires?"

Tommy made a lascivious expression and murmured, "Only that I would be happy to grant them."

Philippa tilted her head. Was she thinking the offer over?

She might only be acting flirtatious to keep up appearances. Then again, if those disturbing facial contortions were her best attempt at *acting*...

Mayhap the rest was real.

"I believe I'll take a stroll in the gardens." Elizabeth leaned on her sword stick. "I've always wanted to explore the 'Dark Walk.'"

"I'll go with you," Marjorie said loudly.

"Baron Vanderbean," said Elizabeth. "Would you and Miss York like to join us?"

Mrs. York gasped. "On the *Dark Walk?*"

"It's not dark," Philippa pointed out. "It's midafternoon."

"But—" Mrs. York flapped her hands. "The things the gossips say happen on those paths after nightfall—"

"Don't worry," said Elizabeth. "The real reason I carry a cane is to knock blackguards unconscious in one swoop."

"And it's sunny," Marjorie added.

"It is a fine afternoon," Mrs. York admitted. "I'll go with you."

"Oh dear," said Chloe. "His Grace and I were hoping you would accompany us for a stroll down the Grand Walk to the Rotunda."

Faircliffe looked as though he'd rather fly off in a balloon than spend another moment with Mrs. York.

Behind Chloe, a few society ladies looked on shamelessly.

"Of course I'm happy to accompany the Duke and Duchess of Faircliffe wherever they wish as their particular favored guest," Mrs. York announced. "Philippa, meet me at the Rotunda in one hour, and not a second later."

"You carry a pocket watch?" Tommy asked Philippa in surprise. "I never noticed."

Philippa dropped her voice. "No. Neither does Mother. She just likes to appear in control in front of her friends."

"I shan't disappoint her." Tommy made a show of consulting her own watch. "It is my honor. We shall deliver your daughter with ten minutes to spare."

"Why did you give up ten of our minutes?" Philippa whispered.

"I didn't," Tommy whispered back. "You just told me she hasn't a pocket watch. I'll set mine to be half an hour late."

As the groups divided in separate directions, a rush of joy filled her at the prospect of having more of Philippa's company.

Courting Philippa was a dream come true, even if it was make-believe.

Baron Vanderbean was the title that gave Tommy the freedom to flirt and dance and make a public claim on Philippa, temporary though it may be. Opportunities she would never have had acting like Miss Thomasina Wynchester, who would not have been welcome among the beau monde. In that role, she and Philippa might never have met.

Oh, if only she could just be Tommy and live as she pleased!

"Come along," called Elizabeth. She and Marjorie led them past the statue of Handel toward the Dark Walk.

The magnificent Triumphal Arches soared up ahead. Tommy *did* feel triumphant. She was here with her sisters and Philippa, away from the crowd and Mrs. York's watchful eyes.

"Chloe mentioned you're forbidden from making literary purchases," Elizabeth said, wasting no time. "We can acquire the other three volumes for you. I'll have Graham look for sellers—"

"I already did." Philippa rubbed her temple. "My mother finally gave me permission to make an acquisition, but it's no use. Northrup manuscript enthusiasts sold theirs years ago, to an individual who no longer resides at that address. No private collectors still own their copies."

"No private collectors." Tommy thought quickly. "What about public collectors?"

"I compiled a depressingly short list of eight organizations and universities with a Northrup manuscript in their collection, from Inverness to Penzance. Cambridge University...Carlton House...Most locations are forbidden to women or closed to guests, and all of them keep their illuminated manuscript collections under lock and key. You'd need an army to get past the guards."

"You're like a...bluestocking Graham," Elizabeth said, impressed. "You would make a good Wynchester."

Tommy ignored her sister. "Did you happen to bring that list?"

Philippa pulled it from her reticule.

Tommy tucked the list into her coat pocket to look over later.

"Now all we need are counterfeit copies." Elizabeth looked at Marjorie.

"You want me to forge four illuminated manuscripts?" Marjorie said, incredulous.

"Just three," Elizabeth reassured her. "Philippa already has one."

Marjorie stared at her. "Do you know how *long* it takes master artists to create each illuminated manuscript? You expect me to just dash a few off in my spare time?"

Elizabeth lifted a shoulder. "It didn't take you long to forge the painting Chloe stole from the Yorks' house."

Philippa tripped and hurried to catch up. "Wait... *What?*"

"Very well," Marjorie said with a sigh. "If Philippa can part with hers, I could create rough copies. They wouldn't fool anyone who looks carefully, but could replace the original on a shelf if no one is paying close attention."

"What painting did Chloe steal?" Philippa demanded.

"*Robin Goodfellow*," Elizabeth answered absently. "The one Chloe's husband gave you as a courting gift."

Tommy tightened her lips at the reminder.

"Oh... all right." Philippa fell back to Tommy's side without further questions or comment.

"You didn't want our painting anyway," Tommy reminded her.

"I remember." Philippa did not look upset at the theft. Nor was she looking at Tommy. She kept her gaze straight ahead, as though hoping she need never again discuss the Duke of Faircliffe or any of her other suitors' attempts to woo her.

Or possibly...hoping she need never suffer any other *gentleman*'s attentions?

"I can also rebind your manuscript, if you'd like," Marjorie offered.

"I trust you to take good care of art," Philippa admitted. "So, yes, that would be wonderful. I am happy to pay for the work."

Marjorie shook her head.

"Unnecessary," Tommy explained. "We don't need your money."

A path beckoned between the trees in front of them.

"Gosh," Marjorie exclaimed. "Have we arrived at the Dark Walk already?"

"By Jove, we have!" Elizabeth exclaimed with far too theatrical a look of surprise. "Why, it *does* look like a splendid spot to conduct a torrid affair."

"Elizabeth..." Tommy said in warning.

Her sisters were already backing away.

"My stars, will you look at that?" Marjorie pulled absolutely nothing out of an imaginary pocket. "The current time is 'leave-Tommy-and-Philippa-unchaperoned o'clock.'"

"Don't come after us." Elizabeth waved her sword stick in their direction. "If you don't take this fine opportunity to make all manner of mischief, you'll both deserve my wrath."

Then they turned and ran off, cackling as loud as a flock of crows.

"Do they always meddle?" Philippa asked.

"*Always*," Tommy said.

"What do they expect us to do now?"

Tommy paused. "Was it unclear?"

"They cannot really expect something like that." Philippa laughed, then looked startled. "Can they?"

"They're probably watching us to see what we'll do, the

minxes." Tommy held out her elbow. "Shall we promenade in a staid, un-ravish-like manner?"

Philippa looped her arm through Tommy's. "That'll show them."

It would not, actually, show them. It wouldn't show anybody anything. Elizabeth and Marjorie were hoping Tommy would take this opportunity to give Philippa incontrovertible, empirical proof of Tommy's interest.

"Did I tell you how lovely you look today?" she asked.

"Baron Vanderbean did," Philippa replied. "Multiple times."

"Baron Vanderbean has the unfortunate habit of blurting out the first thing that comes to his mind."

"Am I the first thing that comes to his mind?"

"Yes." Tommy swallowed. "Every minute of every day. Should he tell you about it less?"

"No," Philippa said softly. "I find I like it."

Tommy's heart stuttered. "I'll let him know."

A breeze rustled the tall trees flanking them on both sides. The shade lent the illusion that they had walked into a tunnel. Long and cool, with no other souls about. Just enough dappled sunlight filtered through the restless leaves to light the shady path.

Philippa bit her lip. "Did I tell you how dashing you look today?"

"Me, or Baron Vanderbean?"

"Both," Philippa answered. "But mostly you."

Mostly you.

Philippa looked at her with her breeches and frock coat and short hair and saw *Tommy*. Tommy's throat went dry. "You did a fine job with the list and the drawing."

A smile flitted across Philippa's lips. "Are you going to tell me I'd make a good Wynchester, too?"

"My opinion is irrelevant," Tommy said dryly. "I appear to be outvoted."

"Not to me," Philippa said. "Your opinion is the only one that matters. I'll have to try harder to impress you."

"Have you been trying to impress me?"

"Has it not been working?"

"Oh, it works," Tommy said. "It's been working since before you were trying."

Philippa grinned. "Was my eye-fluttering really that dreadful?"

"'Dreadful' is a harsh word," Tommy said. "And yet even a harsh word like 'dreadful' fails to fully encapsulate the horror in which—"

Philippa smacked her shoulder. "I won't do it again."

"You can do it whenever you want. You can do *anything* with me." Tommy slanted her a look, but Philippa's gaze was fixed on the path ahead. At this hour, the shadows were not quite dark enough to make watching one's step necessary. The Dark Walk was visible and smooth. The unclear path was where to go next with Philippa.

They weren't acting now, were they? They were alone. Marjorie and Elizabeth had seen to that. They would be standing guard at a calculated distance. The air was calm and cool. No one else was on the path. No one was watching or listening. If ever there was a moment when all pretenses could be dropped, surely this was it.

Why was the prospect so terrifying?

Perhaps because Tommy was rarely herself. She always left home in one guise or another. Yes, Philippa was now *aware* of the role...but she also *wanted* the role. She hadn't said, "Oh, how I long to be close to Tommy Wynchester." She'd said, "Can you pretend to be Baron Vanderbean for the next three months?"

What if she *didn't* want Tommy?

If their playful banter was a game, if she had misread the admittedly ambiguous signs, she would not only lose Philippa forever.

She'd be rejected as *herself*.

That would hurt so much more than just going along with the charade.

"My mother thinks I wear too much lace." Philippa looked down at her gown, then up at Tommy. "What do you think?"

Tommy waggled her brows. "I think I'd be happy to help you take it off."

Philippa narrowed her eyes. "That's what Baron Vanderbean would be happy to do. What does Tommy Wynchester think?"

"Everything the baron thinks, but more ardently."

Philippa stopped walking.

Tommy released Philippa's arm so that she could face her.

Philippa's blue eyes met hers. "The baron flirts with a lot of women."

"He does," Tommy agreed. "He may have a checkered past as a rakish scoundrel."

"Is that all it is?" Philippa asked. "Just flirting?"

"He might have a checkered past as an *accomplished* rakish scoundrel," Tommy admitted carefully. "But there's been no one else for him from the moment he glimpsed an absolute angel just over a year ago."

"A year ago." Philippa's gaze fell. "Who is it?"

Did she still doubt the truth?

Tommy could have told Philippa every detail about the first time she'd laid eyes on her, or the first time Tommy had heard Philippa speak and realized how clever she was, or the first time Tommy had heard about Philippa's charitable endeavors and realized how kind she was, or the first time Tommy had seen Philippa light up with her reading circle and realized how much she valued her friends, and how beloved she was by them in return.

But words were never as good as action.

"I'll show you who I've longed for all this time." Tommy lifted Philippa's chin. "Empirically."

And she lowered her lips to Philippa's.

19

***

*P*hilippa held herself perfectly still as Tommy's lips touched hers. Her heart raced fast and wild.

This was what she had wanted. To try. To *know*.

This was not Philippa's first kiss, but it was the first time she had *wanted* a kiss. That alone was enough to turn what she thought she knew about herself upside down. Philippa York didn't feel passion or desire a lover's touch.

And yet she'd spent the past week with every inch of her flesh prickling with anticipation for a kiss she'd hoped—yes, she'd definitely hoped—would come.

Tommy's mouth was soft against hers. Confident, but gentle. As though Tommy wouldn't go where she wasn't wanted, but if she *was* wanted, she had several good ideas of what to do about it.

Philippa felt as though she wasn't getting a full kiss, but rather the promise of one. The way Gunter's Tea Shop let her sample a new flavor of ice to decide if she wanted more. And in this case...

The answer was yes. Philippa wanted more.

"Should I stop?" Tommy had lifted her lips, but only barely.

"No." Was that Philippa's voice? Wispy and breathless? "Don't stop."

Every moment with Tommy felt reckless and daring, whether they were waltzing in front of the entire ton at a ball or stealing kisses alone on a secluded path.

"May I touch you?" Tommy asked softly.

Philippa's pulse quickened. "Please do. I've been waiting for it all day."

"Ah." Tommy's thumb brushed Philippa's cheek. "I won't make us wait any longer."

This kiss was different from the one before. It was a cornucopia of kisses, a dizzying number, made even more overwhelming by the feel of Tommy's palm cupping the side of Philippa's face, her other arm wrapping firmly about Philippa's waist.

Tommy was taller, but not awkwardly so. Tall enough that Philippa had to lift her chin high to kiss her, but not so tall that Philippa need balance on her toes. A comfortable amount of tall. Just enough to ensure Philippa was actively participating in the kiss.

She wasn't certain what to do with her hands. She had never let a kiss go on this long before. Never *wanted* to keep it going for as long as possible.

Tentatively, she placed her hands on Tommy's upper arms. It felt as possessive as Tommy's arm around her waist. Indecent. Naughty. Decadent.

The greenery and flowers around them made it feel like the first night they'd been alone in a garden. As though this kiss was a continuation of the one they hadn't taken.

Then, Philippa hadn't known what she was missing. Now that she did, she—

Oh. Something new was happening.

Tommy's lips parted, encouraging Philippa to do the same. When she did, the tip of Tommy's tongue touched hers. Shock flashed along Philippa's nerves. A new kind of shock. A shock of awareness. A shock that galvanized a coil of desire inside her and made her want to generate the same bolt of electricity in Tommy.

She tried it: the tip of her tongue licking against Tommy's, inside Tommy's mouth this time. Tasting her. Performing the act was just as exhilarating as when it had been done to her. Perhaps more so. Philippa's entire body was reacting. Her breasts felt heavier, her nipples harder. She was suddenly aware of them pushing at her bodice to brush against Tommy's coat.

The soft black lapels hid Tommy's breasts. Philippa could not help but wonder if they were reacting in the same way. If nothing more than the thickness of two soft lapels was preventing her from knowing the sensation of her breasts grazing Tommy's.

These thoughts only made Philippa's kisses hungrier. More demanding. Her hands were no longer resting on Tommy's upper arms, but rather twined about her neck, locking her in place. She was not in control of her thoughts and sensations, which put her at sixes and sevens.

Philippa's flesh tingled, as though it could feel each of Tommy's kisses all over her body. A brush of the lips here, an openmouthed kiss there. Or perhaps it was Tommy's hands that Philippa wanted to feel on her body. Or hands and kisses both, never knowing how or where the next delicious contact might land.

It occurred to her that *she* could be the one to touch and to kiss Tommy's body. The thought filled her with power and terror and desire. Philippa wasn't certain which would be better—exploring or being explored. She wanted to do both. Perhaps at the same time. She wanted to know what else Tommy's hands and mouth could do, and then she wanted to try those tricks herself. To make Tommy feel the quickening that was building inside her, a sort of throbbing between her legs.

Her heart wasn't cold and dead after all, she realized with joy. No part of her was. Her body had just been waiting for Tommy. She pressed closer.

Distant footsteps sounded behind them. "Tommy!"

She and Philippa broke apart and spun to look.

Marjorie Wynchester raced onto the path, waving her arms. Elizabeth was not far behind her. Marjorie made several strange hand gestures as she ran.

"Your mother is coming," Tommy said. "Apparently Faircliffe had all the amusement he could handle."

Philippa stared at her. "You got that from a hand gesture?"

"Signs," Tommy corrected. "Marjorie can hear, but not well. The entire family learned to sign in case her hearing worsened, and it turned out to be a wonderful method of communication."

"Should I speak louder around her?"

"Just face her. Don't shout or exaggerate your diction, because that makes it harder for her to understand."

Philippa nodded. "Thank you for telling me."

Marjorie had paused several yards away to wait for her sister to catch up.

"Your mother," Elizabeth called out, panting. "Two hundred yards."

"I know. That's what Marjorie just said."

Philippa made a mental note to acquire literature on signs as soon as possible and learn it, too. She never wanted Marjorie to feel left out of a conversation.

She and Tommy hurried to join Elizabeth and Marjorie. It was a good thing they did, because Philippa's mother strode onto the path a scant moment later.

"There you are," she said. "Come along, Philippa. That's

enough Wynchesters for one day. In fact, once a week is more than enough."

The back of Tommy's hand grazed Philippa's. "We can talk about this later," she murmured.

Could they? Should they?

No. Philippa was supposed to be in control of herself. She *was* in control of herself. This experiment could not be repeated. She might want Tommy, but she couldn't have her. It didn't matter that Philippa's body had come alive and pulsed with want.

Tommy wasn't a baron, and Philippa would be forbidden from marrying her even if she were. Tommy wasn't even a man. And yet Philippa was strangely glad of it. She didn't need Tommy to have male parts. She just wanted Tommy.

But there was no road forward. Only a brick wall and a forced detour in another direction.

"There's nothing to discuss," Philippa said. "It was nothing."

"It felt like something to me." Tommy's voice was soft.

"*Philippa*," Mother shrilled. "Answer when you're spoken to!"

"I have to go," Philippa said, then called out, "Yes, Mother, I'm coming now."

She forced herself to hurry away from Tommy, to stride past Elizabeth and Marjorie, to accept the picnic basket from her mother and pretend her interruption hadn't been the absolute worst timing in the long and storied history of her mother's unwanted interruptions.

Was this how her friend Gracie felt when she sneaked off for stolen kisses with the rake of the week? Until Tommy, Philippa hadn't known she *could* feel this way.

She felt as though she'd been lied to her entire life. She'd missed out on so much. Philippa *liked* dancing with the right person, and kissing, and touching. She even liked banter and being giggly. It was fun and romantic.

The only way to make it through the rest of her life was to pretend this hadn't happened. That she was still emotionless Philippa with the cold dead heart.

She *hadn't* liked the rules she'd been born to follow, but she'd known how to navigate them. Mother had implied a nice library was the best a bluestocking could hope for.

Philippa's acceptance of her staid life was predicated on that assumption. That there *wasn't* something better, something different she could have. That "a nice library" was a fair trade for the autonomy of her body, a vessel for which she had little use anyway. Why not let some man climb atop her and then raise his children? It was how things were done. It was the way the world worked.

Except sometimes…it *didn't*. Sometimes things turned out differently than expected. Sometimes there was a twist in Act Two that you never saw coming.

It would perhaps have been better never to realize that she could feel passion than to know she must spend the rest of her life without moments like these. That first garden, where Tommy had almost kissed her. This garden, where it had finally happened.

Now that she'd experienced passion, she *wanted* it.

And the world wasn't built to let her have it.

She could not unlearn this new facet of herself, but she could refuse to indulge it. At least until she'd had time to give these new discoveries proper consideration. She could then decide what to do—or perhaps decide it was best not to change anything at all.

In the meantime, there was plenty else to keep her busy. The illuminated manuscripts, for example. Damaris needed her help. So did Agnes and Katherine. Philippa would concentrate on that.

"I have devised the perfect plan," Mother said when they were out of earshot.

Trepidation slithered in Philippa's stomach. "You did?"

"I did." Mother's eyes shone. "I've just the fish for you to catch. He's untitled at the moment, which means the others have overlooked him in their hunt to marry well. But *you*, my darling... *You* will strike before the iron is hot, and become a viscountess *after* the fact."

Philippa's flesh went cold and her palms clammy. "You cannot mean..."

"Of course I do." Mother beamed at her. "*You* will marry Captain Northrup."

20

Today would be different from the last five days. Today would be better.

Tommy hoped.

Five days ago, she had conquered her doubts and given in to her desires and kissed Philippa. And Philippa had kissed her back! Extensively. Exquisitely. They had been locked in each other's embrace for several long, perfect minutes.

And then Philippa's mother had limited the baron's interactions to once a week.

Part of Tommy couldn't bear to be without Philippa for a single day. The other part worried about reception when she appeared on Philippa's doorstep days early.

The reading circle felt different now. Before, when the bluestockings discussed topics Tommy didn't remotely understand, it didn't matter. No one expected Great-Aunt Wynchester to follow along. She'd devised this costume specifically to be allowed to attend without requiring contribution. Tommy enjoyed sitting back and watching Philippa be extraordinarily clever.

Now that she and Philippa were actively conversing—and kissing—Tommy wished she were just as clever. She didn't have esoteric knowledge to share, or a gift with ancient languages, or a collection of rare tomes. She was a costumed orphan who happened to be good at pretending to belong in places she did not.

A few months ago, the situation would have been easier. When Chloe still lived at home, she would have been happy to explain bookish things to Tommy over a plate of cakes and glasses of lemonade spiked with gin.

Those days were gone. Thursday afternoon reading circles were not only Tommy's chance to see Philippa, but also part of her newly finite time with her sister. Chloe and Faircliffe visited the Wynchester home for suppers, but moments like this—moments of just Tommy and Chloe—had become few and precious indeed.

The carriage pulled to a stop before the York residence.

Her sister alighted from the coach, wicker basket in hand. Tommy followed her up the manicured path to the York town house.

Mr. Underwood opened the front door. Before he could greet them, Mrs. York all but knocked him aside with her hip in order to peer at the new arrivals.

"The Duchess of Faircliffe," she squealed, with a glint in her eyes that did not match her obsequious tone. Tommy supposed Mrs. York never would forgive Chloe for "stealing" the Duke of Faircliffe from Philippa. "And you brought your great-aunt. Again."

But Mrs. York moved out of the way. As usual, Tommy was accepted . . . as long as she was someone else.

"Are we early to the ball?" she quavered as she hobbled past the threshold.

Chloe put a protective arm about Tommy's shoulders. "It's not a ball, Aunt. We're attending Miss York's Thursday afternoon reading circle, as we do every week."

"I don't feel like dancing." Tommy patted her white wig. "I think I'll just sit."

"A lovely idea, Aunt. There will be plenty of chairs at the reading circle."

They kept up this patter down the corridor and into the parlor, where Tommy and her sister took their usual seats between the door and the sideboard. Chloe placed her basket on the floor next to their chairs and wandered about, greeting the other ladies in the parlor.

Tommy sat because she was Great-Aunt Wynchester, and Great-Aunt Wynchester had bad knees. And also because the lower angle of a chair gave her a convenient vantage point from which to watch Philippa without being conspicuous herself.

In the five long days since the outing at Vauxhall, Philippa had grown even more beautiful. Her white-and-pink round dress of jaconet muslin was flounced with lace and flowers.

Just the sight of her made Tommy happy, and not solely for her beauty. Tommy adored watching Philippa light up when talking to her friends. It was no wonder at all that these ladies preferred spending their Thursday afternoons in a parlor with Philippa to promenading about Hyde Park with the crème de la crème of the beau monde.

The ladies of the reading circle *were* the best of the best. *These* were the people they most wished to converse with and to impress.

They certainly impressed Tommy. She had never seen so many intelligent and capable people all in one room. Chloe felt the same way, and she'd spent years spying on Parliament.

A familiar pair of calico ears poked out from beneath Philippa's skirts. Tiglet wiggled his whiskers and gave a plaintive miaow, as though miffed that the ladies appeared more interested in books than kittens.

Philippa bent over, scooped him up, and brought him to her bosom without interrupting the heated discussion she was having with Lady Eunice about archery and fletchers.

Tommy couldn't help but smile.

She needed a private conversation with Philippa. Great-Aunt Wynchester did not participate in literary arguments. Tommy's tendency at the reading circle was to stay close to the dessert tray and toss out the occasional inappropriate comment in her best irascible-old-lady voice.

Today, however, her only aim was to present the peace offering she'd brought for Philippa.

Lady Eunice glanced at the clock in one corner. "Where's Jessica?"

Florentia pursed her lips. "Running late like Gracie?"

This launched an immediate and lively debate between those who felt the reading circle's scheduled hour was sacrosanct, and those who believed "out late kissing a rake" was a perfectly acceptable excuse for tardiness.

It was Great-Aunt Wynchester's moment. The meeting hadn't started, Philippa's conversation with Lady Eunice was waning, and the others were distracted by the polemical Gracie discussion.

"Romantic gift, please." Tommy held out her palm toward Chloe.

Chloe handed her the wicker basket.

Tommy pushed to her feet and bent forward myopically as she peered about the room.

"Miss York," she quavered. "Might you show an old lady where to find the necessary?"

A brief frown lined Philippa's brow at being interrupted. Great-Aunt Wynchester knew good and well where to find the water closet, and in any case, Chloe always helped her aunt when she got muddled.

Chloe, however, was far too absorbed in inspecting her fingernails to notice Philippa staring at her pointedly.

"Of course." Philippa handed the kitten to one of her guests, likely for safekeeping. He couldn't resist an open window. "Follow me, please."

Rather than follow Philippa to the water closet, Tommy ducked into the empty dining room instead.

"Oh—not that way, Great-Aunt Wynchester." Philippa reversed course and hurried into the dining room after Tommy. "This is where we dine. The necessary is—"

Tommy shut the door. Philippa's mother was infamous for listening at the parlor keyhole when the reading circle was in session, but she had no reason to imagine the dining room occupied. Convincing the ladies to abandon their books was Mrs. York's lifelong struggle.

Nonetheless, Tommy motioned Philippa away from the door and around the table where they had sat next to each other for tea.

"Great-Aunt Wynchester, really." Philippa visibly tried for patience. "Surely you can see that this is a dining room, not a water closet. I know you're not as vacant as you pretend. Is this about Damaris's case?"

Philippa was simply too adorable. Tommy could barely look at her without remembering what it was like to kiss her, and battled the urge to grab her and kiss her all over again.

But definitely not as Great-Aunt Wynchester.

"It's me," Tommy said.

Her veins rushed with excitement at the prospect of welcoming Philippa into this jest, just like the baron identity. Having Philippa as a co-conspirator would make the farce even more fun. Tommy grinned at her in anticipation.

Philippa smiled gently. "I know you're you. And if you would follow me down the corridor—"

"No. I mean, it's *me*, Tommy."

"T-Tommy?" Philippa stammered in obvious confusion.

It was likely difficult to reconcile dashing Baron Vanderbean with the old lady standing before her. Even though Tommy had ceased hunching and had spoken in her regular voice, the wiry white hair and the deep wrinkles and the hands covered in liver spots all painted a convincing picture.

The cosmetics could not be removed without special oils. The extravagant wig was pinned so tight, a hurricane could not have budged it. Her only hope was to convince Philippa with words.

"It's me, Tommy," she repeated. "Baron Vanderbean, if you prefer. I have never experienced a superior stroll in a garden to the fine afternoon at Vauxhall in which you and I—"

"Tommy?" Philippa squeaked. "*Tommy?*"

She did not look like a mischievous, delighted co-conspirator.

She looked furious.

"I couldn't visit as Baron Vanderbean," Tommy said quickly. "Your mother limited his attentions to a maximum of once per week, remember? I plan to attend the Oglethorpe ball on Saturday, but I thought—"

"You've been Great-Aunt Wynchester this *entire time?*" Philippa backed away, her movements jerky. "You've been Great-Aunt Wynchester for *months?*"

This was not at all going the way Tommy had expected it to.

"When I told you I wasn't really Baron Vanderbean," she said carefully, "you were delighted by the jest."

"I was *in* on the jest," Philippa burst out. "I had just 'met' the man, and he was instantly vulnerable and honest with me. It was both charming and disarming. *This*, on the other hand…" She waved a hand toward Tommy's disguise. "This!"

Tommy set Chloe's basket on the dining table. It clearly was not an opportune moment for romantic gestures.

"I didn't mean to deceive you," Tommy began.

"You didn't mean to," Philippa repeated. "You put on wrinkles and wigs and made a weekly appearance in my parlor every Thursday afternoon...by accident?"

"That was on purpose," Tommy admitted. "What I mean was, when I started, I didn't plan on ever telling you the truth, so there was little chance of you being cross with me for it."

"Cross," Philippa said. "Oh, I'm cross, all right. I'm tempted to toss you right out of this window and throw your little basket at your head. I cannot believe that...*you* of all people..."

To Tommy's horror, Philippa's eyes were glassy with tears.

"Don't cry." Appalled, Tommy felt a strange pricking in her own throat. "Baron Vanderbean trusted you because he *knew* you. When Great-Aunt Wynchester met you, it was for the first time. *Now* I know you can be trusted with a secret. Until the Duke of Faircliffe, my siblings and I had never let an outsider in."

"I'll cry if I want to," Philippa snapped. "These are tears of rage, which I am perfectly entitled to, thank you very much. Everyone always tries to direct my life for me, and frankly I am sick of it."

"We didn't know each other then," Tommy tried again. "You know me now—"

"*Do* I?" Philippa said with obvious skepticism. "If Baron Vanderbean trusted me enough to tell me the truth, why didn't Tommy Wynchester do the same? It would have been a perfect moment to mention we'd already met, and how."

"I see that now," Tommy muttered. "It didn't seem relevant at the time. We were talking about your parents' desire to marry you off, and it wasn't as though Great-Aunt Wynchester figured into those plans—"

"No," Philippa agreed, crossing her arms over her bosom. "She certainly does not."

Sometimes Tommy was so used to playing a part that she forgot the fiction was real to others. Her roles might be temporary, but her actions could leave a lasting impact.

"I'm telling you now," she said frantically. "No matter how much I might wish I had, I cannot confess any sooner than this moment. I was Baron Vanderbean, and I was Great-Aunt Wynchester, but I was always Tommy, who admires you more than everyone else combined."

Philippa swiped at her eyes, which had lost some of their glossiness.

Tommy stepped forward.

"Don't touch me," Philippa warned.

"I wasn't going to kiss you as Great-Aunt Wynchester," Tommy said.

"I don't want you to kiss me as anyone," Philippa said. "It was an experiment that has now concluded. There is no need for further discussion. *I* certainly won't be dwelling upon the experience."

Oh. Tommy stared at her. *Oh.*

The single most shining moment in Tommy's entire adult life meant nothing at all to Philippa. She had tried it. She didn't like it.

"I'm sorry," Tommy said. "I didn't mean to press unwanted advances upon you."

Philippa's lips tightened. "They weren't 'unwanted' in...a *wanting* sense. You...My feelings were unwanted in the sense that I don't want things I shouldn't want." She shook her head. "I cannot disappoint my parents. Not like this."

That was the least eloquent thing Tommy had ever heard

Philippa say, and yet she understood perfectly. Philippa saw what they could have together and preferred not to have it.

"You intend to marry a man, then?"

Philippa sighed. "Every young lady intends to."

"I never did."

"You're not a young lady. You're an old lady and a dapper gentleman and probably also a country milkmaid and the King of Prussia, for all I know. You don't live like other people, Tommy. *I* do. I'm Philippa, no matter what. I cannot hide."

Of course the daughter of a wealthy MP would expect to show her face in all the fashionable places she pleased without being gossiped about, or tossed out, or shunned forever.

What could Tommy possibly offer worth giving up all of that?

Nothing. There was nothing in the world that could make up for the fact that two women were simply not allowed to live and love together. Even if Philippa were willing to try, she'd lose everything she held dear. Her parents' approval, her standing in society, perhaps her friends.

Tommy could love her a thousand times over, and it still wouldn't be enough.

"Besides," Philippa said. "My parents have selected a suitor already."

Tommy's stomach bottomed out. Her chest tightened painfully. They'd been enjoying a fake courtship they'd planned to last the entire season. But then she and Philippa had shared their first kiss, and suddenly Philippa was ready to accept the very next man her mother put in front of her, sooner rather than later. Tommy had tried, and the answer was no.

Philippa had never truly been hers, and never would be.

"Who is he?" Tommy asked, her voice dull and her limbs heavy.

Philippa's mouth twisted. "Captain Northrup."

"*What?*" Tommy burst out. "You cannot possibly—"

"Of course I cannot possibly," Philippa interrupted, her blue eyes flashing. "But until we have the proof to disgrace him or force him to confess, my mother has determined he is the one. Fortunately, I don't expect him to agree. Once he has his coronet and any corresponding annuity and land, he will have plenty of options. Mayhap he'll prefer a higher-born bride."

"And then what?" Tommy said. "You'll find some other man and marry him?"

Philippa's eyes slid away. "Yes."

One word. One syllable. What else was there to say? Finding a suitor for Philippa had always been the plan.

Tommy forced her throat to swallow, and she gave a short nod. If Philippa was set on marrying a man, that was her choice. All Tommy could do was keep her heart and her emotions locked up tight. Behind a wall of stone, so she could not be hurt.

She supposed it was ironic that someone who constantly played roles should hate change. But whenever Tommy removed her wig and cosmetics, things returned to how they were before. She didn't mind temporary changes. It was the permanent ones that caused problems.

"I'll be at the Oglethorpe ball on Saturday," said Philippa. "Northrup has let it be known that he'll be in attendance, and Mother thinks it the perfect opportunity for me to claim him."

"Well," Tommy said. "That sounds horrid."

Philippa nodded. "It will be."

"I have something that will cheer you up." Tommy opened

the lid of the wicker basket. Her big, romantic gesture would no longer lead to romance, but at least *this* would be a welcome surprise. She lifted out the book and handed it to Philippa.

Philippa looked at it blankly. "What is this?"

"Er," said Tommy. "Hopefully one of the Northrup manuscripts."

"I see that," Philippa said. "That's exactly what it is."

Tommy nodded warily. She had expected more in the way of squeals of joy and perhaps a bit of bouncing up and down. Philippa had *just said* what she most wanted was proof to use against Northrup. Tommy had just handed some to her. It was right there. In her hands.

Philippa stared at it. "Where did this come from?"

"Er," said Tommy. "I started with the easiest place on your list."

Philippa looked up. "Which of the forbidden, fortified, or heavily guarded places was the easiest?"

"Cambridge?" Tommy said.

"You removed a protected illuminated manuscript," Philippa said slowly, "from the Cambridge University Royal Library."

Tommy nodded carefully.

"You robbed the Royal Library," Philippa repeated. "*Without* me."

"Er," Tommy said again.

Philippa dropped the valuable and extremely stolen illuminated manuscript onto the dining table with a thud.

"You're not pleased," Tommy ventured.

"I'm not pleased," Philippa agreed.

Tommy's chest hurt. "I'm trying. I would give you what you want if you would just tell me what it is."

"I don't want to be the passive recipient of someone else's

decisions," Philippa said. "I don't want you to bring me flowers. I want to help pick them. I want to hold the shears from time to time."

"To be fair," Tommy mumbled. "It's not flowers."

Philippa's eyes sparked. "You want me to believe I am the person you most admire? It didn't occur to you to stop lying to me about Great-Aunt Wynchester. It didn't occur to you I might want to be consulted on the plans I helped you to create, despite the fact that I *begged* you to let me be a part of the adventure." Her voice shook. "I didn't occur to you at all."

"That's not true," Tommy said. "You're the only thing that does occur to me. You're the reason I did it."

"No," Philippa corrected. "You stole it because that's what Wynchesters *do*. You solve problems and save the day. You're always the heroes. Well, I don't want to hear about your daring deeds secondhand. This is *my* case, too. I brought it to you. Damaris is *my* friend. *I* found the hidden letter. *I'm* the one expected to smile and simper at Northrup's smug, duplicitous face. But you don't see me as a resource. Not even to talk it over."

"I..." said Tommy.

That was as much of an argument as she had.

Philippa was right. Including her in the operation *hadn't* occurred to Tommy or her siblings. They'd always done everything on their own. They each had their particular expertise, and they worked seamlessly together. Tommy certainly wouldn't have tried to insert her into a *robbery*.

"It's not just you. I'm tired of everyone making decisions for me. I've had a lifetime of it." Philippa's shoulders deflated. "I suppose you expect me to sit around quietly whilst you gad about stealing more manuscripts."

"Er," said Tommy. That was exactly the plan. Or had been.

"I'm grateful," Philippa said. "Even if I'm disappointed. I

might've thought if the wild Wynchesters can do impossible things, surely you could have devised a method to *communicate* with me. A reverse homing kitten. A messenger falcon."

"There might be a messenger falcon," Tommy mumbled. "I didn't think—"

Philippa's eyes were glassy. "I don't want to be the fair maiden to your knight. If you can be your own heroine, why shouldn't I want it, too? I thought you of all people would understand."

The dining room door swung open and Mrs. York burst inside.

"What is the meaning of this impudence?" she demanded. "I will inform you when I am ready to preside over formal tea."

"No tea necessary, Mother," Philippa said. "Perhaps you can show Great-Aunt Wynchester to the door. She was just leaving. And I must return to my friends."

21

⚜

$\mathcal{F}$rom the moment Philippa was announced at the Ogle-thorpe ball, her senses were alert for any sign of Tommy. Would she come? Or would she stay away because of their row? Once Philippa had calmed, she regretted sending Tommy off like that, and had wished she could call her back.Tonight would be their first chance to make up. Presuming Tommy wanted to do so.

Philippa lifted herself onto her toes, then returned to her heels before her mother caught her behaving inappropriately. The entire reason she had accepted her mother's tall stack of invitations was out of hope Tommy would be at the same events. And now...

Philippa was supposed to be hunting Captain Northrup.

He was laughably simple to locate, holding court with a bevy of sycophants eager to claim they had long been particular friends of the new viscount, even before he was awarded his title.

Baron Vanderbean should have been just as easy to spot, if for different reasons. Rather than positioning herself in the center of an adoring crowd, Tommy tended to swagger right past them with little more than a word and wink, because her eyes were only for Philippa.

At least, they *had* been.

"I hope you're not looking for that upstart Vanderbean," said Mother. "You're not to dance with anyone until after you've had your set with Captain Northrup."

"Technically," said Philippa, "Northrup is the upstart. Baron Vanderbean was always his father's heir. *Northrup* is the newcomer to rank and consequence. Or will be. He doesn't yet have his title. I suppose that makes him a not-even-started."

"Technically," said her mother, "I don't give a jot what your dictionaries say. *I* say you're to dance with Northrup before you even look at Vanderbean."

"The baron isn't here," said Philippa. "It appears you'll get your wish."

But she couldn't stop looking for Tommy.

Philippa lowered her heels. What was wrong with her? She was angry with Tommy and at the same time desperate to see her again. Going days without a sign was torment. What was Tommy doing? Glooming out of her rain-spattered window like Philippa? Or off scaling battlements and stealing illuminated manuscripts?

The worst part was, after several hours of throwing herself into charity work to numb her hurt at not figuring in Tommy's plans, Philippa was forced to admit that she was an illogical choice for a partner in daring escapades. She *wasn't* a Wynchester. She *didn't* have practical experience, or any sort of special skills to aid and abet a burglary in progress. She would be an anchor, not an asset, weighing down the team when they most needed to be agile.

Inviting Philippa along on a caper would have been the least practical, most inefficient decision Tommy could have possibly made.

And yet Philippa wished she'd made it anyway.

She sent her anxious gaze about the ballroom for the

hundredth time. What if Tommy was here tonight as a great-aunt rather than a gentleman? Might Philippa have missed her? Or what if she'd come not as belligerent, colorful Great-Aunt Wynchester, but as . . . Miss Thomasina? What might that look like? Would Philippa even recognize her?

Her eyes scanned and discarded each person in turn. Young, old, male, female, fat, thin—

The voice of the Oglethorpes' butler rang out. "Baron Vanderbean."

Philippa's head jerked toward the entrance on the opposite side of the ballroom.

"Humph," said her mother. "The evening only wanted this."

Philippa certainly had wanted it.

Her heart galloped furiously. Tommy had come, and she looked magnificent.

Black breeches clung to tightly muscled thighs that moved with confidence. An emerald green waistcoat disguised the chest that had brushed tantalizingly close to hers. The black superfine of Tommy's tailcoat hid the arms that had once wrapped tightly about Philippa. The dazzlingly white cravat drew the eye up to Tommy's supple mouth, and to the baron's usual expression of impishness and amusement. Either her argument with Philippa hadn't bothered her, or the coy looks Tommy gave others had always been an act. Perhaps Outrageous Flirt was just as much a mask as Great-Aunt Wynchester.

Philippa could no longer claim to be passionless. She had spent years trying to solve the wrong puzzle. It wasn't a matter of "finding the right man" after all.

Was that why she had surrounded herself with other ladies all her life? But she hadn't been romantically attracted to any of her friends. And Tommy wasn't a lady. At first, it had been hard to understand how Tommy could feel like a man *and* a woman. "Both and neither," she'd said. Philippa admired and desired Tommy exactly as she was. Perhaps Tommy was what Philippa had been looking for all along.

Her entire body was pitter-pattering from the inside out. Philippa's veins thrummed with one rhythm, her breath hitched with another. Her palms were clammy, her cheeks flushed. Her legs pressed together.

Baron Vanderbean made his leisurely rounds. Every woman he passed earned a smile and a murmur, and probably one of those ridiculously charming eyebrow winks that made a woman feel so giddy on the inside.

Would Philippa be the last person Baron Vanderbean bowed to? Or would Tommy not greet her at all, after Philippa had all but run off after their kiss at Vauxhall, then forced Tommy out of her house?

Philippa twisted a drooping curl about her finger just in case, and borrowed her mother's ivory fan so no one would glimpse her pinching her cheeks for color. She handed the fan back to her mother just in time.

"Mrs. York, Miss York." Tommy made a handsome leg. "I believe a new set is just beginning. If you're not promised elsewhere, might I have this dance?"

"Actually," said Mother. "Philippa—"

"—would be honored," Philippa said in a rush.

The flash of ire in Mother's face indicated this disobedience would not go unpunished.

Philippa would worry about that later. At the moment, she had an opportunity to be back in Tommy's arms.

The moment they were in the relative seclusion of a crowded dance floor, Tommy lifted Philippa's hand and placed her own against Philippa's side.

"Do you forgive me?" Tommy asked.

"No," Philippa said. "Do you forgive me?"

"There's nothing to forgive," Tommy answered.

"Of course there is," Philippa said. "You shouldn't forgive me until I've apologized properly for my role in our row the other day. I should not have spoken to you so harshly and sent you away without giving you the chance to respond. I let emotion cloud my logic."

Tommy's dark gaze held hers. "And I apologize for not including you in a crime that could have sent you to the gallows if you were caught."

"That's a dreadful apology," said Philippa. "I was disappointed to be left behind, but I was hurt not to be consulted, at least."

"'Tis better to be discarded after careful consideration than dismissed summarily?"

"Something like that."

"You have never been out of my thoughts from the moment I first met you."

Philippa's heart fluttered. Would she ever grow used to such romantic words? "I accept your apology. You were only trying to help. I am sorry I reacted to the situation as poorly as I did."

"I would have been devastated if my siblings pulled off a caper without including me. It should have occurred to me you might feel the same way. I accept your apology."

"Good. Thank you."

"May I kiss you now?"

Philippa stumbled. "We're in the middle of a ballroom!"

"What if we weren't?" asked Tommy. "Could I kiss you then?"

"No," Philippa forced herself to answer. "That part stays the same."

Tommy gave a crooked smile. "I was foolish to hope your feelings had changed."

They hadn't changed at all, which was a large part of Philippa's problem. Even if she and Tommy never saw each other again after the season was through, there would always be a hollow place in Philippa's chest where Tommy had once been.

She doubted she would ever fully recover from this tendre.

"Ah, well." Tommy waggled her eyebrows. "I hope you don't expect Baron Vanderbean to stop flirting with you."

"He can do so," Philippa said. "Just to keep up appearances."

The way things were was the way they had to be. There was too much at stake to allow something as foolish as a heart to make decisions. The life she lived. Her parents' love. She could not bear to lose her family.

"How about you?" Tommy asked. "Have I crossed your mind these past few days?"

Only every single second.

"Baron Vanderbean is the flirt," Philippa replied. "Not Miss Philippa York."

"I thought you might write," said Tommy. "Perhaps with news about the manuscript."

"My mother reads my correspondence."

"You could have sent Tiglet," Tommy pointed out. "He's trained to return home."

"I noticed," Philippa said wryly. "If that kitten so much as senses an open window, he's off like a shot. Underwood must oil the hinges of the door twice a day so that Tiglet doesn't hear it opening. I'll lose three stone if I keep chasing after him like this."

"Then give him back," said Tommy. "I don't want you to lose a single curve. You're perfect as you are."

"No reneging," Philippa said. "Tiglet is mine until we secure justice for Damaris."

In fact, she had spent several lonely nights trying to counter-train Tiglet into recognizing Philippa's chambers as his new home. It was not working.

"I have news," she said. "About the manuscript."

Tommy's eyes were cautious. "Tell me."

"The decorations on the edges are *different*."

"Um." Tommy's forehead wrinkled. "Why wouldn't they be? You did study it close enough to realize it's a different volume in the set of four?"

"Not the chivalric tales inside," Philippa explained. "When the book is closed, an illustration appears on the edges of the pages. It's hidden from sight whilst the book is nestled in a shelf, and obscured when opened to read. Mixed in with the violets and pomegranates are strange markings I wondered could be symbols."

"Are they?"

"Yes," Philippa said with satisfaction.

"How?"

"Katherine and Agnes were devious enough to leave a secret message in plain sight. Well, not quite plain sight," Philippa amended. "The page edges are the part of a book looked at the least. First would be the spine, facing out from the shelf, and then the pages themselves, with their tales of chivalry."

Tommy nodded her understanding. "To most, illustrated edges are just a whimsical touch. Pretty enough, but easily forgotten."

"Just so. These are arranged at exactly the same intervals. Flourishes obfuscate the important markings, but parts of the symbols repeat. It's like a cipher."

"What does it say?"

"I haven't a clue," Philippa admitted. "Even Damaris couldn't decipher it. We'd need all four volumes to have the entire message. At the moment, we possess book two and book four, which means what we have doesn't even go in order."

"Then we steal the entire set," Tommy said.

Philippa pressed her lips together. This "we" was probably the "we" of the Wynchesters. Philippa despaired at being excluded, though she understood why. Her involvement was a terrible idea.

And she would have said yes in a heartbeat.

"I have news as well," Tommy said. "Graham was able to trace Northrup's family history through parish registers."

"Were Agnes and Katherine Sir Reginald's daughters?"

"It doesn't look like it," Tommy answered. "He only had sons."

Philippa frowned. "Are they relatives?"

"Maybe. I don't know. Graham is working on it. According to servant gossip, Captain Northrup's family Bible was destroyed in an unfortunate 'accident' having to do with placing it in the fireplace and pouring whiskey on top."

"He destroyed a Bible? There must have been something in it he didn't want anyone to find."

Such as proof of Agnes and Katherine's existence. And perhaps more.

"That will just make Graham try harder," Tommy said. "He'll hunt for baptism, marriage, and death records in the places where Sir Reginald lived. If there's anything there, my brother will find it."

"There's something to find," Philippa said firmly. Was that true? Or did she so long for adventure that she was seeing symbols and conspiracy where there was nothing?

The dance drew to a close, and a reel began.

"Shall we find partners or shall we take a turn in the garden?" Tommy asked.

Garden. Without a doubt.

"Neither," Philippa said glumly. "You should return me to my mother. I am forbidden from dancing with you until I've stood up with Northrup. Perhaps she'll forgive me if I only disobey for half a set."

"Shall I find you after you dance with him?"

"*Please*," Philippa said. After suffering through Northrup's touch, she would need the comforting feel of Tommy's arms about her.

Philippa was beginning to suspect she would always long for Tommy's embrace.

Tommy had barely brought her back into her mother's orbit when Mother snatched Philippa to her side with far more force than was seemly.

"That will do," she seethed at Tommy. "No more sets with Philippa this evening."

Tommy inclined her head. "As you wish, madam."

"Humph." Mother barely waited for Tommy to walk away before berating Philippa beneath her breath. "What were you thinking? I told you to use him as a stepping-stone, not cling to him like lichen. You'll never attract Captain Northrup if you don't put yourself in his line of sight."

Yes. That sounded like a lovely plan.

Stay out of Northrup's sight.

"Dancing makes me very visible," Philippa murmured. "Everyone was watching. And I didn't wish to be rude to the baron."

"It is rude to disobey one's parents," her mother snapped. "For *that* insubordination, our parlor is hereby forbidden to the members of your little reading circle. There's a bigger fish than Baron Vanderbean on the line."

Philippa's muscles twitched with panic. "But—"

"The entire house, daughter. No one but gentlemen callers shall cross our threshold until you are betrothed. And don't think for a second that I mean Baron Vanderbean. He is limited to once per month, which means I expect four weeks of bliss before that foreigner darkens our door again."

Philippa sucked in a breath. "But—"

"I am doing this for *you*," her mother said. "You are clearly incapable of making a suitable match on your own. Three and twenty, Philippa. On the shelf, long in the tooth, ape leader. Do you think I want these things said about my child? Viscountess has a much nicer ring to it. No one will dare mistreat my daughter then."

Philippa blinked. "People are calling me 'ape leader'?"

"Why do you think your father and I have rejected all the proposals from common fortune hunters?"

"Because they're... common fortune hunters?"

"Because they weren't right for *you*. A wallflower as shy and awkward as you are needs a title as a shield. You won't always have me to protect you. Your name has to be protection itself."

"But Captain Northrup—"

"—is the first man that actually suits you," Mother finished. "He's new to the title, which means he's not been drilled with a lifetime of expectations of what his future viscountess must be like. He'll be honored by the Prince Regent himself, which makes Northrup's reputation the opposite of those disreputable Wynchesters. Of equal import, Captain Northrup enjoys puzzles and books and illuminated manuscripts. Just like *you*, darling. It's a perfect match!"

Of equal import.

Mother considered Philippa's future husband's opinions about books and puzzles to be of equal importance to his reputation and title.

Philippa's stomach twisted with guilt. Her parents weren't punishing her. All ton mothers wanted a titled suitor for their daughters. Philippa's parents believed they were doing her a favor. In their way, they were trying to ensure their daughter had not just a title, but a happy life.

"I will make the best match that I can," she promised

her mother. It wouldn't be Northrup, but if her parents could compromise in order to make Philippa happy, she could do no less for them. Perhaps she could find a gentleman who shared Tommy's qualities. And if not...

Betrothed, Philippa could see her reading circle again. Her throat grew thick. Although not all were "shy and awkward" like she was, her friends counted on those cherished hours together as much as she did.

There was Lady Eunice, whose titled parents pinned even more hopes on their spinster daughter than Philippa's did on hers. At home, Florentia was considered the unmarriageable sister and advised never to call attention to herself. She flourished in the reading circle with her fellow bluestockings. Jessica had been dragged along by Gracie, only to discover wine and books and debate and charity work the highlight of her week. Sybil, whose home was unpredictable, clung to charts and schedules, doing her best to ensure this group of friends was the most stable thing in her life.

"Straighten your shoulders," Mother hissed. "Captain Northrup is walking in our direction."

Philippa straightened obediently. "Captain Northrup hasn't spoken to me since my come-out. He won't start now."

That was the one silver lining. Northrup was as disinterested in Philippa as she was in him.

"Pinch your cheeks," Mother whispered.

Philippa did not pinch her cheeks. Northrup was going to walk right past them to the card room and—

"Mrs. York, Miss York." Northrup made a bow, then held out his hand to Philippa. "Might you honor me with the next waltz?"

Bloody hell.

Northrup *was* interested. And she was forbidden from seeing Tommy for an entire month.

22

*P*hilippa poured a dram of milk into a bowl for Tiglet before the maid removed the breakfast tray. Although he was hiding under a piece of furniture, she was comforted knowing he was somewhere in the room.

Breakfast in bed was supposed to make one feel cosseted, but for Philippa it had always been...lonely.

For the past fortnight, her habit of rising early and alone had improved immeasurably with the company of a naughty kitten. Tiglet enjoyed waking her up by pawing at her hair or settling on the adjacent pillow to stare at her, so that the first sight when she awoke was the kitten's enormous eyes, inches from her own.

Other mornings, like this one, Tiglet slept late, often tucked out of sight beneath Philippa's dressing table or her bed or the wardrobe.

Philippa could not sleep. When she did, she dreamed of Tommy. She ought to have been dreaming of how to decipher the markings on the edges of the manuscripts. But they only reminded her of how isolated she was from Tommy. Even if Philippa could concentrate long enough to discover something, she had no way to send word. Mother had halted outgoing correspondence until Philippa was properly betrothed.

She wasn't just prohibited from hosting her Thursday afternoon reading circle. She was cut off from her friends altogether. Even Great-Aunt Wynchester.

Philippa moved her stool a little closer to her dressing table and looked at the illuminated manuscript before her. It was in splendid condition. So splendid, she was hesitant to poke at the sturdy binding even with a gloved finger. There was no way to tell by touch whether it contained reused scraps or another hidden letter.

Nor could she destroy such a perfect specimen to satisfy her curiosity. Especially when said specimen had been stolen from the Cambridge University Royal Library.

The Wynchesters intended to return this illuminated manuscript in the same pristine condition in which it had been found... didn't they?

There. That was a professional, not-remotely-related-to-kissing reason to contact Tommy Wynchester. The public might take interest in the chivalric tales involved in the famous cipher, which would increase the value of the set. The theft had not yet been discovered, but it could only be a matter of time.

And then what? Philippa was the one in possession of stolen goods, not that anyone would think her capable of sneaking into Cambridge for a spot of burglary. Wallflowers were rarely suspected of conspiring with criminal masterminds.

Or kissing them, which she was definitely not thinking about.

Having a tendre was torture.

It was nine thirty, and all she'd done this Sunday morning was watch the clock and think of Tommy.

She wished she could write to her. Better yet, Philippa wished Tommy would write to *her*. She wished Tommy would appear on the doorstep as... well, anyone. The disguise didn't matter. Philippa missed *Tommy*.

Perhaps Philippa should release Tiglet.

Should she? The kitten was asleep somewhere. Surely it was rude to awaken a sleeping kitten. But Tiglet was a *trained* cat. A professional homing kitten, specifically placed in Philippa's possession in the event she wished to summon Tommy.

Philippa quickly wrapped the precious illuminated manuscript for safekeeping and tucked it back into its hiding spot at the back of her wardrobe. She checked for Tiglet behind each stack of neatly folded clothes, then shut the wardrobe.

"Tiglet," she called. "Come and drink your milk before your long journey."

Tiglet did not come. The milk beside her dressing table remained untouched.

Philippa lifted her skirts and sank to her knees in order to peer beneath her four-poster bed. Nothing, except a few tufts of fur.

She lifted her head and looked over the mattress at her bedchamber door. It was closed. Tiglet had to be in here somewhere...Didn't he? Nervousness fluttered in Philippa's stomach as she lifted pillows and moved curtains aside as she searched.

Wherever Tiglet was, he wasn't here in her bedroom. Despite leaving her windows closed and her door shut, she had lost her only companion. Perhaps when the maid had brought the breakfast tray.

Philippa ran out into the corridor and looked both ways. All the doors were closed. She shut hers and then hurried downstairs. Because it was late October, most of the windows should be closed, too.

Underwood stopped her as she dashed from room to room. "There you are, Miss York. A letter has just arrived for you."

Philippa hurried to the silver tray before her mother intercepted incoming correspondence as well. "Have you seen Tiglet?"

"I have not," Underwood replied. He glanced over Philippa's shoulder at a passing maid. "Have you seen the kitten, Fidelia?"

"I found fur in the bluestocking parlor," Fidelia replied. "We were airing it out since it hasn't been used in a while."

Because there was no reading circle anymore.

And now, no Tiglet.

Perhaps the letter was from Tommy! Philippa took it from the tray. The letter was franked by the Duke of Faircliffe. Since recipients paid postage and many of the Wynchesters' clients were poor, Faircliffe might be providing franked covers. It would be wonderful irony for Philippa's prior suitor to pay for what she desperately hoped was a love letter from someone else.

> *My dearest Philippa,*
>
> *Pardon the short notice, but the most wonderful opportunity has emerged. You must come to a ladies' breakfast at my residence at once, after which we will depart for a lovely afternoon of volunteering at orphanages for charity.*
>
> *Do say you'll come, dear. Don't keep good works waiting.*
>
> *Ever yours,*
>
> *Chloe Faircliffe*

Not Tommy, then. Philippa's shoulders sagged, but only briefly. She liked Chloe, and she was passionate about charity work...*if* that was really the plan. Even if it was, spending the day with children would be a far more appealing prospect than returning to the makeshift desk in her empty dressing room.

"May I send the footman back with your response?" Underwood inquired.

Philippa's head jerked up. *Just* arrived, he had said. Perhaps this wasn't a proper invitation at all, but rather a ruse. Heart pounding, she dashed past Underwood and flung open the door.

"Tommy?" she said breathlessly.

A very startled, very-not-Tommy footman dressed in Faircliffe livery blinked back at her in confusion. "Jackson, I'm afraid. Sent by Her Grace."

"Oh." Philippa's face flamed with heat. "Please tell Her Grace that I would be honored—"

"What is the meaning of this?" scratched Mother's voice from the hall behind her. "Who are you speaking to at this ungodly hour?"

"Their Graces' footman, Mother." Philippa stepped away from the door so that Jackson and his ducal livery were visible. "Chloe has just invited me to a ladies' breakfast and charity outing."

Now that she said the words aloud, she realized just how much she needed this opportunity to escape her ordinary life, if only for a few hours. One more day locked in her bedchamber to avoid hearing Mother's endless stratagems on how to best capture Captain Northrup, and Philippa would go out the window just like Tiglet.

"A breakfast?" Mother said dubiously. "At this hour?"

"Is nine o'clock too early or too late for breakfast?"

"It's appalling," Mother answered. "Proper morning calls shouldn't begin until at least one o'clock in the afternoon."

Philippa refrained from pointing out that the ton's afternoon morning calls were a contradiction in terms. Her mother might be silly, but she wasn't alone. Philippa was the odd one who wanted the world to make sense.

She handed her mother the invitation. "You said never to insult anyone with a title. Won't a duchess's sponsorship reflect well on our family?"

"Very well," said Mother after she'd finished reading the letter. "Summon the carriage. I won't have you arriving on foot like a pauper."

"Their town house is across the square from ours." Philippa pointed through the open door. "Look. You can see it from here. Surely I can walk two hundred yards without anyone thinking we've lost our fortune."

"The *orphanage* is not inside their town house," Mother said triumphantly. "If you walk, you must walk right back here after the breakfast."

"You want me to tell a duchess in front of all of her guests that my mother gave me permission to eat her food but forbade me from acts of charity to others?"

"Augh!" Mother tossed the letter back toward Philippa. "You bluestockings always have an answer for everything."

"Oh, leave her be," came Father's voice from the stairs. Only his slippers were visible. "This will prove there's no bad blood between their family and ours. Philippa has always done as expected, even when she'd rather not. She's a good daughter and will not embarrass us."

Philippa sagged with relief.

"She didn't land the duke," Mother said petulantly.

"She'll make up for that with Captain Northrup," Father responded. "Go with the footman, Philippa. He'll see that you arrive safely. The duchess can deliver you to the front door after your charity outing."

"Yes, Father." She accepted a pelisse and bonnet from Underwood and hastened from the house before her parents could change their minds.

Jackson escorted her across Grosvenor Square, into the Faircliffe town house, and out through a rear door, where an unmarked carriage was waiting.

"W-what?" Philippa said.

The carriage door opened and Chloe's head poked out. "Oh, thank God, I thought Jackson had got lost crossing the square. Climb in!"

"Er," said Philippa. "Is there no breakfast?"

"There's breakfast," said a low, familiar voice that sent pleasurable shivers of anticipation along her skin.

Jackson helped her into the coach. Tommy was inside, dressed as Baron Vanderbean.

Philippa tried to smooth the wrinkles from her skirt, caused by her ill-fated attempt to search under her bed for Tiglet...who was licking his paws on the seat next to Chloe. It would be churlish to move him.

There was nowhere to sit but next to Tommy, who immediately tilted a basket full of small packets in Philippa's direction. "Care for a meat pie?"

She wasn't certain *what* she wanted, other than to be with Tommy. Happiness suffused her as the carriage pulled away.

"Ladies' breakfast," Chloe said between bites. "And now we're off to volunteer for our latest charity, Justice for Damaris. I hope you don't mind. It was Tommy's idea."

"And if you do mind," Tommy said tentatively, "then it was Tiglet's idea."

Philippa stilled. Tommy was saving her yet again, but this time, the rescue was a marvelous surprise. She'd *wanted* to be saved. Philippa realized this made her both hypocritical and confusing. How was Tommy to know when her Tommy-ness would or would not be welcome? It was Philippa who had not been fair.

She accepted a pie. "Tiglet is a scamp. Thank you for rescuing me from my lonesome tower, fair knight."

Tommy's muscles relaxed visibly.

"Splendid," said Chloe. "For we're on our way to Islington."

Philippa's breath caught and her pulse skipped faster.

Tommy grinned. "I'm taking you home."

Philippa's cheeks flushed. She tried not to gaze too adoringly at Tommy. "Are these meat pies like the ones you used to steal?"

"We didn't steal the pies," Tommy said. "We stole the penny we paid for them with."

Chloe looked at Tommy in surprise. "You told her?"

Tommy lifted her brows. "Does Faircliffe know?"

"Touché," Chloe murmured. "Of course you should share whatever you like."

Tommy's gaze cut to Philippa's. Tommy's eyes were full of heat, as if what she was thinking of sharing were not meat pies, but scorching kisses.

Philippa tried her best not to notice, but it was impossible. All she could think about was how close they were. She could lay her head on Tommy's shoulders or tumble right into Tommy's lap. Their bodies within touching distance, their lips within *kissing* distance. She could smell the bergamot and clove of the pomade in Tommy's hair.

"The pies are delicious," Philippa blurted out. There. That didn't sound self-conscious at all.

She needed something that was actually distracting. She needed Tiglet. He was twisting side to side on his back. She finished her pie and scooped the kitten onto her lap. He purred when she rubbed behind his ears. There. Now she had something to think about besides Tommy.

"I intended to wait until we had news," Tommy said. "But when I received your message, I moved our plans to today."

Philippa's message. Ha. She narrowed her eyes at the purring kitten. Even Tiglet ran off and made important decisions without consulting her.

"It's a good thing you didn't wait. I don't know when we'd be able to meet privately. There are to be no more reading circles until I'm betrothed."

Tommy's face jerked over toward Chloe.

Chloe gave a subtle nod. "Done."

Philippa dug her fingernails into her palms. Why was it so impossible to be included, even now? "Could you please decide *with* me instead of *for* me?"

"I'm sorry." Tommy looked stricken. "I thought you would like the reading circle to stay together."

"I would like that," Philippa said. "I'm the hostess and the leader, and yet whatever you two have just decided makes me not part of the circle at all."

"You can still be both," Chloe said quickly. "As long as you don't mind doing so from my home instead of yours. We can tell your mother it's *my* gathering, so she doesn't stop you from attending but your friends will know the truth."

Philippa stroked Tiglet's soft fur, his purr rumbling into her fingertips. She probably sounded ridiculous to the Wynchesters. They were so used to being captains of their own ships. To *having* their own ships and somewhere to sail them. Philippa appreciated being taken along, but she wanted to be a fellow sailor.

"We don't mean to take charge," Tommy said. "Or rather, we've *had* to take charge of ourselves and each other from such a very young age, we don't know any other way."

Philippa glanced at the basket. Meat pies.

Chloe and Tommy hadn't lived her charmed life. The

adults who were supposed to be taking care of them hadn't even been feeding them properly. Philippa might be stifled by her parents and their ambition, but at least she *had* parents. She hadn't been faced with the choice to steal or starve, as Chloe and Tommy had.

She lifted her gaze. Her community project was no longer for lonely girls like she herself had once been. It was for the Chloes and Tommys who had no one to rely on but each other... and for the children who had no one at all. Philippa could not provide each child with a Baron Vanderbean, but she could give them a small escape, and knowledge, and hope.

Chloe's expression was full of love. "There was no one else I'd rather eat a meat pie with."

Tommy grinned. "Now we have an entire family of rapacious rogues and miscreants. And at least two dozen equally roguish beasts being trained out in Jacob's barn."

"Rogues like Tiglet," Chloe cooed and patted her legs.

The kitten leapt from Philippa's lap to Chloe's.

Philippa tried not to be jealous. Of everything. Of their bond. Their family. Their love.

"Chloe misses Tiglet," Tommy whispered. "They were inseparable before Chloe married Faircliffe."

Philippa nodded. She understood. The kitten had been Chloe's first. *Tommy* was Chloe's first.

And Philippa would not get to keep either of them.

23

*C*hloe clapped her hands together. "We've arrived!"

A footman was there to help the ladies out of the coach, but Tommy reached for Philippa first. Philippa pretended not to notice the tickle beneath her clothes at the feel of Tommy's hand on hers or her desire to throw herself into Tommy's arms.

"Follow me." Tommy's eyes sparkled.

Philippa held Piglet to her chest. "Where are we going?"

"To the Planning Parlor," Chloe answered.

Their butler opened the front door to welcome them inside.

"You're the first non-Wynchester to be invited into the parlor," Tommy whispered as they climbed the stairs.

Philippa's head swam with pleasure. Invited. Included. Her heart beat erratically. She had only ever seen part of the ground floor, and had long wondered what the rest of the Wynchesters' home must be like.

The Planning Parlor surpassed her every imagining.

Instead of parquet or a luxurious carpet, they walked into an enormous room with a floor made of slate. Chalk drawings covered a large part of it—a map here, a timetable of some sort there.

A large walnut-and-burl table commanded one half of the

room. In the other half were a variety of chairs and sofas, not facing the fireplace but rather each other, much like how Philippa arranged the chairs in her reading circle to aid discussion.

There were five tall mullioned windows, their thick calico curtains tied back to allow in the morning sun. Bookcases lined the other walls. No, not just bookcases—some were map cases and every other kind of case. Philippa could spend a year exploring every nook and cranny, and likely still not uncover every surprise.

In fact, if she lived here, she doubted exploring the parlor to her heart's content would raise so much as an eyebrow. The Wynchesters did not feel bad about their idiosyncrasies. They indulged them.

Two paintings above the fireplace caught her eye. One was a portrait of a white-haired gentleman with a droll expression. The other was the painting of Puck and his fellow imps that the Duke of Faircliffe had once given Philippa as a courting gift. She hadn't expected it to end up here.

At Philippa's obvious surprise, Chloe burst out laughing. "Oh, the painting? It's a long story. The portrait next to it is of Bean. That is, our original Baron Vanderbean. He's the one who designed our Planning Parlor."

"It's wonderful," Philippa said. "What an impressive library."

"Oh, it's not the library," Tommy said. "We don't actually have one. These are Graham's almanacs and albums and journals and ledgers, and who knows what else."

Not . . . actually . . . have . . . a library?

"No touching my albums," warned a deep voice behind Philippa.

She turned to see the rest of the Wynchester clan file into the room.

Graham, with his springy black curls and a profusion of notebooks and newspapers clutched to his chest. Elizabeth, with her sword stick and a pile of blankets thrown over one shoulder. Marjorie, the smallest and palest, with bits of colored paint on her fingers.

And Jacob, with his gorgeous brown skin and a trio of what looked like... baby hedgehogs?

"Do not juggle the hedgehogs," Graham commanded. "Only I shall juggle livestock in this family."

"I forbid you from touching any of my animals, ever." Jacob ignored the chairs and the sofas and settled on an unchalked patch of slate instead.

Elizabeth and Marjorie encircled him and his hedgehogs with rolled blankets, creating a makeshift pen.

Graham threw himself into a chair and opened a broadsheet as though the spectacle before him was as interesting as waiting for a kettle to boil.

"Are you reading the personal advertisements?" Tommy asked.

"What else? The news isn't interesting," Graham answered. "I learned all the good bits before breakfast."

"And regaled us with every minute detail," Elizabeth said, sotto voce.

"You eat breakfast together?" Longing shot through Philippa. It sounded chaotic and wonderful.

"Every meal when we're home at the same time," Tommy answered. "Some appear at the table with their gossip or their osprey, but the rest of us are civilized."

"I'm not civilized," said Elizabeth. "I resent that accusation."

"Osprey?" Philippa asked doubtfully.

Jacob glanced up from his hedgehogs. "A large bird of prey with a wingspan of six feet and a lifespan of ten to twenty years, in danger of being hunted to extinction here in England. I rescued mine. Her name is Caelum."

"I know what an osprey is," Philippa said. "Should it be near Tiglet?"

"It shouldn't be around any small animal you don't want it to eat," Jacob said. "Which is why I shall release mine back into the wild as soon as her wing heals."

"Aargh." Graham shook his broadsheet. "Why aren't the secret messages ever interesting? Lady who lost her garter inside a catacomb, gentleman seeking same for friendship or more, coordinates for tracking a parcel, notice for a runaway bride: 'Please come home; you can have your violin back.'"

"Those things . . . aren't interesting?" Philippa managed.

"Bah," said Graham. "Who hasn't lost a garter or two? I'm waiting for someone to be kidnapped atop an unreachable spire, thus requiring my daring rescue."

Philippa hesitated. "If the spire is unreachable . . ."

"Ignore him," Tommy said. "He thinks all of that is fascinating, no matter his claims to the contrary. That's why he never stops reading it."

"I pause on occasion." A book came flying out from behind his broadsheet. "There's the intelligence on Northrup."

Tommy caught it with her left hand and handed it to Philippa.

The last dozen pages contained an extremely detailed family tree, and the rest were filled with answers to every possible query anyone could think of to have about Captain Northrup. Philippa paged through it in wonder.

"He dislikes chocolate?" she asked.

Elizabeth shuddered. "He's a monster."

"We already knew that," Graham said. "In fact, Northrup's commanding officer, one Brigadier-General Boswick, doubted Northrup had invented the cipher on his own. According to my sources, Boswick made inquiries as to who might have helped, but nothing came of it. In the absence of evidence to the contrary, he and other doubters were forced to accept Northrup's claim as truth."

"Aargh." Philippa clenched her fingers. "I know no one will listen to the unpopular opinions of a bluestocking, but—"

Another book came flying out from behind Graham's newspaper. Tommy caught it with her right hand and handed it to Philippa.

Graham lowered his broadsheet. "You don't think the intelligence you provide is just as valuable as mine?"

"No...I..." Philippa paged through the journal. Even her observations of the markings on her illuminated manuscript had been faithfully re-created, probably by Marjorie. All of the Wynchesters' contributions were annotated. All of the Wynchesters...and Philippa.

She was important. *She* had contributed to the Wynchesters' intelligence gathering. Her heart warmed.

"At the ball, I saw you stand for a set with Northrup," Tommy said. "Did he say anything that might be of use?"

"Only that my father spoke to him." Philippa grimaced. "It's supposed to be the other way around. Northrup assures me he's not disinterested in a union but is not yet ready to make an official offer."

"That sounds like there *will* be an official offer." Tommy frowned. "Perhaps sooner than we'd like."

"We cannot send him to the devil." Jacob cupped a baby hedgehog in his palm. "Not yet."

Graham tilted his head and considered Philippa. "Your excellent reputation is another asset."

She sat up straighter. Her bland, unobjectionable reputation had always been her most important attribute, according to her parents. Society's opinion was more important than Philippa the person. She thrilled at the idea her pristine reputation might be used for exacting justice. That it was a tool she possessed, but her entire person was helpful and valued.

"In two months, Northrup will have land and a title, but no money. I'm the money," she said. "I have my own inheritance from my grandmother, and my dowry is significant. My parents will trip over themselves to give their approval, and he likely knows it. The only reason he hasn't asked yet is because he's receiving so much attention as an eligible bachelor."

"With luck, he'll wait to ask until he's been made a viscount," Elizabeth said. "Or until he can no longer make purchases on credit."

"She shan't really marry him," said Marjorie. "Will she?"

Everyone turned to look at Philippa.

"I must marry *someone* this season, but I will not accept Captain Northrup."

"What if you don't accept anyone?" Elizabeth asked. "You don't *have* to marry a man if you don't wish to. Why not decide to be a scandalous spinster?"

"Because scandal would reflect badly on my parents," Philippa said quietly. "As well as any friends and organizations who wish to continue to associate with me."

If she lost her standing, she would lose her friends, her reading circle, her cooperative charity endeavors, the last vestiges of her parents' respect, and any hope of founding community reading libraries to bring blessed escape to those who needed it most...

Tommy met Philippa's eyes. "Then we get justice for Damaris before you're forced to cause a scandal."

"Damaris and Agnes and Katherine," Elizabeth amended. "Whilst Graham's associates are trying to find the original document Northrup produced or someone who saw it, we shall collect the other volumes for further analysis."

"Won't there be a commotion when the papers report a string of very specific robberies?" Philippa asked. "The replicas will not fool the world forever."

"Which is why we cannot dally," Tommy agreed.

Philippa's skin prickled. Her time grew shorter every day. At first, she was to have had her freedom until the end of her last season in June. Next, they had needed to avenge Damaris before the season opening celebration in January. Then her parents had decided she must marry Northrup. And now, her and the Wynchesters' plans to help Damaris could fall apart at any moment.

She no longer had two months. She had *weeks*. Possibly even days.

"You're right." Her limbs felt clumsy. She hugged herself to calm them. The manuscripts could be the key. "What is the next step?"

Graham tapped the end of his pencil against his jaw. "You possess volumes two and four. We've identified the simplest target for volume three."

Jacob tickled the hedgehog's belly. "The private library of the Electi Society for the Intellectually Elite."

"Notice the name fails to specify *gentlemen*," Philippa said. "And yet they refuse to allow any of my female friends on their premises."

"Bah," said Elizabeth. "Who needs permission?"

"Er," said Philippa. "Everyone? They've a rigorous qualifying process for membership, followed by a vote all members must be present for . . . The patronesses of Almack's *wish* they were so discerning. The club is so secretive and exclusive, they won't allow nonmembers even to cross their threshold."

"If they know you're coming," said Elizabeth.

Graham nodded. "The Electi Society meets for supper

during the season, followed by wine and lively discourse until the wee hours of the morning on the subjects of ancient and natural philosophy." He tucked his pencil in his pocket. "We're not interested in any of that."

"I am," muttered Philippa.

Jacob set down his hedgehog. "The season has not yet begun, making this an optimal time to strike."

"Not all members of the Society are fashionable enough to have somewhere to go during the summers," Philippa said. "They may still take suppers there, if unofficially."

"Which is why we'll sneak inside in broad daylight," Tommy said. "Long before supper time. The club will be empty."

"Of gentlemen," Philippa acknowledged. "What about maids or other staff?"

Graham held up a journal. "I've annotated timetables for each employee. Staff has a holiday on Sundays until late afternoon, so the butler has been guarding his ale at the pub instead."

Jacob gestured at a shelf across the room. "Tommy has sketched extensive maps of the area."

"Marjorie completed her decoy forgeries," Elizabeth added. "We need little more than half an hour to break in, make the switch, and walk out."

"Not forgeries," Marjorie said. "Decorative replicas."

"It sounds as though you have a plan for everything," Philippa said. Of course they did. They were Wynchesters.

"It's ten o'clock," Elizabeth said.

"On Sunday morning," Graham added meaningfully.

Philippa's mind felt giddy. They meant to strike at this precise moment.

"I want to see the new manuscript before Philippa takes it home." Marjorie turned toward the door.

Jacob gathered his hedgehogs to his chest and pushed to his feet. "Hear that little noise they're making? It's mealtime."

"I'll help feed them," Elizabeth said.

"Wait," Philippa stammered. "Aren't you going to break into the Electi Society?"

"We all help in our own way, depending on our specific talents," Chloe explained. "Marjorie is wonderful at creating forgeries, but awful at sneaking about undetected. Being part of a family doesn't mean everyone does everything. It means everyone does their part."

Graham lifted the journal. "Such as your comprehensive list of the few remaining collectors in England still in possession of a Northrup manuscript. That allowed us to act swiftly."

He was trying to say... When Tommy had dressed as Great-Aunt Wynchester to bring her the Cambridge volume, she hadn't been trying to *exclude* Philippa. Tommy wouldn't have known where to begin *without* her. Philippa had already played her part. Tommy was just doing hers.

The Wynchesters hadn't merely invited her today. She was part of the plan. They'd gone as far as to create a ruse to abduct her and bring her into the heart of the operation. They had used her information, had forged a replica based on her manuscript.

Her chest filled with joy. She was not a useless, passive bystander. She was a part of the team.

Philippa made a rueful expression at Tommy. "I apologize again for how I reacted when you stole the Cambridge manuscript. Is this your way of telling me I've done my bit and should leave the rest to the experts?"

"No," Tommy said. "It's our way of telling you that you're as much a part of this as we are. You can be as involved—or not—as you please."

"I can go *with* you?" Philippa squealed in excitement. She

immediately sobered. "I want to be included more than anything, but I've no idea what I'm doing. Aren't you afraid I'll make a hash of things?"

"*I* am," said Graham. "Tommy believes you're worth the risk."

Tommy's eyes held Philippa's. "We were all new and inexperienced once. If you want in, then you're in. The decision is yours."

"I'm in," Philippa said to Tommy. "If you want me."

She held her breath. Tommy's dark gaze did not waver.

"Oh, she wants you." Graham lifted his newspaper. "Be ready in an hour."

Philippa's cheeks flushed. It had not escaped her notice that the Wynchester siblings appeared to be playing matchmaker. They clearly knew and accepted Tommy as she was. And Philippa, too. But now was not the time to ruminate on such things. She had to be ready—whatever that entailed—within the hour.

Chloe lifted the kitten. "Tiglet and I will make haste to the orphanage. I'll give him back to you when you return."

Philippa gave him a final rub between the ears. "The charity outing is real?"

"It is now. I'm off to create your alibi." Chloe clasped her hands to her bosom and affected an overly earnest voice. "'Oh, yes, Mrs. Smith. This gift is from my dear friend Miss Philippa York, who is in the corridor just behind me. She must be playing with the children.' There will be dozens of witnesses to your kindness and generosity."

"She goes every month," Tommy said. "You've just given her an additional reason."

Chloe waved her fingers and sailed from the Planning Parlor.

"Now what?" Philippa asked.

Tommy smiled. "Now we put on our disguises."

Philippa glanced at Graham, who was half hidden behind a large broadsheet.

"Not him," Tommy said. "He won't be seen. Come with me."

As they left the parlor, Philippa sent another look over her shoulder. "No one will see your brother on a public street in broad daylight?"

"Ah," Tommy said. "Unlike you and me, Graham needn't limit his travel to streets. He'll be the one to gain access to the building. You and I shall lie in wait until it is time to plant the replica. Ours may not be the most interesting of roles—"

"It's terribly exciting." Philippa's heart beat far too fast. Her legs were trembling with anticipation. "I've never lain in wait before. I feel positively roguish."

She also felt.. honored. Tommy was placing a great deal of trust in her, and the Wynchester siblings were placing a great deal of trust in Tommy. It was breathtaking for someone to assume Philippa was capable and clever and worth the risk, as she learned and improved and became useful.

"We're here," Tommy said.

Philippa blinked at a large mahogany door. "We're where?"

"My boudoir." With an exaggerated leer, Tommy opened the door and beckoned her in.

24

*P*hilippa stepped inside one of the largest dressing rooms she had ever seen. Enormous wardrobes covered every wall. It was like a library, but of clothes. And... wigs?

Tommy gestured at the many shelves in her open wardrobes. "Shoes, wigs, 'fashionable buck,' laborer, soldier, lady, country miss, lower class, royalty, livery, cosmetics and prostheses, jewelry and accoutrements."

"I...see," Philippa said faintly. Each wardrobe appeared to contain a little of everything.

On one side of the room were three tall looking glasses. Just beyond, half a dozen comfortable-looking chairs surrounded a massive dressing table with an equally massive mirror.

"Sit anywhere you please," Tommy offered.

Philippa chose the armchair closest to the dressing table. It was indeed as plush and comfortable as it appeared. "Why so many chairs? Were you expecting spectators?"

"My siblings enjoy watching me turn into someone else. They're making themselves scarce to give us privacy."

Philippa could not fathom what it must be like to have the Wynchesters in one's dressing room. The opposite of lonely,

she supposed. This house must seem like a home. Tommy
and her siblings—

Tommy shrugged off her frock coat and folded it over the
back of an armchair. The white linen of her sleeves billowed
about her arms.

"What are you doing?" Philippa stammered, her mouth
suddenly dry.

"I'll put my disguise on first." Tommy loosened her cravat.
One knot at a time. Slowly, she unwound the soft white
material to reveal a long, graceful neck with a thrumming
pulse point at its base. Idly, as though she had not stolen
Philippa's very breath, Tommy dropped the cravat atop her
discarded coat.

Was she going to *undress*? Here? At this moment? In front
of Philippa?

Philippa's lungs struggled for air. Did she want Tommy to
stop? Did she want her to keep going?

Tommy looked magnificent in gentlemen's dishabille.
Casual and dissolute. Philippa tried hard not to look, and then
gave up and looked. It was impossible to say without closer
inspection, but Philippa thought she could make out the outline of small, firm breasts and the shadows of nipples when
the light from the windows hit the cambric just so—

Tommy turned toward her and raised an eyebrow.

Philippa's cheeks flushed with heat. She sent her mortified
gaze anywhere but in Tommy's direction. My, what a lovely
ceiling. Yes, Philippa was fascinated by white ceilings. Flat.
Boring. Nonsexual.

"Is there a question?" Tommy asked.

"I wondered if you bound your breasts," Philippa blurted
out. "I see you do not."

Heaven help her. Had she really just admitted—

"I've bound them in the past," Tommy said, as though

inquiring about her breasts was perfectly acceptable. "I'm fortunate such a step is rarely necessary. Someone with slightly larger breasts would definitely have to bind theirs. And someone as blessed as you would have no hope of hiding her beautiful curves."

Oh God. Now they were talking about *Philippa's* breasts?

"Tell me about your disguise," she said in a rush. "Today's costume. What is the plan?"

Tommy's heated brown eyes trapped hers for a moment before she turned for a basket of supplies. She set it atop her dressing table and settled into her chair.

"We begin with skin tone." She pulled out little jars and sponges. "One must achieve the correct base color before adding any flourishes."

Philippa nodded as though she had any idea what to do with cosmetics.

She watched in fascination as Tommy covered her face and neck in a color almost the same as her own, but slightly more sallow, less vibrant.

"I am in awe of you." The words were out of Philippa's mouth before she could stop them. "I have spent the past twenty years *reading* about intrepid heroes, but you and your family actually go out and *be* them."

Tommy's sponge paused at her throat. "You learned to read when you were three?"

"And that's all I've done," said Philippa. "Until now. Today I'm going to be part of the story. It's exhilarating."

"When I was three, I did not learn to read," Tommy said. "I learned when to be small and silent, and when to be loud or run fast. But we are perhaps not as different as you think. My family and I execute complex plans to help others. You've dedicated your adulthood to charity work. You do Wynchestery things with your purse and your pen."

"I'm glad of any part I can play," Philippa said. "But sewing blankets and writing letters is not exactly swashbuckling adventure. My home is still and quiet until I want to scream. I am almost always alone, except for Thursday afternoons with my reading circle. Your house, on the other hand, is—"

"Chaotic?"

"Delightful," she said firmly. "Exciting. A constant joy. I am at once jealous and deeply appreciative that you're including me today. I treasure all moments spent in the company of a Wynchester."

She really meant, *I cherish all time spent with* you, *Tommy,* but dared not say so. Such confessions could not alter one's destiny.

"Your family is so capable and fearless," she said instead.

"Do you think so?" Tommy added a faint shadow along her jaw. Not the brown of Baron Vanderbean's, but a mottled gray. "*I* am not."

"You?" Philippa said in disbelief. "You are changing into an entirely new person before my eyes in preparation to steal an illuminated manuscript from a so-called gentlemen's club."

"Costumes are easy to hide behind," Tommy answered. "They can mask anything. Age, sex, class, fear. No one sees anxiety when it is concealed behind layers of cosmetics and a distractingly flamboyant frock coat."

Philippa stared at her. "You're always so confident."

"Always?" Tommy cleaned her sponge. "What about the year I spent admiring you from afar because I could not work up the courage to speak to you directly and face rejection?"

"You admired me...for a year?"

Philippa thought back. Great-Aunt Wynchester had first appeared at the reading circle the prior autumn. It *had* been a year. Tommy would have had plenty of time to learn more about Philippa. Time in which she failed to introduce herself...or have any meaningful conversation at all. Out of bashfulness?

"Or what about that night at Faircliffe's end-of-season gala?" Tommy continued wryly. "I managed to plant myself directly in front of you, close enough to touch, and then my face combusted with embarrassment and I ran off in mortification."

"That was *you?*" Philippa let out a startled laugh. "That was the most interesting thing that happened to me all evening. Possibly all season."

Tommy slanted her a look. "More interesting than being courted by and subsequently rejecting the suit of an eligible duke?"

"Yes," Philippa answered honestly. "I wasn't interested in the duke. I very much wanted to know who the person was who had almost spoken to me, and what I had done to chase her off. I thought of that moment for months afterward."

"You hadn't done anything. It was me. When I am anxious or nervous, my brain thinks up all the ways a thing can go wrong and plays them for me over and over. By the time I was in front of you, I was certain that if I so much as opened my mouth, you'd toss your lemonade in my face."

"I do that, too," Philippa admitted. "I stand up for others without issue, but in my own life, stasis is so much safer than change. Society has its rules, and I memorized them all. I even sent out inquiries about a Balcovian equivalent to *Debrett's Peerage* so that I could learn those rules, as well."

"Did you find one?" Tommy asked with interest.

Philippa shook her head. "Apparently, not all countries publish annual volumes listing their peers."

"Pity. I would have liked to read about Bean." Tommy

sighed. "I suppose it doesn't matter. I had the *real* Bean, for a time. What would words change? All good things are temporary. Book or no book, he would still be gone."

Philippa frowned. What would words change? She herself had discounted confessing her feelings, but she disliked hearing the sentiment from Tommy. Words were powerful. *That* was why Philippa did not want to use them. They changed things. Sometimes forever.

Communication was the engine behind her reading circle. The power of building a network of community libraries. And it was also a conversation between two people. She was glad Tommy had finally approached her. This past month together comprised the best days of Philippa's life.

She would never have guessed that Tommy had been afraid to take that first step. Now that she knew, Philippa liked her even more. Bravery wasn't doing the things that came easy. Bravery meant pressing forward even when you were scared silly.

"And now, for the crowning touch." From a box, Tommy pulled out what looked like the fluffy tail of a squirrel.

Philippa reared back, then laughed to realize what she was looking at was not an animal, but rather thick red-brown hair forming a pair of truly egregious side whiskers.

"Just wait," Tommy said. "They're even more impressive on."

Philippa leaned farther away. "Please tell me those are not made from squirrel fur."

"One hundred percent human hair," Tommy assured her. "Probably."

She applied some sort of gummy glue to one of the bushy whiskers and pressed it against her cheek.

As diverting as Tommy was bound to look when she finished, the sight of her wearing only one whisker was even funnier. Wild hair protruded between her fingers, from just below her temple almost to her jaw.

With her free hand, she turned over a small hourglass.

"I must hold them in place for several minutes for it to set properly," she explained. She applied adhesive to the other whisker and carefully pressed it to her cheek, using both palms to keep the false hair in place.

"Is it strange to have me here watching you?" Philippa asked.

"I'm used to an audience," Tommy answered. "The peculiar part is no longer having Chloe."

"Did she help?"

"She can work wonders with curling tongs," Tommy said. "But it's more than that. Our cots were side by side in the orphanage. For as long as I've had memories, she's never been more than an arm's length away. And now she's gone."

"I'm sorry," Philippa said softly. "I can only imagine how heart-wrenching that must be."

"I thought I would be sad forever, but I don't resent Faircliffe anymore. They make each other so happy. It is vexingly adorable. Ask her where she got that hideous bonnet."

"The one in the caricatures?"

"The very one." Tommy eyed the hourglass. Half of the sand now pooled at the bottom. "Chloe always reminds me that change can be for the better. We found each other. Then Bean. Then our siblings. Then I found you."

"Those are wonderful changes," Philippa said. "I especially like the last one."

"Finding is fun," Tommy agreed. "It's losing that's difficult. At first it was impossibly hard to be without Bean. Then just as impossible for me to try to replace him, however temporarily, as his imaginary heir."

Philippa blinked. "I had not thought of that. It must have

taken extra courage to approach me in public as the baron. And to hear his name, again and again."

Tommy dusted her whiskers with hair powder. "I prefer being me, without any costume at all. That is, when I'm not being…Great-Uncle Wynchester."

She grinned and lowered her hands. Gray-brown whiskers burst from her cheeks in untamed glory.

Philippa snorted with laughter. "You look as though you've not seen your valet in decades."

"Then it's perfect."

"Should you look so particular?" Philippa peered at the whiskers in fascination. "Won't a pair of squirrels growing out of your face make you memorable?"

"Unforgettable," Tommy agreed. "Which is often the best disguise. If witnesses are asked to describe me, they'll all say exactly the same thing: they saw an old man with an abundance of whiskers. They won't have the least idea of any detail that might actually identify me."

It was quite clever, and an embarrassing observation about human nature.

Tommy put down her mirror. "How do I look?"

"Incongruous," Philippa admitted. "You've a young man's hair, an old man's whiskers, and a mostly Tommy face."

"Ah," said Tommy. "Then it's time for the next step."

Powdering her short hair gray with patches of white at the temple took no time at all. "I'll have my hat on the entire time," Tommy explained. "But even if someone notices my hair is powdered, they'll think nothing of it…at my age."

Philippa stared in wonder as Tommy carefully added wrinkles all over her face. Deep grooves in her forehead and a dimpled bit of skin between her eyebrows, just above the bridge of her nose. Laugh lines at the corners of her eyes. Grooves from the sides of her nostrils down past the corners of her mouth. Smudges of sallow purple-gray, creating the illusion of drooping bags beneath her eyes.

"You look ancient," Philippa said. "And exhausted."

"I'll wait to do my hands until last." Tommy added tufts of hair to her eyebrows, then waggled them at Philippa. "How do you do, young lady? Come sit on my lap before I fall asleep."

Philippa burst out laughing. "Does that ever work?"

"There's always a first time." Tommy preened. "You're saying I won't cut the same swath Baron Vanderbean did?"

"Oh, you'll make an impression, all right."

"Excellent." Tommy wiped her fingers on a cloth and stood up. "Your turn."

Philippa's heart skipped. "What? I could never pass as a gentleman."

Tommy pulled her to her feet. "I know."

Her face was inches from Philippa's. Even with the springy eyebrows and the deep wrinkles and the frightening side whiskers, she was still magnificently Tommy. Philippa had to turn her face away, lest she be tempted to climb into Great-Uncle Wynchester's lap after all.

"Over here." Tommy led her to an armchair. "This spot has better light from the window."

Hesitant, Philippa started to sit down in the chair.

"Wait," Tommy said. "You'll want to take off your over-dress."

Philippa raised her brows skeptically.

"When applying cosmetics," Tommy explained, "never wear anything you don't want covered in them."

Breath shaky, Philippa turned around to let Tommy loosen the ties of her lace overdress.

She had been undressed before, by her lady's maid. That was done swiftly, the task over in a blink, the gown neatly folded and back in the wardrobe or set aside to be washed and ironed. It was ordinary work for the maid and unremarkable for Philippa.

But this. *This.* Tommy changed in and out of costumes at a moment's notice, yet her competent fingers took their time with Philippa's overdress. The boring little bow at the back was untied lovingly. The basic white ribbon eased free, inch by inch, widening the gap between the lace panels.

Philippa felt more exposed by the second.

The jittery pounding of her heart was ridiculous. It was not only an overdress, but a *lace* overdress, and by definition already transparent. Tommy wasn't glimpsing any more of Philippa's body by removing its outermost shell.

Yet it felt that way. As though Tommy were learning her contours in a way that wasn't visual. Philippa's shoulder blades were hidden beneath muslin, but they felt each brush of Tommy's knuckles as though the material were nonexistent.

Her back and spine were behind a thick wall of whalebone stays, a shift, and an underdress. She couldn't *really* feel Tommy's fingers...could she? It was surely her imagination. There were only eight loops to the ties of her overdress, all right there between her shoulder blades. There was no reason to feel a shiver along her flesh or down her spine.

This act was innocent, Philippa told herself firmly.

Well, not *innocent*—their aim was to steal someone else's property—but certainly nonsexual. It wasn't as though Tommy would risk marring her carefully applied cosmetics by touching Philippa any more than necessary. This slow, sensual disrobing wasn't a *seduction*.

No matter what it felt like.

As soon as the overdress was loose enough, Philippa stepped hastily away from Tommy to remove the garment herself. Her fingers shook.

Tommy's dark eyes watched her in silence from a face that appeared to be a man old enough to be Philippa's grandfather. It should feel strange to be in dishabille in such circumstances. But the knowledge that Tommy was *Tommy* overrode any disguise. Philippa yearned to be in her arms no matter what costume she wore.

Just because a thing wasn't a seduction didn't mean it hadn't worked.

Philippa tried to pretend she was unaffected. She folded her overdress with trembling hands, and placed it on one of the many empty armchairs before taking her seat at the dressing table.

"What would you like me to become?" she asked nervously.

Tommy's knuckles brushed gently down the side of Philippa's cheek. "My wife."

Philippa swallowed. "You mean...an old lady?"

"If that's what you want me to mean." Rather than take the chair in front of her, Tommy stepped out of sight behind Philippa. "I'm afraid I shall have to dismantle your lovely hair arrangement if I'm to fit you with a wig."

"You can't," Philippa said in alarm. "My mother will notice immediately if my hair is no longer *à la Grecque*."

Tommy's voice was wry. "If I can turn you into someone else, I can certainly turn you back into Philippa."

"Oh," she said softly. "Right. I'm not used to needing a disguise. Being me is usually deflection enough. People see me and assume I cannot possibly be up to anything."

Tommy eased the pins from her hair. "Then I have excellent news. Your day as a nefarious miscreant has finally come."

As Tommy combed through her long hair, Philippa tried not to purr like a cat. She loved the sensation of Tommy brushing her hair. It felt...intimate. Tommy's strokes were confident and sure, but also gentle and reverent. As though she was luxuriating in this moment every bit as much as Philippa.

Carefully, Tommy plaited Philippa's hair in two segments. She wound each around Philippa's head and pinned them in place.

"Now cosmetics, before I attach your wig."

Philippa straightened. "Great-Aunt Wynchester's wig?"

"You have too much hair. Besides, hers won't have the right impact. You need a bigger wig."

"Bigger than Great-Aunt Wynchester's wig?" Philippa repeated in disbelief. This was going to be hilarious.

"Shh," Tommy said. "Don't move while I apply these wrinkles."

Philippa held as still as possible.

Tommy's touch with the cosmetics was the same as how she'd brushed Philippa's hair: confident but gentle. It felt as though she was covering Philippa's face with a thousand tiny caresses.

Tommy stepped back to admire her handiwork and gave a pleased nod. "That'll do."

Philippa jerked her gaze to the looking glass and almost startled herself right out of her chair. Even without the wig, she looked as though she'd aged fifty years. She lifted her fingers to touch one of her sagging new wrinkles, then pulled her hand away before making contact.

"The cosmetics won't come off without a special oil," Tommy said. "But all the same, it's best not to touch them. They may smudge when freshly applied."

Philippa looked away from the mirror. If she could no longer see her shocking transformation, perhaps she wouldn't be tempted to touch it.

"Put this on." Tommy handed Philippa a shapeless, boring dove-colored gown devoid of gauze and lace.

"It's too small," Philippa said without unfolding it.

"It's not too small," Tommy said. "It was made for Elizabeth. You just don't want to wear it."

Philippa sent a longing look over the dressing table at her abandoned overdress.

"Don't even think about it." Tommy shook a finger at her. "Your lace overdresses are the Philippa-est things in London. You'll look like your own great-grandmother."

Philippa accepted the dull gray material reluctantly. "Now I'll look colorless and shapeless."

"You have the best shape I've ever seen. There's no hiding it. Drab will have to do."

Philippa flushed and slid on the ugly overdress.

Tommy rummaged through a wardrobe and produced a thick gray wig with light brown undertones. It took a prodigious number of pins, but she managed to affix it securely to Philippa's head.

"Final step: age spots for both of us." Tommy placed Philippa's hands on the center of the dressing table and leaned over it from the other side to apply the cosmetics. "I always thought my temporary disguises were great fun. Turns out, costuming the both of us is even more amusing."

Her voice was casual, but she didn't meet Philippa's eyes.

Philippa bit her lip, then spoke in a rush. "Spending time with you may be the most fun I've ever had, too."

Tommy lifted her gaze from Philippa's hands.

She was *right there*. Almost close enough to kiss. If they both happened to lean over at the same moment...

Graham knocked on the door. "Ready?"

Philippa leapt to her feet. "Ready!"

She was not ready in the least. For anything. But it was time to go.

25

Tommy and Philippa meandered down St. James's Street at a pace that could barely be detected with the naked eye.

After each halting step, they paused to remark upon this window or that cloud overhead or this section of pavement or that blade of grass. At this rate, it would take an hour to travel one hundred yards.

Which was exactly the plan.

If anyone glimpsed them from a window or a passing carriage, all they would see was an elderly couple doing exactly nothing. She and Philippa were conspicuous enough not to look furtive and ordinary enough to register as little more than part of the scenery.

"Are you certain the basket isn't too heavy?" Tommy quavered in an irascible-old-man voice. "I can carry it and give you the cane."

"I'm not your sister," Philippa replied in a surprisingly convincing old-lady voice. "If trouble comes, I wouldn't have the least notion what to do with a sword stick. Other than drop it at my feet and run screaming. Besides, this basket weighs little. *You* didn't spend your youth toting large stacks of books up and down countless stairs."

Tommy grinned at the idea that beneath Philippa's soft, voluptuous curves lay a hidden core of muscle. She was like a sword stick. Pretty on the outside and dangerously capable beneath. Tommy yearned to unsheathe the blade and gaze upon its beauty.

"Are you certain your sister won't miss her cane?" Philippa asked.

Tommy scoffed. "Her dressing room contains an entire armory of sword sticks and who knows what else. I wouldn't be surprised to learn she wears chain mail over her shift."

"All the more reason for her to care very much," Philippa said. "I own many books, and each one is precious to me."

"You wouldn't loan one to a friend?"

"Only if I could trust her to return it in the same condition."

"I have returned every sword stick I've ever borrowed, and never in a condition soap and water couldn't cure. If Elizabeth is disgruntled about anything, it is that she rarely has cause to use the hidden rapier."

"'Rarely'?" Philippa's eyes widened. "You mean she really does attack people?"

"Only when they deserve it," Tommy assured her.

They were ever so slowly drawing closer to the rooms of the Electi Society for the Intellectually Elite. Coaches occasionally passed, but she and Philippa were the only pedestrians on the street. It was impossible to know where Graham was at this moment. Somewhere on the roofs overhead. He'd identified a likely entrance point days ago.

"'Intellectually elite,'" Philippa muttered. "All they do is smoke cigars and drink port. I'd like to exchange all of the books in their library for replicas with blank pages and see how long those pretentious geniuses take to notice the difference."

"That is good to know," Tommy murmured back. "I was wondering what gift to give you for Christmas."

"You have already given me the perfect gift," Philippa said. "You trusted me enough to include me in your plans, and you allowed me to take part in the adventure."

Yes, and it terrified Tommy.

Not just because she had never invited a non-Wynchester into their tight circle, but because if something went wrong, the consequences for Philippa could be catastrophic. If her reputation was ruined and her parents disowned her, Tommy would of course offer her a home. But she wanted to *be* Philippa's choice, freely given. Not as a last resort when all else failed.

"Thank you again." Philippa smiled up at her. "For including me. You are the most skillful and daring person I know. I long to be remarkable, too."

Tommy's chest constricted with conflicting emotions. Of course Philippa deserved to be in charge of her own life. But along with the very practical reasons against bringing her into an illegal scheme, she had just given Tommy a new worry.

If Philippa did everything Tommy did, then Tommy wouldn't seem special anymore. What if allowing Philippa *in* ended up pushing her away?

A wiry man with a tall top hat emerged from the Athenaeum. He turned to look up and down the cobblestone street. He blinked when he saw Tommy and Philippa.

Quickly, Tommy banged her cane on the pavement. "I say no winter was better than the one in '88. 'Twas the best Frost Fair the Thames ever had."

"Pah, you old fool," Philippa replied. "Last winter was the best winter. It dragged on for a year and a half. Clearly it is the winner."

"No, the Frost Fair." Tommy shook her cane belligerently.

"No winter can be the best winter without elephants crossing a river, I always say."

"You always say a load of poppycock, is what you always say." Philippa shook a crooked finger. "A Frost Fair might make the wintertime *amusing*, but the Year Without a Summer by definition excelled at being *winter*. It was indubitably the wintriest winter that ever wintered."

The gentleman in the tall top hat climbed into a hackney and rolled off down the street.

Philippa burst into giggles.

Girlish giggles coming from a face that appeared a hundred years old should have been incongruous.

Instead, they warmed Tommy's heart.

She hoped Philippa would still giggle when she got away with naughtiness, no matter how many years passed by. It made her look youthful despite the wrinkles lining her face. Tommy could barely look at her without wanting to kiss her. She suspected that feeling would never go away. Philippa would be just as alluring as an old woman as she was as a young lady.

"Do you think your brother is inside yet?"

Tommy consulted her pocket watch. "He's inside. He's looking for the library."

"What if the library is locked?"

Tommy leaned casually against the red brick of the Electi Society building. Just an old man catching his breath. "Graham has tools to help. He can't scale walls and leap from building to building with an illuminated manuscript under one arm"—she gestured at Philippa's basket, which contained the replica Marjorie had made—"but he has a leather belt with secure pouches for carrying small things."

"I hope these manuscripts prove what I think they do," Philippa whispered.

Tommy didn't address the unspoken questions.

What if the manuscripts proved useless? What if Graham's network found no evidence to support Damaris, and Northrup was honored for deeds he did not perform? What if, in the absence of a comeuppance, Philippa's parents married her to Northrup after all?

Tommy wanted to hold Philippa tight while she still could. To make the most of what little time they had together, whether it was months or weeks or days.

A series of soft knocks sounded on the window pane next to their heads.

Philippa jumped. "Graham?"

Tommy nodded. "It's time."

She held out her elbow for Philippa and they ambled the last three yards to the front door, making the same show of being slow and easily distracted as before.

Tommy placed the basket flush against the door. Under the guise of bending to brush dirt from her shin, she tipped up the lid of the basket. As she stood, Tommy subtly arranged their bodies so that she faced Philippa, and Philippa's spine was toward the door.

Philippa's voluminous skirts hid the basket from any curious eyes across the street. She and Tommy would appear to be an elderly couple embracing in public. Unusual enough that if anyone glanced this direction, the kiss Tommy was about to take would be all a witness remembered from this moment.

"We're just pretending," she murmured as she lowered her mouth to Philippa's. "You don't have to kiss me back."

Philippa twined her arms about Tommy's neck and kissed her fiercely.

Tommy had to grip the handle of the sword stick to stay upright. This was a taste of what she wanted. She wished she could toss the cane aside and kiss Philippa for the next hour...or perhaps eternity.

She could not cup Philippa's face because of her carefully applied cosmetics. Nor could she sink her fingers into Philippa's hair because it hid beneath a bushy gray wig.

All Tommy could do was stand there, dying to touch and feel and caress, only able to show her passion through the insatiable hunger of her kisses.

Vaguely, she heard the door unlocking, and the lock sliding into place after it closed again. Graham had switched the false manuscript for the real one and was now spiriting the replica up to the library before disappearing across the rooftops the way he had come.

Tommy wasn't going anywhere. For as long as Philippa wished to keep kissing, Tommy was absolutely ready and willing to volunteer every minute of her time.

Her free hand curved against Philippa's side. There were far too many layers of clothes between Tommy's palm and Philippa's flesh, but even this much was heaven. Tommy hadn't expected to kiss Philippa like this again. The possibility that Philippa had yearned for this just as wantonly fanned the flames of Tommy's desire even higher.

Philippa might not *want* to want Tommy...but she *did* want her.

Tommy would think through her emotions on that later. She was far too busy enjoying the sweetness of Philippa's mouth to spoil a kiss with something so meddlesome as feelings.

For as long as Philippa's mouth melded with hers, she would—

The staccato slap of boots against the pavement yanked Tommy out of her haze of desire. She jerked her head toward the receding footsteps in time to see a young lad sprinting off with their basket hooked under his arm.

Shite. That ruffian was stealing what *they* had stolen!

"Stay here." Tommy took off at high speed, her supposedly gouty legs and rheumy eyes be damned.

Philippa did not *stay there*. From the sound of her breath and her boots, she was right behind Tommy.

Tommy didn't turn around to see. She was gaining on the boy, who was realizing that the ancient gulls from whom he'd just nicked a heavy basket were spryer old birds than anticipated.

He leapt over puddles and skidded through mud and gravel, dodging her outstretched cane.

Tommy swiped the tip of her cane against his arm, leaving a streak of mud but failing to dislodge the basket. She wouldn't wound a child—her sister Chloe had once *been* this child— but that illuminated manuscript would mean little to him and everything to Tommy and Philippa.

He slowed to duck down an alleyway.

"Run past!" came Philippa's breathless shout from just behind Tommy. "I've a plan!"

The boy sent a terrified look over his shoulder, causing him to trip and stumble.

Tommy put on a burst of speed and shot past the boy. She could have tackled him, but she didn't want to cause him physical harm—and Philippa had a plan. Nonetheless, Tommy unsheathed the blade to signal the boy ought to co-operate. She flung her arms wide, the sharp sword ready in one hand and the long wooden sheath outstretched in the other, blocking his path forward.

The boy clutched the basket to his chest.

"Them's my fresh apples!" Philippa quavered loudly. "They're for me. These are for you!"

She hurled something small and pink over his shoulder.

Rather than catch it, the lad flinched and ducked.

The reticule exploded against the rough brick lining the alley, sending a half-dozen guineas and shillings flying.

The lad dropped the basket into the dirt and scrambled to collect the coins.

"Over here," came a distant shout from the street behind them. It was Graham, hanging out of a hackney, with Jacob at the reins.

Philippa scooped up the basket and ran toward him.

Tommy sheathed the sword as she sprinted to the carriage. The wheels had already started moving when she leapt inside the open door.

Her last glimpse of the boy was him on his knees in the dirt, scrabbling for silver and gold. She hoped he ate well tonight.

Tommy fell back against the squab, her heart still racing.

"Well," Graham said. "That was subtle."

Through the open curtain, Jacob's broad shoulders could be seen shaking with laughter.

"If I did have apples in this basket, I would throw them at you," Philippa muttered.

"That's the spirit," Tommy agreed. "Throw a shoe at him. We'll deal with Jacob when we arrive."

But the problem wasn't her brothers.

They had come painfully close to executing a flawless mission, and Tommy had almost ruined everything by paying more attention to Philippa's mouth than to their surroundings. Kissing was *dangerous*.

"Might I inquire," said Philippa, "why there appears to be a stray rabbit inside this carriage?"

"It's Jacob's," Graham answered, as though that explained the matter.

If anything, they were lucky the carriage contained only a rabbit, rather than hawks or a Highland tiger.

"That's Lord Fluffinghop," Jacob called from the driver's seat. "Be glad you don't have apples. His Lordship would already be inside your basket, consuming them."

"At least Lord Fluffinghop isn't an attack rabbit," said Graham.

Philippa rolled her eyes. "There's no such creature as an 'attack rabbit.'"

Tommy and Graham looked at her.

"Er…is there?" Philippa stammered.

"First rule of Jacob," Tommy said. "Never assume anything."

"He's too old," Jacob explained. "If you want an attack rabbit, you have to train them young."

"Don't ask how he knows," Graham whispered.

26

*A*lmost home," Jacob called.

Home. For Tommy and her siblings. But as soon as she removed Philippa's wig and cosmetics, it would be time to return her to Mayfair and to her real life as a proper young lady.

Philippa rubbed her hands together. "I cannot wait to inspect the new volume for hidden messages."

Tommy gazed at her. She wasn't ready for their time to end.

Graham lifted his brows. "Do you think every volume contains a hidden letter?"

"*My* copy did," Philippa answered. "It might not be the only one."

He grinned. "Tommy will steal you as many books as you like."

"Philippa can help," Tommy said quickly. "I shan't nick a single illuminated manuscript without her."

More to the point, Tommy didn't wish to endure another day without Philippa. Then again, her presence had led to kissing—the highlight of the adventure—and the kissing had led to almost ruining the entire mission. If she'd let that happen, there wouldn't have been any future kisses.

The carriage pulled to a stop beside the Wynchesters' home. Jacob handed off the reins and opened the door to take possession of Lord Fluffinghop.

Graham waited for Tommy and Philippa to exit, and then entered their home not through a door, but by scaling the rear wall.

As soon as they entered the house, Philippa turned to Tommy and took a deep breath.

"I must apologize," she said. "My actions—"

"*Your* actions?" Tommy interrupted humorlessly. "I am the one who owes you an apology. I have never been less a Wynchester than the moment I allowed a child to make off with the thing I ought to be protecting. If it hadn't been for your quick thinking—"

"I finally *stopped* thinking," Philippa said. "All I do is think, and it gets me nowhere. *Thinking* is what kept me away from you, when all I want is to be back in your arms."

"When you...what?" Tommy stammered. Her chest lightened.

"I'll belong to some lord by the end of the season," Philippa said. "But until then, I don't want to waste a minute more of the time we *do* have together."

"W-what?" Tommy said again, even less elegantly. "You do want me?"

"Is it not obvious?" Philippa's expression was wry. "It wasn't to me. Not at first. That said, I've come across enough Sapphic literature to imagine sexual female relationships—"

"You *have?*" Clearly Tommy had been attending all the wrong reading circles.

"I have *now*. I researched the topic after I met you. All my life I believed I could not feel physical attraction because I had never felt that way about a man. I could become aroused...er...on my own..." Her face went bright red.

Tommy touched Philippa's fingers.

Philippa took her hand and held on tight. "I got to know you and trust you. The closer we became, the more...*fluttery* I felt inside. Perhaps I needed to feel connected to you and trust you before I could relax and unlock my desire. It's not that I don't 'mind' that you can be both a man and a woman. I *like* that about you. You're the first puzzle piece that fits. My feelings are real. I'm glad to have found them."

Tommy had tried so hard to keep her own inconvenient emotions tucked away where they would not bother Philippa. She could not quite credit that it wasn't a bother at all. That Philippa wanted her. That she felt the same. That she understood Tommy would never be Miss Thomasina or Horace Wynchester and liked her exactly for who and how she was. Sometimes masculine, sometimes feminine, and always Tommy.

Her voice was rough. "May I kiss you?"

"Yes." Philippa lifted her face and smiled. "I would like that very much."

Tommy claimed her mouth with a kiss.

The maps she had created in her mind of Philippa's kisses seemed inadequate for this new terrain. It was more intimate than before. This wasn't a tentative kiss between acquaintances testing each other, but the possessive kiss of two lovers who knew each other's mouths very well. Who returned time and again because there was nowhere else they'd rather be but locked in these arms, in this kiss.

There was nothing more courageous than admitting one's innermost feelings to another person. She loved Philippa more at this moment than she ever had before. What little hope she'd had of keeping her emotions buried was now gone forever.

This kiss was a kiss of truth. Of *I want you*, and *I accept you*. A kiss of honesty. Despite the wigs and the wrinkles, they were truly themselves. Vulnerable to each other in a way they never had been before.

It wasn't a game anymore, or flirtation or curiosity. It was real. It was Tommy and Philippa. Together at last, with nothing holding them back.

Until some eligible gentleman took Philippa away for good.

27

*P*hilippa adjusted the positioning of the circle of arm-chairs in the Duke of Faircliffe's ballroom. No one sniffed in disapproval or scolded her that moving a chair was conduct unbefitting a future viscountess. She was free to be Philippa.

Her reading circle would arrive in half an hour. Er, that was, the *Duchess of Faircliffe's* inaugural reading circle, which just happened to take place on the same day, at the same time, with the same people.

Philippa wanted everything to be perfect.

The room was empty other than the chairs and a pianoforte upon the dais. It wasn't quite the same feel as a room filled with books, but there was plenty of space for her friends.

"Thank you," she said to Tommy for the tenth time.

"I told you." Tommy swaggered up to her with an exagger-ated leer. "I shan't accept words. Only kisses."

Philippa grinned. "Even though I know better, it's difficult to remember that you're really Tommy and not Great-Aunt Wynchester."

"Does that mean no torrid kisses?" Tommy quavered in her old-lady voice.

"I'll allow *one*," Philippa answered primly.

Tommy wasted no time closing the distance between them. She pressed her lips to Philippa's. Everything else disappeared, until all that existed was Tommy's sweet kiss. Her mouth was hot, her lips soft and yielding.

Philippa knew these kisses now, gloried in them. They made her feel like a flower coming to bloom. Tilting toward the sun and unfurling each petal, presenting her innermost self for the taking. Kissing Tommy was like opening a window on the first day of spring and breathing in the scent of nature quickening to life.

Her favorite moments were the ones in which her arms were locked about Tommy, and their mouths were lost in a kiss. It didn't matter whether Tommy was old or young, man or woman. She felt and tasted like Tommy. Her embrace was warm and secure, her mouth sweet.

The feel of Tommy's tongue against hers awakened Philippa's body in ways she had once believed inaccessible. Her breasts felt larger, heavier, her nipples straining as if in search of even greater closeness. Desire pooled between Philippa's legs. Tommy wasn't even touching her there, and it was happening.

Every part of Philippa's body was flickering to life.

But time was running out. Philippa's parents would marry her off before the end of the season. She was determined to grab on to Tommy with both hands for as long as she could.

"You realize you could attend this reading circle as Miss Thomasina," she said when at last they pulled away from each other. "My mother isn't here, and Chloe's door is always open to Wynchesters."

Tommy shrugged. "If I must disguise my true self to attend either way, then what does it matter which role I choose? Great-Aunt Wynchester is more fun than Miss Thomasina."

Philippa's lips parted. Tommy's ease with costumes was a

good point. An excellent point. In fact...choosing the right one might matter very much.

After all, it wasn't as though Miss Thomasina could propose. But if Philippa rejected Captain Northrup and all other offers, mayhap her parents would then consent to a courtship with a baron.

"What is that clever brain of yours ruminating about?" Tommy tilted her head. "You're making the queerest expression."

"I was thinking how unfair it was that only men can propose to women."

Tommy grinned. "Who needs to be married? The 'Ladies of Llangollen' have lived happily together for four decades and counting. They are both mistresses of their shared home, and exemplary hostesses to fashionable and unfashionable alike. Lord Byron, the Duke of Wellington, and so on. And then there are romantic partners like the actresses who—"

Philippa understood Tommy's point. Of course she had heard of the famous Irish lesbians who, Philippa refrained from pointing out, left their homes because they could no longer live *in* society and were now relegated to the fringes of it. Celebrated writers and poets like Byron and Shelley and Wordsworth needn't follow the same rules as a young lady of the ton.

The couples Tommy named needn't worry about the censure of Patronesses. Nor did they run a reading circle whose membership contained many other young ladies whose standing in society would be jeopardized by even the hint of scandal. If Philippa was ruined, association with her could tarnish her friends' reputations, risk their charity projects, and jeopardize Philippa's carefully cultivated alliances with other philanthropic ladies and organizations.

It wasn't just Philippa's reputation hanging in the balance. The lives and well-being of children and the less fortunate were at stake as well.

As much as she might dream of being the sort of person with no ties or cares, who could just move to North Wales with her lover and not give a fig what the rest of the world thought about it, that was simply not her reality. She couldn't be *happy* knowing she chose herself over her friends, her family, and the futures of those who needed her aid the most.

Philippa shook her head. "First, we need to stop Captain Northrup. Securing his public confession will be justice for Damaris, and also have the splendid secondary effect of his losing favor in the eyes of my parents."

At that point, if Baron Vanderbean swooped in, Philippa and Tommy could do as they pleased with no one the wiser. A young man stealing a kiss from his betrothed was hardly the stuff of scandal broth.

Philippa and Tommy could just...*live*.

Chloe strode into the room with Tiglet in her arms. Several members of the reading circle followed close behind.

"I was so worried." Sybil rushed into the room. "I feared our sisterhood was to be disbanded indefinitely without our leader. And what about the libraries? Philippa is the one who comes up with the ideas and makes the arrangements. I just make the charts."

Philippa's chest filled with pleasure. "Your charts hold us together and keep us on schedule."

Sybil grinned. "Can you say that louder for Florentia's sake?"

Florentia rolled her eyes. "Philippa is wonderful. Your charts aren't terrible."

Sybil fanned herself. "High praise indeed."

Philippa took Tiglet from Chloe. "Where are Gracie and Jessica?"

"Gracie is late." Florentia lowered her voice. "Jessica wasn't allowed to attend. Chloe is a duchess now but still a Wynchester."

Philippa winced. Poor Chloe. And...poor Baron Vanderbean. If a duchess was not acceptable to all, then a foreign baron would fare even worse. As would his baroness—and the people who counted on her.

She hugged herself. A courtship with the imaginary baron was a fantasy. Marrying well was the only solution, just as her mother had preached for years. Even if it meant a lifetime of grieving the opportunity she would rather have had.

If Philippa forged a public connection with the Wynchesters, she would lose many of the people she loved—and let down thousands more.

She took a deep breath. "I'm very sorry to hear about Jessica. If you don't mind, Chloe, I'd like to pen her a letter while I'm here."

"It's no problem." Chloe and Tommy exchanged troubled glances, likely coming to the same conclusion Philippa had just reached.

She rolled back her shoulders. "Let's begin our meeting."

Damaris stepped forward. "Have you learned anything else from the manuscripts? Did you uncover information about Agnes and Katherine?"

"Unfortunately," Philippa said, "the binding of our new book does not appear to be hiding secret letters. We are forced to look for clues elsewhere."

"But fortunately," Chloe continued. "My brother's informants discovered references to poor relations in parish records. Two spinster cousins living in a cottage on the property. They were apparently lifelong tenants. Sir Reginald Northrup left no record of their involvement with the illuminated manuscripts, but he controlled the younger woman's inheritance. It was how she paid her rent."

"Cousins," Sybil repeated. "They were both Northrups?"

"Agnes Northrup and Katherine Claybourne," Philippa answered.

Damaris frowned. "Different surnames. Were the ladies related on their maternal side, like Captain Northrup and I are?"

"Mayhap," Tommy said as Great-Aunt Wynchester. "Mayhap not."

"Intriguingly," Philippa continued, "we have uncovered no eyewitness account of Sir Reginald actively working on any manuscripts. He spent his days making merry."

Sybil frowned. "But if there is no account of Agnes and Katherine's involvement, either—"

"Clean your ears," barked Great-Aunt Wynchester. "Sir *Reginald* left no such record."

Florentia's gaze sharpened. "You mean..."

Philippa nodded. "The spinster...cousins...were well known in the village for their good works and artistic talent. Graham discovered old letters and a diary that mentions the frequent sight of both ladies surrounded by ink and parchment at a table in the cottage. Sir Reginald was the trustee for Agnes's inheritance—and her landlord."

"Convenient," Florentia muttered. "For Sir Reginald."

Philippa nodded grimly. "When he realized the commercial value of their unique talents, the ladies were thereafter kept so busy, they were rarely seen in the village again."

Sybil's eyes widened. "Did you bring the diary and letters?"

"Second best." Philippa handed out the copies Marjorie had made.

"Maybe they're not cousins," Sybil whispered to Florentia in excitement. "Maybe they were in love."

"Or good friends," Florentia responded. "Either way, their neighbors won't have written it down for you to ogle over."

"Some of us can read between lines," Sybil informed her. "Philippa, what do you think? Were Agnes and Katherine—"

"I'm late!" Gracie rushed into the ballroom with her bonnet hanging half off her head. "What did I miss?"

"Thank God," Philippa muttered. She was not ready to discuss lifelong Sapphic relationships with her reading circle, hypothetical or otherwise.

Lady Eunice handed Gracie one of the letters. "Fraud is in Captain Northrup's blood."

Florentia curled her lip. "Sir Reginald was no artist. He was a liar and an opportunist, just like his disreputable descendant who blithely stole from Damaris."

Sybil pulled Tiglet away from her earrings. "The Prince Regent is about to christen a chamber of the Royal Military Academy after an unethical landlord whose only contribution to illuminated manuscripts was stealing credit from the female artists who created them."

Gracie drew herself up tall. "Can we stop him?"

"We have two months until the season opening celebration." Florentia answered.

"We have less than that," Philippa corrected. "The replacements for the...er...*borrowed* manuscripts won't pass close inspection. That could mean weeks or days. We must act quickly."

"Act quickly by doing what?" Lady Eunice took Tiglet from Sybil. "We have no proof of Northrup's perfidy."

"We do have it," Philippa said. "In a hidden message."

All gazes swung in her direction.

"That is, we have three-fourths of it," she amended. "I've

brought two consecutive volumes. You remember the decorative markings on the edges? Watch what happens to the parts that appear to swirl off into nothing."

After putting on her gloves, she stood the Cambridge manuscript next to the Electi Society manuscript and turned the books toward the reading circle.

Two columns of five equidistant half-moons of extravagantly decorative flourishes dotted along the vertical edges of each book. Each half-moon measured two inches tall and one inch wide... until two volumes aligned next to each other.

Gracie gasped. "They match up!"

The half-moons became full circles, each pair combining to form a single cohesive decorative element. If they had all four volumes to place tightly together, three long rows of circular flourishes would form along the edges, in a five-by-three grid.

Florentia tilted her head. "It reminds me of our cipher. Is there a pattern to the symbols?"

"It is not a cipher. Here, this will help." Philippa stacked the books on their sides, making three horizontal rows of flourishes. "The loops and swirls and ivy disguise the meaning." She unfolded the letter from Katherine and pointed at the similar floral illustrations at the beginning and end. "What do you see here?"

"The top one is an A," Damaris said at once. "And the bottom one is a K."

"There they are again!" Gracie pointed at the edge of the manuscripts with excitement. "I see it now. If you ignore the pomegranates and ivy and the extra swirls, they're letters."

"The spinsters weren't master cryptographers," Damaris said. "They hid the truth in the open."

Lady Eunice gazed in wonder. "Their message is elegant in its simplicity. Incomplete without its partner, and disguised in beauty. It only makes sense when pressed close together."

"We still need the first volume," Philippa said with a sigh.

"We've contacted every club, library, and manuscript collector in England," Chloe explained. "No collections still contain one."

Damaris's eyes narrowed. "Uncle Northrup has that volume. It was the one I based the cipher on. Small wonder all the other copies disappeared. Uncle won't let his out of the house. He locks his manuscript in a strongbox inside his library."

"A wooden strongbox?" Chloe said hopefully. "One we could take an axe to?"

"An iron one, I'm afraid. He keeps the key around his neck."

"That's excellent news," Tommy said.

The bluestockings looked at her with expressions of befuddlement.

"What part of 'kept in an iron strongbox' is good news, Great-Aunt Wynchester?" Sybil asked.

"The hardest bit is solved," Tommy answered. "We know where to find the book and the key." She looked at Chloe. "Have you got a plan yet?"

"I'm working on it," she murmured. "As soon as we call the others to the Planning Parlor—"

"I believe a mother ought to be allowed to see her *daughter*," shrilled a falsely jovial female voice from the corridor.

Philippa wanted to sink into the parquet. What in the dickens was her mother doing here?

She wrapped up the manuscripts and placed them back into their large basket. The lid closed just in time. Mother burst through the open doorway with a triumphant expression, followed immediately by the Faircliffe's stone-faced butler . . . and Captain Northrup.

"Uncle," Damaris said in surprise. "Why are you here?"

"I didn't mean to be," he said in obvious confusion. "I called at the York residence, hoping for a moment with the daughter...Ah, yes, there you are, Miss York."

"'The daughter'?" Tommy blustered in outrage as Great-Aunt Wynchester. "Green bucks with no sense of romance. Why, in my day——"

"That'll do, Aunt," Chloe interrupted smoothly. "As you can see, sir, you've caught us in the middle of a ladies' reading circle, as I've no doubt Mrs. York must have informed you."

"She forgot to mention that detail." Captain Northrup slanted Philippa's mother a dry look, but made no move to bow and apologize for the interruption. Instead, he swaggered farther into the ballroom. "Shall I pull up a chair?"

"*Ladies'* reading circle," Tommy repeated belligerently. "Perhaps this young pup requires an ear trumpet."

"As I told you, Captain," Mother said quickly, "Philippa is very popular and important. She is the bosom friend of the duke and duchess."

"*I'd like* to befriend your bosom," Tommy murmured in Philippa's ear.

Philippa elbowed Great-Aunt Wynchester in the side.

Lady Eunice set Tiglet on the floor and gave the kitten's backside a little pat. "Go," she whispered. "Fetch the key."

Tiglet shot past Captain Northrup and out through the open doorway.

"Brilliant," Chloe said. "Now Tiglet is halfway to Islington."

"It was worth a try," Lady Eunice muttered.

"*Homing kitten*," Tommy whispered. "Not 'attack bunny.'"

"I would offer both of you a chair," Chloe informed the interlopers, "if I weren't entertaining invited guests."

Philippa winced. "Oof," she whispered to Tommy. "If Mother despised your sister *before*..."

"It's Chloe," Tommy whispered back. "She has a plan."

"I suppose Captain Northrup might stay for a cup of tea," Chloe continued. Her eyes were not on Northrup, but rather Philippa's mother. "Between me and my darling aunt, Philippa is *so* well chaperoned, wouldn't you say, Mrs. York? Surely a mother wouldn't wish to stifle a blossoming romance with a relative's unnecessary presence."

"Stifle?" Mother stammered. "No, I...Yes, naturally you and your aunt are fine chaperones. I'll just...I'll just nip back on home, then. I was only pointing out the house to dear Captain Northrup, that's all."

"Of course," Chloe agreed. "I wouldn't have thought otherwise. I am happy to escort you to the door. And because we're such fine chaperones, you can have no objection to Philippa accompanying me tomorrow to visit a dear friend? I'll return Philippa the very next evening. She'll only be away for one night."

"I...Well...That is..." Mother stared around the room helplessly.

Chloe had trapped her neatly. Mother could not object to Chloe's chaperonage, now that she believed Philippa and Northrup had a blossoming romance.

"Bring her home before supper time," Mother said, as if they were the sort of family who took their meals together.

Philippa's chest lightened. Thirty-six hours of freedom awaited!

"I'll see to it." Chloe herded Mrs. York out of the ballroom. "If you'll follow me, please."

From the corridor, Mother twisted to send meaningful looks over her shoulder at Philippa.

Philippa stared back blankly.

Mother's mouth moved in exaggeration. *Hook him.*

Chloe dragged her out of sight.

"Well?" Captain Northrup prompted. "Wasn't I to be served tea?"

"It's over there on the sideboard," Tommy barked as Great-Aunt Wynchester. "Mayhap the captain needs an opera glass as well as an ear trumpet."

"Whatever tea is on the sideboard is *cold*," Northrup said with obvious disdain.

"And you're an uninvited guest," Damaris shot back. "Not everyone adulates you, Uncle. If you wish to be fawned over, I'm sure you've a tall stack of calling cards to return."

Northrup's smile was icy. "You're right. I have too many cards to possibly respond to them all. So I've planned a small gathering of one hundred close friends next week. Your mother has agreed to play hostess at my town house and assures me *you* will be part of the receiving line."

Damaris sputtered incoherently.

"And you, Miss York." Northrup struck what he likely believed to be an impressive pose. "I shall save *you* the first dance."

Tommy dry-heaved dramatically.

Everyone turned to look at her.

She stopped mid-heave and patted the corners of her mouth with a handkerchief. "I saw the cat do it and thought I'd give it a try."

Philippa wished she could pretend to cough up a fur ball every time Northrup glanced her direction.

Her voice shook with fury. "I cannot believe you would flaunt your treachery in front of poor Damaris."

Northrup arched his brows. "What treachery? I'm a hero."

"*Damaris* created that cipher. She shared it with this very reading circle long before she shared it with *you*."

Northrup smirked. "Is that how you remember it? Ladies' inferior brains are notoriously unreliable."

Philippa straightened. "We'll swear to it."

"To whom, pet? No one's asking you." Northrup looked bored. "I told the brigadier general the idea had come to me whilst explaining my illustrious family history to my niece. That must be how she learned of it."

"I learned of it," Damaris said through obviously clenched teeth, "because it was my idea, which I voluntarily taught to you and suggested might be helpful in the war."

"There, you see?" Northrup smirked at her. "No hard feelings all around. My niece voluntarily relinquished all rights to it—"

"That's not what I—"

"—and I claimed them," Northrup finished. "*My* cipher. *My* reward."

Chloe swept back into the ballroom, took one look at the furious expressions, and held her arm out toward Northrup. "Oh, Captain, surely you'll do a duchess the honor of allowing her to escort you to the door. Dare I hope I'm to have the second set at your soirée?"

"Share the second dance with a duchess?" Northrup placed Chloe's hand around the crook of his arm. "I believe I can make room on my list."

"How can he have thought that offer was sincere?" Florentia burst out the moment Northrup was out of sight. "She was sweeping him out of the house like the rubbish he is."

"I won't do it," Damaris spat. "I won't be in the receiving line at a party in which he's to be idolized for something *I* did."

"You have to," Tommy said. "It's our chance."

"A slim one," Florentia said. "He'll be on high alert. He already kept the manuscript under lock and key. After the reception we gave him this afternoon, he knows not to trust any of us."

"He trusts Chloe," Tommy said. "And he wants Philippa."

"He wants my dowry and knows I am honor-bound to obey my parents," Philippa corrected. "Marrying me gives him control."

"Good riddance." Chloe reentered the room and lowered her voice. "I've a plan. We'll work out the details with the others tomorrow."

Philippa arched a brow. "Didn't you just tell my mother you were stealing me away for a couple days, to visit a 'friend' in the country?"

"Islington is absolutely part of a country. And did I say we'd spend the night with a 'friend'? I meant 'close relative.'" Chloe's eyes sparkled with mischief. "I thought you might like to visit my dear sibling Tommy."

28

The long, wide Wynchester dining table was full of food and surrounded by Wynchesters. Next to Chloe was her husband, the Duke of Faircliffe. And next to Tommy was Philippa, whose cheeks flushed pink from laughing so hard. It was a delight to have her at the table. Her reactions to the Wynchesters' tales were priceless.

"I barely escaped the Circuit Court with my wig intact that summer." Tommy sent a dark look across the table. "Thanks to Jacob and his meddling beasts."

He pointed his fork at her. "I believe you mean, 'Thank you, Jacob, for the trained ferrets who were instrumental in our client's acquittal.'"

Footmen approached the table to replace the supper trays with dessert platters. Tiglet scampered behind them.

Graham sagged back in his chair. "I can't eat another bite."

Philippa's eyes lit up at a tray of almond cakes. "I volunteer to take up his slack."

"I told you she'd make a fine Wynchester," said Elizabeth. "A better one than Graham. What self-respecting Wynchester declines cake?"

"An ex-Wynchester." Marjorie's eyes shone. "Philippa can take his place."

"What?" Graham slapped the table in mock outrage. "There's no voting *out*. There's only voting *in*."

"Is that why this table is so large?" Faircliffe waggled his brows at Chloe. "It's meant to accommodate future Wynchesters? I suppose we can help with that."

Tommy glanced at Philippa. Faircliffe referred not to romantic partners, but to their future children. Was that something Philippa wanted? It would be just one more thing Tommy could not give her.

"This enormous house holds more than mere Wynchesters." Jacob accepted a large portion of fruit and gingerbread. "We also entertain friends and host the occasional supper party."

"You *do?*" Philippa sent a surprised gaze toward Tommy. "I've not heard even a whisper of such an event."

"Because we don't invite the bon ton," Elizabeth said.

"Don't worry," said Tommy. "You can be bad ton, like me."

Elizabeth grinned. "Philippa, you are officially a disreputable party. You were wonderfully terrible at stealing the Electi Society manuscript."

"*I* stole the Electi manuscript," Graham said.

"And Tommy and Philippa allowed a *child* to make off with the booty. How? Were the two of you...distracted?" Marjorie widened her eyes innocently, as though she hadn't already had the story from Graham. "Whatever could have held your attention?"

Philippa's face went bright red. "It was Tommy's fault."

"Absolutely my fault," Tommy agreed. "And I would do it again. Indeed, if you're ever to be bested by a child, 'I was busy kissing my accomplice' is a fine excuse."

Philippa made a choking sound and buried her face in her hands.

"So noted," Graham said.

"Unless your accomplice is a hedgehog," Jacob added.

"Or the time . . . " Marjorie began.

And her siblings were off again, laughing and exaggerating their exploits—not that many of their adventures left much room for exaggeration.

Faircliffe was not looking at Tommy and Philippa in horror or even prurient curiosity. Chloe must have already told him about their romantic interest in each other. The duke appeared to have taken the news in stride. Perhaps he was happier than ever that Philippa had rejected his suit. Tommy certainly was. Philippa would not be here with Tommy and her siblings otherwise.

"Are they too much?" she asked Philippa.

Philippa's eyes widened, and she shook her head. "After a lifetime of dining alone, I doubt I shall ever experience 'too much' fun. Are they truly this marvelous all the time?"

"They can't help themselves." Tommy grinned. "Elizabeth has even woken herself up giggling maniacally."

"Not maniacally," Elizabeth said from across the table. "Giggling with cold calculation."

"There's no privacy at the dinner table," Tommy whispered.

The corner of Philippa's mouth twitched. "Maybe later."

Tommy's pulse leapt. A year ago, when she'd first laid eyes on Philippa, Tommy had never imagined she would one day invite her into their home and sit about the family dinner table as herself.

Tonight she was not Great-Aunt Wynchester or Baron Vanderbean. She was just Tommy. No wigs, no cosmetics. She wore trousers and a frock coat because they were comfortable, and no cravat because starch was not comfortable at all. She didn't look like a man or a woman. She looked and felt like herself.

Being accepted and loved had always been a dream of hers. She'd known she was different from a young age. If she could not be like the others, then she would be different on purpose. She could be anyone she pleased.

Lately, she realized the person she most wanted to be was herself. She was already a legion of other characters and caricatures. The only place she could take off her disguise was at home with her family.

And now, with Philippa.

One supper was not the same as pledging a lifetime together. But it was more than Tommy had hoped for and enough to awaken dormant dreams again.

Philippa wiped the corner of her mouth. "Those were the best almond cakes I've ever tasted."

Tommy had forgotten about dessert. All she wanted to taste were Philippa's kisses. There was nothing sweeter.

"Shall we remove to the sitting room?" asked Elizabeth.

Graham rose to his feet.

"Not us." Chloe made a suspiciously bland expression. "It has been a lovely evening, but Lawrence and I are required at home."

Tommy waited but did not feel the usual pang at Chloe leaving early. Philippa was here. Tommy was thinking of sneaking away, too. She and Chloe were still part of each other's lives, but those lives had expanded to include more people.

"Mm-hm," Elizabeth said, wiggling her eyebrows. "'Required' at home. Very busy schedules at nine p.m. whilst Parliament is conveniently not in session."

"*Very* busy," Chloe said firmly. The look she exchanged with Lawrence could have set the house on fire. "We'll see you at Northrup's soirée."

"Northrup." Elizabeth rolled her eyes. "Don't remind me."

"Remind *me* as much as you like." Philippa's blue eyes shone. "I cannot wait for that smug liar to get his come-uppance."

"Did you bring the manuscript?" Jacob asked.

"I did. It's with my valise, which is... Where is my valise?"

"Upstairs." Tommy willed her cheeks not to heat. "In your guest chamber, which is not my bedroom."

"But *is* next door to it," Elizabeth whispered.

With their usual noise and affection, the siblings managed to wish Chloe and Lawrence goodbye and then relocate to the large sitting room.

"There you are!" Philippa scooped Tiglet up from the floor and cradled the kitten to her chest. "He was tranquil as could be in the carriage, and then shot out through the open window as soon as your house came into sight. I keep waiting for him to stop running away from me."

"He doesn't run away," Jacob reminded her. "He goes home."

"I was taking him there," Philippa said. "On my lap."

"He gets excited," Elizabeth said. "He wants to be a good kitty."

"He *is* a good kitty," Jacob said firmly. "All animals are very good at being exactly what they are."

Tommy wished it were just as easy for people like her. She didn't want to play a role. She wanted to be exactly who she was. Especially today.

Philippa spending the night seemed so... *official*. Tommy wished it could be the start of many more just like this one.

In the sitting room, the siblings dispersed to their usual pursuits.

Graham flung himself onto a sofa between two end tables piled high with magazines and newspapers. Elizabeth leaned her sword stick against the pianoforte and began to play an aria from her favorite operetta. Jacob lay on his stomach, trying to coax what Tommy hoped was a sweet cuddly hamster and not a snake out from under a sofa.

Marjorie escaped upstairs, likely to nick Philippa's manuscript and take it up to her attic studio to practice some light forgery.

"This would be a lovely room to read in," Philippa said wistfully.

"We have an entire shelf of books." Graham gestured toward the wall behind him. "You're welcome to read them."

Philippa cast him a sorrowful look, as though the idea of a single shelf for books was embarrassing, and moved to a bay window filled with cushions. "Chloe told me I was welcome to her nook."

"Try it." The words flew from Tommy's mouth without hesitation, surprising her more than anyone.

It was *Chloe's* spot. No one had sat in it since Chloe had left. But now, as Philippa settled on the yellow cushion and none of the other siblings took any particular notice, Tommy realized they had all adjusted to Chloe's absence.

It wasn't that the window seat was no longer important. It was that it could now be important for new people and new reasons.

"How is the reading nook?" she asked.

Philippa patted the cushion beside her. "Come and find out."

Tommy sat next to Philippa in the bay window, hips and shoulders touching. It was dark outside, so the curtains were closed, making the nook seem even cozier. "This *is* nice."

Not just the seating arrangements. The moment. Having Philippa fit in as though she were made to be part of Tommy's life…it was splendid.

"Your siblings aren't looking," Philippa whispered. "You can kiss me."

"Her siblings are listening," Graham said without lowering his broadsheet. "But don't let that stop you."

At Philippa's mortified expression, Tommy kissed both

sides of Philippa's mouth, then rubbed her nose against Philippa's. "Ignore them."

"Ha!" Jacob pulled something from beneath the sofa. "I've got you now, Apophis, my boy."

"Whatever you do," Tommy whispered to Philippa, "do not look to see what Jacob pulled out from under the furniture."

Philippa immediately glanced over Tommy's shoulder and her eyes widened.

"Whatever you do," Tommy amended, "do not tell *me* what he found."

Philippa grinned at Tommy. "I'd like to know what *you* normally do here in the sitting room."

Graham's hand poked up from atop his broadsheet and pointed toward the bookshelf again.

"I'll show you." Tommy retrieved her messy pile of pencils and foolscap from the shelf and brought it to a writing desk near the windows. Her blood seemed to rush beneath her skin, like racing a horse bareback on a bright spring day.

Dancing with Philippa was magical, kissing her, holding her, but so were moments like these. Quiet togetherness with the family. Philippa taking part in Tommy's world, instead of Tommy putting on a costume to be part of Philippa's.

Philippa peered at the stack of papers on the desk. "What is it?"

"Nude drawings I made of you," Tommy whispered back.

"What?" Philippa squeaked.

"Maps," Elizabeth called out. "Tommy is a cartographer."

Philippa stared at her. "You *are?*"

"I don't often sail to distant shores," Tommy admitted. "My specialty is more mundane."

"She can tell you the height and width of every door and window in Carlton House," said Graham. "How many paces from one room to the other, which hinges are rusted, which floorboards squeak..."

"Mundane," Philippa repeated. "I see."

"Carlton House is a silly example," Tommy said. "Those maps are only partially complete." She flipped through the loose pages until she found a sequence of eight drawings and handed them to Philippa.

Philippa paged through them in wonder. "This is my parents' town house. The ground floor in every detail. You know it better than I do. Were you going to break in and steal something else?"

"You, if necessary." Tommy shrugged. "Your parents are always locking you in your room for some imagined slight. If you need to be rescued, I want to be prepared."

"They don't *lock* me in my room," Philippa said. "They send me there when I disappoint them, but usually I keep myself shuttered up on my own. It's easier for everyone."

"Do you want me to sneak in and kidnap your parents?"

"No," Philippa said with a laugh. "They're not perfect, but they're the only ones I have and I'd like to keep them. Maybe the key is compromise. Behave *very* badly, but without anyone noticing."

Tommy gave Philippa her most disreputable leer. "Tell me more about how badly you'd like to behave."

"Baron Vanderbean, for example," Philippa said casually. "His title makes him marginally acceptable, which pleases my parents. And he's actually *you*, which pleases *me*."

"He's not me. If the aim is more time together, a better costume would be Great-Aunt Wynchester or even Baron Vanderbean's sister, Miss Honoria Wynchester. Then we wouldn't even need a chaperone. I could pose as Miss Thomasina, the One Reputable Wynchester. That name has never been mentioned in a scandal column."

Philippa wrinkled her nose. "None of those would be good enough for my family, scandal columns or no. 'Baron Vanderbean' is a societally acceptable suitor whom I enjoy spending time with. If my parents agreed to a courtship, that is a middle ground I could live with."

Tommy could not.

She tried not to be disappointed at Philippa's quick dismissal of the idea. Tommy had gained her interest by pretending to be Horace Wynchester, and mayhap could only keep it by continuing the charade.

It was her own fault, she supposed. She'd begun as Baron Vanderbean and proven it could work, so of course Philippa would wish to continue on. If only Tommy had taken her family's advice and introduced herself *as* herself to begin with…

Philippa gave a little smile. "You said that he was the most comfortable disguise."

Yes. "Horace" was an easy costume.

But Tommy wanted to live and love without a disguise.

"I haven't forgotten our agreement," she heard herself say. "Publicly, Baron Vanderbean shall be at your disposal through the grand celebration in January."

Philippa dropped her voice. "Privately, all I need is Tommy Wynchester and her torrid kisses. Now. Tonight."

"Torrid, are they?" Tommy gave an extra swagger. "You haven't seen torrid yet."

She pressed her lips to Philippa's, coaxing them to part so that Tommy could show her with her tongue just how torrid things could be.

"No seductions in the sitting room," Elizabeth called out.

Tommy burst out laughing and pulled away.

Philippa didn't laugh. Her gaze was hot on Tommy's, and her smile was slow and wicked. "Shall we go upstairs?"

29

*P*hilippa didn't really mean to do the sensual things Tommy yearned to do with her...Did she?

Tommy's limbs were unsteady as she led the way to the marble stairs. Philippa's mother didn't expect her home until the following evening. Night had fallen hours ago.

Her brain was whirring like a malfunctioning clock, a thousand gears spinning at once. It was difficult to reconcile the mundanity of climbing stairs with the reality of having Philippa right next to her as she did so. Philippa was close enough to touch. To kiss.

Tommy brushed her fingers against Philippa's. They interlocked, caught. Now Philippa's hand was in hers, their fingers laced together. When they reached the landing, Tommy took Philippa's other hand and pulled her close. Tommy smiled as she lowered her mouth to Philippa's. Like Tommy's siblings, the Wynchesters' servants were trustworthy and accepting. She and Philippa needn't hurry, nor hide. They could savor this kiss.

Tonight, the magic could last as long as they wished.

Philippa's mouth was soft and pliant. Her kisses were familiar now, which made them all the more special. This was *Philippa's* welcoming mouth, *Philippa's* eager tongue. She felt like home.

Tommy was with the person she dreamed about. Each detail was too precious to forget, so Tommy committed them all to memory. She felt the warmth of Philippa's skin, smelled the orange blossoms and vanilla in her hair.

Every time they kissed, she refined the map in her mind of Philippa. The precise distance between one corner of her mouth and the other. The round curve of her cheek, the pert angle of her nose, the warm softness of the lobe of her ear and the beckoning flutter of the pulse point just behind it. All the places their lips had tasted, as well as all the places yet to come.

One day. If Tommy was lucky.

She forced herself to lift her lips just enough to break the kiss. "I suppose I should show you to your guest chamber."

"I suppose that is what we ought to do," Philippa answered, her face still tilted upward toward Tommy, as if hoping for another kiss.

Tommy gave her one. Two. Ten. It was impossible to pull away.

"Or," she said when she had once again gathered the mental fortitude to separate her mouth from Philippa's. "You could sleep with me. If you wished."

Philippa's eyes widened and her breath audibly caught.

"It could just be sleep," Tommy added in a rush. "It wouldn't have to be anything more."

Philippa brushed her lips against Tommy's. "But it *could* be, if I wanted more?"

"Um...yes." Tommy's heart was beating too quickly to allow for rational thought. Philippa had just said—what that meant was—"Yes, 'more' is a definite possibility."

"I choose that," Philippa said. "I want more. With you."

"You...*do*." Tommy nodded jerkily. "So do I. I choose you. I choose us."

Philippa squeezed Tommy's hand, then turned to face the corridor. "Show me the way."

With their entwined fingers, Tommy pointed out each door as they passed by. "Elizabeth's rooms. Marjorie's rooms. Guest rooms which contain your valise and a bed that you are welcome to sleep in though I hope you do not. And my rooms, just on the other side of yours."

She paused at the threshold to Philippa's guest chamber.

The four-poster bed was there in the center, perfectly made, fringed silk hangings tied. The windows had been drawn, but a low fire behind the screen cast enough light to see her tall valise beside a large dressing table with plenty of space to work.

"It looks very inviting," Philippa observed.

Tommy nodded. "I shall compliment the maids on your behalf. They will be pleased to hear it."

"What will they say when they enter in the morning and everything is just how they left it?"

"They'll say, 'My work here is done. What an accommodating houseguest. Tommy should invite that wonderful Miss York more often.'"

"In that case...We should leave it fully untouched." Philippa moved toward her valise. "I presume Marjorie has already made off with the manuscript."

"Undoubtedly." Tommy rushed forward to pick up the valise. "As soon as she scampered upstairs, I knew she had found it."

"Does your overflowing dressing room have space for my valise?" Philippa teased.

"I will toss all of my wardrobes from the window if necessary," Tommy promised.

"What will the neighbors say?"

"We're Wynchesters. A flying wardrobe or two won't be

half as unusual as the acrobatics they've glimpsed Graham doing. They might even think it was part of his act."

Philippa's brows shot up. "Act?"

"He was a performer in a circus until Bean found him. I mean, Baron Vanderbean. *Our* Baron Vanderbean." Tommy opened the door to her bedchamber.

"*Is* there a Baron Vanderbean?" Philippa followed Tommy inside. "A current one, that is?"

Philippa was asking about one of the family's most tightly kept secrets. But at this point, she already knew Tommy *wasn't* Baron Vanderbean, and had no doubt begun to suspect the truth.

"No," Tommy admitted. She placed Philippa's valise next to the bed. "There's just me."

Philippa's eyes sparkled. "Exactly as I suspected. I admit I am delighted. Thank you for trusting me with the truth."

"Trusting people is hard. And scary. For the longest time, I only trusted members of my family. But I trust you, too. And I..."

...want you to be part of my family.

Tommy crossed to the door before Philippa could see her face. After securing the lock, she left the key in the hole so that Philippa could leave whenever she pleased. But in the meantime, no maids would accidentally walk in on them.

"Now what?" Philippa asked. "Do we help each other into our night rails?"

"*I* do not require assistance undressing, because I am wearing exceedingly practical trousers." Tommy gave a ribald leer. "But I shall be delighted to help *you* out of any clothing you wish to shed."

"You'll have to." Philippa's voice was shy. "None of my gowns were designed for a woman to don or doff by herself.

I'm beginning to suspect it's all part of a plot to keep us helpless."

"Or to make moments like these," Tommy said. "Perhaps ladies' clothing was designed with seduction in mind. *I* shall certainly feel very seduced with each ribbon I untie."

"And then we'll do...anything I want?"

"Only what you want, and everything that you want," Tommy promised. "You need merely say the word, and your wish shall be granted."

Philippa paled. "Say the words...aloud?"

Tommy hesitated. Philippa thought she wanted more, but did she really? Reading Sapphic literature—in books that Tommy hoped to get her hands on—was not at all the same as doing the things it described. Perhaps they were moving too fast.

Kissing was relatively tame. What if the next step frightened Philippa and caused her to run away again?

"I shall remove my boots," Tommy said, narrating aloud to show Philippa there was nothing to fear from spoken words. She sat on the edge of her bed. "I often do this in my dressing room, but today I'm dressed as me, so there are no cosmetics to remove, or a costume to put away."

The wariness in Philippa's eyes was replaced by curiosity. "Dressing as a man is dressing as you?"

"I'm not dressed as a man," Tommy said. "I'm a person in trousers and a comfortable shirt. If I were dressed as a man, I would be wearing a neckcloth that could double as a picnic blanket, and side whiskers furrier than your kitten."

Philippa snickered. "*Your* kitten."

"*Our* kitten," Tommy allowed. She placed her boots beside the fireplace and stepped back to the warmth of her thick carpet. "You can leave your boots on if you like, or you can remove them yourself. Or you can order me to my knees and bid me to remove them for you."

"I cannot *command* you," Philippa stammered. "Can I?"

Tommy smiled. "You might find you like it very much."

Philippa's cheeks flushed and she hurried to the armchair. "I'll take them off myself. I am not completely helpless, no matter what my clothes might suggest."

"Asking for help doesn't make you helpless."

"Not even if it's something I could do myself?"

Tommy arched her brows. "*Could* you boil your own water for tea, if you wanted to?"

Philippa made a face.

"Before you tell me that's different," Tommy said, "ask yourself why. How will anyone know what you want, and where, and how, unless you tell them?"

"It's that simple?" Philippa said doubtfully. "I just say 'kiss me' and you'll kiss me?"

"Every time." Tommy grinned. "Try it."

Philippa stood, set her boots beside the fireplace, and turned back around with determination. "Kiss me."

Tommy strode to meet her but did not reach for her. "Where shall I kiss you? On the top of your head? On your elbow?"

Philippa's eyes widened and her lips parted.

"Ah," Tommy said softly. "Your big brain just had the most magnificent ideas. I very much want to kiss you in all of the secret places that just crossed your mind. Where shall I begin?"

This time, Philippa did not wait for Tommy to cease her teasing. She reached for her and kissed her deeply. Tommy, in trousers and stockings.

Desire rushed through her—the heady sensation of being wanted exactly as and for who she was.

Tommy's arms wrapped tightly about the pretty bluestocking who never left her mind.

"I'm glad you came," she murmured between kisses. "Great-Aunt Wynchester adores you and Baron Vanderbean is smitten by you, but it is Tommy Wynchester's heart you hold in your hands. I want you to know that whatever happens tonight means just as much to me as every other moment we have shared."

Philippa pulled back just far enough to meet Tommy's eyes. "I like you, too. All of you. The roles you put on and the person you always are inside."

Tommy touched her cheek. "I would court you openly if I could."

"Court me in private," Philippa said. "Court me here and now. You'll find you've already won me."

"No, I haven't." Tommy kissed the corner of Philippa's lips. "We're just getting started."

"Show me." Philippa's gaze did not leave Tommy's. She bit her lip, her eyes twinkling. "I command you."

Tommy pulled Philippa back into her arms. "Watch this."

30

❧

*D*izzy with sensation, Philippa wrapped her arms about Tommy's neck and lost herself to the kiss.

She had thought there was nothing she loved more than learning. As it turned out, what she adored most was learning *Tommy*. How her body felt, how her kisses tasted, the little sounds she made when Philippa stroked her tongue against Tommy's.

Everything about the moment felt luxurious and fresh. The decadent sensation of her stockinged toes in the lush carpet, the warm crackle of the low fire, the delightfully unfamiliar bed beckoning two paces behind them.

Tommy was different and new tonight, too. She was wooing Philippa as herself. Philippa hadn't realized how much that vulnerability would mean. To know that this was the real Tommy touching her, kissing her, courting her. Their flirtation was not a role Tommy was playing, but true. This was what they *both* wished. She ran her palms lightly down Tommy's arms, feeling their strength and warmth through the fine linen.

Philippa had woken from several dreams imagining what it would be like if they could ever meet as lovers did. And here they were! She was about to discover how close her imagination had come to reality, as well as learn all the other things she hadn't even known to imagine.

Tommy feathered kisses up Philippa's throat to the hollow behind her ear. It tickled in the best possible way. She felt it in her toes. Tommy touched the tip of her tongue to Philippa's neck, tasting her there. Her breath caught at the erotic sensation.

"Would you like me to remove your gown?" Tommy's breath was soft against Philippa's sensitive skin.

Philippa nodded. She could feel Tommy smile in response. "Tell me."

This was something Philippa hadn't known to imagine. Tommy's husky insistence that Philippa state precisely what she wanted, with words, *aloud*. Or that the thought of doing so would increase her arousal. Center her even more in the moment.

Her breath came faster. She had yearned to be the heroine of her own story. For others to cease making decisions on her behalf without consulting or caring about her opinion. She was about to have her most secret fantasies come to life. But only if she was brave enough to put them into words.

"I want you to remove my gown." Philippa's voice only shook a little. "And to kiss me again afterward. On my mouth and my... neck."

She did it. *She said it.* Each spoken word was terrifying and exciting and freeing.

Tommy was giving Philippa the ability to decide for herself, to *be* herself, to control her own fate—if only for their lovemaking here tonight. Tommy turned Philippa toward the bed.

As far as Philippa was concerned, this would be the night she lost her virginity, technicalities be damned. She wanted it to be Tommy, not some stranger she neither knew nor liked. She wanted a first time and a second time and a third time. She wished her night with Tommy could last forever.

Philippa stepped closer to the bed, so that her fingertips could graze the indigo quilt. The material was soft and warm. The sort of down blanket that would be lovely to snuggle up inside on a cool autumn's night. Or to lie naked atop because the low fire and her lover's touch provided more than enough heat.

Her hair was piled atop her head in artful braids and ringlets, leaving her neck bare for Tommy's explorations. From behind, Tommy dipped her face to the curve of Philippa's neck and began a new onslaught of kisses.

Philippa scarcely registered the slow, deliberate descent of Tommy's fingers at her spine. Her brain could barely process the new sensation of light, sensual kisses where there had never been kisses before. Behind her ear, along the ticklish hairline at her nape, down the back of her neck to where the top of her dress *ought* to be, but no longer was.

Shivers erupted on her flesh. Tommy's kisses continued lower down the back of Philippa's neck until they reached the top of Philippa's shift, an utterly ordinary article of clothing normally hidden from others' eyes. The simple linen garment was no longer ordinary nor hidden. It felt provocative and indecent. Philippa's hands fell from the bed to her sides.

Tommy slid down the lace-and-satin gown ever so slowly. Over Philippa's breasts…hips…calves…A trail of kisses followed the path of Philippa's spine, ending just above the curve of her derrière, where there was nothing between Philippa's flesh and Tommy's mouth save the linen of her shift.

"Step," Tommy said softly.

Philippa gripped the bed for balance as the gown was whisked away.

"Now what?" Tommy asked, her voice rough.

"N-now what?" Philippa repeated. "Don't you have ideas?"

She turned to face Tommy, deliciously aware that her shift barely covered her bosom. Philippa's stays lifted her breasts to improbable heights, two plump offerings begging to be tasted.

"Mm." Tommy ran her curved fingers lovingly down Philippa's side. "More ideas than would fit into a single night. But I want to know about yours. You researched the subject, did you not? What did your Sapphic literature suggest might be an agreeable way for two half-naked people to pass the time?"

"The...literature," Philippa stammered, "was not explicit enough to obtain a clear picture. The etchings, on the other hand..."

Tommy's eyebrows shot up. "There are etchings? Did you bring them? Please tell me your valise is bursting with forbidden erotic artwork."

Philippa shook her head. "They...I hid them..."

"Pity. If you want me to try it, you'll have to describe to me what you saw."

"You're very cruel," Philippa said. "You know what I want."

"That's not true." Tommy kissed the corners of Philippa's lips. "Everyone likes different things. The mystery is part of the pleasure. Even with acts most parties adore, each person will have their own preferences. I'm not trying to punish you. I want to grant your desires."

Philippa could not bear to describe her forbidden images aloud. There had to be a way to turn the tables. "Then...what I want...is for you to try things, and if I like them, we shall keep doing them."

Tommy's slow grin melted Philippa's knees. She suspected her desperate bargain had not been so clever after all, but rather opened the door to a new kind of sensual torment. Her blood thrummed faster.

"As you wish." Tommy trailed the tip of her finger up the back of Philippa's hand, over her wrist, and up her arm, leaving gooseflesh in its wake. "You like kisses. Shall we begin there?"

Philippa managed to nod. She wanted that very much.

Tommy raised Philippa's hand and pressed a soft kiss to the palm. Barely lifting her mouth, she moved to the sensitive skin on the inside of Philippa's wrist, lingering there for a long moment as though drawn to the scent and taste of the rapidly fluttering pulse point there.

Leisurely, teasingly, Tommy's kisses made their way up Philippa's arm to her shoulder. Tommy touched her tongue to Philippa's clavicle before lowering her lips to the ridiculously high shelf of Philippa's bosom. Her breasts swelled and tightened in anticipation of Tommy's warm lips against her flesh.

Lips... and tongue. Tommy was not just kissing her but tasting her. Slowly. Reverently. As though savoring the flavor of each new inch and curve and crease. But most of Philippa's bosom—the best, most interesting parts that yearned to be touched—were hidden away.

"You can take off my stays," she said in a rush.

"I shall be delighted to."

Rather than turn Philippa around, Tommy stepped closer and kissed her. Their bosoms touched. Philippa could feel it now, the tips of her nipples straining through her shift to brush against the curved silk of Tommy's waistcoat.

It was wanton and wonderful.

Tommy took her time unlacing the ribbon, as though committing every detail of the moment to memory. Philippa was doing the same. The first loop. The second. The soft scrape of cording sliding against gooseflesh as Tommy exposed each new inch.

When Philippa's stays were loose enough to set her bosom free beneath the linen shift, her nipples tightened in the cool air. Or perhaps it was because she was rubbing them against Tommy's chest as they kissed.

Knowing the hard peaks of her breasts were now clearly visible, Philippa cast her stays to the floor beside the bed.

"This is too slow," she blurted out, her heart pounding in nervousness and excitement. "I want to be in the bed. With you."

"As you please."

Tommy removed her waistcoat. Three small buttons, wrapped in the same emerald fabric. She slipped the waistcoat from her shoulders and dropped it atop Philippa's discarded stays. It landed with the faint rustle of one fabric kissing another. Her breasts were small and unbound, the dusky nipples visible through the thin cambric. Tommy slipped off her trousers and tossed them aside. She was now clad only in silk stockings and a billowing gentlemen's shirt that fluttered to mid-thigh.

Philippa had never imagined that seeing Tommy dressed in nothing but a man's shirt could be so erotic. It felt daring, like everything Tommy did. Reckless and free, she was at her most attractive when she was just being herself.

Tommy's lack of inhibition made Philippa feel bold, too. She grabbed Tommy and pulled her close. Their hips came together. Their mouths met in a searing kiss. This time, there was nothing but soft linen separating their bodies. The tips of Philippa's breasts brushed the underside of Tommy's, touching with her nipples where she had not yet caressed with her hands

Tommy's smile was slow and seductive. "The bed, you said?"

Philippa nodded breathlessly. She unwound her hands from Tommy's neck and scrambled backward up onto the mattress, not wanting to divert her gaze for even a moment. She wanted to learn everything there was to know about Tommy's body. Its silhouette against the orange firelight. The hills and valley of her breasts visible above the gapping neck of her men's shirt as she climbed atop the bed to join Philippa.

Tommy's mouth caught hers, but only briefly. "Stop or continue?"

"Continue." Philippa's head fell back against the pillow.

Tommy slid beside her. Her lithe, warm body touched Philippa's from shoulder to toe. Tommy bent her top leg, resting her smooth thigh atop Philippa's. The welcome weight of Tommy's leg felt possessive and intimate. As though they were branding each other with their bodies. Tommy hooked an arm around Philippa's midsection, just beneath her breasts. Not quite sexual...but adjacent. As though her touch *could* be sexual, if Philippa wanted it to.

"Stop or continue?"

"C-continue."

Tommy shifted so that she was atop Philippa. Not lying on her, exactly. Their legs were entwined and their pelvises touched, but Tommy's arms propped her up so that there was a gap between their breasts.

Philippa stammered, "What are you..."

Tommy slid toward the foot of the bed. Not far—a few inches. Just enough to allow her mouth to reach the spot where the hem of Philippa's neckline met the plump curve of her breast. Tommy dropped soft, slow kisses along that line from one edge of Philippa's bodice to the other. The first row of kisses was on the exposed flesh of Philippa's breasts. The second row of kisses was just below the hem, along the thin linen.

Having a layer of linen between Tommy's kisses and Philippa's skin should have felt more chaste. Instead, her nipples tightened in awareness that Tommy's mouth was drawing ever closer.

Tommy paused when her mouth was so close to Philippa's nipple that she could feel Tommy's breath through her shift. "Stop or continue?"

"*Continue.*" The word came out raw, a shameless, helpless plea.

"Kisses or touching?"

"Both," Philippa whispered. "Please."

Breathy little one-word answers were far from eloquent, but Tommy did not seem to mind. Instead, she resumed her slow, heated kisses, down the hill of one breast, into the valley between, up the other side, ever so close to the trembling peak there.

The tantalizing trajectory of Tommy's mouth consumed Philippa's attention until Tommy's slender fingers cupped her other breast, trapping the engorged nipple. She began to play. Philippa's body reacted instantly. Every muscle galvanized.

While Tommy's left hand stroked Philippa's breast, Tommy's mouth closed over the other, teasing through the fabric with her lips and teeth and tongue.

This was a kiss of a different sort. Deliciously unsatisfying, serving only to make Philippa's body all the more restless. A coil of want began to curl between her legs. Her clitoris felt swollen and needy, eager to be the next body part visited.

"May I...touch you?" she asked.

"I told you." Tommy's eyes met hers. "You can touch me whenever, wherever."

"You can touch me everywhere, too." Philippa desperately

hoped Tommy would take her true meaning and not force her to specify whether she referred to her toes or her vulva.

Tommy tugged down Philippa's shift, exposing her breasts to the cool air...and the heat of Tommy's mouth. Philippa closed her eyes and tilted her head back, only to realize that she was arching her back to raise her breasts toward Tommy. If she'd had an etching of this moment, it would have been erotic indeed.

She reveled in the sensation of Tommy's fingers against her bare nipple, Tommy's wet tongue scraping against the other, only to suck it into her mouth.

Heat and excitement suffused Philippa's body. She wanted to see, to touch.

She placed her hands on Tommy's back and fisted her fingers in the soft shirt. The action caused the hem to rise, revealing the alluring shape of Tommy's buttocks.

Without lifting her mouth from Philippa's bare nipple, Tommy's fingers trailed down Philippa's abdomen, over her hip, to tug up the bottom hem of her shift. Tommy yanked the linen up bit by bit. Uncovering Philippa's calves, then knees, then thighs.

Philippa held her breath. Would Tommy push it all of the way up to Philippa's waist, displaying the part of her that ached for Tommy's touch? Or would she—

Conscious thought fled as Tommy slid her slim hand between Philippa's legs, cupping her where she was hot and slick. Her flesh felt swollen and sensitive, eager to be touched. When Tommy reached Philippa's clitoris, a shock of pleasure shot through her. This was so much better than doing it herself while dreaming of Tommy. So much faster.

Tommy's fingers rolled against her, once, twice, thrice, until they were slick and slid easily. Dipping now, confident, exploring, *finding*.

Philippa moved restlessly, her hips bucking as she sought to deepen the touch, no longer rational enough to be self-conscious. Tommy's hand matched the rhythm. Philippa's entire body felt tighter, on edge, waiting breathlessly as the familiar pressure climbed within her, in a wholly unfamiliar way.

Doing it *with* Tommy, feeling the climax build *because* of Tommy.

While her fingers stroked Philippa's clitoris, Tommy lifted her mouth from Philippa's breast to her lips. Philippa met the kiss hungrily, greedily, sucking Tommy's tongue as Tommy's fingers toyed and dipped, teased and pierced, bringing her ever closer to an arousal so intense, she teetered on the precipice of satisfaction.

The pressure exploded into pleasure. Philippa reached her peak with Tommy's fingers still driving inside her, sending mindless waves spiraling throughout Philippa's body.

When at last Tommy removed her hand, Philippa caught it in hers. She felt the slickness coat her own fingers. They had done this together. They could do it again. Philippa could bring the same pleasure to Tommy.

"I want to do it to you," she rasped, her heart still banging too fast to think properly.

"Hurry." Tommy licked Philippa's lip. "I'm close just from doing it to you."

Was that true? Was it possible? Philippa reached beneath Tommy's shirt to cup her in the same intimate manner.

The sensation was similar to what she felt when she touched herself, but the angle was different. Tommy's vulva was indeed slick and ready. Philippa was not quite certain what to do or how to go about it, so she explored the way Tommy had. Rolling her fingers, then circling with just the fingertips and then—*ah*. There was the clitoris.

Tommy's mouth crushed into hers and they rolled slightly so that Philippa was on her side and Tommy was on her back, her toned legs splaying for easier access.

Philippa stroked, lightly, tentatively. "Like this?"

"More." Tommy ground herself against Philippa's fingers, punctuating their kisses with sensual little moans.

Philippa tested dipping a finger inside. Tommy gasped for air. Philippa thrilled to learn which speed and which strokes earned the best little whimpers.

She broke the kiss and traveled instead down the svelte column of Tommy's neck toward her small breasts, tasting as she went. The slight salt of sweat, the citrusy bergamot of Tommy's perfume, the heat of her flesh.

Experimentally, Philippa licked one of Tommy's dark, erect nipples. She was immediately rewarded by the muscles of Tommy's vulva clamping briefly about her fingers. Philippa took the breast into her mouth, swirling her tongue the way Tommy had shown her, while stroking with her fingers the way she now knew drove Tommy to the edge.

"I . . ." Tommy gasped. Her slender hips bucked and she ground faster until her inner muscles spasmed rhythmically about Philippa's fingers.

Tommy collapsed and pulled Philippa into her embrace with an exhausted, but contented, sigh. Philippa wrapped her arms about Tommy and held on tight.

"To be clear," Tommy said drowsily. "We can do that all night long if you want."

Philippa's heart lurched as though it, too, wished to get closer to Tommy with every fluttering beat. Her lips curved. Neither her heart nor her body was cold or dead or broken. Philippa's heart was in *love*. With the person whose arms she was in, whose bed she was sharing.

Lovemaking had been more than she'd dreamed. She wanted to do this with Tommy every day. Not just the marvelous sensual parts, but *this*. The snuggling, after.

It was a miracle . . . and a disaster. How was she supposed to continue on with an ordinary life, after experiencing *this?*

31

With her wig and wrinkles in place and a wicker basket clutched in one liver-spotted hand, Tommy accepted the Duke of Faircliffe's assistance from his carriage.

"Can Northrup's town house hold this many people?" Chloe gestured at the queue of coaches behind them. "Wouldn't guests have been more comfortable if he held a smaller fête?"

"And detract from his glory?" the Duke of Faircliffe asked dryly as he held out an elbow to each lady. "With Northrup's ballroom full to bursting, gossips will label it a major 'crush of the season' even before the season has properly begun."

"I cannot wait to give the gossips something even bigger to talk about," Tommy said. "The 'scandal of the season,' starring the soon-to-be-disgraced Captain Northrup. Tonight, we put the final gear in motion. Are you ready?"

"Of course I'm ready," Chloe answered. "Is Philippa ready?"

"Philippa needn't do anything," Tommy said firmly. "She has a reputation to mind and will serve as a distraction whilst we dabble in a little light burglary."

The Duke of Faircliffe slanted his wife a look of exaggerated shock. "Does not a *duchess* also have a reputation to mind?"

"Pah," said Tommy. "Not *your* duchess. Besides, Chloe's been nicking things since she was five years old. She can do it in her sleep. Of course she can do it in a crowded ball-room. You look after Philippa and leave the thievery to the experts."

"I'll look after all of my ladies." He gave his wife a look of such heat and tenderness, Tommy rather doubted Faircliffe capable of noticing anyone else.

"And another thing," she quavered at full volume, once they were within earshot of the door. "Young bucks like you, Faircliffe—"

"Why, look, Aunt," Chloe said soothingly. "We've arrived at Captain Northrup's residence. Isn't it lovely? This fine man must be the butler. Here are our cards, good sir. These are gifts for Miss Damaris Urqhart. We'll present them to her ourselves. I am anxious to be rid of my coat and bonnet. Aunt, may we assist you with yours?"

"I'll help her," Faircliffe said.

Tommy cackled and sent a salacious look at the butler. "Any excuse to be manhandled by a duke, I always say. Don't you agree?"

The butler's startled eyes flared wide. "I...what..."

"Come along, Aunt," Chloe coaxed. "They'll read our names, and then we can greet our hosts."

Tommy tottered next to Faircliffe and Chloe, being sure to peer about myopically and bump into anyone who passed within arm's length of her.

The most effective part of the Great-Aunt Wynchester disguise was not her wig or her cosmetics, but the impression of helpless senility. One look, and she was immediately discounted as harmless.

...And more than a touch embarrassing. The sort of person one would be relieved to see disappear from a fancy soirée.

There would be no search party, nor any particular surprise, if an old lady were to be discovered roaming the halls in confusion. The trick was not to be caught until *after* she'd found the manuscript. Only then would she be ready to make her grand re-entrance to the ball.

"A captain, you say?" she blustered when they reached Northrup. "You remind me of an insolent pup who once barged into a ladies' private reading circle without an invitation. I should hope that cad was no relative of yours."

"Come along, Aunt," said Chloe. "Give your basket to Damaris, and let's greet the other guests, shall we? Look, there are Mr. and Mrs. York and their daughter, Philippa. Doesn't she look charming tonight?"

"A treat." Tommy licked her lips as she tottered away from the receiving line. "A soft, succulent peach of a girl. A ripe, plump, dare I say juicy—"

Chloe snorted. "You're lucky only I can hear you now."

"And I," the Duke of Faircliffe said. "I am less lucky."

"Pah," Tommy said. "You have your own peach right here. Take her to the refreshment table for a nice cup of gin while I charm the stockings off my future father-in-law."

"Please leave his stockings alone," Faircliffe murmured. "Which direction is the gin?"

Chloe hooked her arm through his and led him toward the refreshments.

Tommy patted her wiry white wig and peered in all directions before hobbling toward the York family.

"I suppose you young things plan to dance until dawn," she quavered at Mr. and Mrs. York in lieu of a greeting.

They exchanged startled glances. Likely because, according to the journal Graham kept on the Yorks, the MP and his wife were rarely seen within arm's reach of one another. There was no recorded instance of them dancing together.

"Young love," Tommy said with a shake of her head, then turned to Philippa. "Why, aren't you just the sweetest thing with your pinchable cheeks and all this lace. Is it your come-out tonight?"

"It is not her come-out," Mrs. York snapped. "That is Philippa, whom you have seen every Thursday afternoon for several months in a row—"

"Not lately," Mr. York said. "Didn't you forbid her from having friends some weeks ago?"

"*I?*" Mrs. York turned to him in affront. "Is it not *your* ambition that requires Philippa's future husband to be a member of Parliament or eligible for the House of Lords?"

"My political ambition is not half so grasping as your social ambition," Mr. York shot back. "If I have to hear one more word about how mortifying you find our lack of title, and how all of your hopes are pinned upon a bookish wallflower who after five long seasons cannot even..."

Good God. Tommy sent Philippa a horrified glance. Was *this* twaddle what Philippa heard all day when she was at home?

Philippa lifted one shoulder almost imperceptibly, as if to say she had mastered the art of blocking out their voices long ago.

"You look beautiful," Tommy whispered. "Delectable, some might say."

"You're the only one who might say," Philippa whispered back, letting the tips of her fingers brush Tommy's. "And shh."

If Tommy were Baron Vanderbean right now instead of Great-Aunt Wynchester, she could pull Philippa into her arms the moment the music began and—

"...at least Captain Northrup is *English*," Mrs. York finished, as though settling an age-old argument. "What good is Baron Vanderbean? He's ineligible for Parliament, and just barely considered bon ton. It's a fine thing he isn't present tonight, or I daresay Philippa would make calf's eyes at him and spoil her chances with Northrup."

"Just because he's to be a viscount doesn't mean Northrup will take his seat in the House of Lords," Mr. York said. "We should limit the pool to active statesmen. The Speaker of the House is a future viscount, and he's in want of a wife."

"He's not in want of a wife," Mrs. York said in exasperation. "He's in *mourning* for one. Who knows when he'll wed again! Northrup is the bird in hand. He's standing up with Philippa for the very first dance."

"I suppose he'll stand up with all of the other unmarried ladies for every other dance," said Mr. York.

"He will and should, as is proper. But the *first* dance is symbolic." Mrs. York turned jubilant eyes on her daughter. "The wait is almost over, darling. Tomorrow, I expect the captain to pay a formal call upon your father."

"Well, where is he, then?" Tommy barked. "Hasn't forgotten about our dear Pippa, has he? That's the orchestra setting up. You might want to go and put a bug in his ear, lest your captain forget all about his grand symbolic gesture."

Alarmed, Mrs. York glanced over her shoulder at the receiving line, which now contained only Damaris and her mother. At the edge of the dance floor, Northrup stood among a clump of admirers. He puffed up his chest and spoke more heartily than usual, clearly intending to be observed.

"Well!" Mrs. York harrumphed and hooked her hand in her husband's arm. "Come, Mr. York. We cannot allow his new airs to cause him to shirk his duty to Philippa."

"Dear me," Philippa said emotionlessly. "I am so upset."

"Go on then," Tommy barked at Philippa's parents. "Bring

that soon-to-be viscount to heel. I can play duenna to this pip until you've put things to rights."

Mrs. York looked as though she might say something, but a violinist took that moment to draw her bow across a string to tune her instrument. With renewed haste, Mrs. York dragged her husband across the ballroom toward Captain Northrup.

Tommy turned back to Philippa and lowered her voice. "Tell me more about the parts of you I've set a-quiver."

Philippa's lips curved in a remarkably wicked smile. "You'll discover them for yourself if we ever have another moment alone together."

"Oh, is that all we need? I'll clear the ballroom posthaste." Tommy patted her false bosom. "Where did I put that tinderbox? A small fire ought to do the trick. Plenty of wood to be found in a ballroom."

"No setting fires until we find the manuscript," Philippa scolded her.

"It's in an iron strongbox upstairs," Tommy said. "Perfectly safe from a wee little strategic ballroom inferno. Just think how much easier it will be to nick if everyone's already run off screaming."

"I see why we always put *Chloe* in charge of the plans," Philippa teased.

Tommy grinned at her. They were a *we*. It thrilled her.

"My sister's logical plans lack a certain...*flair*," she protested. "We should really put Graham in charge. He's always wanting to leap from the backs of horses or scale turrets with a rose clamped in his teeth. Or Jacob! Now, *there's* an unpredictable plan full of pythons and poetry."

"I can only imagine." Philippa's mouth twitched. "He'd have filled the ballroom with beasts by now."

Tommy nodded. "And *then* Graham could swing down

from a tightrope, snatch up a plate of meat pies, and launch himself back into the sky amidst a flutter of flower petals."

"This is a fancy party," Philippa reminded her. "There are no meat pies. He would be forced to retrieve the actual object of the mission instead."

"Pah," Tommy said. "Never let the men have all of the fun. Retrieving the manuscript is *my* bit."

"And here comes mine," Philippa said with a grimace. "Mother must have worked her magic."

Tommy turned to see Northrup swaggering in their direction.

Philippa shuddered. "Ugh, I would marry any man but that one."

Tommy's bravado faltered.

Even now, after the night they'd shared, Philippa still planned to marry some lord. Tommy would be nothing more than a funny thing Philippa had once done the autumn before she got married and settled into a *real* life.

"There you are," Northrup said, as though Philippa's conspicuous position alongside the dance floor had made her difficult to spot. "Shall we lead the way?"

Tommy glared at the strutting captain as he ushered Philippa to the center of the ballroom.

Perhaps it was best if Great-Aunt Wynchester did not sulk broodingly at the gentleman of the hour and his pretty partner.

"Aren't they such a lovely couple?" came a low female voice just behind her.

"I heard they're betrothed already, or close enough to it," came the whispered reply.

"Her parents must be *so* proud," the first voice said dreamily.

Tommy clenched her hands. She was definitely glowering, and there wasn't a bloody thing she could do to stop it.

Philippa's husband would not be Captain Northrup if Tommy had any say in the matter, but it would be *some* gentleman or other. Tommy did not figure into the equation.

She swallowed. She could not be upset. Philippa had made no promises, nor had Tommy asked for any. If their connection was to be nothing more than a shared secret, then Tommy would at least keep it for as long as she could. She would not stand here watching Philippa and Northrup or listen to the gossips' fawning approval of this godawful match.

She made her way to the refreshment table instead. There was no platter of meat pies, but there was dessert, which could do in a pinch.

Tommy was engaged in consuming fresh lemon cakes when the interminable first set finally ended. Since Philippa had been standing with her ancient chaperone when Northrup arrived to claim his dance, he brought her back to Tommy.

"Where's that duchess?" Northrup glanced over his shoulders. "She promised me the second set. What was her name again?"

"Her name is 'Your Grace,'" Tommy barked. "You green lads, with no sense of respect for ladies—"

"No." Captain Northrup scowled. "I meant her title. She's the Duchess of—"

"Faircliffe," Chloe said smoothly, materializing from nowhere to slip her hand around Northrup's arm. She winked at Tommy. "I believe this is my dance?"

"So it is." Northrup puffed up his chest again and strutted out onto the dance floor with exaggerated slowness, so that everyone could see him with a duchess on his arm.

"Oh, he's bon ton," Philippa muttered darkly. "Overflowing with *je ne sais quoi*."

"It's 'shite,'" Tommy whispered. "He's overflowing with shite."

"If only my parents had felt this passionately about marrying me off to Baron Vanderbean," Philippa said with a sigh.

Tommy shook her head. The ton's opinions of Baron Vanderbean were irrelevant. He wouldn't be marrying anyone. She didn't want to have to pose as her father's namesake to earn her lover's acceptance. She wanted to live as *Tommy.* Chosen for herself, and nothing else.

"It's been almost a full minute," Tommy said. "Chloe's done by now. It's my turn."

"What?" Philippa spun to face the dancers. "How?"

"I'll return posthaste," Tommy said. "I have to bump into my niece."

She placed her spectacles in her wig and bumbled onto the parquet, hunched and squinting. She narrowly avoided the other dancing couples then collided with Chloe.

"There you are," she barked. "I can't find my spectacles."

Northrup's face turned so purple, Tommy hoped he might explode.

"Aunt…" Chloe said gently. "They're on your head. Please go wait for me elsewhere. I'm dancing with Captain Northrup."

Tommy patted the spectacles on her head, harrumphed, and tottered away without another word. She adjusted the fichu covering her bodice. The key was now inside her false bosom.

Hurrying, Philippa caught up with her halfway to the door.

"What are you doing?" Tommy motioned for her to stay in the ballroom, where it was safe. "Chloe will ensure he doesn't notice anything amiss until he's at least finished his set with her, but that gives me barely thirty minutes. Wait here."

"No." Philippa did not slow her pace. "I'm coming with you."

32

You're not coming with me." Tommy staggered backward in obvious horror. "You don't have an excuse to be wandering the corridors—"

"I do," Philippa said, keeping her voice low but firm. "Northrup gave me the excuse. He told me where to find his bedchamber and heavily intimated our second set of the night could take place upstairs."

Tommy's mouth fell open. "*What?* That may be an excuse, but it's still scandalous. If I am caught, no one will think anything of it. But if *you* are caught, you won't have the life that you want."

"I don't have the life I want now." Philippa's voice shook from three and twenty interminable years of being excluded from what she wanted most. "Please do not make my choices for me."

"I'm not trying to," Tommy said. "I just don't see—"

"Once I am wed, I won't have opportunities like this, to do something important and to help my friends. I may not be allowed to *have* my friends. Agnes and Katherine had no one to stand up for them. I want to be that person, whilst I can."

Tommy nodded slowly. "I understand wanting to decide your future and the desire to be useful."

Philippa's shoulders relaxed. Even their disagreements were tolerable. Tommy listened to Philippa's viewpoint and believed her feelings to be relevant and important. It was heady and empowering.

She seized her chance. "Like you said, no one will think twice if Great-Aunt Wynchester is seen wandering the halls. Northrup already thinks you're my chaperone. If I notice your absence, it's the most natural thing in the world for me to go and find you."

"Your logic holds," Tommy admitted. She drew in a visible breath. "You are your own person, making your own decision."

"No," Philippa said softly. "We are a team, making decisions together. Two brains are better than one."

"Yours is undoubtedly the cleverest." Tommy tilted her head. "Come along, you knavish bluestocking wench. Show me where you will absolutely not be meeting that despicable blackguard later."

Philippa's legs wobbled with relief. Tonight, *she* would be a heroine. An active participant in the adventure. Even if such a moment never repeated, she would always remember with pride the time she brought justice to Damaris and public recognition to Agnes and Katherine.

She hurried out into the corridor. "Come along, Aunt. Tut-tut."

"I'm not *your* aunt," Tommy muttered, but hobbled quickly for an arthritic old lady with poor vision. She pulled a folded parchment from a hidden pocket and handed it to Philippa. "This map is based on Damaris's recollection."

Philippa looked at the sketch. The style was like the other loose maps she'd seen at Tommy's residence. The difference being, she must have scouted those herself. Philippa hoped Damaris's memory was as keen as her cryptography.

She considered the map. "We need only go to the end of this corridor, make a left, and the library will be the third door on the right."

Tommy pulled out her pocket watch. "We must hurry. Half-hour sets are only an approximation, and we've already used five of our minutes."

"Northrup might not miss his key all night," Philippa said. "Then again, when he finishes this set, he might notice my absence and wonder if I'm awaiting him in his chamber."

"You won't be anywhere near there," Tommy said firmly. "But you're right. It's another reason to hurry. Chloe will do her best to distract him for as long as—"

A quartet of footmen bearing heavy trays piled high with refreshments strode around the very corner Philippa and Tommy were walking toward. Philippa stopped in her tracks.

"Ladies," said the youngest of the footmen. "The ballroom is—"

Tommy pointed at his chest.

"He was here," she quavered, her entire manner bewildered. "My husband was standing right there until you walked straight into him."

"I..." The young man exchanged baffled glances with the other footmen

"He's a ghost," Philippa stage-whispered. "Mr. Wynchester has been gone for thirty years." She waved for them to continue. "Carry on. I'll bring her back as soon as she's convinced his spirit has been frightened from the building."

The footmen hesitated, but the trays of food and libations expected in the ballroom won out. They hurried on without another word.

Tommy continued peering at the wall in confusion until the corridor cleared. Then she turned and grinned at Philippa. "We make excellent partners."

Philippa flushed. She folded the map and hid it in her reticule.

"I'll follow your lead," she whispered.

Tommy stuck her spectacles in her wig at an even more topsy-turvy angle, hunched her back and shoulders, and tottered off down the corridor.

Philippa tried to stop her lips from curving, but her whole body felt like smiling every time she looked at Tommy. Being in her presence was always a treat, but being by her *side*, being her equal, her partner... It felt like something more important than a team. Something bigger. Something better.

Something she wished could last forever.

"Here's our left," Tommy whispered. "If something goes wrong, blame it on Great-Aunt Wynchester."

Philippa nodded her understanding. And, she thought, perhaps she *did* understand Tommy a little better than before.

Tommy didn't charge off headfirst into adventures because she wished to leave Philippa behind, or because Philippa hadn't entered into her mind. The opposite. Tommy constantly thought of Philippa. She was willing to take any risk that gave a greater chance of Philippa's future happiness.

Unlike Philippa's parents, who wanted the best for their daughter only insofar as it benefitted them. The man Philippa would be forced to share her body with for the rest of her life was a cog in the machinery of her father's political ambitions, one more stepping-stone for her mother's social climbing. If her parents hadn't rejected commoners in hope of personal gain, Philippa might have married years ago.

She also would never have met Tommy.

"Third door," Tommy said. She pressed her ear to the smooth pine. "I don't hear anyone inside."

Philippa stepped forward. "I'll peek through the keyhole."

Who knew her mother's trick would come in handy?

Rapid footsteps sounded around the corner.

"Yes, I did see them," came a male voice. "They were talking about ghosts—"

"No time," Tommy whispered. She reached for the handle, flung open the door, and pulled Philippa inside after her. She shut the door with a whoosh.

The room was a servant workroom, not a library. Three startled maids ceased ironing napkins and tablecloths at once.

"Shite," Tommy said.

"Oh, how dastardly!" Philippa swept ahead, shaking out the map with one hand. "Our map contains *false clues*. Or are everyone's maps suspect?" She turned to the maids and gave them her most earnest expression. "Are we the first to get this far?"

"To get...to the ironing room?" stammered one of the maids.

"Why are you here?" asked another.

"For the treasure hunt, of course!" Philippa beamed at them. "The National Bluestocking Society is on the hunt for an antique astrolabe the hostess has hidden somewhere on the ground floor. I deduced we would find it amongst the books, but this does not appear to be a library."

"Brilliant deduction," muttered the other maid.

Her companion snorted softly. " '*Bluestockings.*' "

"Have a look." Philippa held up the wrinkled paper, map facing the maids. "It says the library should be the third door on the right."

"Second door," said the first maid. "Library is the next room."

"But it's locked," said one of her companions. "We just finished cleaning it."

"Oh!" Philippa flung the map at Tommy and clapped her hands together with excitement. "Then you have a key! This is splendid luck. We'll be the first to the astrolabe and I shall become Bluestocking of the Year. There's to be a special geological formation named after the winner!"

The maids glanced at each other with obvious amusement but showed no indication of being eager to unlock the door.

"Oh, my stars." Philippa gave a trilling laugh. "Aunt, how much does the treasure map indicate fair passage costs?"

Tommy peered at the paper for a long moment, turning it from side to side before glancing up in triumph. "One guinea."

"A guinea! I have a guinea here in my reticule." Philippa made a show of opening her reticule, in such a way that the coins inside clinked against each other loudly. "My goodness, I have *three* guineas. One for each of you! That is, if one of you will do us the great honor of assisting the future Bluestocking of the Year in her noble quest?"

"I'll do it," two of the maids said at once.

"Let Rufina," said the third maid. "She has the key. Bring our guineas back, girl."

Rufina all but scampered out of the workroom to lead Tommy and Philippa to the library. She had the door open in a trice.

"There's an extra guinea here for you," Philippa whispered as she dropped four coins in into the girl's palm. "If any of the other teams make it this far, pretend you haven't seen us."

The girl nodded effusively, then dashed back to the workroom. Muffled giggles could be heard through the wall.

"That was lucky," Philippa said under her breath. "I didn't think they'd believe the ruse."

"Pah," Tommy said. "It was human nature. Servants don't think much of the brain capacity of older women *or* the beau monde."

"Well, I'm not leaving this library without the illuminated manuscript."

Philippa glanced around the room. The book was in a heavy strongbox, which made it unlikely to be stored overhead, or on a shelf at all. It was most likely low to the floor, or on a sturdy surface.

Tommy consulted her pocket watch. "Twenty minutes."

For a library, there were dashed few books. Most of the shelves were filled with bottles of wine and sherry, and varying styles of glasses to drink from.

"Here." Tommy ducked behind a sofa.

Philippa joined her at a gap between the bookshelves.

Together, they managed to tug the iron strongbox free from its snug hollow. Tommy fit the key into the lock. Nothing happened. Philippa wrung her hands to stop them from trembling. If they had come all this way, only for it to be the wrong box or the wrong key—

Tommy wiggled the key again, more forcefully this time, and the lock sprang open.

Philippa sagged with relief. Of course it was the right box, and of course Tommy would be able to open it. Tommy probably could have picked the lock with a quill from a porcupine if it had come to that. Knowing Jacob, releasing porcupines down the chimney had probably been the contingency plan. Luckily, the key had worked. Philippa leaned forward.

Tommy lifted the lid to the strongbox. Because the volume was too wide to lay properly on the bottom, the priceless illuminated manuscript was stuffed inside at a diagonal. Its gilt spine was shoved against one corner and the painstakingly illustrated pages were curled and bent.

"That *noddcock*." Philippa reached for the poor, abused manuscript. She ran a gloved finger lightly along the edge that had borne the weight against the side of the iron box and did her best to straighten the bent sections. "If one does not know how to treat books with care, one should not have them."

Tommy nodded gravely. "This is why I don't own any books."

Philippa shook her head. "You would take care of something that mattered to you."

Tommy snorted. "Have you seen my map collection? Graham swears he spends half of his time piling them back on the shelf whenever there's a strong breeze from the open windows. Is the manuscript as you hoped?"

Philippa set the volume on the shelf with the glass tumblers in order to examine the markings along the edge. She pulled Marjorie's reproductions of the other manuscripts' edge illustrations from her reticule and held the copies of volumes two through four next to Northrup's volume one.

"It is *exactly* as I hoped," she replied with satisfaction. "I won't have to destroy perfect bindings in search of hidden letters after all. We have everything we need to share Agnes and Katherine's talent with the world."

Tommy held up loose papers from the bottom of the strongbox. "Do you recognize these?"

"They look like instructions for the cipher." Philippa frowned. "Damaris exhorted us to toss the directions into the fire once we'd memorized the trick."

"Some don't seem like Damaris's handwriting." Tommy handed her the papers.

Philippa flipped through them. "You're right. The instructions are incomplete. This one skips a line. And that one is even worse. They must belong to Captain Northrup."

Damaris's uncle must not have paid close attention when he'd copied his niece's ideas in order to present them as his own.

Her foot bounced with excitement. "We can *prove* he didn't invent a thing."

She shot to her feet to glance wildly about the library.

Tommy leapt to her feet as well. "What are we looking for?"

"Paper," said Philippa. "A desk, an escritoire, a writing slope, quill and ink, *anything*."

There was nothing of the sort.

This was truly the worst library Philippa had ever seen.

Tommy pulled a pencil out of Great-Aunt Wynchester's white wig and handed Philippa the paper with the map. "Can you use the back of that?"

Philippa moved wine and sherry bottles to create a writing surface. She paused every few characters to consult various pages of the manuscript as she filled out a careful grid.

Tommy peered over her shoulder. "What in the world is that?"

"A simple substitution cipher," Philippa answered. "Made exponentially more complex by writing the letters in a diagonal. Unless you know the pattern as well as the sequence of characters used as punctuation, it's all but impossible to decipher."

33

*P*hilippa tucked the code inside the illuminated manuscript and rose to her feet. Her chest swelled with satisfaction. "Today, justice will be served. Damaris, Agnes, and Katherine are brilliant women who will finally receive the credit they deserve for their indispensable contributions."

"Not today," Tommy said. "Tomorrow morning. Graham has associates inside printing offices in every corner of England. You and Damaris can draft the perfect exposé, which will be at the top of every newspaper in the morning."

"No." Philippa lifted the rescued book. "Poor Damaris is suffering in that ballroom. She's putting on a brave face to honor a man who merits no such accolades. We do this here, tonight, in front of witnesses. Let the gossips write their own scandal columns. We end this now."

Tommy raced to block the closed library door. "He will not be kind to you."

"Let him be cruel." Philippa lifted her chin. "Being a wallflower has been my protection for far too long. People dismiss me. They think bluestockings are boring and worthless."

Tommy still blocked the door.

"We're *not* boring. We're *brave*. We're clever. We're capable.

And *we're* the reason that smug, lying plagiarist will *not* be crowned for someone else's achievements."

"Even if he tries to take you down with him?"

"He cannot take away who I am. I shall be the Venus flytrap of wallflowers. The bluestocking whose books reveal the truth and demolish fraud. And we'll do it in front of those he most wishes to impress. The people he's been lying to all along."

Tommy considered this, then dropped her hand from the door. "All right, then. Let's shatter illusions."

The moment Tommy opened the door, her posture and manner transformed back to Great-Aunt Wynchester. She peered out of the cracked door in both directions, one trembling hand cupped above her squinting eyes, as though the sconces in the corridor were bright as the sun.

"I don't see my dead husband anywhere," she quavered loudly, and tottered into the hall.

Philippa kept her head down. She did not think the maids would ask further questions, but it was best to make haste.

After they passed the ironing room, they hurried down the corridor to the open doorway that led to the dancing.

Philippa strode into the ballroom as though she were the chivalric knight here to champion a lady in need.

Nobody turned to look. Sweeping about with an ornate, bejeweled, Elizabethan book in her hand made her no more interesting than any other day.

The thought of standing at the edge of the dance floor for the next quarter hour waiting for the song to end so that she could dramatically face down a fraudulent cryptographer was a depressing comedown.

"Should I feign an apoplexy?" Tommy whispered.

Philippa shook her head. She'd just caught sight of Captain Northrup. He was not dancing the reel, but rather, surrounded by a circle of sycophants between the musicians and the refreshments table.

Interrupting a round of loud bragging was not *quite* the same as winning a jousting tournament or winning a kingdom.

But it would do.

"Follow me." She led Tommy between the queue for the refreshments table and the edge of the dance floor.

"I can recall any number I hear, no matter how large," Northrup was informing his profusion of admirers. "I'm told I was not only the best shot of my division, I also possess the strongest muscles. Due to my superior blood, of course *I* was the only one who could—"

He caught sight of Philippa, which she supposed was a minor miracle in itself.

When Northrup leered blatantly, she realized it was not her countenance that had animated him, but rather the thought of despoiling her upstairs in his bedroom while everyone else was engaged in a country dance. He was about to be disappointed.

His worshipers turned to see what had caught their deity's attention.

Northrup's leer faded at the sight of his ancestor's manuscript in Philippa's gloved hands. No. The manuscript belonged to his ancestor's tenants, whose efforts Sir Reginald had claimed as his own.

Northrup patted his chest in growing horror.

Tommy held up the missing key and bellowed, "I believe you dropped this, pup!"

Now they held the attention of the entire refreshment queue, as well as the dancers closest to this edge of the parquet.

"I didn't lose it." Northrup stormed through his admirers, knocking them out of his way. "You *stole* it from me, you crazy old bat—"

"So you confirm that she is holding your key and that this is your manuscript?" Philippa asked archly.

The dancers stumbled as more of them tried to stare.

"Obviously it's my book," Northrup said peevishly. "My great-great-et-cetera-grandfather, Sir Reginald Northrup, penned every stroke of that illuminated manuscript by hand. He was the most revered Elizabethan scribe, and the most important artist to all of us here today."

"More important than Sir Walter Raleigh?" Tommy barked. "More revered than William Shakespeare?"

"Was Sir Reginald half as intelligent as the great Captain Northrup?" Philippa lifted the cover of the manuscript and pulled out the cipher she had created. She held the paper out toward Northrup. "As you have reminded us all on many occasions, you are the cleverest man in the room. Can you tell me what this says?"

He snatched the paper from her hand and stared at the grid of symbols, then flipped to the side with the map, then back to the side with the perfect square in neat rows and columns.

"It's gibberish," he said in disgust. "Did *you* write this?"

"Yes, I did," she replied. "In cipher."

Damaris broke through the refreshment line as planned. She set a basket at Philippa's feet and held out her hand to Northrup. "May I see it, Uncle?"

"Who cares what it says?" He shoved the paper into his niece's palm with enough force to crumple it. "I am busy speaking to other men. Can't you bluestockings entertain yourselves elsewhere if you cannot entice a man to dance?"

The dancers who were too far away to hear edged closer. Their steps no longer matched the reel but were a blatant attempt to come within earshot of what appeared to be the most exciting moment of the night.

"May I?" Damaris asked.

Philippa handed her the manuscript.

Damaris flipped through the pages with astonishing speed, pausing only every half second or so to glance at the wrinkled cipher.

The violinists lowered their instruments because no one was left on the parquet to dance. They, too, inched closer to watch.

Damaris closed the book and handed it back to Philippa, then shook out the parchment and began to read. "'Northrup is a liar and a fraud. If he had created this cipher, he would be able to read it.'"

"Let me see that," a masculine voice boomed out.

Everyone turned as one of Northrup's colleagues edged his way to the front. Not a colleague—his commanding officer, Brigadier-General Boswick.

The brigadier-general took the page from Damaris's hand respectfully and produced a quizzing glass from his pocket.

"We made alterations to the cipher before sending it into the field," he explained to the crowd. "But the core principles are the same. If I could see the manuscript?"

Damaris handed it to him.

His gloved hands treated the volume with obvious care. He consulted Philippa's cipher before turning to this page and that with deliberate precision. At last, he closed the manuscript.

"What does it say?" called Lady Eunice from somewhere behind them.

Philippa grinned. Her friends no doubt already guessed what it must say.

The brigadier-general cleared his throat. "It says... 'Northrup is a liar and a fraud. If he had created this cipher, he would be able to read it. With love, Damaris, Philippa, Agnes, and Katherine.'"

Gasps rippled through the ballroom.

Northrup's face mottled. "Who the devil are Agnes and Katherine?"

"One is your great-great-cousin, many times removed," Philippa said. "And the other was her...companion. *They* were the artists who illustrated the Northrup manuscripts. Your ancestor had nothing to do with it."

"*They* are the ones who are nothing," Northrup thundered. "I've never heard those names before!"

"Is that why you destroyed your family Bible?" Philippa asked. "In an attempt to erase all evidence of Agnes Northrup, the true heroine in your family?"

"I..." Captain Northrup spluttered. "How did you..."

"Much like our military have not heard Damaris's name before, even though *she* was the one who invented the cipher that helped to win the war. Your ancestor was just as unscrupulous a liar as you are."

Northrup paled, his nostrils flaring. "How dare you suggest—'

"She's not 'suggesting' anything," Tommy snapped. "Your general just *proved* you haven't the least notion how to read a cipher you allegedly created."

All eyes swung back to Captain Northrup.

"That doesn't prove anything about my ancestor," Northrup said quickly. "Sir Reginald was well respected and known throughout his parish."

"Indeed." Damaris reached into the basket and pulled out the old letters and yellowed diary Graham had unearthed. "Known as a particularly heartless landlord and bully, whose only use for his cousin was to siphon her inheritance and steal her credit as an artist."

"See here," said Northrup. "Who cares if he had outside help? Even the great Renaissance masters had apprentices."

"You just said Sir Reginald penned every stroke himself," Sybil called out. "Which is it?"

Northrup waved his hand impatiently. "I said it because it's true. If there were any evidence to the contrary, it would have been found long before now. Sir Reginald deserves to be honored as the namesake of the grand Northrup Salon at the Royal Military Academy."

"There absolutely ought to be a grand Northrup Salon," Damaris agreed. "But not for him. For the splendid female artist Miss *Agnes* Northrup. She and her partner were the ones who created the chivalric tales."

"As I said," Northrup ground out. "If you had proof—"

Philippa gestured to an empty table. "If we might use that surface for a demonstration?"

The young footman Philippa and Tommy had passed in the corridor rushed forward to brush the spotless table with a handkerchief.

Damaris placed her uncle's illuminated manuscript on its side, spine facing the onlookers. "Volume one."

Philippa carried the heavy basket over to the table and removed its contents one by one. "Volume two, volume three, and volume four."

"How on earth did you amass a complete collection?" Brigadier-General Boswick narrowed his eyes in suspicion. "We purchased all privately held copies, barring the handful owned by conspicuous organizations who—"

"Never mind," Philippa said quickly. "How is irrelevant. What is important is that all sets are signed by the artists."

"They are?" Northrup paled. "I mean, that's wonderful. Point out my ancestor's signature and we will put paid to this pageantry at once."

Philippa turned the pile of perfectly aligned manuscripts so that their edges faced the audience.

"Adorable," Northrup said with a roll of his eyes. "So clever, the way the little flourishes are only complete when nestled against their partner. But it hardly proves—"

"They're letters," Damaris said. "Fancy ones, so pretty that it's easy to miss the truth. The lines without leaves and petals are the lines of the letter. Do you see this A?"

"There are multiple," Lady Eunice called out. "I can see two A's."

Damaris pointed each one out for the crowd.

"I can see them, too!" several guests called out.

"I think I see a K," said another lady.

Philippa nodded. "The five-by-three grid has no spaces, but the message it spells out is simple enough. Even Captain Northrup must see it."

Brigadier-General Boswick cleared his throat. "It says, 'Agnes & Katherine.'"

The crowd gasped.

Sweat beaded upon Northrup's brow. "You painted this on yourself. You *added* it, to try and humiliate me!"

Philippa shook her head. "These four come from different sets, and they match perfectly. *All* the Northrup volumes are likely signed in this manner. With the unique signature of the original artists, Agnes Northrup and Katherine Claybourne."

Captain Northrup's face went bright red. "I…"

Philippa touched the topmost volume. "There is no denying who should be honored for their artistic talent and their genius, and who should not."

"She means *not you*, pup," Tommy barked at Captain Northrup. "Three cheers for Agnes, Katherine, and Miss Damaris Urqhart, lady cryptographer!"

Philippa's reading circle cheered first and loudest. The rest of the women in the ballroom joined in the cheer.

Damaris's mother linked arms with her daughter and glared at her brother in stony silence.

The brigadier-general turned to Northrup. "You stole the cipher from your niece."

"Just like his knavish ancestor!" Tommy quavered helpfully. "Supplanting women for personal gain is in this swindler's blood."

"Can there still be a Northrup Salon?" Philippa asked. "Is 'In honor of Agnes Northrup and Katherine Claybourne' too long to fit on a plaque?"

"I cannot fathom what actions the Prince Regent may take," said Brigadier-General Boswick. The cold look he gave Northrup indicated the brigadier-general referred to consequences far beyond whether the Royal Military Academy would rechristen one of its chambers. "Perhaps he'll start by canceling your pension."

"I see there won't be a new viscount in January after all," Tommy said loud enough to be heard in every corner of the ballroom. "Unless lady cryptographers can be viscounts, too?"

"That would be wonderful, Aunt," Chloe said, materializing at Tommy's side. "I hope we all send letters of support to encourage Parliament to crown her a peeress in her own right. In the meantime, I imagine any hostess worth her salt will be certain to have Damaris's name at the top of her guest list."

"I hope you come to *my* musicale, Miss Urqhart," Lady Southwell blurted out.

"And *my* supper party," said Lady Ainsworth. "My daughter would love to speak to you."

Northrup's circle of onetime admirers dispersed, putting physical distance between themselves and their erstwhile idol. For him, it appeared the ball was over.

For Damaris, it was just beginning. She hugged Philippa tight. "Thank you."

The rest of the reading circle joined them, before Damaris's mother pulled her away to bask in her newfound popularity.

"You did it," Tommy said to Philippa. "I had no idea tearing a tiny hole in patriarchal coverture would make my nether regions so excited."

Philippa elbowed her in the ribs and tried not to laugh with joy. She had done it. *They* had done it.

They were heroines!

34

✽

$\mathcal{W}$arm sunlight streamed through Philippa's bedroom window at eight o'clock the following morning. She awoke with Tiglet curled into her side. A smile took over her face. She felt as though illuminated manuscripts with tales of chivalry and heroic knights had been written about *her*.

She had slain the dragon! *She* had brought a happy ending to not one, but three fair maidens! Triumph was not a feeling Philippa was accustomed to. She loved it. She was happier this morning than on the day of her come-out, or the night she first used her Almack's voucher.

Tommy's family must awaken with this sense of pride and justice every day of their lives.

The joy came from knowing Philippa had made a difference. She'd been part of a team that nudged the world in a better direction than it had been going yesterday. A *far* better accomplishment than "can use watercolors" or "knows five melodies at the pianoforte."

Rightful credit had been given to three talented women who deserved it. The reading circle was euphoric. Damaris was the belle of the ball—due to her *cryptography*. A so-called unladylike pastime that had helped to win the war.

This sudden popularity should also help with the reading

circle's charity endeavors. After Philippa broke her fast, she intended to write to all the ladies who had previously declined to take part in collaborative charity work with a group of bluestockings. Perhaps now they would be eager to help.

Philippa's dream to bring lending libraries to every neighborhood in London could actually come to fruition. What lady wouldn't wish to join causes with women who stood up for other women? Perhaps the reading circle would even grow twofold!

Her lips curving in what felt like a permanent grin, Philippa dressed and made her way lightly down the steps. By now, Tommy and her siblings would have returned the "borrowed" manuscripts. At this hour in Philippa's home, only the servants would be awake. But even without friends to talk to, nothing could dampen her sunny mood.

To her surprise, the muffled sound of her mother's voice came from the cerulean sitting room. Philippa paused. She gave up on her plan to read alone and headed to her mother's sitting room instead.

Philippa's jaw dropped when she walked through the door. Not only was her father out of his study and seated beside the fire, but every surface of the salon was covered with gifts. Flowers, sweets, wine, pile after pile of letters...

"What *is* this?" Philippa said in wonder. "Is it for me?"

Her mother rounded to face her, countenance pale save for two bright spots in her cheeks.

"It would appear so," Father said from behind his broadsheet.

"There's nothing from any *suitors*," Mother said acidly, "so don't get your hopes up. All of this nonsense was sent by your foolish bluestockings."

Now that Mother mentioned it, fine Madeira *was* an

unusual choice from a gentleman, but made perfect sense if the sender was Lady Eunice.

Philippa crossed to the overflowing sideboard. She recognized the handwriting on the letters as being from ladies who attended her reading circle. All two dozen of them must have sent a note or a gift. She picked up the bottle of wine. A note was attached to the neck with a sunny yellow ribbon. Philippa removed it carefully and unfolded the letter to reveal several paragraphs of Lady Eunice's elegant handwriting.

Darlingest Philippa—

Mother snatched the letter from Philippa's hand and tossed it into the fire.

"I was *reading* that!" Philippa clenched her fists as the fire consumed the kind words. "It was from a friend."

"Not anymore." Mother drew herself up to her full height—an inch taller than Philippa's admittedly short frame. Mother crossed her arms over her chest and lifted her nose. "There shall be no more reading circle and no more bluestocking nonsense."

"*What?*" Philippa's chest constricted. "Why?"

"Because you're ruined," Mother burst out. "What did you think you were doing?"

"The right thing!" Philippa snapped up straight. "I didn't ruin *my* reputation. It is Captain Northrup who lied to everyone and stole his niece's cipher."

"Captain Northrup, celebrated war hero and personal favorite of the Prince Regent, who planned to bestow a viscountcy upon Northrup to honor him, and now shall not."

"He shan't?" Philippa brightened. "It *did* work."

"It worked to paint you as poisonous to the gentlemen of

the ton," Mother snapped. "Why single him out? There isn't a man alive who hasn't done something he regrets."

"I certainly have," Father muttered from behind his broadsheet.

Mother ignored this. "Fashionable gentlemen no longer wish to be under the same roof as Philippa. Not when her presence could spell doom or scandal."

Philippa's happiness faded. This was the worst possible outcome of the best thing she had ever done.

"There are *no more suitors*," Mother whispered, pressing her hands to her chest in horror.

No. That was not the worst thing. Philippa didn't give a fig about receiving the cut direct from men. She liked the idea that her mere presence could cause arrogant bucks to tremble in their champagne-shined Hessians. "Bringer of Doom" was an even better sobriquet than bluestocking.

But if Philippa was persona non grata to the men, then she had become persona non grata for the ladies, too. The female half of the ton had brothers, fathers, husbands, sons. Some would forbid contact with her. Others had never wished to rub elbows and now had even more excuse to ostracize her. Philippa's stomach sank.

The citywide lending library was not going to happen. The charity collaborations were as ephemeral as smoke. In fact…there were *eighteen* letters and gifts, not twenty-four. Her grand triumph might have cost her several of her dearest friends.

Lady Eunice had sneaked out one letter and a bottle of Madeira, but her very proper parents had no doubt forbidden her from any further acquaintance with Philippa.

"*You're* not canceling my reading circle," she said bleakly.

"I've no need to," said her mother. "We'll be lucky if the *newspaper* still comes."

"I am literally reading it at this very moment," Father said from behind his broadsheet. "Or rather, was attempting to do so before I was interrupted."

Of course the newspaper would still come. And the milk cart, and their servants, and so forth. But many, if not most, of Philippa's friends would not be permitted to risk their reputations.

And she had only herself to blame.

She noticed a letter written in a strange hand. It bore no name but her own. She turned it over: the wax was unmarked. Philippa broke the seal and scanned only the first few lines before tossing it into the flames herself.

"Yes," Mother said softly. "Some of your letters are anonymous, and they were not penned by admirers."

"I've told her a hundred times to cease reading your correspondence," Father said from behind his newspaper.

"Philippa doesn't want to read that rubbish either," Mother said. "You would have seen her throw it into the fire if you had put down your broadsheet."

"I'm reading about our daughter," Father said. "She is the topic of a scandal column."

"*Me?*" The word scratched Philippa's throat. She'd known she would be mentioned, but Damaris was the heroine of the story—and the villain was her uncle. "What happened to Captain Northrup?"

"Oh, he's ruined as well." Father shook out his paper. "You're infamous for coldly engineering the downfall of a celebrated gentleman of Polite Society."

"I...Well, I...definitely did that," Philippa admitted. "I would do so again."

Her concern had been the women who had been wronged. A man like Northrup would only grow worse once he became a lord.

"You should have gone along with him," Mother bit out

bitterly. "You would have had a *famous* husband, and a *title*. What the dickens is wrong with you?"

"Why can't you see that something was wrong with *Northrup?*"

"Like 'being the Prince's favorite'?" Mother asked sarcastically. "Or, 'soon to be honored publicly, with his betrothed at his side'?"

"Not everyone withdrew their suits," Father said from behind his broadsheet.

"And that is where we find ourselves." Mother's lip curled in disgust. "Left with a handful of fortune hunters too eager for your dowry to care what kind of woman they wed. At this point, we must marry you off to anyone who will take you."

"It's not a difficult decision," said Father. "The 'handful' is gone. There's only one man left."

"The dregs of the dregs, I'm sure," Mother spat. "You could have married a *lord*, Philippa. You chose to ruin him instead. The social consequences of your rash behavior—"

"It's *my* life," Philippa burst out. "I'm the one who must live with the consequences."

"It's *not* your life," Mother said coldly. "It's all of our lives. You are not the only person in this household to receive vile correspondence. Did you pause to think how your behavior would affect your mother and your father? I have received several notes retracting prior invitations. Some from the wives of men your poor father *believed* to be staunch allies."

Philippa's lungs were suddenly devoid of air.

The fatherly voice behind the broadsheet did not come to her defense.

Losing the very friends Philippa had wished to protect was a horrid unintended consequence. Discovering she'd managed to lower her parents' consequence in the process...Possibly even ruin her father's carefully constructed alliances in the

House of Commons...Philippa wrapped her arms about her stomach.

"Who is the last fortune hunter remaining?" Mother asked.

"Lord Whiddleburr," Father's voice replied.

Mother turned to Philippa. "What good fortune, darling! You'll become a lady after all. That is, so long as the marquess does not hear of your scandal."

"He doesn't hear very well at all," Father murmured. "He's older than I am."

"I've no wish to marry Lord Whiddleburr," Philippa said with horror.

"You didn't want to marry Captain Northrup, and you got that wish," Mother said. "Now we will take charge. Go upstairs and stay in your bedchamber until your father has had a chance to finish the marriage plans."

"Finish?" Philippa stammered. "You didn't even know who it was until a few moments ago."

"If we obtain his signature in the next few hours, perhaps the betrothal will stick. Whiddleburr and his heirs will be important allies in Parliament. With a special license, you could be married tomorrow."

Philippa's flesh went clammy. "Tomorrow?"

"You should be thanking us," Mother said. "His title will elevate your nonexistent status and help mend the damage done to ours as well. Lord Whiddleburr will make a fine parliamentary ally for your father. After all of the trouble you've caused, it is the right—and only—thing to do."

Philippa's fingernails dug into her palms, but she kept her jaw tightly shut. If choosing Lord Whiddleburr over a life of love or happiness could repair the harm done, perhaps it *was* the "right" thing to do. She *had* caused this damage. She *did* hurt her parents.

She wasn't the white knight after all.

Eyes blurring, Philippa turned and ran back up the stairs to her private chamber. She dropped to her knees to search beneath the mattress for Tiglet. The homing kitten was nowhere to be found. After a frantic search through her rooms, she gave up and slipped down the rear stairs to the servants' entrance. Philippa ignored their startled gazes as she rushed out of the house and to the street to flag down a hackney.

The November wind was cold and unforgiving. Philippa's entire body was shivering by the time she climbed inside the carriage.

This time, she wasn't running away. She was running *to* someone. If her remaining freedom could be counted in hours, she wanted to spend every minute of it with Tommy. They might never see each other again.

When she reached the Wynchester residence in Islington, their butler held the front door open wide the moment Philippa alighted from the hackney.

"She's upstairs," said the butler, as if Tommy had left standing orders that Philippa was to be admitted at any hour of any day.

"Thank you." Philippa raced up the stairs.

She poked her head into the Planning Parlor first. It was empty except for Graham, who was reading his usual pile of newspapers. Unlike Philippa's father, Graham tossed his broadsheets aside at once.

"Philippa! Just the person I both dreaded and hoped to see. Your parcel arrived today. And I wanted to personally—"

"Thank you," she interrupted, accepting the brown paper package. There had been more than enough unexpected gifts for one day. "Have you seen Tommy?"

"She just returned from Battersea Park," Graham said. "She'll be in her dressing room, changing out of her livery. But I wanted you to know—"

Philippa didn't need information. She needed Tommy.

35

⚜

$\mathcal{T}$ommy returned her white wig to its box and yanked off her cravat. As always, today's mission had been fun and rewarding, but she was eager to doff her uncomfortable livery and be herself again. There was a map she was excited to finish before next week's assignment.

Most of all, she needed to see Philippa. Tiglet had arrived while Tommy was out, and the morning's papers had not been kind. As soon as Tommy was back in her usual clothes, she planned to—

The door flew open. Tommy spun around. Philippa burst into the dressing room, dropped a brown paper parcel to the floor, and threw herself straight into Tommy's arms.

Tommy held her tight for several long moments without saying anything at all. When Philippa let out a muffled sob, Tommy murmured, "*None* of Graham's associates wrote a negative word about you."

Philippa choked and pulled away.

Tommy's stomach twisted. "Our footmen bring him the first copies of the main newspapers, but by then it was too late."

"It wouldn't have mattered," Philippa said dully. "The papers are only repeating what everyone else is saying. I received letters upbraiding me for my impudence in daring to come between a man and his undeserved glory. And my parents..."

Tommy stilled. "Are they all right?"

Philippa let out a sound somewhere between a laugh and a sob. "Of course you'd be more concerned about the well-being of my parents than they are about the well-being of their own daughter. Wynchesters are wonderful. My parents are unhappy with me."

"You did nothing wrong," Tommy said firmly. "I mean, you broke a few rules and maybe a couple of laws, but nothing you should feel bad about. Helping others is a *good* thing. Damaris, Agnes, and Katherine deserved credit. And Northrup deserved to be taken down. Propositioning you in the middle of a ball, for God's sake."

"It doesn't matter who deserved what," Philippa said. "I cannot undo what I've done, nor would I do so if I could. But I did not mean to cause—"

A *miaow* sounded from beneath a discarded frock coat. Tiglet poked his nose and whiskers out from under a lapel.

"You little scamp." Philippa scooped up the kitten and cuddled him to her chest. "No matter how hard I try to make him happy, he keeps running away."

"He doesn't run away," Tommy reminded her. "He comes home. It's what he's trained to do."

"Which means it's hopeless." Philippa looked distraught. "There's nothing I can do to make him feel at home with me. Tiglet and I are not meant to be together."

"Or," Tommy said hesitantly, "perhaps it's a sign that you *are*. The Wynchester family can afford to grow." *She* had learned to grow. "What if... what if this were your home, too?"

Philippa lay her cheek against the kitten's calico fur. "I wish it were. Thank you for asking. But we both know I'm not a Wynchester."

"Because you're a York?" Tommy scoffed. "I was something else before I was a Wynchester, too. All of us were. Besides, you know I'm not talking about changing your name. I'm talking about changing your address."

"My parents already have a plan to change both. It's underway as we speak." Philippa twisted her lips. "I'm to be a wife. That is what proper young misses grow up to do."

"You don't have to be a 'proper miss' or 'wallflower' or 'wife' or any other such label. You're Philippa." Tommy touched her arm. "It's fine to play a role, but never forget that it *is* a role. It's always better to be you."

"I'll be the me that's married to Lord Whiddleburr," Philippa mumbled. "Marchioness to an old roué I barely even know. But I cannot defy my parents again."

"Good Lord. You cannot possibly want Whiddleburr." Tommy shuddered and stepped back. The future was clear. "Nor shall you defy your parents."

Philippa looked up in shock. "You think I should marry him?"

"No. I cannot agree with your assumption that they can control your life. You're three and twenty. Two years past the age of majority. Disappointing your parents is not the same as defying them. They're the ones disappointing *you*."

Philippa clutched Tiglet to her chest and closed her eyes.

"If they're sorry they raised a wonderful daughter with a mind of her own, then they are the ones with the problem." Tommy stepped forward and brushed the pad of her thumb across Philippa's cheek. "The decision must be something *you* can live with."

"I cannot live with ruining my parents' lives," Philippa said in a small voice. "I longed to make them proud. Instead...It's not just them. My reading circle is in danger, too. Our charity work. The women and children who were counting on us.

Even the laws my father is trying to pass in Parliament. That's not what...I was trying to put wrongs to right, not cause new ones."

"And you did both at once. Actions have consequences."

"I want different consequences." Philippa swallowed. "A different life. If I'm to be a wife, a baroness would be splendid. I realize you cannot *really* marry me...Unless you can? I'd much rather be with you than Lord Whiddleburr."

"No," said Tommy. "You'd rather have Baron Vanderbean."

This was not the proposal of her dreams.

Philippa *did* want her...but only disguised as someone else. Tommy's shoulders curved, her exquisite gold-and-blue livery awkward and heavy.

She had been so looking forward to taking her regalia off and being herself again. Then here came the woman she loved, pleading for Tommy to put a disguise back on.

Tommy had *asked* Philippa to stay. To make this her home, just as Tommy and her siblings had. To be herself. *Philippa.* Not any label society or her parents tried to place upon her.

That wasn't good enough. *Tommy* wasn't good enough. The baron identity was the dressing that made their relationship palatable. Her stomach churned with acid.

Philippa wanted her only if Tommy could be someone else.

"You want me to put on my tail coat and go and beg your father for your hand?"

Philippa's brow furrowed. "It would take some begging. Lord Whiddleburr outranks you. Outranks Baron Vanderbean, I mean. And you're not in Parliament. But at least the baron is near my age and not a fortune hunter."

He wasn't anything. He wasn't *real*.

"That's all I would have to do?"

"Well, obviously you would need to *keep* being the baron," Philippa said. "He cannot disappear the moment we're betrothed. The ruse will only work if people believe it. You'd have to be the baron in public and anywhere he would reasonably be expected to be present."

"Obviously," Tommy repeated, her voice dull and empty.

Her skin prickled beneath her livery. Was it worth it? Was getting to keep Philippa worth giving up herself? Being forced to answer to her father's name forevermore?

It wasn't Happy Ever After if only one person was happy with who they were ever after. She didn't want to be the lesser evil in the choice between Lord Whiddleburr and Baron Vanderbean.

If Tommy wasn't chosen for herself...then she wasn't being chosen at all.

"No," she said quietly. "I'm *not* Baron Vanderbean. I'm Tommy. I asked you to stay with *me*."

"I *would* be with you," Philippa said.

"You'd be with Baron Vanderbean," Tommy said. "Anywhere he might reasonably be expected. Which is everywhere *you* are. In public. At private gatherings. At home."

"I rarely attend society events," Philippa pointed out, "and the baron is famously reclusive. Besides, my own parents are rarely seen together. I could spend most of *my* time with my sister-in-law."

Tommy closed her eyes. "Miss Thomasina" was *also* a disguise.

"In any case, you make an excellent Baron Vanderbean. His costume is very comfortable, remember?"

"Any costume is unbearable if it cannot be removed. Theater is an enjoyable pastime because it *ends*. Four hours, then the curtain closes. But everywhere I went would be my theater. Every day. Constantly onstage, even at home."

"*I* would know you were really you. Your family would know you were really you."

"My family would never ask me to hide myself for the rest of my life," Tommy said quietly. "They love me. They would never prefer a fictional character over the real Tommy."

Philippa blanched. "I—"

"I want to be wanted for me. *As* me. Doesn't everyone?" Tommy opened her arms wide in supplication. "Or did you think I own so many disguises because there's nothing underneath?"

Philippa's voice shook. "That's not fair."

"*I'm* not fair?" Tommy said in disbelief. "How can you ask me to marry you as Baron Vanderbean? There *is* no Baron Vanderbean."

"But you have wardrobes full of—"

"Being caught dressed as a chimneysweep wouldn't matter. Being caught impersonating one's conspicuously absent benefactor, however…The ramifications could be severe."

Philippa's face drained of color. "But if you—"

"It is one thing to don temporary disguises for our clients when the circumstances warrant," Tommy said quietly, "but I was not planning to live a lie for the rest of time."

Or to continue using Bean's name as if it were her own.

Philippa's eyes were wide, her cheeks pallid.

Tommy kept her voice even. "I thank you for your kind offer. I must decline. I want my partner to be the person I can be myself with." She now despaired of such a dream ever coming true. "Even if that means it cannot be you."

"I didn't mean…" Philippa's voice wobbled. "It seemed like…a compromise…"

"I don't want a compromise," Tommy said. "I want to be loved. I want forever. I want it all. And I want you."

Philippa's gaze jerked back to hers. "What?"

"I love you," Tommy said simply. "I love Miss Philippa York, without qualification or limitations." Her ribs ached.

"Saying no to you is the hardest thing I've ever had to do. I hope my counteroffer is one we can both say yes to."

"What counteroffer?"

"This: I'll be Tommy, and you'll be Philippa, and we'll live here, together, happily ever after."

Philippa's face twisted in anguish. She let out a long, shuddering breath. "I can't."

Those two words sliced through Tommy as though she had been run through with a blade. "You can't or you don't want to?"

Philippa stepped forward, her face beseeching. "My parents expect—"

"Aren't you sick of your parents' expectations?" Tommy burst out. "Don't you expect better of *them?*"

"They are trying their best," Philippa said in misery. "I'm the one who is not. I have shamed them. And if I were to...With *you*..."

Tommy turned away before her blurring eyes could blot out Philippa's face.

Anyone but Tommy Wynchester. She was leave-able. Abandonable. Unimportant. A fine distraction for a month or two, but ultimately unnecessary. She was not nearly as enticing as the roles she played. Fiction was better than the real person.

"The 'new' Baron Vanderbean is a lie," Tommy ground out, "and marrying him is a fairy tale. It is not reality."

"Tommy—"

"I am flesh-and-blood. I don't want to only be useful when playing a role. I've been acting my entire life. I am real. I want to be myself with the woman I love."

"You said you were happy to be Baron Vanderbean," Philippa said. "The word we used was 'indefinitely.'"

"We were talking about this season. I was willing to play a

baron as much as you needed within the context of those three months. 'Ninety-one days,' you said. I agreed to a *temporary* ruse. I did not agree to cease being Tommy for the rest of my natural life. It was just supposed to be—"

Tommy raked a hand through her hair. What had she expected? Philippa was a Proper Young Lady. Used to giving orders and having every whim granted. She was haut ton. Born with the silver spoon. And everyone knew Polite Society did not mingle with Wynchesters.

Much less voluntarily give up their high social class for a dalliance.

There was no possibility of Philippa choosing Tommy for herself.

Tommy had just wanted it to be true so much that she'd let herself keep dreaming.

It was time to wake up.

"If we cannot both be ourselves," she said, her chest tight. "If we both don't *want* each other for ourselves, then we shouldn't be together."

Philippa's eyes were glassy as she slowly set the kitten on a chair and gave his head one final pat. "I'll see myself out."

36

~~~

Philippa took a step toward the door, then turned around. "I wouldn't *rather* have Baron Vanderbean. It's that I can only accept—"

The stoic expression on Tommy's face was more than eloquent. The answer was no. No to Philippa's wild, desperate proposal. No to Philippa. There was nothing to be said, nothing that could be done. She had made a hash of it, and her time with Tommy was over.

She stumbled across the dressing room to the door.

"Philippa…" Tommy's voice was raw, but she made no move to chase after her.

Good. Philippa was already on the move. Already running. Already—

—smacking headlong into Graham Wynchester, knocking a tall stack of his precious albums clattering to the floor, and sending a spray of broadsheets into the air in all directions.

Philippa let out a choking sob. She dropped to the floor to pick up the fallen papers. The man was just trying to exit his bedchamber, and she'd managed to botch *that* for him as well. The best thing she could do for this family was never to bother them again. Her words had wounded Tommy, and her very presence was enough to—

Graham swept his journals and papers into his room with his foot and touched Philippa's elbow. "Where are you going? *Why* are you going?"

"I'm leaving," she blurted out. "I'm...I'm sorry. Look at what I did to your books!"

"One could argue the fault is mine." Graham sent a rueful glance over his shoulder. "I cannot tell you how many times Bean told me not to walk with a stack so high it obstructs my vision. Are you certain it wasn't me who ran into you?"

"Pretty certain," Philippa mumbled.

"Come with me." He shut the door to his bedchamber and led her down the corridor. "This is the Planning Parlor."

"I remember." Even if it had been Philippa's first time in the room, the enormous table with its myriad compartments, the wide array of globes and maps, the bookcases full of intelligence gathered, the chalk outline of what appeared to be an escape route from a dairy farm drawn upon the slate floor...it *looked* like a room where plans were made.

"Sit." Graham released her wrist and pointed at the chairs and settees arranged artfully about the fireplace.

Philippa waited to see which armchair Graham would take before choosing one opposite him.

"Aren't you worried about your books and papers lying in disarray?" she asked in a small voice.

"I'm more worried about you," Graham said. "Books and papers can be replaced."

Philippa's eyes prickled and she darted her gaze away while she blinked extra hard.

Graham leaned back in his chair. "A little bird told me you have the dreadful custom of running away from things you care about at the first sign of conflict."

Philippa stammered, "Tommy said that?"

"Elizabeth and Marjorie," Graham replied. "They apparently witnessed your technique in action at Vauxhall Gardens."

Philippa's cheeks burned with shame. There was no glib answer that could absolve her.

"This is the Planning Parlor," Graham said again. "This is where we come to work problems out. If you still wish to run away after you've analyzed the problem logically, let it be a strategic choice rather than cowardice."

Philippa winced. The picture he painted of her was not pretty...but it *was* a hopeful one. He would not have brought her here unless he did believe there was a solution just waiting to be fathomed out.

Graham folded his arms across his broad chest. "Were you running away from my sister?"

Philippa nodded once.

"Did you intend to come back to her?"

Philippa clenched her teeth and shook her head.

"It's all right to feel confused," he said.

"I am not confused," Philippa replied. "I understand the nuances of my situation perfectly well, which is the reason I walked—ran—away. Sometimes the wisest thing to do is to recognize when you are defeated. I am out of choices and I am out of time."

Graham raised his brows. "Your parents cannot still intend to betroth you to Northrup."

"Lord Whiddleburr," she muttered.

He looked appalled. "Let me loan you the journal I compiled on that family. You may change your mind."

"I already don't want him," Philippa ground out. "I want Tommy."

"But Tommy tossed you from her chambers in repulsion?"

"No, she did not."

"She screamed at you and cursed your name?"

"*No.*"

"She made a rude comment about your favorite author?"

Philippa glared at him. Brothers were apparently horrid beasts. "You make it sound as though I brought on my own heartache all by myself."

Graham gazed back at her without responding.

Heat traveled up the back of Philippa's neck.

Tommy *had* asked her to stay. Philippa *had* chosen to run instead. She had very much caused the current situation herself.

"I want her, but I cannot have her," she said glumly. "Young ladies in Polite Society only have one accepted path. Marry well or be mocked and pitied as a spinster."

"Fascinating," Graham said. "I had no idea how remarkably stupid clever people could be."

Philippa's mouth fell open. "That is very rude."

"So is running away from the person who loves you most." He lifted a shoulder. "This will be the shortest planning session this parlor has ever seen. You've already given yourself a plethora of potential answers. Don't be a lady. Travel the improper path. Don't marry well. Live on the margins of society as a spinster who does exactly what she wants."

"I would if it were just my life in the balance." Philippa's voice scratched. "My choices reflect on my family, my friends, and my charity work. I am not *Philippa* without those things. They need me and I—I need them."

"Must you give them up?"

"I *tried* to find a way," Philippa said, defeated. "To please my parents and to please society and to live with myself. I thought perhaps everyone might be happy if I married Baron Vanderbean."

"Not Tommy?"

"Tommy *is* Baron Vanderbean."

"No. She's Tommy. She's been courting you as Baron Vanderbean because it's what *you* want. She's been trying to please *you*. Even if she's miserable knowing you'll only accept her if she's someone else."

"Not *my* preference," Philippa stammered. "It's..."

But it *was* her, ultimately. It had been Philippa standing in front of Tommy, Philippa saying Tommy wasn't acceptable as herself, Philippa saying only Baron Vanderbean would be good enough for her.

Philippa hurting the person she loved more than any other.

She hadn't even said the most important words. She had been so busy explaining what sort of partner would or would not do, that she'd missed the opportunity to mention the tiny little fact that Philippa was hopelessly in love with Tommy. Just Tommy.

Baron Vanderbean had seemed such an easy solution. It had not occurred to Philippa that asking might be hurtful. That it might have *been* hurtful all along.

She rubbed her face. Not only had she asked Tommy to permanently play the role of someone she was not...Philippa would have become Baroness Vanderbean, taking social precedence over the actual Wynchesters. It wasn't much of a compromise if Philippa was the only one to come out on top.

One of the things Philippa had always cherished about Tommy was her empathy. Yet Philippa had not shown the same character. She had been selfish as a partner, as a lover, as a friend...Her shoulders crumpled.

Tommy had mentioned that every time she took on the role of the false Baron Vanderbean, she was reminded of her *real* Bean. It made her uncomfortable and sad. How could she be expected to submit to a lifetime of such conflict and memories?

"Brothers may not be horrid beasts after all," she mumbled. "*I* might be the horrid beast."

Graham inclined his head. "Admitting it sounds like the first step of a promising new plan."

Philippa's throat thickened and she averted her gaze.

"We cannot choose whom we love," Graham said, "but we can choose what to do about it. If you and Tommy found joy, then you should hold on to each other. I want both of you to be happy."

He would. The Wynchesters were the loveliest family Philippa had ever met. How she wished her own felt that way about her.

"We want the same for you," Graham added. "You should, too."

She stared at him, startled. It was as though he had read her thoughts and gave her what she most needed.

Graham smiled gently. "You are within your rights to seek your own joy. Of course you wish no ill upon your friends or family. They should feel the same about you. If they do not, what are you really missing?"

Love.

He was right. Friends and family should want the best for each other. If Philippa's parents did not care about her happiness, then it was up to her to find her own. She was uncertain what would happen with her charity projects, but highborn ladies were not the only possible benefactors. Wynchesters did impossible things every day.

It was time Philippa did, too.

Starting with making up for one very bad mistake.

"I hurt Tommy," Philippa said wretchedly. "I didn't mean to, but I did. This mess...I did it to myself. Instead of just saying yes to what I really wanted. *Her.*"

Graham's dark eyes were grave.

Philippa drew in a shuddering breath. Her stomach felt leaden. She could not imagine how badly she'd wounded Tommy by not accepting her as herself. By not *appreciating* her for herself. By not letting her know there was no one else Philippa loved and admired more.

She yearned to be the one who gave Tommy what she wanted, what she needed, what she deserved. As wild and free as she always seemed, how often had Philippa stopped to ask Tommy what *she* wanted? What *she* needed?

Philippa hung her head. "Asking your sister to permanently and publicly be someone she's not was no better than my parents' constant demands that I be something I'm not."

"Which is why *you* shouldn't do it, either." Graham's voice was soft. "Sacrificing your own happiness and needs to satisfy your family's selfish wants is just as unfair. It isn't noble to coddle them at the expense of your own happiness."

Philippa twisted her hands.

"Trust yourself. Believe in yourself. Live for yourself." Graham gave her a brotherly smile. "No matter what your parents told you, it's *all right* to have the things you want in life. You can reach out and grab them."

Freedom. Love. Tommy.

Running away was not the answer. The only acceptable path forward was for both Philippa and Tommy to be themselves.

Even if it meant disappointing her parents. Even if it meant the loss of her reputation. Even if it meant no longer being part of Polite Society. Love was worth it.

Tommy was worth it.

"*Carpe diem*," Philippa said. "*Carpe vitam. Carpe amorem.*"

"That's the stuff." Graham held out his hand and pulled her to her feet. "Seize the day, seize life, and seize love."

As he had suggested from the beginning.

"Do Wynchesters always win?" Philippa grumbled.

"You'll find out. If you manage to become one of us."

Philippa rolled her shoulders. It might be impossible. It might be too late. She might have already destroyed Tommy's trust in her.

But she wouldn't walk away again without doing everything in her power to prove to Tommy just how much Philippa loved her.

"Before I go…" She bit her lip. "Might I ask for one tiny, peculiar favor?"

Graham's brown eyes glittered with mischief. "Anything."

37

Tommy flung herself atop her freshly made bed and stared up at the canopy.

She could not bear to make small talk with her siblings, who were all having a perfectly fine day and had not just watched the woman they loved fleeing in horror at the thought of being together as partners.

Philippa had left half an hour ago. Tommy *could* have gone after her. Would have, once. But if Philippa didn't love her—not enough to want Tommy for and as herself—then what good was chasing a dream that was already over?

A knock sounded at the door.

She ignored it. One's private chambers were sacred space. If Tommy had wanted to come out of her room, she would have done so. She was not ready for smiles or hugs or well-meaning optimism.

The knock came again.

Tommy placed her pillow over her face. At least she didn't have curls to ruin or cosmetics to smear. She was just Tommy.

Alone. Again.

The banging at the door penetrated the feathers of her pillow.

Tommy cast the cushion aside and lurched toward the closed door.

"Not now, Graham!" Had her voice cracked? Oh God, it had cracked. Now he would never leave her alone. He would sit out there in the corridor, his back against her door so that he would tumble inside the moment she opened it—

"It's not Graham," came a muffled voice. "It's me, Sir... Philip."

Tommy's heart banged against her chest in hope and confusion. She ran a hand over her hopelessly tousled hair and opened the door. "Sir... Philip?"

Philippa swaggered into the bedroom with her blond ringlets shoved inside a beaver hat and what looked like Graham's frock coat over her lace dress. A glass of port dangled from her fingers and a large cigar protruded from one corner of her mouth.

Tommy tried her best not to be charmed.

"You look ridiculous," she said flatly. "You are not remotely convincing as a man about town."

"I know." Philippa let her cigar tumble from her mouth into her glass of port. "*You* would be splendid at it. But being splendid at something does not mean a body is obliged to do it."

Tommy crossed her arms, but edged aside enough to allow Philippa farther into the room.

Philippa stared down at her goblet. "My parents have always believed I'd be a fine countess or duchess. They're probably right. Yet I never wanted that life." She looked up and met Tommy's eyes. "I have no right to saddle *you* with a role you don't wish to have, either. No matter how well we might play the part."

Hope filtered through the cracks in Tommy's defenses.

"I am so sorry." Philippa's pretty face twisted in agony. "I did not mean to hurt you, but I did. I was thoughtless and selfish. I so wanted to find a path to 'forever' with the person I love more than any other, all I could think about was—"

"Wait." Tommy's heart beat faster. "What did you just say?"

"I love you. I've loved you for longer than I've dared to admit it, even to myself. Saying the words aloud terrifies me. I'll say them again anyway. I *love* you, Tommy Wynchester. *You.* You haven't left my mind from the moment you blushed and ran away from me at Faircliffe's gala. I was halfway in love with 'Baron Vanderbean' and I don't even *like* men. It was you who won me, from the start."

"You love me?" Tommy repeated. Her head swam. "The real me?"

"With all my heart. I understand if you don't love me back anymore," Philippa said. "If I lost your love when I lost your trust, it's no more than I deserve. I'm sorry I hurt you. I'm sorry I disappointed you."

"You did hurt me." Tommy hugged herself. She loved Philippa madly, but was no longer willing to settle for temporary. She wanted it all. "You made me feel less than a fictional character. I wasn't even second best. When you couldn't have him, you left me without another word."

"It is indefensible." Philippa placed her goblet on a side table and pressed a hand to her heart. "I wasn't even running from *you*. I was running from my fears and my insecurities and my embarrassment."

Tommy knew what it was like to let one's fears guide one's actions. She had fled rather than speak to Philippa at the end-of-season gala. And it had taken her siblings' intervention and several false starts to prance up to the York carriage at Hyde Park and introduce herself.

But they hadn't known each other yet. From that moment on, Tommy had made their growing relationship a priority. There was no running away from something you wanted to make work. You put in the effort even when it was difficult or uncomfortable. Especially then. Love wasn't one person putting the other first, but rather all parties taking care of each other.

Always. Not just when it was convenient.

Tommy compressed her lips. "What will you do the next time you're afraid or embarrassed?"

"I don't know," Philippa said honestly. "But I won't do it alone. Whatever happens, we'll work it out together. My place is at your side...if you'll have me."

"You won't be tempted to run away?"

"*With* you, but not *from* you. You are the person I wish to have and to belong to. Every single day for the rest of my life." With shaking fingers, Philippa removed her top hat and dropped to one knee.

Tommy's heart began to clatter.

"My beloved Tommy Wynchester." Eyes beseeching, Philippa lifted Tommy's hand to her lips for a kiss. "You are perfect exactly as you are. I love you for who you are, not who you pretend to be. With me, you can always be Tommy, and it will always be more than enough."

Tommy wanted to believe it. Needed to believe it.

Was *terrified* of letting herself believe it.

Philippa pressed Tommy's fingers to her chest. "Please allow me to spend the rest of my life with you."

Tommy shoved her hands in her pockets. "Your parents—"

"—will not approve, no. I am done trying to be someone I am not for people I can never please. You and I can be exactly who we are, and please each other."

"What about Polite Society?"

" 'Polite'? They are unconscionably rude and selfish. And yes, I was once a lot like them. I gladly choose being a Wynchester over returning to that world."

"One cannot choose to be a Wynchester." Tommy's voice scratched. "Wynchesters must choose *you*."

"Do *you* choose me?"

"I might."

"Then I'll tell you a secret," Philippa said. "I can live with it if the rest of the world never chooses me. What I cannot imagine is a life without you. I love you, Tommy. You have my heart, and you *are* my heart. I don't care who knows it or what the gossips say. *I* choose *you*."

Tommy stared at Philippa, her eyes pricking and her heart beating far too fast.

"Please," Philippa said softly. "Let's determine our future together. Lovers and partners forevermore."

"Well," Tommy said. "I suppose I could think it over."

Philippa made a garbled sound.

Tommy pulled Philippa up and into her arms. "Yes, my beloved bluestocking. Yes, I'll spend my life with you. I choose *us*."

"Thank God." Philippa pressed her lips to Tommy's.

Tommy answered the kiss with hunger, wrapping her arms tight about Philippa.

Their other kisses had been kisses of *perhaps* and *mayhap* and *maybe*. This was the first kiss of *yes*. The first kiss of *always and forevermore*. It was a kiss to savor, and also the first of many just like it. The future stretched far and bright, lit with a constellation of kisses.

"Oh!" Philippa pulled her mouth away, breathless. "I almost forgot. I have a gift for you."

"Please tell me it's not the cigar slowly turning into sludge in your glass of port."

"It's even better," Philippa promised. She held up a finger. "Wait here."

Tommy waited in bemusement as Philippa sprinted into the adjoining dressing room and emerged with a brown paper package.

"I *did* forget you'd walked in with that," Tommy admitted. "What is it?"

"Open it and see." Philippa handed her the parcel.

Tommy sat on the edge of her mattress. She untied the twine, then unfolded the brown paper.

It was a handsome leather book, brand-new and expensive, with a gold monogram embossed onto the cover. She ran her fingers over the gilded "TW" in awe.

"It's gorgeous," she murmured.

Philippa bounced on her toes. "Open it!"

Gently, Tommy lifted the cover. The first page was blank. She turned it. The second page was blank, and the third, and the fourth. The entire book was pristine and empty.

"You brought me…a blank album?"

"It's for your *maps*," Philippa said. "They shall live jumbled no more. See these little folded bits? They're corners that can be glued at the exact dimensions you need. Each map slides right in, allowing it to be easily mounted and just as easily removed when it is needed for a mission. If you'd like, I'd be happy to design a cataloging system for you. We could work on it together."

A laugh of delight escaped Tommy's lips. "It's stunning, and thoughtful, and useful. Rather like the bluestocking minx who arranged it for me."

Philippa gave her a shy smile. "Shall we take it downstairs and organize your poor homeless maps at once?"

"No." Tommy placed the album on the side table next to

her bed with care and then opened her arms for Philippa. "I have other ideas. Prurient, obscene ideas."

"Mm, tell me more." Philippa pulled off her half-boots and launched herself into Tommy's embrace. "Or better yet, show me. I love to practice what I learn."

It took no time at all for their clothes to be piled upon the floor.

"Our life doesn't have to be scandalous." Tommy kissed Philippa's breasts. "We can be two eccentric spinsters who happen to live together. Just like Agnes and Katherine."

Those were the last words for several minutes. Instead, Tommy concentrated her eloquence on what her tongue was doing to Philippa. She trailed her kisses lower, down Philippa's stomach, past her hip, between her thighs.

Tommy loved the heat of Philippa's skin, her scent, her taste. The way her muscles tightened and the little sounds she made at the back of her throat when she was close to her peak.

It all went directly onto the Philippa map in Tommy's mind. Each curve and crevice, each slick surface and the swollen nub at its apex. Every moan. She could reach up with her hands and, without looking, know exactly where and how to stroke Philippa's breasts to bring her to the edge.

She did so now, enjoying the knowledge that not only was she the first to do this, she would be Philippa's only lover. Tommy's tongue was—

Philippa's fingers clutched Tommy's hair as her climax took her. Tommy didn't stop licking until she was finished and spent. Only then did she haul herself up to Philippa's side.

"I want...I want to do it to you," Philippa panted.

Tommy kissed her. "You can do anything to me that you like."

Philippa shook her head, her gaze heated. "No. I want to do everything that *you* want."

Tommy's body quickened in awareness. "You want to do...what I want?"

"I want to do *everything* you want." Philippa sat up and started to push Tommy onto the cushions, then stopped herself. "Give me orders."

Tommy's pulse raced. "Orders?"

"Commands. Explicit instructions. I am a quick study. There is nothing I am more interested in than bringing you pleasure. Tell me what you like, so that I can do it to you. Do you *want* to lie down? Is there a position you'd prefer this time?"

There were suddenly about four hundred positions Tommy would prefer. Her head grew dizzy at the reminder that this was no temporary liaison. This was not their one and only chance to slake their lust, but rather one more of many. They belonged to each other now. They'd made love before and would *keep* making love, whenever and however they pleased.

It was the most seductive idea she had ever contemplated.

"Push me onto the cushions," Tommy commanded. "Hold me down so that I cannot touch you. Torment me with kisses that rarely go exactly where I want nor for quite as long as I would like."

A smile curved Philippa's lips. She pushed Tommy's shoulders back onto the bed and pinned her wrists against the pillow on either side of her head. Tommy's blood rushed with excitement.

Philippa pressed a kiss to the wildly beating pulse point in the hollow beneath Tommy's ear. "You said I can touch you anywhere." Philippa trailed kisses down Tommy's throat and around the base of Tommy's small, pert breasts. "Tell me if I'm starting in the right place."

This wasn't a game, Tommy realized. It was a promise. A new beginning. Philippa was showing with her kisses that she accepted Tommy for who she was and accepted her exactly *as* she was. There was no need to hide behind a disguise. Tommy could be fully herself with Philippa, out of the bedroom and in.

All she need do was let Philippa know what she wanted, and Tommy could have it.

"My breasts." Her voice was strained, excited. "Suck them."

Her eyes fluttered shut. Philippa's rumpled hair tickled as she dragged her parted lips up Tommy's chest to her straining nipple.

With her eyes closed tight, Tommy could hear the blood rushing in her ears as her voice rasped instructions to pinch and lick and tug and suckle.

Giving commands should have made her feel like the one with the power, but instead it made Tommy feel vulnerable and exposed. She could give orders, but whether and how to respond was up to Philippa. It added a layer of uncertainty and anticipation, followed by a rush of excitement and pleasure when her pleas were heeded.

Philippa followed instructions with enthusiasm and delight, as if Tommy's naked body was a treasure trove full of riches and surprises, each more wonderful than the last. She did not hesitate to touch and lick and stroke anywhere and everywhere Tommy asked.

Philippa's soft ringlets brushed Tommy's tensed thighs as Philippa eagerly used her mouth and hands between Tommy's legs in exactly the manner her hoarse voice begged for. She dug her fingers into the bedclothes as Philippa's fingers and tongue brought her ever closer to climax.

"I want...I'm about to..." Tommy gasped.

Philippa's mouth sent Tommy into an explosion of pleasure,

riding out the shockwaves. Only when the spasms calmed did Philippa finally cease her sweet torture. Tommy hauled Philippa up and into her embrace.

They collapsed into each other's arms and held on, legs entwined, the softness of their breasts flush against their racing hearts.

38

❦

*P*hilippa snuggled into Tommy amid the rumpled sheets. She never wished to leave this bed. Here in Tommy's arms, Philippa felt content and safe, satisfied that her life was finally going exactly as it ought to.

Tommy laid her cheek against Philippa's forehead. "What if we closed the canopy and stayed in bed for the next fortnight?"

Philippa cuddled closer. "Your wish is my command."

"All *I* wish to do," Tommy murmured, "is love you forevermore."

Philippa lifted her head and widened her eyes. "What a happy coincidence! All *I* wish to do is to love *you* forevermore."

"Then so we shall." Tommy grinned at her. "An entire wing of this house is unused. Which means there are plenty of extra rooms if you'd rather not be in the same corridor as the rest of my noisy, meddlesome siblings."

"First," Philippa said, "I adore the idea of being heckled by your noisy, meddlesome siblings. Second, I want to be as close to you as possible."

"My bedchamber and your guest chamber are adjoining rooms. We could make it permanent," Tommy offered.

"May I still sleep with you from time to time?" Philippa teased.

"Actually *using* your bedchamber is completely optional. I hope you do spend every night right here with me." Tommy stroked Philippa's hair. "You're not worried what people say?"

"Your siblings and staff already know the truth, and no one else has any reason to know where I sleep. I shan't hide myself or my love for you in my own home." Joy bubbled inside Philippa. "Oh!—must my bedchamber be a bedchamber?"

"It can be a gambling den or a circus for otters if that's your preference. We've more than enough money to outfit your rooms however you like. What is your heart's one true desire?"

"A study," Philippa said dreamily. "A big, beautiful study, with sunny windows and a large desk and a comfortable arm-chair and a special bookcase for my collection of illuminated manuscripts."

"You have scandalized me," Tommy said. "But I acquiesce. You are to have the bluestocking study of your dreams. And if you like, the largest salon on the ground floor of the other wing can be converted into a library."

"I don't have *that* many books." Philippa thought it over. "Yet. You're right. That's an excellent choice."

"I was thinking you'd have room for your reading circle," Tommy said with a laugh. "You needn't give up your friends just because you've become a Wynchester."

"No." Philippa's voice scratched. "But they may be obliged to give *me* up. A few of them already have. When they find out I'm no longer in Mayfair..."

"They'll no longer wish to be friends with you?"

"No," Philippa admitted. "They still love me. But they

must obey their parents, and after the scandal with Northrup, I'm no longer fashionable."

"Scandal doesn't last forever," Tommy promised her.

Philippa let out a slow breath. "It'll last long enough to ruin my chance of building a network of neighborhood reading libraries."

Tommy frowned. "Are they literal neighborhoods? Do you have directions?"

"We didn't even get that far," she said glumly. "I was still working on finding sponsors. Once we had enough pledges and patronesses, we could work on determining specific addresses for the little libraries."

"Or *I* could work on it," Tommy said. "I can help you map the best locations for each community. If your patronesses don't have to be society ladies, you might discover other possibilities. There could be a solicitors' office that would like to sponsor a location, or a dressmaker, or even a publishing house."

Philippa threw her arms around Tommy and hugged her tight. "Thank you. I would love that above all things."

"I hope not above *all* things," Tommy said. "I have a gift for you that I hope you'll like."

"You do?" Philippa let go in surprise. Tommy's help with the library project was more than gift enough. She did not want for anything else.

Tommy slid out of bed and returned with a small box.

Philippa sat up and opened it carefully. Inside was an elegant pocket watch on a gold chain. Her breath caught. "It's beautiful."

"It's synchronized to mine." Tommy grinned at her. "Now that you're officially a Wynchester, we cannot have our newest member arriving tardy to the family's highly improper and occasionally illegal philanthropic adventures."

Philippa pressed it to her chest, her heart overflowing with happiness. "Thank you so much. And…I think it *is* time. Before we can create a new life together, first I must put paid to the old one. I must inform my parents of my new address."

As she rooted through the discarded clothing on the floor in search of her shift and plum underdress, her hands would not stop trembling.

"Do you want me to come with you?"

"*Please*," Philippa said with feeling.

This ought to feel joyful, like the moment she unmasked Northrup's perfidy, but instead she was filled with dread. When she returned home, Philippa was going to break the impending betrothal to Lord Whiddleburr as well as her parents' hearts.

Her palms were already sticky. But it was time to stand up for herself.

With Tommy at her side.

Tommy laced Philippa's gown. "Who do you want me to be?"

Philippa looked over her shoulder at her. "Whoever you want to be."

"To visit your parents?" Tommy thought it over before disappearing into her dressing room and emerging in shimmering celestial blue satin with matching lace at the hem, thin gold spectacles, and shiny brown hair styled with face-framing ringlets. She was positively gorgeous.

Philippa curtsied. "And whom do I have the pleasure of greeting?"

Tommy handed her a calling card. It read:

TOMMY WYNCHESTER
BLUESTOCKING

Philippa burst out laughing. "You have cards that say *bluestocking?*"

"I have cards that say absolutely everything," Tommy said. "Vintner, wax chandler, Royal Exchange broker, Duke of Wellington…"

Philippa lifted her lips to Tommy's and gave her temporary bluestocking a thorough kiss.

When they clattered down the stairs, Elizabeth and Marjorie were just emerging from the direction of the sitting room. Tiglet pranced just beside them.

Elizabeth pointed at them with the tip of her sword stick. "Where are you going?"

"To confront Philippa's overbearing parents. Well…" Tommy tilted her head. "Philippa is in charge of the confronting. I'm going for support."

"I'll go along to provide personal protection," Elizabeth said.

Marjorie lifted a sketchbook. "I'll capture the ambiance for posterity."

"An image of Philippa standing up to her parents or of Elizabeth attacking them with her sword stick?" Tommy inquired.

"It will all be part of the same memorable moment," Marjorie assured her.

Philippa scooped up Tiglet and grinned at Marjorie and Elizabeth. They hadn't asked what, precisely, Philippa needed to confront her parents about or take a stand against. It didn't matter. They were on her side no matter what.

"Tales of chivalry should be written about you," she informed them.

Elizabeth looked thrilled.

"You should write them," Marjorie said to Philippa. "I'll illustrate."

"Illustrate your way into the carriage." Tommy motioned them out through the front door. "We've dragons to slay and no time to waste."

The Wynchesters' coach-and-four awaited them. A smartly dressed tiger helped the ladies inside.

"To the Yorks, please!" Tommy called out, after arranging herself on the bench next to Philippa and Tiglet.

Marjorie and Elizabeth exchanged knowing glances on the opposite side.

Elizabeth gave an exaggeratedly suggestive wink. "Dare I hope?"

"You may hope," Tommy replied primly, twirling one of her false ringlets.

Philippa cupped her hands to her mouth and whispered, "You would be right."

Marjorie and Elizabeth burst into delighted applause.

"It's about time you became one of us," Elizabeth said. "As soon as we're free from this carriage, I shall unsheathe my sword and dub you a Wynchester."

"There's no such ceremony," Tommy informed Philippa. "Say no if you value your ears. *I* value your ears."

"We should add a knighting ceremony," Elizabeth said. "Just *agreeing* we accept a person into our family lacks panache."

"Any ceremony sounds wonderful to me," Philippa said. "I've never had siblings before. Or lived with anyone who particularly wished to spend time with me. There aren't words to express how much this means to me."

Marjorie brightened. "We have signs to express the things words cannot. When we feel something deeply, or wish to swear upon our souls, we do this."

All three sisters touched their hands to their hearts and lifted their fingers to the sky.

"I am proud to be a Wynchester," Philippa said, and copied the movement.

Elizabeth grinned at her. "Welcome to the family."

"This doesn't mean you two imps are welcome to monopolize her," Tommy warned. "You are preemptively forbidden from spending time with Philippa without submitting your requests to me in advance. We have already arranged our calendar, and we have decided never to leave the bedroom."

"What about breakfast and supper?" Marjorie asked.

"Those are good points," Tommy admitted. "Especially if there are pies."

"What about books?" Elizabeth asked.

"Your sisters are skilled negotiators," Philippa said. "We find ourselves forced to compromise. Tommy can have me sometimes, and the rest of you can have me some other times."

Tommy crossed her arms. "I did not approve this plan."

"You don't have to," said Elizabeth. "We are the Democratic Republic of Wynchesters and our collective vote outnumbers yours."

"We're not that, either," Tommy whispered to Philippa. "If we were, Elizabeth would find a way to legislate daily sword fights."

"I'll teach you." Elizabeth beamed at Philippa. "Tommy won't be half so cocky once you've sliced off a lock of her hair with the tip of your sword."

"I'll illustrate the act." Marjorie held up her sketch pad. "For posterity."

"Do I even want to know what sorts of images one might find amongst those sketches?" Philippa inquired.

"You do not," Tommy said. "But if you do, peruse Graham's shelves. Marjorie has helpfully illustrated a few choice scenes from the intelligence his network has gathered."

"That sounds ominous," Philippa said.

Marjorie smiled at her angelically. "It is."

The carriage drew to a stop. Philippa's stomach lurched. They had arrived at Grosvenor Square. The York town house loomed just outside.

Tommy helped Philippa from the coach. "We'll be with you every step of the way."

"If you require violence, just make the sign," Elizabeth said.

Philippa held Tiglet nervously. "What is the sign?"

"*Any* sign." Elizabeth patted the handle of her sword stick. "Blink if you want mayhem."

Philippa blinked in surprise.

"Perfect." Elizabeth unsheathed her sword. "I'll attack first."

Tommy pushed Elizabeth behind Marjorie.

"Keep her in check," Tommy told Marjorie. "If she kills anyone, it will be your fault."

She nodded. "I won't look away, except when I'm drawing."

Philippa giggled despite herself at their silliness. She knew they were doing it on purpose, to try and ease her nervousness. "Thank you." She straightened her shoulders. "*I'll* attack first."

She sucked in a deep breath and strode up to the front door.

Underwood welcomed her in with a distressed expression. "Your parents are in the cerulean sitting room. *Together.*"

Philippa's eyes widened. It did not bode well that Mr. and Mrs. York were still in each other's company—or had returned to the sitting room to continue arguing over their daughter's fate.

"No swords," she said to Tommy's sisters. "Follow me."

She marched into the parlor with her head held high.

"Where have you been?" snapped her mother.

"We're here if you need us." Tommy pulled her sisters to one side.

"Need *who?*" Mother said.

"The Wynchesters," Elizabeth answered helpfully.

"Philippa, these people are exactly what's wrong with you," Mother hissed.

"No," Philippa said. "They're exactly what's right. Please convey my regrets to Lord Whiddleburr. I shall not be accepting his—or any—suit at this time, or at any time."

"*What?*" Mother burst out. "We have spent *all morning* refining the terms of your settlements—"

"Now you can keep the money," Philippa said. "Not marrying me off will be economically advantageous."

"Not if you're upstairs spending our fortune on old manuscripts," Father said from behind his broadsheet.

"Ah," said Philippa. "That is where you're in luck. I shan't be upstairs at all. From this day forth, I shall be living with the Wynchesters."

"You cannot be serious." Mother let out a high laugh. "Darling, this is your final opportunity to be a lady. Whiddleburr is a *marquess*."

"And yet," said Philippa, "I find myself far more tempted by the idea of remaining a spinster for the rest of my days."

"I told you we should have secured her acquiescence first," Father said without lowering his broadsheet.

"You did?" Philippa said in surprise.

"What good would that have done?" Mother said in exasperation. "The only man she's ever shown any interest in is…Is *that* what this is about? Are you eloping with Baron Vanderbean?"

"I'm afraid Baron Vanderbean was called home to Balcovia," Tommy said. "He has not sent word on when or whether he shall return."

Elizabeth and Marjorie raised their eyebrows at each other.

"Well, that's something, at least," huffed Philippa's mother. "At least I needn't worry you've taken up with a Wynchester."

Philippa concentrated on petting Tiglet and tried very hard not to exchange glances with anyone.

"Now, darling," Mother continued, "if you would just be reasonable. Lord Whiddleburr is likely to retract his offer if you no longer reside here in Mayfair with us."

"There is no offer to retract," Philippa said. "I've already declined it and am not open to considering any others."

Mother wrung her hands. "Think of your father and his potential connections in the House of Lords. Think of your poor mother, and how *close* you are to having a title. When you can rule Polite Society as a lady—"

"The only society I wish to keep are the Wynchesters and my reading circle," Philippa said.

"Darling, you know you cannot have *both* of those. Surely you prefer the reading circle over the company of—" Mother coughed delicately into her hand, seeming to recollect at the last moment that there were three Wynchesters standing in her parlor, two with their arms crossed and one with her hands atop the brass handle of a sword stick.

"Those who wish for my company may still have it," Philippa said quietly. "But if you and Father feel you must punish me to protect your reputations..."

Her father shook his broadsheet without lowering it. "Oh, let her be a spinster in peace. She already was one. I'd as soon see our daughter's nose in a book as stuck up in the air next to Whiddleburr."

Philippa's heart fluttered. "I—you—"

Mother pursed her lips. "I cannot accept such behavior. But it is also clear that I cannot stop you. I do love you, darling. I only wish you needn't be so difficult."

"I'm not trying to be," Philippa said. "As unusual as this seems, life will be simpler. I'll no longer be welcome in the beau monde, but I hope I'll still be welcome here."

"We won't *disown* you," her mother said in shock. "Our house shall always be open to our only child. Why can't you continue living here?"

The newspaper crinkled. "Perhaps because as long as she lives here, you'll never cease attempting to arrange every aspect of her life."

Philippa inclined her head at her father's words. "I have my majority and my inheritance. I'm ready for independence. I love you, Mother—I love both of you—but my happiness lies elsewhere."

Her mother sniffed. "You cannot possibly expect us to visit *Islington*."

Philippa bowed her head. "I would never."

"Thank God," muttered Elizabeth.

Marjorie's skirts fluttered as if she'd kicked her sister.

"Well." Mother harrumphed. "I suppose you've come for your things."

"Our daughter shall not carry her baggage about like a tramp," Father said from behind his newspaper. "Have the maids prepare the trunks and send the footmen over with them in the carriage." He turned the page. "Yes, all the way to Islington."

"Then this is goodbye. Mother, Father," Philippa said. "I hope to see you again soon."

Father shook his newspaper without responding.

It was the same as always, yet so different. He did not have time for her, but he cared about her more than she had ever guessed. Loved her enough to let her go.

Mother followed them to the door, but stopped Philippa before she followed the others outside. She smoothed one of

Philippa's ringlets. "I do hope you'll find someone you can agree to marry one day."

Philippa could not help but a smile. Her muscles felt light and free. "Breathe easy on that score, Mother. Love is definitely in my future."

She nodded to her kindly butler and strode out from the home she'd lived in for as long as she could remember... straight into a solid wall of women.

"W-what," she stammered.

"It's Thursday," Florentia said.

Sybil took Tiglet from Philippa. "It's time for our reading circle."

"When Chloe didn't send out invitations, we assumed we were to come here," said Lady Eunice.

Gracie alighted from a hackney and raced up the path. "Am I late?"

"No," Philippa said in wonder. "For once, you are not. But I'm afraid I don't live here any longer. I am happy to keep hosting the reading circle, but it will need to take place at the Wynchester residence in Islington."

"Mother will *never* let me go there," Gracie said. "I'll say I'm with Sybil."

"I'll say I'm with Florentia," said Sybil.

Florentia nodded. "I'll say I'm with Lady Eunice."

"I do as I please," said Lady Eunice. "That is the single greatest advantage of being a spinster."

"Mayhap not the *single* greatest," Tommy murmured.

Damaris curtseyed. "I shall be honored to attend, wherever we find ourselves."

"I thought.." Philippa stammered. She turned to Lady Eunice. "But... your parents?"

"Have forbidden further interaction," Lady Eunice acknowledged. "However, I am eight and twenty years old and in possession of a significant inheritance. I *could* leave home over this, which would cause far more gossip than they desire. I shall be allowed to continue attending a reading circle."

"I won't be allowed to," said Florentia. "I think most of us will find a way anyway."

"Ooh," said Gracie. "We can all ride together!"

"We won't all fit in one carriage," Sybil pointed out. "I'll make a schedule."

Philippa's heart overflowed. It was the happiest of endings. She had everything she wanted! A happy future with the person she loved, the life she wanted to live, and the best group of bluestockings London had ever seen.

"Meet me next Thursday," she told the ladies. "By then, I'll have had a chance to organize a space for all of us and—"

"Ow, no!" Tiglet leapt from Sybil's chest and sprinted down the Brook Street pavement in the direction of Islington.

"Tiglet! Tig-let!" Philippa called out, though it was no use. "Tig—"

The kitten paused, his calico ears flicking as he glanced over his shoulder at Philippa. Then he turned with his tail in the air and pranced back to her without complaint.

Philippa scooped him up and cuddled him to her chest in disbelief. "But—he's a homing kitten."

"And you're taking him home," Elizabeth said.

Philippa touched her cheek to the kitten's fur and smiled. From now on, there would be no more running away.

Not even for Tiglet.

EPILOGUE

✖

April 1818
Wynchester Residence

A grin curved Tommy's lips at the familiar sound of rau-
cous bluestockings arriving for their Thursday afternoon
reading circle.

Once the ladies were settled on the other side of the house
in Philippa's new library, their joyful, boisterous voices would
no longer be heard from the sitting room, where Tommy was
working on her maps. The cataloging system Philippa had
created was phenomenal. Tommy now had several albums
organized thematically. When they'd needed to infiltrate an
auction house last Tuesday, it had taken mere seconds to pull
the right maps.

With the new system in place, Tommy's maps had multi-
plied. Thanks to Philippa, the Wynchesters could complete
their missions more efficiently than before. There was even a
new album dedicated solely to Philippa's burgeoning network
of community reading libraries.

Marjorie was in her third-floor studio, painting or forging
heaven-knew-what. Jacob and Elizabeth were in the rear
garden, practicing some sort of complicated and extremely
ill-advised maneuver with swords and hedgehogs.

Graham was the only other sibling in the sitting room,
sprawled in his usual sofa with a broadsheet in his hands. He

must be hard at work. Every surface within reach was piled high with journals, correspondence, notes, crisp newspapers waiting to be read, and old newspapers blurred and soft from being read too many times.

"What are you looking for?" Tommy asked.

Graham lowered the broadsheet, his brown eyes sparkling. "News of the parcel."

"The alleged mystery parcel alluded to only obliquely in otherwise innocuous advertisements?" Tommy inquired politely. "Are you *certain* something nefarious is afoot? Perhaps you're simply bored because we've found ourselves between adventures again."

"There *is* a parcel." Graham rubbed a hand over his black curls and let out a tight sigh. "There *was* a parcel. I am certain of it."

"You suspected smugglers, did you not? Perhaps the contraband has reached its destination."

"Smugglers don't smuggle a lone package for a lark. They have bills of lading and illicit vendors and unscrupulous clients. I've found the trail. There is a mystery waiting to be discovered."

"Well, if you need me, I'll be—"

Tiglet jumped onto the table. His paws skidded toward an open bottle of ink. Tommy scooped the curious cat out of the way just in time.

"You're grown now," she scolded him. "No more making kitteny messes. Just for that, I'm taking you to your mistress." But she snuggled him to her lapel all the same.

Quickly, she strode out of the sitting room and across the house to the new library, where the door was wide open. The dozen or so women inside were still waiting for Gracie, but they did not appear to be cross. Lively chatter filled the air.

A small gold plaque next to the door read:

THE AGNES & KATHERINE LIBRARY
FOR WOMEN WHO CAN ACCOMPLISH ANYTHING

The ladies had each donated copies of their favorite volumes. Philippa had used part of her inheritance to stock the rest. Every wall of the salon was lined floor-to-ceiling with bookshelves, with a ladder to reach the topmost titles.

The sideboard contained artful trays of libations and hors d'oeuvres—including pies.

Clad in her usual cloud of lace, with her heart-shaped face framed by golden ringlets, Philippa was easy to spot. She was deep in conversation with Florentia and Lady Eunice. At the sounds of footsteps approaching, she glanced up and smiled at Tommy.

Or perhaps her grin was at the sight of a calico cat burrowing inside Tommy's coat, with only his furry behind and question-mark-shaped tail protruding out.

As always, Tommy's heart warmed every time she glimpsed her.

The unused wing of the house felt alive again. This was Philippa's home as well now, and already felt as though it had always been that way.

And Tommy's chambers upstairs—er, that was, *Tommy and Philippa's* chambers—were the best rooms in the house. Philippa's private study was fit for a queen. Tommy's dressing room contained more disguises than ever, now that Philippa was taking part in the schemes. Their nights were spent in each other's arms, and their days were spent in pursuit of their passions.

Rather than bother with society events, the Wynchesters threw their own parties, where Tommy and Philippa were free to dance as many sets together as their feet allowed.

Philippa now had a dedicated armchair in the Planning

Parlor, and her personal reading nook in the sitting room. She spent hours working on parliamentary speeches with Faircliffe and creating pamphlets for social reform with Chloe, and spent just as much time having passionate discussions with Graham about the shocking lack of care some people took with their books.

"*Miaow*," said Tiglet.

Tommy deposited the cat on the hardwood floor. He immediately darted through the skirts and slippers, making his way straight to Philippa. She scooped him up and winked at Tommy.

Sort of winked. Philippa was trying very hard to learn the trick of what she'd termed Tommy's "rakish eyebrow wink," but so far Philippa managed to look far more adorable than lecherous. Her friends thought the hapless attempts romantic. If Agnes and Katherine were alive, the bluestockings were certain their next grand story would be about Tommy and Philippa.

Today, the ladies were helping with the library project. Damaris, with her newfound fame, recruited more wealthy matrons than Philippa had dreamed possible. Chloe penned pamphlets. The rest of the reading circle used Tommy's maps to explore the communities in pairs, approaching successful local businesses as possible sponsors. Many offered up a spare corner to use for the library itself, either out of goodwill or in hope that some of the additional traffic would become future customers.

Philippa and her friends were changing lives in their beautiful bluestocking way. It was lovely to be part of it as Tommy.

Great-Aunt Wynchester would be proud.

Cat-free for the moment, Tommy made her way back to her maps. But she had scarcely reentered the sitting room when Graham leapt up from his armchair, sending notes and newspapers flying.

"Did Jacob misplace another scorpion?" she asked in alarm.

"What? No. That is, I've no idea, and it's the least of my concerns."

"You're not concerned about loose scorpions?"

"Not when there's an adventure to be had." Graham's golden-brown eyes smoldered with satisfaction. "*I found it.*"

Tommy frowned. "You found the smugglers?"

"I found the clue." He ripped a large piece from the paper. "The parcel is a woman."

Tommy stopped walking. "Someone is smuggling a *woman?*"

"Someone *was* smuggling a woman," Graham corrected. "The package has gone missing."

"Someone *misplaced* a woman?"

Graham yanked on his top hat. "And *I'm* going to find her."

DON'T MISS GRAHAM'S STORY IN

NOBODY'S PRINCESS

Summer 2022

ABOUT THE AUTHOR

Erica Ridley is a *New York Times* and *USA Today* bestselling author of historical romance novels. She lives between two volcanos on a macadamia farm filled with horses, cows, parrots, frogs, and the occasional howler monkey. When not reading or writing romances, Erica can be found eating couscous in Morocco, zip-lining through rain forests in Costa Rica, or getting hopelessly lost in the middle of Budapest.

Please visit **EricaRidley.com/extras** for more Wynchester fun, including coloring pages, research notes, frequently asked questions, and behind-the-scenes secrets.

You can join Erica's VIP List at **Ridley.vip** or find her at:
Twitter @EricaRidley
Facebook.com/EricaRidley
Instagram @EricaRidley

Get swept off your feet by charming dukes,
sharp-witted ladies, and scandalous balls in
Forever's historical romances!

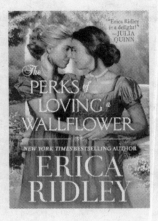

THE PERKS OF LOVING A WALLFLOWER
by Erica Ridley

As a master of disguise, Thomasina Wynchester can be a polite young lady—or a bawdy old man. Anything to solve the case—which this time requires masquerading as a charming baron. Her latest assignment unveils a top-secret military cipher covering up an enigma that goes back centuries. But Tommy's beautiful new client turns out to be the reserved, high-born bluestocking Miss Philippa York, with whom she's secretly smitten. As they decode clues and begin to fall for each other in the process, the mission—as well as their hearts—will be at stake...

Discover bonus content and more on read-forever.com

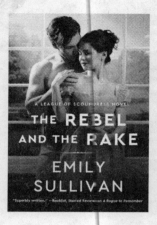

THE REBEL AND THE RAKE
by Emily Sullivan

Though most women would be thrilled to catch the eye of a tall, dark, and dangerously handsome rake like Rafe Davies, Miss Sylvia Sparrow trusted the wrong man once and paid for it dearly. The fiery bluestocking is resolved to avoid Rafe, until a chance encounter reveals the man's unexpected depths—and an attraction impossible to ignore. But once Sylvia suspects she isn't the only one harboring secrets, she realizes that Rafe may pose a risk to far more than her heart...

WEST END EARL
by Bethany Bennett

While most young ladies attend balls and hunt for husbands, Ophelia Hardwick has spent the past ten years masquerading as a man. As the land steward for the Earl of Carlyle, she's found safety from the uncle determined to kill her and the freedoms of which a lady could only dream. Ophelia's situation would be perfect—if she wasn't hopelessly attracted to her employer...

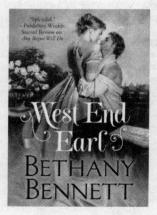

A LADY'S GUIDE TO MISCHIEF AND MAYHEM
by Manda Collins

The widowed Lady Katherine eschews society's "good" opinion to write about crimes against women. But when her reporting jeopardizes an investigation, attractive Detective Inspector Andrew Eversham criticizes her interference. Before Kate can make amends, she stumbles upon another victim—in the same case. With their focus on the killer, neither is prepared for the other risk the case poses—to their hearts.

A DUKE WORTH FIGHTING FOR
by Christina Britton

Margery Kitteridge has been mourning her husband for years, and while she's not ready to consider marriage again, she does miss intimacy with a partner. When Daniel asks for help navigating the Isle of Synne's social scene and they accidentally kiss, she realizes he's the perfect person with whom to have an affair. As they begin to confide in each other, Daniel discovers that he's unexpectedly connected to Margery's late husband, and she will have to decide if she can let her old love go for the promise of a new one.

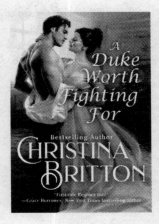

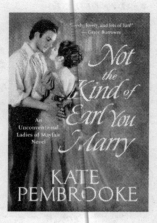

NOT THE KIND OF EARL YOU MARRY
by Kate Pembrooke

When William Atherton, Earl of Norwood, learns of his betrothal in the morning paper, he's furious that the shrewd marriage trap could affect his political campaign. Until he realizes that a fake engagement might help rather than harm...Miss Charlotte Hurst may be a wallflower, but she's no shrinking violet. She would never attempt such an underhanded scheme, especially not with a man as haughty or sought-after as Norwood. And yet...the longer they pretend, the more undeniably real their feelings become.

A NIGHT WITH A ROGUE
(2-in-1 Edition)
by Julie Anne Long

Enjoy these two stunning, sensual historical romances! In *Beauty and the Spy*, when odd accidents endanger London darling Susannah Makepeace, who better than Viscount Kit Whitelaw, the best spy in His Majesty's secret service, to unravel the secrets threatening her? In *Ways to Be Wicked*, a chance to find her lost family sends Parisian ballerina Sylvie Lamoureux fleeing across the English Channel—and into the arms of the notorious Tom Shaughnessy. Can she trust this wicked man with her heart?

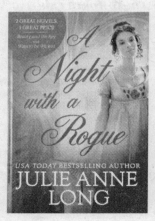